THE DRATSIE DILEMMA

BY GAIL CARRIGER

Tinkered Starsong
Divinity 36 | Demigod 12 | Dome 6

The Tinkered Stars
Crudrat

The Finishing School Series
Etiquette & Espionage | Curtsies & Conspiracies
Waistcoats & Weaponry | Manners & Mutiny

The Parasol Protectorate Series
Soulless | Changeless | Blameless | Heartless | Timeless
prequel: *Meat Cute*

The Custard Protocol Series
Prudence | Imprudence | Competence | Reticence

Parasolverse Tie-in Books & Novellas
Poison or Protect | Defy or Defend | Ambush or Adore
Romancing the Werewolf | Romancing the Inventor
How to Marry a Werewolf
Dear Lord Akeldama (direct from Gail only)

AS G. L. CARRIGER

A Tinkered Stars Mystery
The 5th Gender

The San Andreas Shifters Series
The Sumage Solution | The Omega Objection
The Enforcer Enigma | The Dratsie Dilemma

Newsletter exclusives: *Marine Biology | Vixen Ecology*

THE DRATSIE DILEMMA

SAN ANDREAS SHIFTERS

G. L. CARRIGER

"It is an odd thing, but everyone who disappears is said to be seen in San Francisco."

~ Oscar Wilde

CHAPTER ONE

DRY HUMOR

The Past: Sato in a Box

Sato sat in the box called a *room*, inside the bigger box called a *house*, and glared at his dumb legs – hating all of it. To be fair, they were perfectly good legs, if legs were what you wanted, but Sato missed his tail.

The box was warm and a little damp, but not in the right way. Not wet with salt, no matter how close to the ocean the box squatted. The box was forcing Sato to face up to the fact that he was beached, alone and lonely, with a body that felt heavy because in addition to the legs and the box, it turned out he also wasn't wild about gravity.

Gravity wasn't wild about him, either. He'd already fallen down the stairs in this dumb box... twice. It felt like he was aware of all his bones for the first time. And those bones did not want to listen to him.

His room was quiet, but not the muffled friendly quiet of the Deep. It was the quiet of an abandoned human space. A quiet that came coupled with all the vastness of an overwhelming sky just outside. Just above. More infinite than the ocean.

Or, *this* box was quiet.

The box next door had other ideas.

The neighbors, as it turned out, were loud.

His sire had said, in that soft abrupt way he had of talking, that the neighbors were *difficult*. Sato must learn to ignore them. Because everyone on the block ignored them, otherwise there would be *trouble*.

How did one ignore something so noisy and boisterous? It was as if the air vibrated with currents of spiky sound. Everything was too sharp here. It was maddening.

Sato went to his window and, after some fiddling, raised it up. The loud box was right there, with only a limp weed-tree between them. The noise increased but it was no warmer or cooler inside with the window open.

"Hi!"

Directly across from him was a similar window, on the second level of the noisy box, also open. A small boy was leaning out of it precariously and talking, evidently, to him. Sato didn't know what to do about any of it.

Apparently the small boy did. He kept talking. "You're the new kid! Mr Sato's surprise son." He waved his arms around like sea kelp as he spoke. It was almost pretty.

Sato wondered how the child knew. So far as he could tell, his sire didn't talk to anyone, didn't have any friends. He wasn't the type.

The boy was small and extremely... what? What was the correct word to describe him? Like a brightly colored nudibranch. He had round soft pink cheeks, huge dark eyes, a big forehead, and a shock of hair the color of sun coral.

Cute was the word. The child-creature was almost unbearably cute. And sparkly. Sato was merfolk enough to like sparkly things.

"I'm Patrick!" said, apparently, Patrick. "Patrick Inis. I'm your neighbor. Well, obviously. What am I saying? Why do you have to look so... just so... ugh! Anyway. Where was I? Hi! We're, ya know, *that* family. The ones that the whole neighborhood talks about. The noisy ones. And the nosy ones. The problem house. We like to know what's happening or we like to *be* what's happening. Usually both. That's how I knew you were coming.

My brother told me. I've lots of brothers. And sisters, for that matter. It was Con who told me, I think, the one closest to me in age. He's hoping it will get me out of his hair. If I have a friend next door, who's my own age. You see, Con isn't actually *that* close to me in age. He's an adult now, barely tolerates me. I'm – what do they call it? – oh yeah, *the oops baby*. Only not really an oops. *Every Inis is wanted,* my ma always says. Maybe not *remembered,* but *wanted.* Frankly, there are way too many of us. I guess we *are* wanted, but only in a sack of potatoes kinda way. It's one of the reasons we're so noisy. Not that potatoes generally cause a ruckus."

Sato stared at the boy. Patrick's mouth never seemed to stop moving. His cheeks were getting pinker. He was as relentless as the waves on the shore.

"Do you not speak English? Aren't you gonna say anything?" Patrick asked.

"Are you gonna let me?"

The boy's cheeks went lobster red but he giggled. "Hard to ever get a word in edgewise in my fam. I got carried away by all the free air space. I guess I gotta stop if I want you to answer." He paused. "Also, you're gorgeous."

Sato thought that, as a merman, *that* was a given. Of course he was gorgeous. But it was Patrick who had eyes like one of the deep sea trenches. They seemed to go on forever, but also they had a bit of surface shine to them.

Patrick pursed his lips and made a *ptttt* motorboat noise. Sato had met a seal once who could make a noise like that. Impressive.

"Are you not a big talker?" asked Patrick.

"No idea," said Sato. Nothing had ever whipped him into a verbal frenzy except, apparently, Patrick's eyes, but that seemed to be confined to the inside of his own head. Thankfully.

"What's your name?" asked Patrick.

"You didn't find that bit out already?"

"Not for lack of trying. Have you any idea how exciting it is to have a boy my own age move in next door?"

Sato could not believe that. Patrick looked a lot smaller and younger. "We are *not* the same age."

Patrick sort of puffed up a little, like an affronted blowfish. "Inis run small. It's a *thing*. I can explain if you like. But I probably shouldn't do it yelling between houses. Can I come over?"

Sato didn't say anything. Was that something humans did? Just invited themselves into each other's boxes?

"So, your name?" Patrick pressed again.

"Why?"

"So I can ask for you when I knock."

That sounded like human interactive guest practices, so he said, "Sato."

"Isn't that your father's name?"

"Yes."

"Oh, so you're like Sato Junior?"

Sato did know this part. His mother had made him memorize it before she chucked him up onto the shore – a beached-wood child no longer wanted by the sea. Returning him to the land, so far altered from any land-bound state that he was now to be called by a new name. "No. I'm Sato Daiki. He's Sato Kenta."

Patrick tilted his head, lips pressed together. "Confusing, but that's cool. Be right over."

Sato gave an expressive look at the tree between their two houses. He'd heard that humans did strange things like climb trees – was this kid proposing to transfer between their boxes that way?

Patrick laughed. "Oh, I think not. I'm water-born too. I don't climb. Or I do, but then I usually get stuck. It's not pretty or fun for anyone. I'll come in through the door like a proper friend."

"Friend?"

"You and I are gonna be friends. I can tell already."

Sato had never had a friend before.

The window across from him slammed shut.

The house remained loud.

Sato closed his own window and went to his bedroom door. Opened it carefully.

His sire had shown him to this room, *his* room, and told him, curtly, to "settle in." That he would "call him down for dinner."

Sato took that to mean he was to stay in his room until summoned, but it wasn't like he had anything to unpack. The pod had sent him to surface with nothing but one set of clothing, too big, a mermaid's purse of pearls, and his DURPS paperwork. Well, it was a DURPS authentication shell, but it could become paperwork when needed. He wore it around his neck, strung on a piece of braided fishing net, never to be removed. Like he'd been caught by them, by the humans.

It was up to a merman's human father to provide anything beyond the shell. Sometimes fatherhood might be purchased, for the price of an egg case full of pearls. If the father declined, died, or disappeared, then the merman would have to make it on his own two feet. Sato was considered one of the lucky ones. His sire at least felt compelled to put a roof over his head. A box around him. Had taken the pearls away with a heavy sigh, like their value worried him. Had asked him about his mother. Asked if he would ever see her again.

Sato knew sirens' law. The sires, the better ones, the ones who retained any connection to the sea, they always asked. One night with a mermaid and they never forgot, they never stopped wanting her, they never let go, and they never settled for anything less. They never settled for anything *human*. They'd live in their boxes looking out at the sea for the rest of their lives, remembering one night. Not knowing that sex with mermaids had consequences, and sometimes those consequences turned up on their doorsteps ten years later.

Sometimes, the sea spat a pubescent mer-boy back out at them. A boy who shared half their genes – born of the sea but who that sea no longer wanted. A good sire raised that boy until the sea reclaimed him.

His sire, Sato Kenta, was one of the good ones.

And Sato Daiki was supposed to be grateful for it.

Instead he stood at the top of the staircase, that he'd slipped on twice, and listened.

"Who are you?" His sire's voice at the door.

"Hi! I'm Patrick. I live next door. In the problem house. I'm decent, though, I promise. Although, to be fair, I'm also kinda loud. I'm here to visit Sato. I'm his new best friend."

"What?"

"Well, I'm gonna be. You just wait."

"What are you?"

"Friendly."

"Is this a kid thing?"

"It's okay, Mr Sato, you're new to being a father. You'll figure it out soon enough. Sorry about my family, they think playing country music really loudly will help them fit in. I hope you don't mind the Dixie Chickens."

"Chicken?"

"It's this new band, very hip."

"Hip?"

"Ah, I see. Nevermind. You're making dinner, right? That's part of parental obligation."

"Yes, catfish katsu. Kids like fried food, yes?"

"We do! Well done, you. Let us know when it's ready."

"You are staying for dinner?"

"Most definitely. We never get anything as fancy as stew made by cats. Training your cats to cook sounds awesome, but also kinda labor intensive. Imma go up to Sato now. You two have the same first name but different last names, that's wild, you realize? Very innovative." The boy stumbled over the word. "Mad props and all."

"It's Japanese. We say the last name first."

"Then why do you call it a *last* name?"

"We don't call it that, you do… oh never mind. Just go up."

"Thanks, Mr Sato, sir."

"Sato-san."

"Oh, so you *do* have a different first name! See."

"No, that's… shoes off, please."

"Oh? You don't like 'em? But these have hardly any holes. They're my *good* pair."

"No shoes inside."

"Like inside *the house*? Cool idea. Easier to keep clean."

"Just leave them by the door."

"I dig it. Socks are cool. Shoes are dumb."

Sato watched a small figure dart in from the open doorway, slide across the floor. "Wheeee!"

There came a faint thud as the boy hit… something, and then Patrick was bounding up the stairs. He was a lot better at stairs than Sato.

Sato met Patrick at the top, looking down at him. He was so small and sparkly. No actual sparkles like scales, but sparkly in the way he moved and smiled. Huge shining eyes, flashing white teeth, rosy cheeks, a full head shorter than Sato, and Sato wasn't big by human standards. Probably about half his weight as well. But mermen were extra dense on land.

Patrick twinkled up at him. "Hi!"

"Are we really the same age?"

"You're starting fifth grade?"

"I guess so."

"Then no, we're not *technically* the same age."

"Technically?"

Patrick hung his head and whispered. "I'm two years younger. But can you pretend I'm not? I'm so tired of being the youngest."

"Only two years?" That meant he was eight. Sato was used to a lunar calendar but still, Patrick seemed undersized.

"Like I said, we run small."

"We?"

"My people. My family. Us. Trouble. Let's go into your room and talk about it. I don't think your father should hear. I really just call you *Sato*?"

Sato dipped his head. "Maybe eventually you'll use Daiki."

"I have to, like, earn the privilege?"

"I guess. I just learned the rules myself."

Patrick straightened up. His jaw tensed. "Okay, I can do that. What did *they* call you, the people you were with before you moved here?"

Sato thought about his pod. Or not really *his* anymore, now just the pod that had raised him. "Daiki." He put the siren song shriek into it, but not enough to bleed human ears. Still, Patrick winced. "But everything worked differently there."

"Under the sea?"

Sato started. Patrick knew? This strange cute child-boy *knew* what he was? But that was supposed to be a secret. From humans. Only his father should know. Well, DURPS because registration was required, but no one else. That was the whole point. He was supposed to learn how to pass as a human. How had he already given himself away, just talking between boxes, when he'd barely said anything?

"How could you possibly know—?"

"I told you, my family makes it their business to know. Particularly about...," Patrick lowered his voice conspiratorially, "...*shifters*. This your room?"

Patrick opened the door as if he were the one who lived there. Sato wondered if all human boxes had the same layout.

He followed Patrick inside.

Patrick launched himself onto Sato's futon.

"It smells like the sea," announced Patrick.

Sato had been lying on it earlier, staring up at the ceiling. He didn't have a very good sense of smell, but he loved the way Patrick's little nose twitched. He wasn't sure anything should be allowed to be *that* cute.

Patrick instantly bounced back up again, began investigating the small freestanding plastic wardrobe – empty. The tiny desk and shelves – bare. The one set of drawers – empty.

"You arrived with nothing?"

Sato nodded once.

"I'll have to take you shopping before school starts. Will Mr Sato give you a clothing allowance? Oh – supplies too. I mean, I can show you how to pinch the necessities, but you probably shouldn't risk being arrested until you've found your land legs."

"Tell me how you know?"

"That you're merfolk? Local selkie saw your pod dropping you off. Reported it to my dad by way of gossip exchange. He told the family. Not that my fam cares much for a merman in our town, especially a male pup – you have so little power in the grand scheme of things. But like I said. The fam likes to know, ya know, who's who in the local shifter community."

"Why?"

"Why do we care? Well, otters are usually up in everyone's business. We come by it naturally. But my family likes to think we're big water-dogs in this part of the Mississippi delta. Ya know, *movers and shakers* via land, river, and sea. It's a good thing we're in the middle of nowhere so far from New Orleans. Less competition. Here we get to be *important*. Basically? We run a lot of import-export ops. All that noise right now? Moonshine party."

Sato frowned. More words he did not understand, but basically what Patrick was saying was, "You're not human either?"

Patrick finished his perusal of the room, threw himself back down on Sato's bed, writhed about a bit. Not like he was trying to get comfortable but just because, like talking, movement seemed to be his natural state. He was squirmy and bouncy. Like a squid. Spurts of activity and then a lot of wiggling. Sato liked it. Sato liked him. Liked him there, in his strange box room in this strange dry surface-world of oppressive weight and sharp sounds. This was the first time he'd felt comfortable in his skin-without-scales since he'd left the sea.

Sato moved cautiously, perched on a corner of the futon, focused on Patrick. Fascinated.

Patrick stared back at him, silent for a change, eyes big. Then he sort of shook himself and sat up, leaned against the frame.

"We're dobhar-chú! You know – otter shifters. Dratsie? Heard of us?"

"Yes. But only sea otters. You're not that, are you?"

"Technically river otter, but we can swim in both. Not like you."

"Like me what?"

"Merfolk are salt-triggered, right?"

"Oh, yeah." Fresh water, large amounts of it, was a strange idea to Sato. The concept that there would be enough fresh water collected in one place for him to get fully inside and not sprout tail was, frankly, terrifying. How was he supposed to swim without a tail? The surface world was insane.

Patrick wrinkled his cute little nose again. "I can change form at will. Dobhar-chú are lucky that way."

Sato wondered if Patrick would change for him right then and there, in his bedroom.

"Wanna go swimming sometime?" Patrick asked, sounding hopeful, eyes huge. His cheeks less pink now.

"Yes." Sato thought there was nothing he would like more. He wondered what Patrick's otter form looked like. Probably just as cute as his human one. He couldn't possibly be any cuter.

Patrick bounced, went pink again. "Awesome!"

The box next door emitted a metallic crashing noise. Then went back to a kind of twangy whump whumpping.

"Your house is very loud," said Sato.

"Sorry about that. Imagine growing up inside it! I mean, I know I'm a chatterbox, but I assure you I'm the quietest one. I have nine older sibs. *Nine!* Someone should've stopped my parents at some point. They started with two sets of twins *and* then triplets. That's just excessive. Plus assorted aunts, uncles, and cousins. You should know, it's mostly shifters but the fam deals with humans too. Nasty ones."

"What is it they do?"

"My parents? Lots of stuff, most of it illegal. So the humans that do visit are some of the worst. Cops too occasionally, but Pa pays them off. So on the bright side, everyone tends to keep lots of secrets. Your identity isn't important to them. Still, I wouldn't recommend letting anyone else in town know what you are, if you can help it." He gave a chin nod to Sato's webbed hands.

"But your whole family knows?"

"Yeah and the local selkie. But they won't tell unless it's to their advantage. And it's only advantageous if you develop power in shifter circles or human government. You're not thinking about a career in politics, are you?"

"I'm ten, Patrick."

Patrick pursed his lips, looking both wise and rather silly. "And I can already tell you aren't a fan of public speaking. Stay off their radar and you'll be fine. Just another shifter kid that no one wants. No offense."

"None taken. It's true."

"Being a merman kinda sucks? Like being the youngest in a big dobhar-chú family?"

Sato didn't know if that was correlative, but being a merman did *kinda suck*.

Patrick was looking at him closely out of those shiny deep sea eyes. "Do you miss it?"

"What?"

"Your mer-family, your… what do you call it?"

"Pod."

"Yeah, that. Do you miss your pod?"

"No. Maybe I miss my little sister. She's cute." Fun. Chatty and adorable. Like Patrick. Only he thought Patrick was even cuter and more his. More than his own sister had been. Meymey had belonged to his mother first and the sea second. She had loved him, but had always known she would lose him to the land. So she was his sister, but never *his*. Patrick seemed to be something different. Like this room, Patrick had been gifted to Sato. Lonely and waiting. No pearls required.

Sato had no idea how he knew that. It was just the way Patrick looked at him. Like he couldn't quite believe Sato existed. Like he was inhaling, after holding his breath underwater for too long. Even as he moved and darted glances, quick and sharp and restless around Sato's space, he was comfortable in it. Like Sato was both a new exciting thing and a mooring point.

"I do miss the sea," admitted Sato.

"That's easy to solve. After dinner, let's go swimming."

"We're allowed to do that?"

"I don't see why not. I know all the beaches. Most of them are deserted at night. I can show you how to shift and not get caught."

"That sounds nice," said Sato, because it did.

"So we're gonna be friends?" asked Patrick.

Sato thought they already were, so he inclined his head at his first friend.

Patrick ejected himself forward and across the futon, scrambling to the corner where Sato sat.

Sato found himself wrapped in skinny, oddly strong arms, squeezed from behind.

The kid was like a barnacle. Was it an otter thing or a Patrick thing?

"What?" Sato asked, confused. He didn't know what to do with his hands, so he clenched them at his sides.

"This is a hug. It's nice. You'll get used to it."

Sato wasn't sure he liked it, but Patrick seemed to, and that mattered.

Later, years later, Sato liked to think he'd known it from the start. From that very moment. It was Patrick. For him, it was Patrick, and it would be Patrick, and that was just *it*. Like he'd somehow known and decided on forever, in that one moment.

Sato liked to think he was decisive and confident and sure of himself. Even at ten. Even as a terrified abandoned sea-child in an alien world of gravity and legs, cutting sounds and fathers who were not fathers, with horrible sad eyes.

Would he have made it? On land? Among humans? At a human school? In the human world? Without Patrick?

Fortunately, he never had to find out.

CHAPTER TWO

20,000 LATTES NEAR THE SEA

The Present: Trick inside Bean There, Froth That Cafe, Sausalito

On his better days, Trick liked to pretend that it wasn't his fault. He'd been adopted by a pack of werewolves, technically it was all downhill from there. *Literally*, since the pack lived at the top of a very steep hill.

Trick forced himself to remember that he lived there with them. No longer footloose and fancy free (sleeping each night in the back of his old car). Now Trick resided in an *actual* room. In an *actual* house. Trick the dratsie and a pack of werewolves, together. And one very powerful magistar. And occasionally a kitsune drag queen named Mana. And most often a merman named Marvin.

Which was where the real problem lay. Trick liked Marvin a lot. But he had serious issues with mermen.

It was weird that years later, decades even, he was somehow full circle in another small town, on another coast, with another merman in his life. Although this one didn't want to screw him silly at the slightest opportunity. Marvin had Alec for that.

So far as strange circumstances and terrible situations that were entirely his own fault were concerned, this was probably one of the better ones. Merman notwithstanding.

It had all started when one of those werewolves had plonked himself down at a corner table and began studying in Trick's café, Bean There, Froth That. Yes, werewolves study. And no, Trick didn't own the cafe, but it was *his* territory. Otters were territorial about transitional social spaces.

Then, because Colin was there, Judd started showing up. Wherever Judd went, his fellow enforcer, Kevin, inevitably followed. Once the two enforcers were around, well, the Alpha had to come check out what was drawing them regularly to the local cafe on the waterfront. Then the Beta popped in, and then Max, all powerful Beta-mate.

Actually Max had been one of the first to frequent the Bean, but at the time Trick thought he was just one of the world's sexiest human joggers. Trick would never have guessed that Max was part of a pack. No, Max was a godling – gifted unto spandex and gay men. But because Trick brewed a mean coffee and was willing to cater to Max's ridiculous sweet tooth, the magistar started making regular stops at the Bean, after his morning run.

All of which is to say, eventually and inevitably all of the San Andreas pack showed up in Trick's cafe including the Alpha-mate, Marvin the merman.

That was when things got fishy. Because Trick might not be accustomed to werewolves but he was *overly* comfortable around mermen. And he genuinely liked Marvin. Marvin was a hoot and a half. He had a fantastic wardrobe and killer style for a man who should be more comfortable in scales than sequins.

Then, because they were around and causing a ruckus, and Trick was naturally attracted to ruckuses, Trick got involved with the pack. And because they were werewolves, they then got involved in his life. Suddenly there were bear shifter policemen, money laundry (yes, *laundry*, not laundering) investigations, werewolf country music singers with sinister agendas, and one incredibly gorgeous gold-spangled jacket.

And Trick found himself diving into the ocean, with Marvin the merman, on the tail of some selkie bad guys with offshore accounts and mafia connections.

As you do.

Especially if you're Trick.

Ultimately, because the werewolf pack found out that he was sleeping in his car, and they did *not* like that idea, Trick ended up living with them whether he liked it or not.

Now Marvin, whenever he wasn't working but his Alpha-mate was (which seemed to be an inordinate amount of the time), had installed himself amongst the regulars at Trick's cafe, just as if he'd always been there.

Today he was occupying the front table, in the big window, wearing a tight cropped aqua t-shirt with a lettuce hem and "princess" scrawled across the front in glitter. He had on baggy ripped low-slung acid-washed jeans, and approximately four hundred jelly bracelets, purple glitter platform jelly shoes with a floating fish scape in the soles, elaborate teal and turquoise eye makeup (which brought out his eyes), and pale purple glittery lip gloss. He looked fantastic.

Trick, of course, had dressed to complement. They often coordinated their outfits these days. Marvin had given Trick full access to his wardrobe. They were about the same size. Trick was wearing the same makeup, a ribbed lavender bodysuit with over-sized white cargo pants, rainbow laced turquoise boots, and a pair of silver glitter earrings, one of which said "queen" and the other "bitch." And his apron, of course.

The Bean was buzzing with activity, just as Trick liked it. He was feeling particularly twirly, since someone had put retro stylings on the jukebox. (Okay, it was Trick, but he liked to pretend he had a mystic musical benefactor with fantastic taste.)

The bell chimed as a very large personage entered Trick's cafe. At six foot ten, he automatically ducked his head as he entered, giving him the aura of gentlemanly behavior. Deputy Kettil had arrived.

The bear shifter looked annoyed and surprised to find Trick behind the counter. Even though Trick was the main barista and was *always* behind the counter.

At one time Trick had doubted Deputy Kettil's sexuality because his closet was so deep it was practically a walk-in. It probably housed Turkish delight instead of mothballs. Trick didn't doubt anymore. The big man's eyes were always laser-focused on Trick, hot and interested. Trick was all too familiar with that expression. The cop had been a problem for Trick from the get-go. He was protective, repressed, and clearly liked Trick a lot. Unfortunately, Trick had a weakness for all those things in a man. He loved the attention, too. Of course he did. But Kettil was still a cop and Trick was, technically, illegal, not to mention he came by his hatred of cops honestly. Most importantly, a hot pot of Trick's spice and fabulousness didn't do closets, even if it was big enough to fit Marvin's whole wardrobe.

A man couldn't hide his sexuality and date Trick. He shuddered to even contemplate walking around town next to an off-duty Deputy Kettil. Apart from the incongruity in their sizes, the act of them being out on a date together would instantly render Kettil's closet null and void.

Trick may not take himself seriously, but he expected his lovers to at least try to honor his existence, as rarely as this lasted, and as poor as his track record may be.

That too wasn't his fault. Trick suffered from Sato-comparison-itis. The thing he missed most (not that Trick would ever admit to missing anything about Sato at all, *of course!*) was the intensity of focus. Sato's eyes on him, Sato's care over him. Sato had always looked at him like he was the greatest thing ever. No matter what he wore. No matter what he said. No matter how much trouble he got into.

"Where's your better half?" asked Trick. Technically, the bear shifter had a partner on the force, but he always seemed to have shaken himself loose when the time came to get coffee.

No response from the deputy, just a hard stare.

Trick tried again. "Helllloooo there, officer, what can I do you for today?"

Deputy Kettil blushed becomingly.

"You never stop, do you?" he growled in a tone guaranteed to cause Trick to shiver slightly, in a good way. Trick reminded himself that he wasn't up for coaching a three-hundred- pound slab of yummy through a sexual identity crisis.

"I was born with a full head of hair, an innate love of oysters, and no sense of shame whatsoever."

"A hardened flirt from the get-go?"

"Hardened indeed. So, Deputy Snookums, you feeling pot or black this morning?"

"What?" grumbled the bear shifter.

Trick sighed. The man had no sense of humor. "A whole pot of black coffee for you today or just your usual thimbleful of depression?"

Deputy Kettil always studiously avoided the shifter side of the menu for some unknown reason and simply got a shot of espresso when he got anything at all. Trick was confused by this. And a little hurt. After all, the shifter's menu was where his true genius lay. There was a rosemary, honey, and lemon toddy with a salmon oil float that was specifically designed with bear shifters in mind. Maybe Trick had even been thinking about Kettil when he invented it.

Then again, maybe the bear shifter really wanted an excuse to come into The Bean, growl at Trick, order a drink he hated, and leave. Who was Trick to judge what bear shifters did for fun?

"Just a shot of espresso and none of your nonsense."

"You're no fun."

"You're only just now figuring that out?"

Trick teased the bear out of habit; he wasn't sold on Deputy Kettil. Even if Kettil was out, policemen were a difficult dating proposition for a dratsie with a devoutly criminal family and a record including trumped-up charges from corrupt cops.

Trick wrinkled his nose and reached for the bean. "It's Kona today."

Deputy Kettil grunted approval, Hawaiian was his favorite.

Trick liked them too, but he didn't admit to it. Hawaii was a place he'd never visited but deeply resented. Hawaii had been the start of the end. Hawaii meant loss. Wasn't the beans' fault where they came from, but he always specified *Kona* because saying Hawaii made him angry. Also, Kona indicated that lovely chocolatey note and he *needed* everyone to be educated about bean origin flavor profiles. It was a barista's moral imperative.

Kettil began examining the pastry case.

Trick plonked down the espresso.

Kettil shot it down. Winced.

Trick tilted his head at the case. "You want something *more*? Don't strain yourself."

"That salmon?"

Trick grinned big and batted his lashes. "Salmon sarriette with capers and cream cheese."

A curt nod. "To go, please."

"Look at you, branching out. So brave."

Kettil glared at him.

"You want it warmed?"

"No, thank you."

"So polite." Trick popped the pastry into a paper baggie.

The bear turned and walked out without another word.

"Bye bye now," trilled Trick at his massive back.

Trick caught Marvin turning to watch Kettil leave. The merman had observed the entire interchange with interest.

Trick felt suddenly exhausted. He wished he had better taste and a different type.

Floyd, who was so much a part of the cafe furniture that Trick forgot he existed half the time, said, "Deputy Kettil seems interested in you, kid. You gonna tap that?"

"Floyd! Language! How old do you think you are?" Varyenite, sitting at the back, waved a silver-and-amber-bedecked hand at Floyd, who was at least eighty years old if he was a day. She had a grey mohawk and ran the tarot, incense, and crystal shop three doors down because, as she put it, she "went woo and lesbian in the eighties and saw absolutely no reason to correct for a lifetime of spiritual growth." She came to Trick's cafe every morning for his turmeric, citron, and cayenne herbal restorative. She got a shot of espresso in it, though, and her pastry preference was an old-fashioned doughnut because, as she reminded Trick often, she lived the stereotype but wasn't defined by it.

"So?" Varyenite turned sharp eyes onto Trick, "*are* you going to tap that?"

Trick began wiping down the espresso machine in annoyance. "I don't know. He's a bear shifter. He's a cop. He's closeted."

"Come to think of it, we've never really seen you date, have we?" Varyenite nibbled at the extra-glazed crunchy edge of her doughnut.

Floyd's knitting needles clacked with interest. "You don't date, kid?"

Trick glared at his two most loyal customers. "I've been known to. But I'm more of a catch-and-release type." *Easier to leave them first.*

Marvin, of course, entered the conversation at that juncture. "Oh thank goodness, I knew you were a fabulous slut!"

Trick blew kisses at him. "Honored, of course."

Floyd squinted his eyes behind his thick specs in understanding. "Organ focused, just not the heart?"

"Floyd, really!" said Varyenite, but only because she felt she ought.

Trick grinned. "What can I say, the flesh is willing but the spirit is weak."

"Burned?" suggested Varyenite, perceptively.

Trick let out a dramatic sigh. "Badly. Heart and soul shattered into a million opalescent pieces and scattered all over the Mississippi Delta, like Louisiana's Osiris."

Varyenite nodded sagely. "Dildo origin story."

Trick made victory fingers at her understanding of Egyptian mythology.

"So are you gonna catch and release the bear?" Floyd was relentless. He was kept alive on a diet of cappuccinos and other people's business.

"I'm not sure he would know what to do with me." Trick gestured at his own slender frame then spun like he was on an ice rink. "*This* is not *intro-level* gay."

"The boy has a point," said Floyd to Varyenite.

"The boy is all points and rainbow facets," she replied, brushing crumbs off her fingertips and standing up. "See you tomorrow, gentleman, when no doubt nothing will have changed."

Marvin stood as well. "Well this has been an enlightening morning but sadly, I too must work today." Marvin worked as an adjunct to the Coast Guard, of all things. He was currently half occupied with collecting remains in conjunction with a mass murder investigation, and half occupied trying to persuade the Coast Guard that, as their primary submersible contract worker, he should be allowed to wear a robe instead of a uniform. One that he was designing of course, modeled after a boxer's robe, only with more sparkle.

The Coast Guard was very unsure about the pugilist robe scheme, but they loved what Marvin could do for them once he was in the water. Unlike any other sea shifter, Marvin retained his ability for human vocal communication, and that was invaluable. He was, despite everything, remarkably good at his job – mostly search, rescue, and salvage (not murder). So the Coast Guard was disposed to put up with Marvin, his sparkles, and his eccentricities. So far, though, no robe.

Marvin held out hope.

Marvin was gathering up his mock-croc shoulder bag, teal of course, when suddenly he caught sight of someone out on the sidewalk, and pivoted slowly to track them as they came into the cafe.

Trick looked up, alert because Marvin was. At the tinkling bell he expected to see one of the pack or a very handsome stranger with loads of muscles.

Instead, it was a stunningly beautiful woman. *Woman* being the operative word. Trick could appreciate female beauty, of course he could, but he'd never known Marvin to give any woman a second glance – who wasn't friend or family. This one was neither.

In fact, she seemed a stranger to the Bay Area. She was wearing impractical shoes and a skirt suit. Not a tourist but a professional. No one ever came to Sausalito on *business*. Trick couldn't remember the last time he'd even seen a skirt suit in person.

Marvin looked at her hard for a long moment.

"Oh, hell *no*," he said, and then promptly dashed out of the cafe.

"Rude!" said the woman, before approaching Trick's counter. She flicked a lock of salt-crusted hair behind her shoulder with one webbed hand. She had a length of black pearls coiled around her wrist.

Great, first Deputy Kettil and now... mermaids. And Trick had woken up in such a good mood that morning.

The Present: Sato, who hates politics, dealing with mermaid politicians

The grand assembly halls of the True Deep are nothing like a human might expect, had any two-legged ever been allowed to visit. Which they most definitely had not.

They are not beautiful. There are no sculptures. There are no crystal hallways to swim through, decorated with pearls and seashells. They are pretty in their bioluminescence, the way the lantern fish drift throughout, lighting the way. The assembly halls are made up of anemone gardens and kelp forests, they have no floors or ceilings, nothing is intentionally built or decorated.

The Deep is merely an idea, a designated temporary sea-zone claimed by the Soteria while they conspire and plan, before they move on.

What is beautiful about the Deep is the merfolk who inhabit it. They need no grand architectural gestures to attract the minds of men. They never have. There is nothing the land could produce more stunning than an average mermaid.

And they know it.

The mermen are beautiful too.

But no one cares about them.

The mermaids are the pearls that truly decorate the Deep. It matters not what surrounds them because few can look away. The stunning colors of their tails, the delicate see-through fins, the perfect symmetry in faces, the beautiful luster patterns on some and the iridescent skin on others. Sirens indeed.

Sato Daiki thought it was a pity, since it was all wasted on him. He kind of, just a little bit hated them for all of it.

Irony that he, one of the few males in attendance, really didn't want to be there. He suffered the whims of the Soteria's current because occasionally it took him to land. To his hunting grounds. Away from the deep.

He had traded his freedom for opportunity. But it meant all too often he was trapped in the middle of the ocean by bureaucracy.

"How much longer?" he signed at Meymey, hiding his hands behind his dorsal fin.

Meymey only flicked him to stay still and silent. The gesture was annoying and offensive.

A lull in debate and his sister swam before the council and took up position. Among her peers, she looked particularly young.

"Oh I see, our little Paralia wishes to speak, how cute," said the Ogress.

"The humans are having a gathering." Meymey started in on her speech without acknowledging the older member.

Only to be immediately interrupted by the Anax. "The humans can never not have gatherings, there are so many of them. What matters this particular one to us?"

"It is around a topic of great interest to the merfolk," insisted Meymey.

"What do they know of things that interest us?" the Anax persisted.

Meymey puffed out her cheeks, frustrated. She was the youngest there and Sato wondered, not for the first time, how his mother had managed to get her into such a powerful position.

"Let the child sing." That was the Klepsydra. From what Sato had deduced, she was not exactly allied with his mother's pod but she wasn't in opposition either. She did not always vote alongside his sister, and was probably weighing in at this instance simply to keep things moving. She was, after all, the official timekeeper.

Meymey pressed on. "It is a gathering around something called *marine biology*."

"They have those all the time." The Anax was fierce and barbed always. "This is nothing new or special. Perhaps you do not realize because you are so young." She had a temper that could boil water. Sato did not like her.

"This one will be focused on the breeding and procreation of sea creatures and something the humans call population statistics." Meymey always swam her intended current firmly, fighting for her voice and vote.

The other four members of the Soteria were suddenly interested in what she had to say.

"*Breeding*? Are you certain?" That was the Sibyl speaking, the oldest of the Soteria and the only one among them approaching infertility and obsolescence.

Meymey fluttered her hands in mermaid agreement. "And all matters connected to it."

"But for fish."

"And sea mammals," pressed Meymey. "Are merfolk not mammals of the sea?"

"We are *people* of the sea. We do *not* behave the same way."

Especially not around breeding, thought Sato. He had grown, during his time living among humans, to believe that merfolk had a truly impractical way of perpetuating their species. Mermaids having to hunt down and fuck human males once a month. This was something that required migration, like salmon swimming upstream, only mermaids swam into a two-legged form and beached themselves in pursuit of sex. Since, aside from vangill, all mermen were sterile, a whole other species had been unwittingly recruited to participate. There simply weren't enough vangill to go around. It was a system that codified the outcast state of mermen and rejected mermaids who couldn't breed as useless. It was unpleasant. Sato often felt merfolk deserved to die out. Perpetuating the species was mean-spirited and complicated. Why bother?

But it was all the ruling mermaids cared about.

Meymey made her big political play then. "I should attend this gathering openly as Paralia of the Deep."

"Send a merman in your stead." The Anax looked pointedly at Sato.

He blinked slowly back at her. He would like that. He could hunt for Patrick untroubled by mermaids and their agenda.

Meymey glanced at him.

Sato twitched his tail in a faintly accepting way.

"Mermen do not care enough for our concerns around this matter, as a species," she replied. She wanted to go herself. It was her prerogative. And she was right, Sato didn't care.

"Of course they do not, they are too stupid to care." The Anax sneered at Sato.

Sato's face did not change. He was happy to be thought stupid and unsympathetic. The faces of the four other vangill, each floating close to his respective Soteria, also did not change. They had all heard it many times before. Although only Sato played dull-witted and uncaring on purpose. He had a reputation for violence and he preferred it that way.

"Then send a spy or envoy. A selkie or a dratsie should do." That was the Ogress. Meymey may play for a different political camp, but she was still a mermaid and should not be risked or sullied when others might do the dirty job of actually having to talk with humans.

"You wish me to explain to an *outsider* the full scope of our concerns on this matter?"

"Of course not!"

"Then how would they know what information to look for?" Meymey remained calm and patient, belying her age. The others did not liaise with the transitional shifter species as much as the Paralia. And those like the selkie and the dratsie were intentionally kept in ignorance on the full scope of merfolk population decrease. Other water shifters could not be allowed to realize how dire their numbers, or the mermaids would lose control of the sea.

So far as Sato could gather, after too many years in and out of these damn assemblies, merfolk population numbers were not just declining, but drastically reduced. The mermaids were, at this point, justifiably worried that within three or four generations there would, in fact, simply be no more sea people at all.

Sato was bored by the whole crisis.

"You're saying this is a mermaid's job and only she can do it?"

Meymey fluttered her hands again. "I'm saying this is the Paralia's job. Is it not in my mandate to act as ambassador to the dry world above?"

"You are to be a diplomat to the humans and land-bound shifters when absolutely necessary and when called upon by their governing bodies to represent the oceans. And you are to maintain contact with those sea folk who transition between land and shore. But to walk amongst them *yourself*? To talk with humans one-on-one, not for breeding but for actual communication? To seek *counsel* with them? Surely that is excessive exposure. Surely that is too much to ask. Especially of one so young as you." The Sibyl *sounded* nice. She *sounded* like she was genuinely concerned for innocent little Meymey's well-being. She was being patronizing.

Sato wholly distrusted the Sibyl. Possibly more than any of the other Soteria. She was the only one who had never tried to sleep with him. That was a relief but also why he distrusted her. Mermaids always wanted sex with vangill. They were, after all, the only potent mermen.

Meymey's tail stiffened at the implied incompetence. "There is no one better. Plus I will have Sato for protection. He will keep me safe."

Sato wished she hadn't mentioned him. She had reminded them that he was special, that he was the best, and that they had never had him.

"Your brother with the magic spurs, how could we ever forget." The Ogress's tongue was sharper than Sato's spurs.

Sato knew for a fact she fucked her own vangill regularly, but no child had resulted. Frankly, he knew way too much about the sex lives of the five Soteria of the Deep. It was annoying for a man of his inclination.

"There's a rumor he prefers two legs over tails in all things," shot back the Anax.

Meymey jumped to Sato's defense. "There's a rumor you insult my brother because he doesn't want to breed *you*."

Shocked silence descended at that. The Ogress's vangill coiled his tail slightly, side-eyeing Sato.

Sato ever so subtly let the tips his spurs show, like huge curved deadly teeth down the length of both forearms. His control had only gotten better over the years. He suspected he was always ready to fight these days. He had probably been that way from the moment Patrick left him behind. His spurs lurked in the shallows of his own flesh, easy to access, ready to deploy.

Even more subtly, the other four vangill all backed down. Hovered a little higher in the water, tails forcefully relaxed.

The mermaids may jockey constantly for power and position, alliances may shift as easily and as often as the tides. But the five vangill of the Deep knew which one of them would win a fight, without ever having to actually duke it out. They also all knew that Sato Daiki never stopped training. That his spurs were not just instinct, they were practiced. He went to land regularly. Ran the beaches, interfaced with humans, practiced with their life-guards, and participated in their athletic competitions. He did strange things in the sand like volleyball, matkot, and ssireum. Occasionally he did very strange things *to* the sand, like punching it or running through it.

There were endless rumors around Sato Daiki and what he did when the Soteria were *not* meeting. When the ladies were back with their home pods or on rotation visiting their constituents. He led tuna hunts, and was known to go up against whitetips, makos, and even the occasional bull shark just for the thrill of it. Some even claimed he did not fuck mermaids because he got his sexual thrills from killing. That his unnatural bent was not human women but blood.

Sato let all the rumors flow, cultivated them even. Perhaps he did find solace in shark-infested waters, in using his spurs to kill more often than other vangill. He needed to use them. He'd been frozen in time by those spurs, adolescent and sullen, lost Patrick because of them. He used them to fight the world because of what those spurs had cost him. One dratsie, paid pound by pound in fish flesh. The sea and its inhabitants owed him that much.

Eventually, too long, Sato felt, the Soteria voted.

Meymey got her wish, three to two.

"I will recruit a diplomatic pod and…" Meymey cut herself short, eyes suddenly focused on the Klepsydra's daughter, who was only present because she was still a minor and must stay close to her mother.

"Klepsydra, your child, she is…?"

Sato followed her focus. "Bleeding," he snapped out, sharp and annoyed.

"Congratulations!" said the Sibyl brightly.

The Klepsydra looked indulgent. "She has begun her first courses."

"She should be on land!" sang out Sato, a near shriek.

"Well, yes, but we had a meeting." The Klepsydra was dismissive.

Sato had already turned to scan the surrounding waters. How long had she been bleeding freely? How far did her trail extend? What waters had she swum through to get here?

Behind him there was arguing.

In front of him there was the speck of something familiar moving through the water fast, a shark.

Of course there was.

Some distance away but Sato knew a shark when he saw one. It was no doubt coming toward them in that open-jawed inevitable way that was feeding frenzy from having *scented blood in the water.*

Sato showed his teeth at the threat, pointed like the shark's. Good, he was bored.

His spurs were already out.

He spared a glance to his sister. "Get away from the others.

Go to that cave where we stopped for lunch on the way here. I'll meet you there."

She did not argue or talk back. Not under these circumstances.

Sato assumed the other vangill would see to their charges but he glared at the Klepsydra's merman. "You're an idiot."

One of the other vangill agreed with him. "Get her daughter to land now."

"But she's too—"

"You risked all the Soteria!"

Sato ignored their bickering and braced for the shark attack.

The best thing about sharks was how stupid they were.

The thing came in and at Sato, because Sato stayed ostentatiously in its way. It didn't know whose blood, only that there *was* blood. Its mouth was wide, all those rows of teeth on display, deadly and hungry and intent.

Sato admired the beautiful horror of it, but also wished the sea would occasionally offer up some novelty.

It was great white, but a young one, only about twice as big as he was. Fast, but not fast enough. Sato dodged and dipped down to one side, slashed out with his spurs, going for the gills.

He missed, but got a good slice in.

The shark barely registered. But now, it was bleeding too.

None of the other vangill came to fight alongside Sato. He couldn't blame them. They would be getting their charges to safety.

Had it been anything but blood in the water, Sato would have done the same. But blood meant more sharks.

He caught the back end of the shark with one set of spurs, near its tail, hooked in hard. Then he crawled up the shark's thrashing body with his spurs, poke poke poke, until he was back at its head. He dug firmly in with his left spurs, dangling from that one arm. Riding and floating along the length of the shark's writhing body. Let himself be buffeted. He was positioned so that the shark could not curl around and bite him, because it would have snapped itself in half.

He began stabbing and slashing with his right spurs until

finally he got them into the creature's gills. Now it was in real pain.

The water was white and red and pink with blood and froth.

Anchored into the shark's most sensitive spot, Sato began pumping his tail, driving the shark with power and agony, back the way it had come.

The shark, panicked and suffering and no longer breathing properly, allowed itself to be ridden away.

Now there was a new trail of fresh blood in the water.

Now any sharks that followed would have a new target.

The only way to hide the scent of blood in the Deep was with more blood.

Eventually Sato retracted his spurs, let go of the shark. He charged up to the surface, moving as fast as he could. In case the shark followed. And to wash the blood off of himself.

He took to the air, jetting out of water and spinning, using gravity to fling any shark flesh still attached to him away.

He did it again. And again. Moving even faster through the air than the water. Casting bits of shark to the skies.

He spotted a yacht then, one of the fancy pleasure ones that rich old men bought because after humans acquired too much money they liked to acquire too much risk.

He beached himself on it easily, traded tail for legs.

The boat was not what he expected. It was filled with men in dark clothes and piles of brick-shaped objects stuffed into plastic bags.

Someone shot at him.

Drug runners.

The yacht lurched, hit broadside by an injured great white.

Then, as expected, there came another shark, bigger, also crashing into the yacht.

The men started yelling and running around uselessly. Some of them started shooting over the side of the boat.

They yelled at Sato too, in one of the human languages he did not speak.

Sato shrieked back at them, in the language of the sea. He

couldn't quite make their ears bleed like a mermaid's, but it did hurt and added to the chaos.

The yacht nearly capsized from shark attack.

One of the humans fell over the side.

Some of the drugs fell over the other side.

That upset them more than anything else.

Sato could have swum away. But this was more interesting.

The sharks seemed to be well occupied with each other, and the fallen man, and possibly the drugs. One never knew what a shark swallowed when in a feeding frenzy.

Sato gauged the bulk of the activity. Sharks, humans, blood, all focused in the same place. He ran the length of the yacht and launched himself off the front, diving as far out as he could, clear of the chaos.

He hit the sea, shifted, and swam away.

He met his sister at that small cave with the very narrow mouth which he himself could barely fit through.

"You bleed the shark so it would lure away any others following the scent trail."

Sato hardly need answer the truth.

"You're smarter than you look, brother."

"Can we go now?" asked Sato, trying not to sound pitiful. The land beckoned. He wanted to hunt for Patrick.

His sister chatted about her plans to recruit a diplomatic pod to attend the humans' marine biology gathering with her. It was her first official opportunity to visit the human world. She was apprehensive but excited.

"Scientists should be easy for you. Nerds," he said.

"Nerds?"

"Nerd is a subcategory of human that thinks more than it acts, obsesses more than it loves, and conflates dominance with intellectualism."

"Do we like them?" she asked.

"You will because they are easy to manipulate. I do not care."

"That's a shocker. You, not caring." She had learned all her sarcasm from him.

Sato was proud.

She bumped up against him softly as they swam. "You killed the shark?"

"Maybe. Not sure. I left it to play with some humans."

"Sometimes I wonder if they're right about you."

Sato looked at her.

"Liking it too much."

"Is it wrong to enjoy one's job?" Sometimes he worried about that too. He needed to find Patrick. He missed feeling.

"I think it helps them feel better about themselves to believe you have unnatural preferences and that is the reason you reject them."

"I know."

"Why do you reject them?"

"You actually want to know why your brother doesn't stick dick into your coworkers?"

Meymey blew out bubbles in exasperation. "The Klepsydra at the very least is universally acknowledged as the most beautiful mermaid in all seven seas. And she's obviously fertile."

Sato remained unmoved. "She's of the opposite political party."

"So?"

"My spawn would be raised a Red Tide." And by an idiot who doesn't get her daughter out of the water when she starts her period.

"Never say you actually care about merfolk political factions, Daidai." Sometimes Meymey was far too perceptive.

She didn't know that he never slept with any mermaids, ever. She didn't know he had no children at all swimming the oceans. Irony incarnate. There he was, the strongest of the vangill, aware that merfolk were fading out of existence and that he could help with that. Yet he had never once bothered to increase their numbers.

Didn't want to.

Couldn't do it.

Just wanted Patrick.

When he felt any kind of urge at all, Sato took himself away, to the land. To some solitary beach. To soft sand of the kind

Patrick once drew in. To spend himself on memories. To hate himself a little more for his own needs. Resenting the sea that had kept him from fulfilling one all-important promise a decade earlier. He went to a dry place where he could nurse regrets instead of children, away from the watery world that was now both his prison and his sanctuary.

He'd never admit any of that to Meymey. She was all he had now. His misery would oppress her with another unsolvable problem among many. Perhaps she thought he still grieved a lost love. Or perhaps she thought he went out regularly to sow his powerful vangill seed, just not among the Soteria. Maybe she even believed, or wanted to believe, there were hundreds of young Satos swimming with other pods in other waters.

Sato said only, "You know I will never fuck any of the Soteria. Things would get too complicated for you."

"It's only sex, Daidai."

"Fine, things would get too complicated for *me*."

"Sometimes I think you are the most human of any of us and that is why you are so good with your spurs."

"Explain."

"The human inclination for violence, for advanced weaponry, that was what you really got from them, living with your sire for all those years."

"It's an interesting theory."

"Well, I appreciate the result, whatever the cause." Meymey may not understand him or his choices, but he was her big brother first and foremost, and her protector. She had never been given cause to doubt his abilities or loyalty.

"Where is the landmass we're ultimately swimming to?" he asked, hoping it was a place he hadn't searched before. Hoping for a chance at one missing dratsie.

"It's on the other side of the Pacific Plate. You know, that fault line that gives the humans trouble all the time. What do they call it?"

"Don't all fault lines give humans trouble? The two-legs find it nearly impossible to deal with a quake." Sato thought back to that rescue mission in Hawaii, the one that had kept him from Patrick. It had been the first of many.

Meymey fluttered her tail extra hard, putting on a burst of speed.

Sato caught up with her easily. Her tail was a similar blue color to his, and almost as beautiful, but nowhere near as big or powerful. "Which fault line, Meymey?"

"The one near that famous bridge that's red but the idiot humans call it golden."

Sato put a human geographical map into his head and frowned at the unexpected trivia question. "The San Andreas fault line?" he hazarded.

"Yes, that's the one!"

"Is the human marine biology gathering in the place they call San Francisco?" Sato felt a thrill. It had a reputation for being an accommodating city for shifters and other disenfranchised folk. It was the kind of place he could imagine Patrick settling into.

The hunt was back on.

CHAPTER THREE
THAT'S JUST FLIRTY POOL

The Past: Patrick at the swimming pool

Patrick tried not to completely panic but he was scared. He might even have cried a little, not that there was anyone to see. Super embarrassing if he were caught, though.

A series of stupid decisions having to do with his crazy human friends who wanted to break into the local high school and drink and swim had resulted in Patrick, locked inside the pool, alone on a Saturday night. And he knew that no one was coming to open the darn thing back up again until swim practice started Monday morning.

That's assuming the high school team *had* swim practice on Mondays.

He didn't want to yell because he didn't want to get caught. But he also didn't want to spend the next forty-eight hours at a swimming pool.

Not that anyone would hear him if he yelled. The high school was on the outskirts of town.

His stomach growled.

He looked at the gate again, topped with barbed wire. Decided he better go see if he could find a ladder or something. He hated heights, though.

"Seriously?" A familiar gruff voice made intentionally less pretty by a smoker's burr emanated from outside. Sato materialized out of the shadows on the other side of the gate.

Patrick's tears and fear instantly vanished. He became annoyed with relief and humiliation. *Why did it always have to be Sato rescuing him from dumb shit like this?*

"Oh, it's you."

"It's me." Sato stared for a long moment. His face was as deadpan as always. Beautifully sullen. "What are you doing, Patrick?"

"Oh, ya know, just hanging out."

"If you wanted to go swimming, you coulda just asked."

Patrick crossed his arms. "It's not like that."

"Oh no? What's it *like* then?"

Patrick went on the defensive. "How'd you know I was here? Were you following me?"

"Like I don't have better things to do than tag after a group of idiot middle-schoolers."

"Ah ha! So you *were* following me. Otherwise how'd you know I came with friends?"

"Some friends. They abandoned you."

Patrick bristled. "They were drunk and I was exploring the locker room. I think they forgot about me."

"The locker room? Seriously, Patrick?"

Patrick grinned. "I can't have fantasies?"

"You're twelve. You're a *child*." Sato spoke with all the disgust of a fourteen-year-old.

"Tell that to my hormones." Patrick stuck his tongue out.

Sato gave a very big sigh.

Patrick grinned at him, enjoying the feeling of having gotten the upper hand. Upper fin, maybe?

Sato turned away. "I can leave just as easily as I came. You're the one who's stuck."

Patrick went on the defensive. "Would we say stuck?"

"Yes."

"I'm not your responsibility. You don't have to always look after me like I'm your kid brother."

"You wanna stay there all night? I thought you hated the smell of chlorine."

Patrick wrinkled his nose. "I really do." Also, he was a terrible swimmer. As a human. Ironic, really. That's why he'd been in the locker room and not playing in the pool with the others. Well, that was *partly* why. He did *also* have his fantasies.

The object of them continued to glare. Finally Sato said, "Sit tight," and disappeared off somewhere.

Patrick sat on the cold concrete, as instructed, and waited, as instructed. He only squirmed a little bit. He had no doubt that Sato would return. Sato would never leave him behind. To Sato he was indeed the annoying little brother, always in trouble, always up to no good. Sato's responsibility. Assumed, of course, because Patrick had slotted himself into Sato's life since the moment he moved in next door. Sato had accepted it with a startled grace. Of course he should look after Patrick. Who else would do it?

"Why you still sitting there? Come on." Sato's head was sticking out of the infamous locker room. Patrick's hormones got a sugar rush from that idea alone.

"Wait! What?" said Patrick knowing he sounded like an idiot.

"This is *my* high school, remember? I know how the damn gym is constructed."

Patrick leapt up and trotted over.

Sato hustled him through the door with a webbed hand at the nape of his neck. Guiding him through the dark. Patrick didn't have very good night vision. Neither did Sato, but this was familiar territory to him.

Wait a minute.

How familiar *was* Sato with the boys locker room!

"Clearly you didn't explore very thoroughly," said Sato, prodding Patrick around a pile of wrestling mats. "There's a door to the soccer field on the other side."

"Well yes, but it was locked."

"Now it's unlocked," said Sato, unfussed.

To be precise, now it was broken. Sato never seemed to have much patience, especially if there was a barrier between him and

Patrick. This delighted Patrick. The door was hanging askew. Sato had destroyed the old hinges rather than try for the solid bolts or the handle. Smart boy.

Patrick grinned at him. "You gonna be in trouble for this?"

"You gonna tell on me?"

"No cameras?" Patrick looked around for small red flashy lights or something equally sinister.

"How could a school this rundown afford *cameras*?" Sato scoffed. "You watch too much *Team Werewolf*."

"Fair point. Oh boy, am I looking forward to this hell hole." Patrick was all sarcasm.

"There is no point in being cheeky about it. If you weren't looking forward to high school, you wouldn't have broken into our pool. Stop chattering nonsense."

Patrick pouted. "I told you, it was my friends' idea."

"I *told* you not to listen to humans. Especially not actors."

"But I *like* the drama club."

"This is my surprised face." Sato's surprised face looked exactly like his regular face. So Patrick supposed it was nice of him to point it out.

They walked in silence off school grounds and down the dusty road back toward town.

Finally Sato said, "Locker room, Patrick, really?"

"You've seen my manga collection. It's a *trope*."

Sato arched a sarcastic brow. "You have any idea how gross they are?"

"High school boys," insisted Patrick, "getting naked in locker rooms. What's not to love?"

"High school humans," spat Sato in response, as if that put a stopper on everything.

But you're not human, thought Patrick, but didn't say.

Not that he didn't get to see Sato naked whenever he wanted. They still swam together regularly. Nothing more than swim, sadly. Sato was ever conscious of their age gap. Also, he probably never considered Patrick as anything beyond a sibling.

Also, he was probably straight.

Patrick, even Patrick Mr Word-Biscuits Covered in Sentence-

Gravy himself, had never yet worked up the courage to ask outright. Sato never displayed any sexual inclinations. His room remained as sparsely decorated now as it had been when he first arrived. Oh, there were textbooks and school supplies, but no posters, no manga, no DVDs, nothing that showed interest in anything, really, let alone the opposite sex.

Mermen don't collect stuff was all Sato ever said about it.

Like no matter how many years passed with him on land, living among the humans, he was always about to leave.

"I wanna go swimming," Patrick said. Because he did, but the locker room had made him want to see Sato naked. Because, quite frankly, that never got old and it was all he could get.

"Now? Tonight?"

Patrick nodded vigorously.

"You need to eat. You've had nothing but alcohol."

"Not even that."

"You didn't drink?"

"Naw, that was human fun."

"You don't swim in pools and you didn't drink? What was the point then?"

"*Locker room,*" explained Patrick again, patiently. Sato wasn't very bright.

Sato sighed in a long-suffering way. "Come to my house, there's katsu. We can swim in the morning."

"Can I spend the night?" Patrick walk-flopped to drape himself partly over Sato's back and side, because he loved how solid and dense he was.

"Like you need to ask." Sato snorted, tolerating his contact and his absurd words.

Patrick bounced along happily, still half hugging the merman.

Everything was better now.

The Past: Sato at the Pool Party

. . .

Sato sneered at yet *another* freshman girl trying to flirt with him. The lure of the older boy seemed to be strong with this year's crop. Or maybe they liked his emo image. He hadn't washed his hair in days, and with his current cut the sea made it extra spiky. He had on his ubiquitous leather gloves, to hide the webbing, and he was smoking to put gravel in his voice. Because every part of him – hands, hair, eyes, voice, cheekbones   told the story of what he really was to anyone who knew to look carefully. And he never forgot that, especially not at a party full of humans. It required a lot of effort for mermen to hide among humans. Fortunately, humans were dumb and self-involved and lacked basic observation skills.

Didn't stop Patrick from calling him *an accidental punk meets salt-lick* and *would it kill him to take a proper shower once in a while?*

Sato certainly wasn't interested in human freshman girls coming up to him, awkwardly twirling their dull hair and asking if he wanted a drink.

He was looking for Patrick. Where the hell was he?

The house was packed. Someone was a trust-fund kid. It was one of those super fancy beach bungalows that usually only rich tourists rented, but this one seemed to be owned by one of this year's freshmen. Or the family of said freshman. Sato didn't care which.

Sato ignored them all. Because none of them were Patrick.

He spotted a flurry of activity out the back, near the swimming pool. Because of course there was a big fancy swimming pool and a hot tub. Even though the ocean was *right* the fuck there. Humans were *insane.*

There came a puff of white from the center of the group of humans and someone yelled in surprise. Was that... snow? Sato had never seen snow in real life, only on TV. No? Tiny feathers? Cotton fluff?

Patrick suddenly emerged from amid the group. He was covered in the white fuzz, and had some young human kid of indiscriminate age and gender by the wrist and was dragging them bodily after him.

The kid was *also* covered in white fuzz.

Sato squinted. Definitely feathers. Had the kid molted or something? Shifter of some kind? Did bird shifters have a molting season? Were there even bird shifters?

Patrick brightened at seeing Sato. "You're here."

"I'm here."

"Good, let's go."

"What's going on, Patrick?"

"Jake's brother is home from college and was picking on this one, their youngest sib."

He raised up the attached child's hand. The kid's eyes were round with confusion. One cheek was red in a way that would be a bruise tomorrow.

Sato didn't ask who Jake was, presumably the host of this appalling party. "Siblings bully each other. You know that better than anyone. What's this kid to you?" Patrick's parents barely cared that he existed most of the time. His siblings only noticed him to yell or beat the shit out of him.

Patrick made a face. "It's what they were bullying the kid *about*."

Sato stepped forward to start brushing feathers off Patrick's head and shoulders. His hair was a total mess.

"They used a mean word for *lesbian*," explained the kid, quietly. "It's normal."

"It's disgusting," objected Patrick, "And you shouldn't have to put up with it, just because they're older, and bigger, and jerk-faces."

"Jerk-faces?" Sato teased, annoyed that Patrick had involved himself in human family drama. "What's with the feathers?"

"I might've busted open one of those big pillows. Who knew there were so many feathers inside?"

"At a pool party?"

"I brought the pillow out from inside the house."

"Why?"

"Well, you see—" Patrick was interrupted before being able to relay the details of what Sato was sure was an absolutely riveting, if completely confusing and very long, story.

A couple of large college humans came lumbering at them

with arms akimbo, looking pugnacious and swollen, ripe with testosterone. Waterlogged with ego. They were wearing trucker hats and hockey jerseys – at a pool party. They too, like Patrick and the kid, were covered in feathers.

Sato moved fast. He was between the trucker hats and Patrick as quickly as possible. Protecting the kid too, of course, but Patrick was the one that mattered.

"Who the hell are you?" one of them asked Sato, correctly identifying him as the real threat.

Sato felt absolutely no inclination to answer. Or, indeed, to talk at all. No doubt such humans as these possessed vocabulary levels at an inverse proportion to the amount of hair gel and body spray strewn over their pink bodies.

The front one swung at him with a giant-clam-sized fist.

Sato dodged easily. He was faster in water, of course, but even on land he had good reaction time compared to humans, especially of the large drunken variety. His time of falling down stairs and hating gravity had long since passed. He still didn't love gravity, but he was good at it, or at least good enough to activate it against others.

Yellow trucker hat punched at him next.

Sato dodged again, balancing his weight on the balls of his feet.

Blue trucker hat tried to go around him to get at Patrick or the kid.

Sato tripped him with one foot and then pivoted on that same foot and shoved him in the stomach with the other, sending him into the pool with a satisfying splash.

Patrick, who was never particularly concerned or worried about his own safety, especially if Sato was around – spoiled little thing – suddenly yelled, "Careful! Don't fall in the pool!"

Sato didn't dignify *that* with a response, just gave him a brief, incredulous look. Then went back to dodging trucker hats and pushing them around.

But then Patrick added, "It's one of those newfangled salt-water pools."

Sato hadn't noticed the distinct lack of chlorine smell. Now he did. He quickly moved away from the water, drawing the last remaining trucker hat to follow him toward the house.

It'd be terribly embarrassing if he fell in.

Sato would keep his legs if he fell into a normal swimming pool, and he was a decent swimmer in his human form now. But if he fell into saltwater? He'd spontaneously shift into merform right then and there, in full view of most of the freshman class. And while Sato was proud of his tail – it was *gorgeous*, if he did say so himself – he didn't want to display the damn thing for all the world to see. The point of being a merman among humans was not to be noticed *as a merman*.

The final trucker hat, a red one, seemed to be smaller and meaner than the ones that had come before. Sato had occasion to observe that smaller humans were more vicious than larger ones, like scorpions. Which meant that this human was a bit more on Sato's level.

The vitriol coming out of this human's mouth was colored by all possible slurs – some that Sato hadn't even heard before. And Sato had lived in the South for seven years now, looking like he did with Patrick tagging after him, dressing like *he* did.

Accordingly, Sato did the most logical thing – punched red trucker hat as hard as he could in the mouth to shut him up.

As hard as he could, being an extra dense shifter, probably knocked loose a couple of teeth. Red hat's opinions on all matters gay and Asian would not be altered by a punch, of course, but Sato felt better. He really couldn't be bothered with trying to rectify small human minds. Knocking out small human teeth was easier.

The trucker hats were now all officially down or dripping.

Sato gave the small human kid that he'd sort of rescued a nod and then grabbed Patrick by the wrist, and simply dragged him away from all the threats and out of the house. The human kid was gonna have to figure out its own family drama. Sato had absolutely no inclination to adopt another stray. Patrick was more than enough responsibility.

"Oh, well, I guess we're done with that party, are we?"

Sato gave Patrick a *look*.

Patrick sighed and skipped along beside him, kicking up dust on the side of the road. He was still shedding small white feathers, like dandelion fluff. "It was boring, anyway."

Sato agreed wholeheartedly. Why did Patrick bother hanging out with humans? He didn't ask that, though, because he pretty much knew. Patrick needed people. He *liked* people, all kinds of people. Sato wasn't enough for him. Even in this shit-hole of a small town, Patrick was bound and determined to find his people and collect them, because Patrick didn't really have his family and otters were nothing if not social.

Instead Sato asked, "Why did you have a feather pillow out by a pool, Patrick?"

Patrick gave him a cheeky grin. "Wouldn't you like to know?"

Sato glared, if he didn't want to know, he wouldn't have bothered to ask.

Patrick executed a funny, taunting dance move. Probably from that production of *West Side Story* he was in last summer. Then he stuck out his little pink tongue.

Sato wanted to bite it.

"Boy's gotta have some secrets, Sato-san."

Sato rolled his eyes and resigned himself to another one of Patrick's mysteries. He'd collected a lifetime's worth. Like, how had Patrick gotten stuck in the water tower that one time? Or, why were there two dozen horseshoe crabs in the trunk of Sato's sire's car? Or why had Patrick dressed as Sailor Monsoon, Queen of the Dragon Seas, three Halloweens running when he preferred manga to anime?

"It would have been so funny if you'd fallen into that pool," said Patrick, dark eyes glittering.

"Funnier if you had."

Patrick pouted at that. Unlike Sato, Patrick could change into his otter form at will. He wasn't compelled by salt water to do so. But his family insisted on keeping a low profile. No human was to know they were dobhar-chú. So if he'd fallen in, he certainly would have flailed about and embarrassed himself.

He batted his eyes at Sato. "Would you have jumped in to rescue me, revealing yourself in all your glory?"

Sato changed the subject, because they both knew he would have simply thrown pool noodles at Patrick and let him save himself. Patrick wasn't incompetent, just reckless. "Why'd you antagonize the trucker hats, Patrick?"

"Seemed like a fun thing to do at the time."

"Party was that dull, was it?"

Patrick sashayed a bit. "Exactly. So let's do something even more fun!"

"Swim?" suggested Sato, because it was always his favorite thing to do, especially with Patrick.

"Yes, please!" Patrick sparkled at him, sharp bright teeth and fathomless dark eyes. Sato forgot, briefly, how gravity worked. Stumbled slightly.

Patrick didn't notice. "Can I have a piggy?"

Sato stopped and crouched slightly.

Patrick launched himself onto his back, wrapping his arms tight about Sato's neck, where the gills were when Sato shifted. Wrapped his legs around Sato's hips, where his tail sprouted. A dear familiar weight, as easy and as welcome as those gills or that tail.

Sato waited until the dobhar-chú was safely settled, then stood straight, hoisted Patrick up. Sato let his long legs eat up the dusty road after that, happy with them for a change. Did not mind gravity at all, when it pressed Patrick into his back, a welcome burden.

CHAPTER FOUR

A MOISTNESS OF MERMAIDS

The Present: Sato somewhere in San Francisco Bay

"It's not a good idea." It was all Sato had to say. So it was all he said. Of course it was not enough for Cascade. Nothing ever seemed to be enough for the ineffable Cascade.

"Why not!" She fluttered her fins upward, offended by what she took to be his challenge to her mermaid acumen. Or something.

Sato ignored her and focused on his sister. "Send me if you must." Then he could do some hunting.

"Oh really! Why you?" Cascade pressed.

"Surface reconnaissance should be conducted by a merman," he explained, thinking this should be obvious.

"Why should it?" Cascade hated being contradicted by anyone, let alone a lowly male.

"Because I'm a *merman*. I've lived among humans for years."

"So?"

"I know what to look for. I know their manners and behaviors. I know how to interact without calling attention to myself. I'm familiar with human society and social morays."

Meymey's tone was soft, placating. "This is not the same part of the world as your youth, brother."

That was true. "It is still the same language and the same continent. Some exposure and dry dirt training is better than none."

"I'm part of the merfolk diplomatic core. I've had human etiquette and culture lessons!" Cascade took her duties very seriously. Or at least pretended to.

But you've never walked among them for anything more than a one-night stand, Sato wanted to say, but he knew it would do him no good.

"I thought we were trying for a low profile," he said instead, aware that he was implying she lacked all capacity for secrecy. But that was because she'd be recognized instantly for what she was the moment she went into the public. This was the Bay Area, not some tiny coastal village.

Cascade rose up out of the water, fins fluttering furiously in annoyance. "I can keep a low profile!"

But in Sato's experience, no mermaid could. Still, he stayed silent and turned to his sister, waiting for her decision, unsurprised when it came down against him.

"Let her go, brother."

He inclined his head. "As you wish."

She added, presumably so his feelings wouldn't be hurt, silly child, "I would rather you stay by my side. These are unfamiliar waters full of all manner of shifters. I'd feel safer if you remained close."

Sato dipped his head in tacit agreement. It was her decision he did not need to be coddled. It was the wrong decision, but she needed to make her own mistakes. They all did. As vangill he would now simply prepare for the inevitable fallout.

Cascade looked smug but also nervous. "Do you think I will be in grave danger if I go into one of their cities?"

Sato wasn't going to hold anything back. "Of course, especially the dock area."

"But I have a *business suit* to wear!"

"You're still a mermaid."

"It's a very nice suit. One of my selkie friends has it reserved at a boutique for me."

Sato arched a brow in amusement. Selkie had notoriously expensive but very *bad* taste in suits.

"And is this boutique also located in San Francisco?" Sato asked, just so he knew which part of land he'd most likely have to rescue her from.

"No, I don't think so. It's from a different population center on the edge of a different part of the Bay."

"Which one?"

"Ooh, good question. I suppose I should know that information if I am to go find the suit."

"Yes, you should. I suspect it would be ill advised for a mermaid to go wandering around any local human population wearing a robe looking for a place that sells suits."

"Is that because there are a lot of them?"

"Yes. Remarkably enough, humans have a large number of clothing shops." Sato was being sarcastic, of course, but it rolled right over Cascade.

Meymey gave him a narrow-eyed look.

Sato kept his face deadpan. "The San Francisco Bay Area has a population of over seven million."

Cascade's mouth opened in shock. Then closed again. "That's a lot of people to put clothes on."

"Exactly. So, the name of the town your selkie friend said the store was located?"

Cascade stared off at the watery horizon for a while. Clearly her brain was working overtime. "Something to do with sauce?" she said, finally.

Sato had gone on land and gotten them a burner smart phone the moment they arrived. He'd searched Patrick's name, and for dratsie, in the local area. Not that he expected to find anything online. But he had to start somewhere. Nothing, of course. Then he'd used it to look up a map of the local area to get familiar. The mermaids would need the information, and he needed to strategize a plan of attack. He left it in a locker at a changing hut the rest of the time.

Mermaids, especially well-connected pods like his mother's, always held things like family credit cards, bank accounts, and other means to access funds on land. The pods were generally quite wealthy by human standards, like the selkie that merfolk dealt with in offshore accounts, but they tended to keep theirs legal. It meant large human corporations wishing to profit from sea people relations above docks, as it were, dealt with the pods.

All of which is to say, Sato was familiar with the town in question. "You mean Sausalito?"

"Yes! That's the one. Do you know where it is?"

"Yes. I can guide you there." Privately, Sato was thinking it wasn't a bad spot for Cascade to test her legs. And for him to start hunting.

It was a smaller tourist town, full of low crime rates and yoga pants. Probably a good place for her to pick up a sire, if she wanted to test out the effectiveness of her vaunted suit.

So Sato, and the rest of the diplomatic pod, accompanied Cascade that morning. They watched her swim to shore and dive inside the local dressing hut via the privacy tube. Sato itched to follow her. The town looked promising in a Patrick kind of way. The coastal ones always did.

Only the most progressive beach towns had huts for water shifters returning to land. These provided changing rooms, with showers, towels, plus robes and foot coverings for rent. Sato thought it was a very human thing, to charge for the privilege of forcing other species to obey their own modesty codes, but he had made use of such facilities on more than one occasion himself. Sato, after all, intentionally visited larger human densities more than any other merman. He never stopped looking.

Sato watched until he saw Cascade emerge from the hut wearing a fluffy white robe and pink slippers with ears that looked like a fuzzy prey mammal.

"What an extremely peculiar thing," said Meymey, sounding rather prissy.

"The hut or the tube or those slippers?" wondered Sato.

"All of it. Why?"

"Can't have naked selkie, dratsie, merfolk, and so forth just wandering around a town like this. It would scare off all the tourists."

Meymey said, "Surely not. One would think the opportunity to see the occasional naked mermaid would only attract tourists."

"Fair point. Unfortunately, there are all sorts of laws around body autonomy and display in human cities."

"They can hardly apply to shifters," said one of the youngest members of the pod, Hali. She was even younger than Meymey. Sato wondered who'd been bribed to get her in. It probably had to do with aligning with his mother's pod. Sato grappled with his patience. Or lack thereof.

"Oh, but they do. If we choose to walk amongst humans, the humans are going to have things to say about what we wear when we do so."

"That might be one of the strangest human quirks," said one of the others, Tarni, big eyes on Sato's face.

"It gets weirder," said Sato. "They have restrictions around the *kind* of clothing that the different genders can wear. It encompasses fabrics and in some places, color."

"Humans are bonkers," said Hali, whose tail was an unusual yellow color that mermaids regarded as rather ugly for no good reason. Sato refrained from reminding her of that equally illogical stance.

Sato had gotten accustomed to clothing, living amongst humans, but he'd never really understood what could be worn by whom. Especially as Patrick, his guide in that world, liked to push boundaries. During his *flop on Sato's futon, upset that shifters can't get piercings* phase, Trick had extolled the virtues of kilts. These were, so far as Sato could tell, exactly the same as the pleated skirts worn by girls (and only girls) at Saint Brendan's three towns over. Sato had simply opted for baggy and black, much to Patrick's disgust.

"You should be grateful I bother to wear anything at all," Sato had said at the time.

"There are so many things wrong with that statement," Patrick had replied, giggling.

Sato fluttered his fins to return himself to the present. "Fortunately for us water shifters, pretty much every human culture has figured out some form of a robe. Unfortunately, in most places, we're *also* not supposed to wear a bathrobe in public."

"How can they expect us to keep up with what's acceptable in any given place or time?" One of the other members of the pod sounded justifiably annoyed.

Sato was losing patience. "Hence the huts. Usually there is a clerk who explains the local population's idiosyncrasies with regard to attire. Cascade was smart to use her local selkie contacts to get something lined up."

"Daidai, did you just compliment Cascade?"

Sato had surprised himself. "Better tell the Klepsydra to log it into the oral history of our species. It'll never happen again."

Meymey fluttered her hands in approval of his wit, then said, "The rest of us are also going to need clothing. Should we follow Cascade into this place called Sausalito and buy our own suits?"

Sato shook his head. "I'm pretty certain a town of that size could not withstand the onslaught of an entire pod of mermaids. Certainly not this early in the morning. Let the poor things cope with Cascade first. We'll observe from a safe distance."

"On the other hand, I'd be happy to take you all shopping," said a smoothly mild voice from just behind them. "Haight Street would *love* you."

Sato and the rest of the diplomatic pod, which numbered twelve total, rather comically swiveled in unison to face the stranger.

A merman bobbed facing them.

Sato got the horrible feeling that this stranger had been observing them for a while. He'd likely overheard their entire conversation. Fortunately, it had all been about Cascade and human clothing taboos. No Soteria secrets had been divulged.

Nevertheless, Sato was angry at himself. He'd forgotten how overpopulated the waters were in places like the San Francisco Bay.

Not that he thought one dinky merman was a real challenge to him. This was clearly no vangill.

Still, Sato moved to the front of the pod, vangill position, so that he swam defensively between the mermaids and the intruder.

The specimen facing him was of the undersized northern waters varietal. His were the merfolk with iridescent skin, patina, rather than scale patterns like Sato, luster. To have only patina was thought quite plain by merfolk standards. But this merman was extremely handsome by Sato's personal preferences. A dip beneath the waves proved the stranger had an impressive turquoise tail. He was (for lack of a better word) *pretty*. Sato had a terrible weakness for pretty men. Well, one pretty man. Still he appreciated the aesthetic.

Sadly, this one was looking at them with nothing but hostility and suspicion on that pretty face. He was obviously one of those mermen who had no affection for his own people. Or perhaps it was simply that he had no affection for a strange pod in his waters.

Which attitude he proved with his next statement. "I do love shopping. You'll find human clothing can actually be quite fun. But first, I must insist that you explain who *exactly* you are, and what *exactly* you're doing in my territory."

Meymey bristled. "Mermen do not *have* territory. And there is currently no mermaid pod that claims the San Francisco Bay. We checked."

Aqua, the diplomatic pods' interpreter, was actively upset by the merman's behavior. "Who are *you* to demand any kind of explanation from us? Your role is to give us information and otherwise stay out of our business."

"Oh dear, did you think I had allegiances? I assure you, there is indeed territory in play, but it has nothing to do with the people of the sea."

"We know what the humans like to think, but they have no true authority in these waters. Or in any waters for that matter."

"I do not speak for the humans either, although I number the local Coast Guard among my allies. And they are empowered to act on my call if needed. I promise you I am neither weak nor isolated like most mermen. But the humans are not the claimants to these waters. You are close to the Sausalito shoreline here, and these shallows are under rightful protection by local shifters."

Sato felt suddenly nervous. "Who exactly?"

"The San Andreas pack."

"Werewolves?"

"Predominantly."

Sato considered. He didn't know much about werewolves but he'd thought they tended to stick to their own kind and land, not the sea. This was weird.

The mermaids all scoffed.

Meymey swam to bob next to Sato. "Four legs cannot claim the right of one tail."

Sato wished she wouldn't go so close to the stranger. He raised his forearms.

The pretty merman smiled, hostile, showing all his pretty pointed teeth. "This particular pack numbers water folk allegiances *and members*."

"Which water folk? Tail or web?" Sato thought he was managing to successfully hide his interest with authority.

"Both. And enough to make it very difficult for even you, vangill."

"Selkie allegiance?" speculated Sato. A large enough number of selkie, especially trained fighters, could indeed make it hard on him. But not many other water species could take down a vangill. Dratsie numbered no fighters at all among their ranks, for example.

The merman smiled. "Not the selkie. Merfolk always forget there are *unsalted* waters."

Sato's mind raced. Tails, river-based, powerful enough to beat a vangill.

"Kelpie?" he hazarded, surprised.

The merman inclined his head. "She is not of the pack but we socialize regularly."

"We? You consider *yourself* one of a pack of wolves?" Meymey was truly shocked.

Sato was surprised too, but he hid it better.

The merman did not answer that.

Meymey went fishing for the power dynamic, "So you are the sea singer for this pack and its allied parties in matters of diplomacy?"

The pretty man raised his pretty eyes to the heavens in the manner of the exasperated land-bound. He had clearly spent all his adult life among humans. Sato didn't know whether he envied him that or pitied him. He wondered what he knew of the local dratsie population. Was there a local dratsie population?

"You're a diplomatic pod?" The merman had figured it out.

Meymey smiled this time, showing all her teeth.

He looked hard at Sato. "And you're not just a vangill, you're one of *the* Vangill of the Deep."

Sato didn't need to smile. It was fun to watch him squirm.

But their new acquaintance seemed more resigned than upset. The presence of a Soteria resulted in neither shame nor proper respect; instead he opened that pretty mouth of his and swore a blue streak. Patrick would have been impressed with such mastery of the English language. "What in Seven Seas did the Bay Area do to warrant a visit from the Paralia of All Seas?" At least this merman still knew the Deep well enough to know which Soteria they would send to shore.

"I assure you, I had no idea you existed at all," said Meymey.

"No need to put me in my place, I assure you, Paralia." The merman's stunning changeable blue-green eyes focused hard on Meymey, correctly categorizing her as the one in charge. "I know the rank I swim under all too well. But whether you like it or not, you are in *our* waters now. I am not their custodian. Nor is the kelpie."

"Then who claims to sing for these waters?" Meymey knew her rights. She must speak to the local voice of authority in the area. Whether she acknowledged them or not. Whether they had legitimate claim or not. The politics must be played when a pod strayed into the human world. Knowing she had gone blindly into someone else's territory, legitimate by merfolk standards or not, she must establish her authority and dominance. Which meant Sato's spurs might well be called upon.

"This shoreline belongs to the local werewolf Alpha."

The mermaids, shocked, all just looked at each other for a long moment. Then they all started laughing. Their siren voices were stunning and lyrical, bouncing over the waves. Sato wondered if any humans could hear them, and if, entranced, they were already walking into the ocean.

"Werewolf *alpha*? You can hardly expect me to speak sensibly to a creature that *doggie paddles*!" Meymey was still laughing.

The merman looked like he had expected this reaction. He looked away from them in annoyance. He was facing the shore and his attention became distracted by something there. Something the humans were doing.

Sato would normally never have allowed himself to get distracted by such a thing. He would never have taken his eyes off a strange vangill. But this was an ordinary merman. Any threat was not to their safety but in who he represented. This strange alpha with his pack of misfit allegiances. And that was Meymey's problem, not Sato's. So he turned to see what had caught the merman's eye.

There was a commotion coming from the waterside town, loud enough and excited enough to carry over the waves. A shrieking of distress. The high-pitched whine of human terror.

Sato knew that sound well. Humans were always loud and annoying but they were even louder and more annoying in crisis.

The strange merman, no longer caring about them, dove past the pod with a splash of his powerful turquoise tail and took off toward the shallows in an impressive burst of speed.

The humans were a boiling mess at the end of one of their piers. A few plopped gracelessly off the edge and into the bay. Sato had observed this kind of behavior before. No doubt one of their number, probably an infant, had fallen into the water and could not swim.

Sato glanced back at the pod.

They were still chuckling.

"I will meet you at our designated spot," he said to his sister.

"It is their problem," she replied, not acknowledging that he would dare to instruct her.

"Favors owed," was all Sato replied. He was already swimming backwards. He twisted up and out, using his tail's full strength to jet himself first through air and then through water.

Their strange new acquaintance was fast, but Sato was much faster. He caught up to him and sped past him easily.

The waters of the San Francisco Bay were not pretty. They were mucked-up and dirty, busy with ships, filled with human refuse and buoyant fluids that humans love, like oil. The bay was cloudy with runoff from shore, replete with all the residue that humans leave wherever they go, filthy creatures. Merfolk had, in general, better eyesight than humans, and indeed, better eyesight than most land shifters in their four-legged form. But waters full of sediment and refuse were a thing even good eyesight could not rectify.

So Sato broke the surface occasionally to make sure he was headed in the correct direction, and once he was there, among them, he ignored the human swimmers and looked for something being ripped along by the undertow.

Looked as best he could. Angry at them for dirtying the water and then dropping and losing something important in it.

But Sato had been trained the hard way for search and rescue. He spotted the small figure easily. A human child, fortunately wearing bright colors, caught in some insignificant current, spinning and sinking.

Sato got to him easily, grabbed him up in both arms. Knowing speed was the most important thing with those who could not breathe underwater, he simply propelled himself up out of the water at the edge of the pier.

He cleared the railing of that pier, which had not stopped the child from falling in, so was obviously useless. He beached himself, child still in his grasp, onto the wooden decking, scattering humans out of his way. His tail so long the fin draped over the edge.

He probably bumped more than a few humans. He certainly knocked one over, but no more fell in.

He tipped the child onto its back and looked hopefully around.

They were all just staring at him, dumbfounded.

Stupid humans.

"Do none of you know CPR?" he asked.

Nothing but stunned silence, staring at him, mouths opened. Most of them had likely never seen a merman in fin and flesh before.

Sato sighed. "I will have to break your nudity taboos. I cannot administer it in this form. I have gills."

They all just continued to stare. Some had their mouths open like guppies. So helpful.

One of the women from the crowd rushed to the child. She was shrieking and sobbing over him and plucking at his wet clothes in an utterly ineffectual manner.

Sato shifted forms.

He took to his knees, leaned over the kid, sealed his mouth over and administered five breaths. Then he put one hand to the thin chest and began compressions. Fifteen and then two breaths. It had been so long since he'd done it, he'd forgotten the rules. He remembered how very little force he had to use and to tilt the chin back. He remembered to keep his own breath slow and gentle, watching the corresponding rise in the kid's chest. Frankly, he thought he did pretty good, for a merman.

Soon enough, the child coughed and spit up seawater all over Sato's face.

Sato rolled the kid to one side to drain the rest.

The woman had stopped shrieking and was now half sobbing, half panting in relief, as if she had been the one to swallow seawater.

"Hey, human," Sato explained dispassionately. "Perhaps you should know CPR before you bring your spawn near the ocean."

"But how interesting that you do know it, merman." The stranger merman had, at some point, beached himself next to them. He was still in tail, presumably to protect the delicate human eyes from his manly bits.

Sato felt no such respect for their sensibilities.

He stood, utterly nude, and looked down on the woman and her now wide-eyed coughing child. Then he tilted his head and regarded the useless crowd, judging them wanting.

"No medals," he said. And then for good measure, "Or speeches. I hate speeches."

He heard sirens. Cops were coming. Sato didn't feel like dealing with them. It had already been enough excitement for one morning.

He decided, of all people, the strange merman seemed to hold the most social power in this situation. So he looked down at him.

The merman was grinning up, eye level with Sato's procreative organs. "I knew you would turn out to be the most interesting one."

Sato pointed down at him with two webbed fingers. "This is your problem now. I will come with the Paralia to discuss terms in an hour."

"Terms?"

"This child is alive. I hold a favor owed, merman. You claimed this territory, which means these people are your responsibility. Bring your singer."

"Not possible."

"Your cops will take longer than an hour?" Human authority figures often moved very slowly.

"Probably, but that's not the delay. My Alpha will not be back from the lab until this evening."

"Lab?" Sato heard the heavy beat of large boots coming down the wooden deck. "Wait. No. I do not care. Where and when?"

"The shock-rock near the changing hut." The merman pointed at the shore at a section where there was no beach and no pier, only inhospitable human-made rock, edging a human-made road. "I will bring my Alpha to you, two hours after sunset."

"Done." *My Alpha, was he? From a merman?* Sato turned to leave. But they were surrounded by humans, still staring. Several of the younger ones were taking videos with their dumb phones.

Sato glared at those between him and the edge of the pier. "Move."

Nothing.

"That which I intentionally push into the water does not get rescued." It was an appealing idea.

Still nothing.

He raised his voice. "Move or I will make you."

They made a pathway for him and his two legs to walk through.

Sato took three big strides, climbed to the top of the railing, and dove back into the sea.

He flicked his tail at them as he swam away, hard enough to splash any who might have rushed to the railing with their phones to film him leaving. He hoped some of them dropped those phones into the sea.

He'd forgotten how annoying humans were to deal with.

The Present: Trick inside Bean There, Froth That, Sausalito

Sometimes it sucked to run a shifter-friendly cafe in a seaside town.

Case in point, the (probably human) tourist standing in front of him looking very confused and the (definitely mermaid) sitting in one corner watching the (now even more likely human) man try to navigate Trick and his cafe.

The man was wearing a red baseball cap and white socks. He was also wearing other appalling things in between – although how funny would it have been if he were not? Regardless, those were the two items Trick noticed. The mermaid was probably not upset by the socks – aside from Marvin, very few sea folk held opinions on footwear. For obvious reasons.

"What's your specialty drink today?" the tourist asked, no greeting and no smile.

"Which side of the menu you hail from?" Trick responded politely, because he assumed human from the socks, but didn't want to step on anyone's toes. After all, he didn't have the best sense of smell and sometimes fashion lied. Orange basketball shorts and a white ribbed tank meant this man was living some kind of stereotype, Trick just wasn't sure what or why.

The presumed-human went from confused to annoyed.

Trick gave an expansive and very twirly sort of gesture to the left side of the specials board. "Sweet and smooth," then to the right, "or silken and savory?"

"Savory... drinks?"

Trick wondered if the dude could read or just didn't like to. The script on his board was very neat. Trick had excellent handwriting, if he did say so himself.

Trick turned defensively bratty – it was his natural state, after all. "The bone broth cappuccino with dashi depth charge and furikake sprinkles is currently our most popular drink. It's deeeeeelishious!" He smiled brightly.

The man looked disgusted. His face possessed a certain *something* that made Trick fantasize about bitch-slapping him with a dirty dish towel. And there was only a counter between them and the dish towel was *right there*.

Trick decided to try to get this over with quickly. "Okay, pumpkin-buns, how about trying the Slippery Paris Brest?" He was very proud of that drink. He'd invented and named it himself.

"The what?!"

"It's like a hazelnut cortado but made with condensed milk." It was currently Max's favorite on their menu. Trick made the magistar order it *by name* every time because the town's premier hottie got adorably red and embarrassed. Trick didn't want to admit that was why he'd named it the Slippery Paris Brest, but it certainly was an added bonus to regularly fluster the most powerful mage ever to wear spandex of a morning.

Baseball cap's witty rejoinder was, "I'm still stuck on the bone broth. It's popular, you say. Why? How? With who?"

"Did you not see the stickers in our window?" Trick's tone was becoming sharp. He didn't mind a bit of flirtatious chit chat but he struggled to reconcile himself with indecision when drinks were on the line. Beverages were important and should be taken seriously.

The customer turned to look back at the door. Three large decals decorated the window next to it: a rainbow, a paw print, and a semicolon.

"You welcome fags, pets, and nut jobs?" suggested the dude, turning back to Trick.

Trick sighed. "Sure do, but not shitbags. Get out, please."

"I'm sorry, what?"

"You're not from around here are you? Shoo, fly."

"Excuse me?" Unfortunately, baseball cap was not leaving.

"There is no excuse. Go away and grow a sense of compassion better than your fashion acumen. Until then, you aren't welcome in this establishment. There's a Sunboodle around town somewhere. Go drink there."

The man began to sputter.

"Now now, little barista, why you being so mean to such a handsome man," said the mermaid in a rippling voice, seductive.

Trick had wondered how long it would take her to interfere. The man was red hot mermaid bait – well, orange hot. Snack-colored human. His dick was probably covered with that powdered fluorescent cheese stuff.

To be fair, she actually hadn't been a problem until that moment. She'd been sitting quietly, alone, sipping an Abalone Palmer and looking out at the ocean.

Trick had counted himself lucky that initially she'd seemed to be in a passive mood. Despite Marvin's overwrought reaction. Or perhaps because of it.

But now Trick realized that her calmness was probably because of the lack of human males in his cafe. Aside from Floyd, of course. But Floyd was past breeding age and any mermaid would know the signs of non-viability in human males.

She stood, not bothering to tug down the hem of her skirt, and oiled her way back into line behind the baseball cap. She was acting sexy enough for Trick to realize how sexy she was. And that was pretty darn sexy, since he was gayer than a plucked duck in a party frock. The orange shorts didn't stand a chance.

"I think I'll have another drink myself," she said, not looking at Trick.

"Very well, beautiful, what can I get you?" Trick took her as an excuse to ignore Mr White Socks Species Supremacist. Mermaids expected flattery and attention. Trick gave her both. Despite his snarky banter with the regulars, Trick was actually good at customer service.

Baseball cap took full notice of what was now standing behind him and lost some of his outrage to pure unadulterated lust. He let out an apparently involuntary whistle.

The mermaid preened but pretended to focus on Trick. "I feel like something a little more extravagant this time. What's best?"

Oh dear, here we go again. Straight people are so exhausting. "Well, personally, I love the fish sauce latte with the prawn paste froth." Trick knew his shifter clientele well; that was absolutely the drink sea people would enjoy the most. It was one of Marvin's regular orders.

"The seaweed matcha looks kind of special too."

"That's actually one of my personal favorites. Good choice."

"I didn't say I wanted it. Besides, if that's your favorite, why did you recommend the shrimp thing?"

"I love them all equally. I can't have one drink thinking it's better than the others. It'll get ideas above its station."

The mermaid looked at him like he was insane.

Trick had momentarily forgotten that merfolk, on the main, entirely lacked any sense of humor.

The mermaid swiveled and batted her lashes at the dude. "What would you pick for me, handsome?"

The man's tongue practically lolled out like a cartoon character's.

Trick was amused, but he'd underestimated the man's ego, because dude-bro had a pretty quick response.

"How about the slippery breast?"

The mermaid looked a little shocked.

Trick sputtered out a laugh which he turned into a cough.

Floyd snorted.

"While apt in certain aspects, that's not really my side of the menu, darling," replied the mermaid, stroking the man's arm.

Clearly she had donned legs and come into a human town for one reason and one reason only. Skirt-suit notwithstanding.

The man looked very turned on and faintly confused.

Impasse.

Trick was losing patience with both of them. "Well, if I can't make either of you a drink, I'm gonna dole out some unasked-for advice."

"What?" said the mermaid, looking through her lashes coquettishly at the red baseball cap's red face. Trick wondered how obstructed her vision was under such circumstances.

"I can't tell for certain but I suspect bigotry is an inherited genetic disorder. I wouldn't think this one is very good breeding stock, sweetie."

The mermaid glared at him. "You revealing my endgame?"

"You think he's smart enough to play? Don't you want brains in your daughter?"

"Like I don't have enough brains myself, *plus* the more dominant genetics."

"I'm pretty sure it's 50/50 no matter how you fuck," shot back Trick.

"Excuse me. What *is* this place?" Red cap shook himself, trying to battle the mermaid's thrall. It was cute that he tried, but she was still petting his arm and the crotch of those ugly orange shorts wasn't hiding his interest.

Floyd played his role perfectly at that point. "Is anyone getting a drink? Some of us have knitting to do."

Sometimes Trick really loved Floyd.

The mermaid pretended a little stumble. "I'm not very steady on these legs, you know?"

The human immediately placed one big hand at the small of her back, his fingers straying down to the top of her pert ass. Trick had no doubt she was wearing nothing at all under her little suit; most shifters went commando. It made life easier. A mermaid on the prowl, doubly so.

"I'll be your third leg, honey," he responded, leering.

Apparently, one's anti-shifter moral code went out the window when mermaids were flirting.

Trick hoped she bred a female child. That man would be a thousand times worse to his merman son than Mr Sato's consummate disinterest ever had been to Sato.

"Are you certain?" Trick questioned the mermaid's judgment.

She ignored him, leaning into the man and looking up at him adoringly with big eyes, the kind humans drown in.

The man made a growling noise, which really did not work out of a human mouth, and then bent to press a sloppy kiss to the mermaid's neck. Near where her gills would be, were she in her true form.

"This is a cafe, not a club. You can't make out here!" Trick tried to get ahead of the inevitable.

The mermaid smirked at him. "Spoilsport."

"Do I look like I care for your agenda?"

"So you're not gonna make me a drink anymore?" She was good.

Trick was better. "Is the Slippery Brest in consideration? Or are you gonna actually order something true to your nature? I'd recommend a beverage with soy milk for protein and salmon oil for energy, but then you'll be kissing him with fish-mouth. That's clearly *not* his thing."

The mermaid looked affronted. "Gross. I don't mouth kiss like a two-legged baboon. Speaking of which, what are you, little barbed-tongue beastie?" She couldn't figure it out because merfolk had an even worse sense of smell than dratsie. Plus Trick worked in a seaside cafe for good reason. All that coffee brewing and salt air masked his otter musk. Only shifters with the very best noses who knew dratsie and that they existed at all stood half a chance of identifying him. Which was why the only one to ever deduce what he was unprompted was Judd. And that was because Judd was overly smart for a werewolf enforcer and old enough to have met dratsie before.

Of course, it was now pretty common knowledge amongst the local shifter community that Sausalito housed a dratsie barista. Packs were notorious gossips and could never keep secrets – what one wolf knew, all wolves knew. And the San Andreas pack numbered a Magistar, a drag queen, and one fabulous merman amongst their numbers. Trick was just one more stray they'd picked up among many. He'd been outed to more than one local shifter community as a result. It made him nervous but he was learning to live with it.

The man pivoted to press his now blatant and raging erection to the mermaid's ass. She swayed a bit to encourage it but was otherwise more interested in trading barbs with Trick.

She had netted her prey. The human was caught. He could wait a bit while she satisfied her curiosity. Although if his sweaty face and glazed look were anything to go by, he wasn't gonna wait very long.

It wasn't even nine yet! Trick wasn't a prude by any stretch of the imagination, but this level of heterosexual activity was a bit much for one gay boy to have seared into his eyeballs before breakfast.

"No dice, sweetheart. I'm immune to your charms," Trick said.

"Land shifters are so boring," she replied.

"That's not why I'm immune, water-baby."

She pouted and would have kept asking, but she had under-estimated her prey's impatience.

"Let's get out of this shit-hole and go somewhere a little more private, darling," baseball cap said. "I'm staying at this BnB just down the block."

"So you're not in town for very long?"

"Just for a conference." He started dragging her toward the door.

"What a coincidence! Me too."

Trick frowned. He looked at Floyd. "Since when did Sausalito host conferences? Since when did mermaids go to conferences, for that matter? Not to mention men in polyester sportswear and tube socks."

Floyd waggled bushy gray brows at him. "Wouldn't it be hilarious if it turns out they're going to the *same conference?*"

"The mind boggles," replied Trick, still confused.

"Are you presenting?" the mermaid asked the man as he

politely held the door for her to go through, ogling her backside as he did so.

"No, I'm a reporter for the *Patriot's Monthly Overview*."

"Of course he is," said Trick. The door closed behind the pair.

"What? I missed that bit." Floyd's ears were nowhere near as good as Trick's, for both species and age reasons.

"He's a reporter for some rag or another. Something political is going on." Trick legitimately wondered if both oddballs were in town for the same thing. There were some issues that concerned both shifters and conservatives. Environmental legislation, for example. Was it something like that? In Sausalito?

Trick wondered if he should tell the pack. Merfolk so rarely involved themselves in land-bound business. But if it was something concerning ocean pollution, they might. Should he tell Alec that they had a mermaid in town? Should he give Marvin the chance to do it first? But Marvin had run away. He didn't have as much information as Trick. Pack politics were such a pickle.

Trick sighed. "Floyd, you've lived here for a while. Sausalito doesn't have a convention center, does it?"

"Oh yeah, certainly, right behind the Center for the Arts."

Trick wrinkled his nose. "There's nothing but water behind the... oh, I see, make a joke at the new guy's expense?" Trick had lived in Sausalito for several years, but he was well aware how small towns worked. He would be *the new kid* for decades. Floyd had lived in the same house downtown for over sixty years but he was still *that Ohio guy*. In small towns, locals were born, not transplanted. One couldn't be made local; one could only, eventually, if very lucky, become reluctantly tolerated.

Floyd put down his knitting needles. "Trick, kid, I worry about your social life. Shouldn't you be going into the city regularly?"

Trick frowned. He might *look* like a party boy but he'd never been much for clubs. "What does that have to do with anything?"

"You forget we have a ferry?"

Trick *had* forgotten. He tended to travel *through* the bay, not on top of it. He considered this information. There were plenty of convention centers and event spaces along the waterfront in San Francisco. Someone who knew the area, or liked the water, might choose to ferry in, rather than stay in the city. Still seemed an odd choice for tube socks or a mermaid.

Messy. This was all very messy.

Floyd was smarter than he looked, so Trick decided just to ask him for advice. "Should I tell Alec about the mermaid or see if Marvin does it first?"

"You sure that was a mermaid?"

Perhaps not quite so smart. Trick rolled his eyes. "Floyd, really? How old *are* you?"

"Old enough to know better than to get involved with merfolk." Which was a very smart thing to say.

Trick considered. Marvin probably thought the mermaid was in the Bay Area to breed, but if she really had come for some convention, that meant a whole pod was likely in the Bay at the moment. A whole pod of mermaids would cause quite a stir in any community, not just the dick-first human male contingent. Although they would definitely be the hardest hit.

Hardest. Trick chuckled to himself.

Trick wasn't opposed to the occasional dick-first human male himself. He, like the mermaids, felt they had their uses. Plus, given how vastly humans outnumbered shifters, Trick was just loyal enough to non-humans to believe that mermaids should be allowed their fun when procreation was on the line – even if the heterosexual specifics disgusted him. But if the mermaid was in town for more than just netting a baby, perhaps the werewolf pack should have a presence at this conference? After all, the San Andreas shifters included two water folk among their number, not to mention an Alpha with advanced degrees in marine biology.

"I guess I *must* tell Alec," admitted Trick.

"He probably already knows," said Floyd, being all wise again. Because Floyd may not know a mermaid when one walked into a cafe, but he knew the local pack Alpha pretty well by now.

CHAPTER FIVE

A SPUR IN HAND IS WORTH TWO IN THE DEEP

The Past: Patrick at Bay L'Ours

"I've been summoned." Sato was looking out at the still waters of the bay. Sitting on the empty beach, long human legs sprawled out like he still didn't know what to do with them.

Patrick was drawing shapes in the sand between them, playing around the borders of Sato's fingers, pleased by the strange shape Sato's hands made because of the webbing. Patrick's own hands, when he was not an otter, looked entirely human. Poor Sato, having to wear those black leather gloves even in the summer heat. There were rumors he was a serial arsonist with hands covered in burns. Sato never bothered to correct rumors, quietly amused by the idea of a merman playing with fire.

"What?" Patrick barely registered the casual comment. But then he did, and processed the implication.

Still Sato repeated himself. "The summons. It's come."

"What!"

"I've been called-down by the Deep to serve my time as a vangill. A debt of spurs." Sato raised his forearms and slapped them together, as if to remind Patrick what lay beneath the skin there.

Patrick stared at him, dumbfounded.

"Hawaii, apparently," Sato added, as if the location mattered when he was casually referring to years of separation.

Three whole years!

"How can you just tell this to me out of the blue all of a sudden?"

Sato's lips twitched. "We've known this would happen from the moment I developed spurs."

Patrick thumped the sand. "You should've kept them secret!"

"I had no choice. Sire thought there was something wrong with me."

"I know. I was there."

Sato gave Patrick a look that said as clearly as anything, *Then why are we talking about it?*

Patrick remembered it well, three years ago. They'd been swimming together, probably too far out, and the shark had thought (if sharks thought at all) that Patrick and Sato looked tasty and easy. Apparently, that's all it took to give a merman spurs. Well, to give a merman like Sato spurs. One of the rare ones. Made special by fear and anger and the desperate need to protect. And Sato, who had, until that moment, been just a plain unwanted merman – sterile, and useless, and rejected by his people – had sprouted evil thorns up and down each forearm.

And those thorns changed everything.

They'd gotten away from the shark, with the shark the worse for the encounter, and because Sato didn't know what to do, and because Patrick was freaking out, Sato had asked his father what they meant. Those spurs. His father, who was, if possible, even more stoic than Sato, had said nothing at all. He might've known. He might've been warned. Or he might not've. It was impossible to tell with that man. But he'd done exactly what he was supposed to do as the sire of a merman. He'd sent a message to the Deep. To the people who had rejected both of them.

And the Deep responded.

When he's old enough, we will summon him back. Three years he owes us, for those spurs.

It was a message that came in the shell of the Soteria and it could not be ignored. For the Soteria controlled the sea. If Sato wanted to continue to swim in it, he'd do what they told him.

Sato had looked it up, of course. What exactly it meant to be a *merman with spurs.*

Patrick had looked it up, too. This wasn't the Dark Ages. Everyone had the interwebs now. Things had changed a lot since Sato moved in next door. Even merfolk were known to exist, although of all the shifter species they kept one of the lowest profiles. Still, it meant there were articles and studies online. Blogs hosted by obsessive mermaid fandoms, and even a WooTube channel or two dedicated to the mysterious and gorgeous *people of the sea.* Mermen weren't rated the hottest of the shifter species (mermaids were, but that's typical human gender bias for you) but they certainly had their groupies (who called themselves *guppies*). So there was at least some speculation over those very few mermen who had been spotted with spurs.

Patrick had read all about it, avidly. But none of it told him when or why Sato would leave him. Only that he definitely would.

The spurs, or the shark, or the knowing he was leaving, or the knowing that the people of the sea wanted him back, changed Sato. He watched Patrick much more closely whenever they swam together after that. Like the act of becoming weaponized forced Sato to become a protector whether he liked it or not.

Well, *more* of a protector.

Patrick resented it. Resented those spurs. Resented Sato protecting his otter form. After all, he wasn't without claws or teeth. Never had been. And both of his were sharper than any merfolk could boast. Not as strong as Sato's new spurs, but at least Patrick knew how to use his defenses. He'd had them his whole life.

"They sent a message by dolphin," Sato explained.

Patrick knew his friend well enough to ask, "When did it come?"

"About a month ago."

"And you decided to wait and tell me *now*?"

"You had finals." Sato had graduated (only just) with a strong sense of senioritis. Patrick, on the other hand, was stressed about grades even though he was only a sophomore. It wasn't just finals, either. Patrick was in the school play and on the track team. He liked to be busy, anything to keep him away from his own house and in the company of others. Also he *needed* good grades. They made him different from his family. Better than them.

Sato had no intention of going to college. "You're the smart one," he said whenever Patrick tried to make him study. "It's a human institution anyway. The merfolk will summon me back now that I have spurs."

And they had.

"It's no big deal," said Sato, still staring at the sea and not looking at Patrick.

Of course it was a big deal! Patrick's best friend. His only shifter friend. The only person who had stuck by him through everything. Was leaving.

"You should've said something the moment you got summoned. Does your father know? You aren't going to just tell him the day before you leave, are you?"

Sato was like that. With his father. With most people. Sometimes even with Patrick. That thought made Patrick suddenly terrified.

"How long do we have before you leave?" *Before you leave me behind* was left unsaid, but the whine in Patrick's voice implied it.

Sato wrote the number three in the sand with one webbed finger.

"Three days!"

"Three weeks."

Patrick threw a handful of sand at him.

Sato's eyes were almost cheerful. "Are you trying to start something?"

"How could you keep this from me for a *whole month*?" They'd wasted half of their last summer vacation.

"We spend all our time together either way."

"Daiki!" Patrick was driven to use Sato's given name. "Sato Daiki, seriously?" Patrick cast himself dramatically back onto the sand, flailed his arms open. "You're tired of me, aren't you?"

"You *are* exhausting." Sato wore that tight secret smile that he only ever let Patrick see. "Why are you being dramatic about this? You have tons of friends. You claiming you'll *actually* miss me?"

Patrick sat up. "Of course I won't miss you! You'll be gone, so I won't have to worry about sleeping on your tiny futon or how hard it is to wake you up in the morning. You'll be gone so I won't have to coax you into cracking a book or actually eating vegetables. You'll be gone so I won't need to persuade your lazy ass to get a job or do something useful with your time." *You'll be gone,* said the refrain in Patrick's head.

You'll be gone. This annoying taciturn steadfast companion that Patrick hadn't asked for but had clung to desperately for seven years.

"You won't be able to hide out at my house eating everything in the fridge and chittering about how great my sire's cooking is." Sato said it like it was a good thing, but Patrick could tell he was worried.

"I'll miss his katsu."

"Greedy," said Sato, calm as ever, but that look was in his eyes, the new one. The one that was the opposite of deadpan.

Recently, Sato's stoic face had changed. It became no less stoic, but a tiny glitter had entered those kelp-brown eyes that said Sato had decided, at some point and without notification, that Patrick meant something different to him.

Patrick, who previously found Sato's blank expression comforting, became nervous. Sato had been a restful and unchanging mooring point for years. How dare he alter? Patrick was overrun by teen angst and family drama. That Sato would change too was unacceptable. Especially changing now, right before he left!

Patrick felt like he was being teased. As if Sato had decided not to tell him about the summons because he wanted to see

Patrick overreact. He wanted Patrick to be upset that he was leaving. He wanted to mock the ache Sato's absence would cause. Sato wasn't meant to tease. He was too easily cruel. Teasing was Patrick's job.

Patrick scrubbed out his sand drawings and the number 3 in annoyance. "Can't you get out of it? Ignore the summons? Refuse?"

"Like dodging the draft? As if I were some human with all their vast numbers and landbound populations to hide in?"

"You pass as human most of the time." Patrick pouted.

Sato lifted and examined his webbed hands. "But I would miss the ocean. And you know the moment I swam, they'd find me and drag me down."

"Human form, swimming in rivers or lakes, that wouldn't be enough?"

"All rivers flow to the sea. So too goes information. But no, fresh-water swimming wouldn't be enough. You know how much I love my tail." Sato put one webbed hand to Patrick's sand-burnished knee. "It's already scheduled. This is supposed to be an honor, remember?"

"There will be others, won't there, training with you in Hawaii? Other mermen. Other vangill. Other people. Strangers. You'll hate that."

Sato grunted in agreement.

So far as Patrick could tell, Sato only really liked two people. His little sister, who he hadn't seen in years, and, for some strange reason, Patrick.

"What will I do without you there to stop me from killing all the idiots?"

Patrick smiled at that.

Sato seemed calm, but he had a terrible temper. Only Patrick seemed to notice when it started boiling over. Only Patrick could tease Sato out of it.

"You really think you're prepared, Sato-san?"

"Prepared?"

"For three years without me?"

Sato snorted.

It was so frustrating. Nothing phased Sato. Not even being conscripted to serve as some weird warrior bodyguard to a shifter species that had rejected him.

Patrick flopped back again. Glared at the rapidly darkening sky rather than his annoying best friend. Tried not to cry. Not sure if that was because Sato was leaving or because Sato apparently didn't care that he was abandoning Patrick.

Patrick who had two more years of high school with no Sato.

"Aren't you just cooler than a cucumber?" he accused the sky.

"Sea cucumber?" suggest Sato.

"If I pick you up unexpectedly and squeeze, would you spurt?" Patrick said it before he really thought about it, because his mouth was like that sometimes.

Usually Sato just laughed at him.

Not this time.

Sato was suddenly looming over him, one brow arched in an extremely annoying way. "Wanna find out?"

Patrick found himself being wrestled on the sand in a crude parody of early childhood tussles, when they first became friends. Before Sato had developed spurs. Before Sato started looking at Patrick differently.

They ended with Patrick trapped under Sato, pinned by his bigger, denser body. Human skin cooling and pricked by the evening breeze. Burning hot where they touched. Too hot for water creatures to withstand.

Sato flicked Patrick's forehead sharply with his forefinger. "What did you think would happen? I can't defer it, this isn't a college waitlist. They summon. I go. No discussion. No other option."

Sato was probably thinking, *What else am I good for?* He had no prospects in their small human town. What would he do, get a shit job and wait two years for Patrick to graduate? Then what? It's not like Patrick had grand plans for his own future.

Maybe I should fix that.

Patrick didn't want Sato to see the fear or the disappointment or the tears near the surface.

Patrick was still a shifter. He was svelte and nimble in either human or otter form. Sato may be bigger, faster, and stronger, but Patrick would always be more slippery. Also, he'd been on the wrestling team freshman year. He'd enjoyed torturing the closeted boys and he thought the tight spandex uniforms were sexy.

So he easily wriggled out from under the merman. Twisted around so that Sato ended up being the one pinned.

Patrick expected to simply be bodily lifted up at that point. Except, for once, Sato just lay supine beneath him, a slight smile teasing his lips, that new scary spark in his eyes.

It was a shock.

Sato studying his face.

Sato's gaze drifting to his lips.

Fire was buried in this creature of the sea. It probably wasn't a good idea to let it flame up between them, for it would scald their friendship. Then Patrick would have no Sato and no friendship either.

Patrick was a teenager. He was gay. He was utterly familiar with this need in himself, especially when wrestling. He knew what he felt was desire. He just wasn't sure if Sato knew that's what was happening.

Sato had never done anything to indicate he liked sex, let alone boys – not a single word or deed. He'd tolerated Patrick's wildness and open confessions and crazy talk and blatant flamboyance as if it were as unalterable as a hurricane. Perhaps it was. Perhaps Sato had known Patrick was gay before Patrick did. Perhaps this was *how* he'd known. Perhaps he'd always recognized in Patrick some tiny part of himself. Perhaps the burn had always been mutual and it was Patrick who hadn't noticed. Too tied up in his own identity and burgeoning needs.

Patrick wasn't sure if he wanted to deal with this *plus* Sato leaving. Everything safe, changing at once. If Sato had to leave, shouldn't he do so with them staying exactly as they'd always been?

Patrick leapt up, elbows flailing, and trotted forward into the water, allowing his otter form to take away the human self – the human skin that burned with want, the human heart that hurt with loss. His otter was plain brown and very cute, nothing special, whiskered and mischievous, with dexterous hands and clever instincts. Just a large, silly river creature. Just one of the elusive dobhar-chú, tricksters of the waterways. His otter form made no demands but liquid fun.

He was confident that Sato would follow him into the sea.

Sato did. Catching up easily, his tail a massive glistening spectacle of dark blues, as flamboyant in the water as Patrick was on land. As animated, with its trailing delicate fins and flicking movements, as Patrick could get at his most outrageous. In Sato, any liveliness was only ever there in his tail in the ocean, where only Patrick got to see the beauty of it.

They stayed that way for longer than they usually did. Swimming together, avoiding mankind, the otter and the merman, both of whom had run out of time, neither of whom was ready to grow up.

The Past: Sato at Bay L'Ours

Sato watched Patrick out of the corner of his eye.

He was always watching Patrick. He tried to remember a time when he didn't feel compelled to watch over him – tracking sparkles, tracing the shine in his eyes. Pleased by the way his cheeks flushed the color of a conch shell in embarrassment, or delight. Sato was bigger and older and Patrick was such a sweet, inquisitive little thing. He'd demanded attention and care. The cutest creature Sato had ever seen. Still the cutest, years later.

His sire was home and puttering in the kitchen when they arrived back. The human barely glanced at them, so accustomed to their comings and goings and the salt smell of a recent swim. Both of them in board shorts and flip-flops and nothing else.

Patrick went immediately into the kitchen to see if there were snacks.

Sato's sire casually passed over a small plate piled high with takoyaki.

Patrick, big dark eyes glistening with pleasure, issued a cheerful *thank you* which Sato's sire barely acknowledged. They clattered up the stairs to Sato's room like they'd been doing for seven years. Sato's whole history among humans was him and Patrick, together like this.

Patrick popped two takoyaki into his mouth at the same time, cheeks protruding like a hamster.

"I think my sire won't miss me at all," said Sato, sitting down in his desk chair and spinning it slowly.

Patrick cast himself onto the futon front first, nearly lost the takoyaki off the edge of the plate. Had to stop catastrophe with a hand that instantly got covered in sticky sauce. Patrick started licking it off with his pink tongue, making pleased noises.

Sato had to look away fast and focus on his empty desk.

"Of course he'll miss you. You're his only son."

"I'm his *only* connection to the Deep." They had argued over this before.

Patrick genuinely believed that Sato's sire *loved* him. Like some mythical human father was supposed to love his child. But that was because Patrick needed to believe that the restful calm, cold, simplicity of the Sato household was normal and safe. Since it was his only place of refuge.

But Sato knew it was not.

Sato knew this house was merely a box he'd been trapped in for a while. His sire was one of those who had been taken by the Deep. When a human loves a mermaid, there is no coming back from it. There is no love left for anyone else, even a biological child. His sire looked after him because it was his duty. His sire looked after Patrick because Patrick was there. There was no genuine love or care behind any of it. There was just obligation and the hopeless fantasy that *someday* she would come back for him.

Stupid human.

"I'm going to miss this too." Patrick popped another takoyaki into his mouth. Vibrating with happiness but also clearly sad. He had no subtlety. He showed every emotion on his sweet, currently sticky, face. He would have to learn to stop that and protect himself.

"You can always come back and demand he make them for you."

"Without you? Will he even stay in this dumb town?"

"Of course he'll stay. He's waiting for her."

"And in the meantime he'll make me, some stray otter, takoyaki? I think not."

Sato didn't argue further. Patrick was probably right. There was a good chance his sire would forget Patrick existed entirely. There was a good chance he would forget *Sato* existed.

They were talking about takoyaki because neither of them wanted to talk about Sato not being there anymore. Because Sato didn't want to think about the fact that in going away Patrick would be alone, with no Sato to take care of him, and no place to hide where his family could not get him.

At first, Sato hadn't understood why Patrick was so against his own parents. He hadn't really cared, because it meant Patrick spent all his free time with Sato. But in high school he began to suspect that it was because Patrick's family was involved in something not just shady, but dangerous – all the time. That Patrick was half afraid of the people, strangers and criminals, who were always in and out of his home. That the loud house full of chatter and angry laughter was actually no home at all because of that. Although Patrick always said he was just avoiding the chaos. Since Patrick was an agent of chaos himself, that seemed a weak excuse.

Patrick changed the subject. "At least you'll get to see your sister again."

"If they let her come visit me in Hawaii."

Sato admitted to looking forward to that possibility. His sister was one of the only things he missed about his pod. Half sister by human standards – different sires. Meymey was three years younger than he was, only a little younger than Patrick, and just as good-natured and pleased by life. He thought if he had to go back to the sea and train to be a protector, at least he might get to protect her. Increase her reputation with his vangill status. But really he was mostly interested in the training itself. Vangill were supposed to be the biggest badasses of the ocean. Sato wanted that. He wanted to come back to Patrick stronger, better able to protect him, more worthy of him.

But in the interim, what would Patrick do without him?

Probably be fine, actually. Patrick had loads of friends. Patrick was popular. Sato was the one who struggled to fit in. He expected it would be the same again among the vangill. Just because they all had spurs wouldn't make them like each other.

The real question was: What would Sato do without Patrick?

"Will you swim me out of the bay?" *Will I get a proper goodbye?*

Patrick flopped over, reached out a skinny arm, and pulled at Sato's chair so it rolled and bumped into the futon.

He offered him a takoyaki between two delicate little fingers.

Sato contemplated the offer for a moment. Took it carefully with his teeth.

Then, before Patrick could pull his hand back, Sato grabbed his wrist. Keeping the hand there. Carefully licked those sticky fingers, watched Patrick's dark eyes fill with confusion, and lust, and fear.

The dobhar-chú jerked his hand back fast, stared down at it like it had betrayed him. Looked at Sato with huge eyes.

Sato was delighted to see his little pink tongue dart out to wet dry lips. Sato wanted to bite him (and it) so badly. Way more than the takoyaki.

"I… what were we talking about?" croaked Patrick.

"You're giving me a proper goodbye."

"Of course I'll swim you out! Who else would? Gotta make sure you actually leave and don't wimp out and follow me home."

Patrick probably thought that all along he'd been the one tagging after Sato. Sato knew that it was always he who'd followed Patrick. Trailing behind the shiny one, this lucky piece of adorable he'd landed next to and never been able to let go.

"You'll be fine without me," he said, more to reassure himself.

"Of course I will!" Patrick actually looked offended, which was good. "Maybe I'll finally start dating."

"Over my dead body," replied Sato.

"You won't be here, who's to know?" Patrick was taunting him.

"Get a job, not a boyfriend," suggested Sato.

"Why not both?"

Because you're mine, not some stupid human's who doesn't understand you and can't swim with you and won't protect you. That was what Sato wanted to say.

Instead he said, "Greedy. Feed me the last one."

"You gonna tease me again?"

"Was I teasing?"

Wary, Patrick offered up the last takoyaki. This time Sato used his lips, not his teeth, sucking the two fingers that held it.

Patrick gasped and then started to cough. The now empty plate tilted as he flailed about.

"You'll get crumbs in my bed," reprimanded Sato, softly, loving the impact he'd had. What did he have left to lose now? He was going away, Patrick would be alone and unmoored once more. He wanted to leave some kind of tether behind, something more than just friendship. Something that would make it impossible for Patrick to forget him.

But of course this was Patrick. He should've known to expect what happened next. Instead of retreating or shying away, Patrick grabbed both of Sato's wrists and tugged, one small foot pushing against the chair.

The chair rolled backwards and out from under Sato. He found himself sprawled half on top of Patrick and half on top of the takoyaki plate.

"So much for the crumbs."

"Shut up," said Patrick. And because he was a shifter and quite strong, he muscled Sato over onto his back, the plate now underneath him and easy to ignore. Patrick on top of him and impossible to let go.

He clung to Sato like a barnacle. Like he had when they'd first met.

"So we're gonna be friends?" he'd asked back then.

Sato, confused by this new land of twos and fours, of dry air and cooked food, had agreed dumbly. And found himself wrapped in the skinny arms of a strange, slight creature full of confidence and hope.

Sato wanted to say, this time, in a cheesy parody of Patrick back then, *So we're gonna be boyfriends?* but he was too embarrassed and too afraid that what had been a lifesaver to him, seven years ago, was a spontaneous gesture long forgotten by the boy who'd once wielded it.

Patrick, who always distributed hugs like they were expected. Like they weren't the only hugs Sato ever got. Would ever get. Like they weren't important. Like they were some casual thing. Like there had ever been anything casual about what was between the two of them.

Patrick was feather-light atop him. He gave Sato all his weight without question, complete trust. He pressed his face into Sato's neck. They both still smelled of the sea.

"I don't want you to go."

What could Sato say to that?

Sato ran his hands over Patrick's thin back, strong muscles there and the little bumps of his spine. Would Patrick get enough to eat if he wasn't at Sato's house anymore? He was still growing, after all. And shifters ran high energy, especially otters. He needed lots of protein in his diet but he always just ate whatever he could get hold of, usually carbohydrates and sweets.

Sato shifted Patrick so he was cradled more fully against him, so their bodies shelled into each other.

Patrick squirmed and for once Sato didn't try to hide his response. Just sighed and let him feel how he hardened and heated. Pressed his hips up slightly to remind Patrick he was male.

Patrick squirmed even more, making everything worse, or better. Then he seemed to realize what he was doing, and what was happening.

He gave an adorable little squeak, and tried to jerk away.

But Sato had his arms wrapped tightly around him now. His

forearms like iron bands – extra reinforced, even in his weaker human form, by the hardness of sheathed spurs.

"I'll come back for you," he said. "I'll come back to visit if they let me." Still bitter from the taunting, he added. "You better *not* date anyone while I'm gone."

Patrick recovered his snark faster than his breath. "How else am I to get any kind of experience?"

"There's three weeks before I leave. Get it with me."

"Sato, what is this? You're not gay."

"Says who?" Sato turned his head and nudged Patrick away from his neck, became fascinated by his lips so close.

"I would have known!" insisted the impossible boy. Who should, by virtue of a raging erection, be in very little doubt.

"You're an idiot." Sato bucked under him.

"Well, yes, clearly." Patrick wiggled, intentionally this time. Testing his power.

That was more than enough. Sato flipped them over, and himself off the takoyaki plate, his ass no doubt covered in sauce and crumbs. But at least this way he could start kissing Patrick.

Which he did.

Patrick tasted like sweet sauce and salty octopus. Delicious.

Sato spent a lot of energy forcing himself to stay focused on lips, and face, and neck, and not more or lower. Because they had three weeks to be boyfriends before he left, and while Sato definitely wanted to do everything all at once, Patrick was just fifteen. Sato knew all too well how unpracticed they both were in this matter.

And he still had to contend with his instinct to protect, even now. Against himself.

CHAPTER SIX

ISLAND OF THE BLUE SEQUINS

The Present: Trick in the San Andreas Pack Den, Sausalito

"Oh good, you're home. Come here." Colin waved Trick over as soon as he walked in the door. The smallest of the San Andreas werewolves was nested in one corner of the world's biggest, puffiest couch doing something on his laptop, as usual.

Trick adored Colin but that couch messed with his head. It was a land mass in its own right. He had to cast himself into it, rather than sit down. If he perched on the edge he'd inevitably slide backwards and get eaten by the sheer squish of it all. It wasn't a couch, it was a barge that had eaten too many soft furnishings, then floated into the pack house and taken up residence there.

Colin was adrift on a sea of leather, legs tucked under him, serious and focused.

Trick ignored Colin's summons, hung up his bag and his favorite new coat with the furry leopard print collar (Marvin called it Trick's slutty pimp puffer), and wandered into the kitchen to check on the dinner situation.

"What's up, love muffin?" he sang back at Colin from there.

He didn't wait for an answer, just turned to Lovejoy, who was bopping around the kitchen to some truly terrible music, played blessedly softly on a tiny speaker. "We having a proper sit-down this evening?"

Lovejoy shook his head. "Got a diplomatic thing later, after Alec gets home. No time for a pack gathering. Food is ready if you want. There's rice in the cooker."

Trick checked the huge simmering pot on the stovetop. It contained large hunks of flesh on the bone in a dark sauce with boiled eggs and smelled strongly of five-spice and white pepper. "Moo palo!" He bounced on the balls of his feet. It was one of his absolute favorites.

"Yay!" He hugged Lovejoy, hands full of silky material. His friend had a predilection for satin shirts with bold patterns unbuttoned nearly all the way. It was very mafia chic and slightly ridiculous. But Trick appreciated that the man put in some effort.

Lovejoy chuckled and ruffled his hair with a free hand that smelled strongly of garlic. "You always get so excited when it's Asian food."

"Told you, I was raised on Japanese."

"So you say. Someday you'll tell us why that is, when your accent is both Irish and Southern."

Trick let go of Lovejoy and went to grab a bowl. He doubted he ever *would* tell the pack anything substantial about his upbringing or his family history, but it was nice that they were interested, even if other people's curiosity made him uncomfortable. The San Andreas pack already knew too much about him for anyone's safety – theirs or his.

He distracted everyone by doing a little dance and chanting, "Moo palo, moo palo, rah rah rah!"

Lovejoy was more sensitive than most to the way Trick shut down. The werewolf curved one hand over Trick's shoulder, gentle against Trick's freneticism. "I'll make nikujaga for you once I learn how."

Trick was touched, bounded a little from foot to foot. It hadn't been one of Mr Sato's dishes but he would still love to try it. "You'd do that for me, special?"

Lovejoy resumed dredging or coddling whatever magical

thing he did to make food amazing. "Of course I will, cutie. Especially since you won't request anything specific."

"You know me. I eat anything." Trick's favorite was still takoyaki. He'd never ask Lovejoy for that – it required a special pan. More importantly, he hadn't eaten it since *then*. Since Sato kissed with his sweetly salted mouth and they got sauce on his chest and crumbs on his bed. And ass.

Trick forced himself to miss the takoyaki so he would not miss Sato's kisses. And that meant not asking for it or eating it. He'd relegated the rich salty-sweet taste of both into becoming nothing more than a tiny battered ball of fried memory.

Not that he would ever have the courage to request anything special from this pack. He didn't want any pack member to go out of his way for Trick, ever! He was enough bother already, interloping and staying with them. Taking advantage of their generosity.

He also tried to be always kind and cheerful and upbeat. Pleasant to be around. Of course, he enjoyed the positive attention this garnered him, but he was well aware it was a survival mechanism.

Charming people didn't get lonely. Charming people didn't get left behind. If he were cute and funny enough and never any trouble at all, perhaps he'd get to keep this family. This time.

But in reality? Who knew how long he would be allowed to stay. How long he would be tolerated in their territory. In their *home!* So he also made himself as useful as he could around the house, helping to clean and prepare for the near constant back-yard parties. He paid a tiny amount of rent into the pack fund. Not a lot because he only had his cafe job. Alec said he didn't have to pay anything. But Trick was already eating for free and felt he *must* contribute.

He certainly didn't feel like he'd earned the right to request anything specifically. Especially not a dish that required a special pan to make and kisses to understand.

But he was also one to get enthusiastic over anything he truly loved and enjoyed. He was bouncy and excitable by nature. A hard life hadn't beaten that aspect of his personality out of him.

He was still an otter – playful and joyful and easygoing and maybe a little neurotic. So when Lovejoy, or any of the others, happened upon a dish or a snack that Trick particularly loved, Trick couldn't stop himself from showing appreciation. Usually by clapping, and wiggling, and doing a little dance.

Lovejoy, at least, had figured this out and loved to see him happy. So now there were a couple of regular stews in the pack's monthly meal rotation, like moo palo, that specifically catered to Trick's preferences and happy claps. Trick found this awfully sweet and somewhat embarrassing, but it was too late now.

Trick served himself a bowlful of Lovejoy's moo palo. Trick adored pretty much all Thai food – it had no discoloration from poisoned nostalgia like Japanese cuisine.

He didn't bother with rice, just took his bowl to the huge dining table and plonked it down, splashing only a little. He could talk to Colin from there without having to shout. He tried to prove to them regularly that he was polite and house-trained. Mr Sato had seen to that, somewhat accidentally. The were-wolves didn't seem to care; they were a rowdy bunch.

Colin launched into conversation the moment Trick sat down. "Trick, baby-cakes, you know anything about this hot naked dude saving a kid from drowning this afternoon? Downtown?"

"I'll play your erotic little game," said Trick, chewing in a way he hoped conferred deep interest in the matter of all things hot, naked, and dudely.

"There is a wealth of photographic evidence, and I do mean wealth. Dude is *smoking* hot."

"In *our town, this town, Sausalito,* and I missed it? Worse, no one told me? Emergency response systems must be reworked stat! In Sausalito it should be made abundantly clear to all residents that firemen respond to fires, paramedics to injuries, cops to crime, SBI to shifters, and *me* to naked dudes. Spot a random naked dude, send in Trick."

"You're like a birdwatcher, only for cock?"

"Exactly! After all, cock, technically, also a bird."

"You know in England they call them twitchers?"

"Accurate."

Colin laughed. "Birdwatchers, not cockwatchers."

"Less accurate." Trick waved an airy hand and continued his fake ranting between bites, "The downtown gossips at the very least should have told me about a naked dude. I mean, what good is Floyd if not to tell me when unfettered dick is hanging out in our vicinity? What's my purpose on this earth if not to catch a *smoking* hot dude, as you so eloquently put it, when he is wandering around my neighborhood starkers, I ask you?"

"You're frittering away your entire existence, and it's obviously Floyd's fault," agreed Colin.

"You, however, were at school all day. How did you know when I didn't?" Trick worked some pork off the bone with his spoon. "You got news alerts set up for *Sausalito*?"

"Of course – it's the pack's hometown, after all."

"Sometimes you're more Big Brother than you are little brother," said Kevin to his much smaller and younger brother, walking into the den. He was wearing a short yellow waffle robe and a smug expression. The waffle robe was new and clashed with his red hair, the expression was ubiquitous.

"I resemble that remark," replied Colin, looking equally smug. Aside from coloring, they actually weren't all that similar, except when they smiled or got smug.

Trick swallowed his mouthful of stew. "Colin, this news has me strangely intrigued. Was the cock in question over at the viewpoint past that new seafood place? You're well aware I don't have line of sight to any of the piers from my counter. A mermaid did visit my cafe this morning, though. That was weird." He remembered the white socks and the tented old basketball shorts. "And kinda gross. Sometimes I really don't get breeders."

Silence met that rather obvious statement.

Colin said, "Mermaid? Really. Now that's interesting because this hot naked dude was apparently a hot naked mer*man*."

Trick's stomach whooshed at that information. Sato? Of course not. What would Sato be doing in Sausalito? Still, Trick's mind froze. He pushed down the impossible hope.

Impossible because he'd thought he'd given it up. He scrabbled for a witty response. Reached for sarcasm. His voice dry and squeaky.

"The cock in question was fish-tangential? Did Marvin go for a swim and accidentally rescue a kid after he left my cafe this morning?" Trick suggested the most obvious answer. "No offense to Marvin but I've seen it all before, and like all the most discerning of cockwatchers I'm only interested in new specimens."

Colin shook his head. "It wasn't Marvin."

Kevin was less smug, now wearing his none-of-your-nonsense enforcer expression. "What are you two squirts on about?"

Colin took mercy on his brother. "Apparently this dude plucks this kid out from the undertow, and then shoots himself up out of the water hard enough to clear the rail of that new pier – holding a six-year-old! Flops onto the lookout deck, gives the child CPR, saves his life, struts around naked for a bit, then swims away."

"Sounds like a merman," said Trick, because it did. Not much like Sato, though.

"He's ripped too. Fantastic abs."

"Who has fantastic abs?" asked Judd, coming in then. He was wearing a yellow waffle robe just like his fellow enforcer, only the color looked a lot better on him. He glared in mock jealousy at his mate.

Colin slapped his computer closed. "*You* do, of course, love of my life."

Judd pouted down at Colin. "What, you're not gonna share the pretty?"

Colin made a face at him, crawled to the edge of the couch, escaped to standing, then made his way into the kitchen, probably only just realizing he was hungry. "Would it kill you to get a little jelly?"

"Gingersnap, you've been watching way too many K-dramas lately. Jealousy is a sign of insecurity at best and entitlement at worst. It has very little to do with affection." Judd trailed after

Colin into the kitchen. Draped his huge body over the smaller man while Colin stirred the stew.

"More importantly, it's also a sign of immaturity. Judd is absolutely ancient, remember?" Kevin grinned cheerfully and headed for the kitchen as well.

Lovejoy intercepted the enforcer. "Too crowded already. Go sit down."

Colin said, "Should I dish?"

"By all means, feed the ravening hordes," said Lovejoy, standing with crossed arms and watching until Kevin was safely seated opposite Trick at the dining table.

Then Lovejoy unwound Judd from his mate and shoved the big man in the same direction. Judd pouted but lumbered over as well. No one argued with Lovejoy in the kitchen.

Colin didn't need to ask if the enforcers wanted food. They *always* wanted food.

He dished out a small bowl for himself, and then two large bowls for the enforcers, plus rice and various condiments. He loaded up a tray and took it all to the big dining table. Joined the three already there.

Trick was almost done with his own serving. He looked up as Colin sat. "A strange merman and a strange mermaid in Sausalito at the same time? That can't be a coincidence. And if it isn't a coincidence, it's super weird." He ate the egg he'd saved for last.

"What do you mean?" asked Colin.

"Mermen are solitary and mermaids mostly travel in large groups. Such a pair traveling together would seem to be an anomaly." Trick was probably revealing that he knew too much about the people of the sea. But he didn't think the wolves were smart enough around delta dynamics to understand such nuances.

The pack regularly assumed that Trick would, as a water beast himself, know about all shifters who swam in water. As if the oceans weren't more vast than the land. As if wolves kept tabs on bears or cats or any other shifter population not their own. Also, the pack had never quite figured out that while Trick regularly swam in the bay, technically his shifted form was that of a *river* otter, not a *sea* otter.

They had a lot to learn, poor things.

"Sounds like the start of a joke," said Kevin. "A merman and mermaid walk into Sausalito."

"Technically only one of them walked, the other one flopped," pointed out Colin, having seen the footage.

Trick fidgeted in his chair, wondering yet again if it were Sato. Every time he heard mention of a merman, he wondered. Which, admittedly, wasn't often. The sea people kept a low profile. But it had never been Sato, and Sato traveling with a mermaid? Sato traveling with anyone? Unlikely.

"One merman is a visitor, one mermaid is a hunter, two merfolk at once? That's an aberration. I don't like aberrations." Colin liked things that fit neatly into charts and played well with statistical models and predictable patterns.

"Or an invasion," grumbled Judd.

Marvin came waltzing in at that juncture. He'd been with the coast guard all afternoon for some secret operation, but he'd changed out of his uniform before returning home. The dress robe was still caught up in red tape. He refused to wear his adjunct's uniform at any other time not strictly required by his contract because, as he put it, they wouldn't let him write *Rear Admiral* in glittery puffy paint on the ass of the slacks.

"If you don't like aberrations, sweetie pie, how do you tolerate me?" he asked.

"You're not an aberration, you're a delightful distraction," replied Colin.

"The world's best ravishing incongruity?" suggested Trick, grinning at his friend.

Marvin wiggled his blond eyebrows at them. "I like it! Good drag name too."

"Did *you* hear about the merman saving the kid downtown this morning?" Judd asked Marvin.

"I was there, Captain Velcro," Marvin shot back.

"So you met this visiting merman?" Trick tried not to sound as desperately curious as he was.

"Hm. Would we say *met?* There were no formal introductions. In fact, he was awfully rude." Marvin could be very, very evasive when he felt like it.

"And did you meet Trick's mermaid?"

"Since when has Trick had a mermaid? You changing sides on me, biscuit whiskers?"

Trick got up to take his now empty bowl to the sink. "*Biscuit whiskers,* my gay ass. She's not *my* mermaid in any lifetime – in fact, she would appear to be some dude-bro's mermaid. She went off with this tourist wearing white tube socks and a red baseball cap." He checked to see if there was anything else he could do in the kitchen to help clean. Lovejoy had left it spotless, though. Trick wished they would let him be more useful.

"Tube socks? How *absolutely* revolting." Marvin shuddered.

"Right!" Trick dished out a small bowl of moo palo for the merman, adding fish sauce and seaweed sprinkles to the top.

He carried it back to the table. "Come eat. And I'll consider telling you about the man's shorts."

"*Shorts?* With tube socks! This is like walking roadkill. I'm utterly riveted." Marvin scuttled over.

Trick pursed his lips. "*Orange* basketball shorts and one of those stretched-out white tank tops. And for the sake of truth, I must report faithfully that he did *not* have the body for that."

Marvin sat down and began eating, staring trancelike at Trick. "Does anyone? This is more fascinating and horrifying than that two-week-old body I fished out of Monterey Bay last month. Go on!"

Trick needled him. "You know, if you'd stayed a bit longer this morning, you would have seen the whole thing yourself."

"True, but then I'd have missed the hot merman. I assure you, my scenery was better than yours – no shorts at all, and the body to pull it off. I also wouldn't have known that we have a much bigger problem than just one merman and one mermaid with bad taste in humans."

"Did you miss the bit about the tube socks?" Trick pressed, knowing Marvin.

"No no, you're right, that is a serious problem. Have you considered posting a *no tube socks* sign on the cafe door?"

"I don't think cafes should discriminate." Trick wondered how he could get Marvin back onto the merman.

Marvin shook his head. "Trick, baby-doll, sometimes I think you're too kind and generous. People take advantage of your good nature. You're doomed to get your eyeballs seared by tourists."

"I suffer," agreed Trick.

"It's a curse one must bear in the beverage industry." Marvin took a bite of food.

"What could possibly be more of a problem than an arbitrarily benevolent merman and a bog-standard mermaid in town at the same time?" Colin attempted to get Marvin back on track. A daunting task.

Marvin sighed big and dramatic. "Try *twelve* mermaids."

Trick let out a shaky breath. A whole pod? Definitely not Sato. Sato would never, in a million years, go around with a whole pod of mermaids.

Kevin looked up from his soup. "*Twelve*, did you say?"

"Don't look so hopeful, none of them will be interested in you, snookums. If I've told you once, I've told you a thousand times, mermaids only fuck humans," said Marvin, merciless.

Kevin sighed. "Their loss."

"If they all go into the city at once, there could be riots," pointed out Colin, practically. "This weekend, for example, just imagine them at Fisherman's Wharf."

Trick shuddered. "I'd rather not."

"What's a group of mermaids called again?" asked Lovejoy, finally joining them with his own bowl of food.

"A migraine," said Trick.

"What he said," agreed Marvin, even though they were his people.

"A pod," explained Colin, who was a nice person.

"*Twelve* of them, you say?" That was Judd, who probably had a better idea than any other werewolf about what might be going on. Simply because he'd lived long enough to meet the occasional pod of mermaids before.

"What does it mean?" asked Lovejoy.

"We are well and truly fucked," said Judd.

"Well, not us specifically, but probably lots of local human males," said Colin.

"The ones wearing tube socks, most likely. Do you think tube socks are some kind of mermaid aphrodisiac?" wondered Trick.

"Enough with the tube socks, Trick," said Marvin.

"I thought you were on my side."

"Unfortunately, I am going to have to do something quite out of character at this juncture."

"Oh no, don't change!" wailed Trick, pushing into melodrama. He tucked his hands under the table edge. They were shaking.

"What's that?" asked Colin.

"Get serious. Because there is something even worse going on."

"What's worse than twelve mermaids bobbing about the bay?" wondered Judd.

"Twelve mermaids *and* one merman?" suggested Lovejoy, who had been paying attention.

Marvin pointed two fingers at him, "Bing bing bing! Give the pretty boy a prize. It's what twelve mermaids *and* one merman *means*. Too small for a proper pod and no spawn at all? A fully grown, protective, Alpha-type merman swimming with a dozen grown females and arbitrarily rescuing human children. That doesn't seem weird to you? And you know I don't use the term *Alpha* lightly."

Trick said, "Sure seems weird to me." If Sato had taught him nothing else about the people of the sea, it was that mermen preferred to be solitary, especially from their own kind. Marvin was the only apparent exception.

"Darlings all, the time has come for me to break silence on the matter of the merfolk."

"Oh, must you?" said Kevin.

"Eat your soup, big guy, I must." Marvin stood and struck an orator's pose, hand over his chest. "Gentlefolk of the land-bound world – of beached, bleached, and dry. We are being honored beyond measure by a very austere and important visitor. Yes, my dearest fuzz-butts all, the San Francisco Bay is currently hosting one of the five *Soteria of the Deep*."

"The *what* of the *what* now?" asked Colin.

Trick knew what the Soteria of the Deep meant. He should not know such a thing. He wasn't a mermaid. But he did.

"One of their *leaders* is *here*?" Apparently Judd also knew.

"I know, right? Isn't it amazing?" Marvin was all sarcasm. "Aren't we lucky?"

Trick felt his ears roar slightly. One of *them*. One of the ones who had called Sato away. One of the ones who had kept him. One of the thieves. One of the enemy.

One of those who, if given the right incentive, might be persuaded to tell Trick where Sato was. One of those who might actually know. Or at least have the resources to figure it out.

"Is this why Alec has a meeting tonight?" Trick asked, forcing himself to speak calmly.

"It is."

"Do you want me to come?" Trick barely managed to keep his voice from shaking. Not sure if he was hopeful or terrified.

Suddenly he was a mess. Okay, not so suddenly. He'd started going messy the moment he'd found out about the strange merman.

A mess like the teenager he'd once been.

A mess over Sato. Or the possibility of Sato.

A *hot* mess, of course, but a mess nonetheless.

Because he did and didn't want to know why he'd been abandoned. Why he'd been forgotten. Why the one fixed thing he had trusted in his ever-unstable life, Sato, hadn't come back to him. Why the charm of otter-kind and his clever manipulative ways had failed the one time they'd really mattered. Failed because of a merman. Did anyone ever really want to know why they hadn't been good enough?

"No thank you, Trick," said a new voice from the front door.

Trick was relatively new to being around a werewolf pack.

There was still a lot about it that confused him. But he always found the effect of the Alpha among them *impressive*. A little creepy but impressive.

There they all sat around the big table – at home, relaxed, eating delicious food, enjoying themselves.

Then Alec walked in the door.

The impact was immediately obvious in the body language of every werewolf there. Colin, Kevin, Judd, Lovejoy – their posture just melted slightly. Alec's scent on the air (Trick assumed) and their shoulders were less tense. Alec within their line of sight, and they became a tiny bit less alert, less on their guard, softer. As if Alec were a nice bouquet of flowers, or a pretty sunset, his mere presence a gift to their senses but more importantly a gift to their psyches. A walking, talking antidepressant – that also turned into a raving beast regularly.

To Trick, who possessed very little capacity for relaxation (and never had – otters were notoriously high strung) this was almost magical to watch happen. He had yet to get tired of it, every time Alec walked into a room filled with pack. The way they all reveled in him, like cats basking in sunbeams.

When he let himself, Trick wondered if he'd been that way around Sato. Or if that had been love. Or youth. Or ignorance.

Certainly Alec was still very much *Alpha*. The attention of everyone in that room swiveled toward him, almost imperceptibly, but entirely. They were all his to command, and he knew it, never questioned that, but he was also clearly theirs. He belonged to the pack. And they knew that too.

Marvin, being Marvin the Merman, did not react that way. Instead, he shot up from the table and catapulted himself at his mate, launched himself into the air in a ballet leap, entirely convinced Alec would drop his computer bag and catch him. Alec was tall by Trick's standards, but slight, not huge and beefy like his enforcers. Trick certainly wouldn't have trusted Alec that way.

But Alec dropped his bag and caught his mate easily.

Alec may look like a nerdy lab scientist (which he basically was) but he was still werewolf strong, and he was better-than-werewolf fast.

Trick had had occasion to observe, over his admittedly brief time with the San Andreas pack, that Alpha werewolves were natural leaders, of course. But what made them Alpha was actually not that leadership ability, it was something less obvious. Judd had a greater aura of command and sheer feel of power about him. Kevin was better looking and more charismatic. Lovejoy was more charming. Bryan was more kind. Colin probably had a higher IQ. Tank was bigger than any of them. Tank was bigger than any werewolf Trick had ever seen. And Isaac was, well, Isaac was special.

But Alec? Alec was just… a better *werewolf* than any or all of them. Trick had asked Marvin once what it was that made Alec an Alpha.

Marvin, who loved bragging about his mate, replied, "Alec fights smart. He's not just a human with a PhD, he's a *wolf* with a PhD."

"What does a wolf need a PhD for?" Trick joked.

"You know what I mean."

"The shift doesn't impact his brain meats?"

"Exactly. Grade A brain meats inside my man, at all times. He's Alpha because of who he is, of course, but also *what* he is when he's a wolf. Apparently it's quite impressive. Particularly to other wolves. Particularly to the suckers who end up fighting him. Poor things."

Trick had taken Marvin's word for it because he'd yet to witness Alec really fight and he never felt any of the rest of Alec's aura. Werewolf Alpha power didn't seem to really affect Trick.

But the way all the other werewolves, and occasional other pack-oriented shifters, behaved around Alec? Even Trick could see *that*.

Trick's non-responsiveness had confused Alec at first. Not worried, just confused. The Alpha was so accustomed to those living with him relaxing in his presence, accidentally obeying him without question. Trick never did that.

"Otters have little hierarchy built into their social structure. It's just age and blood relations dictating interpersonal behaviors," Judd had explained to Alec while also directing an inquiring look at Trick.

Trick had nodded. "Yeah, it's just family dynamics and changeable allegiances. We don't really fight for dominance," he'd explained, so that the pack would understand he'd be no good for them in battle. He'd be of no help with Heavy Lifting or bodyguard duties either. He wanted to be useful, but couldn't do that.

"We're lovers, not fighters," he'd added.

In reality, dratsie were tricksters and fraudsters. The dobharchú used weaponized charm and wit way more than claws or teeth. As a species, they were known to be *clever*, not tough. When they were known at all.

In reality Trick may never fully trust Alec because he was too scared to trust like that ever again. Because he'd only relaxed and fully trusted one other dominant Alpha type. And that hadn't worked out so well.

Alec left his computer bag in the doorway, arms full of merman, and carried Marvin into the dining room, sat in a chair with the merman in his lap.

Lovejoy went and got him a bowl of moo palo.

Trick wondered how the Alpha was going to eat stew with a gorgeous blond draped atop him.

Alec continued talking to Trick. "Sweet of you to offer, but it would be better not to overwhelm them with numbers at this first meeting."

Trick wasn't sure what he felt about that, mostly relief. But also a little sad. Yet again, the pack didn't actually seem to need him for anything. Which felt a little like they didn't want him. He shook that off. "So they're in this area for a while? Why?"

"I don't know. I only know they're here." Marvin squirmed around in Alec's lap to sit properly. Alec made a pained expression.

Oblivious to his mate's discomfort, or possible arousal, the merman said, "I claimed Alec as singer for the seas in this area."

Alec puffed out his cheeks. "So you texted. I don't understand."

Marvin explained. "Sort of like the leader of local allegiances. A liaison between sea and land who understands local politics. Technically it should *not* be a four-legger. It should be me, or a selkie, or Ms Trickle, or even Trick."

"Fuck no," said Trick, vehemently.

"But since you have water folk in your pack and number quite a few others as friends in this area, I think I can make the claim stick," said Marvin. "Plus there is Max to consider."

"Max?"

"Mermaids don't respect humans at all. Not even slightly. Mostly they are just annoyed by them or use them for breeding. But mermaids do respect Magistars because they respect quin-tessence and anyone who has the power to harness it. They know what that kind of ability can do to existence, even theirs."

Alec said, "Which is why I'll be taking Marvin, Bryan, and Max with me tonight." He glared at his enforcers. "No one else."

Kevin and Judd exchanged apprehensive looks. "But there are thirteen of them!"

"At least take Isaac," suggested Colin.

"Wouldn't do any good," said Trick and Marvin at the same time.

Marvin swiveled to stare at him. "And how would you know that?"

Trick only shrugged. "Omega wouldn't work on dratsie. I'm assuming he wouldn't work on merfolk either."

Alec looked suddenly interested. It was just like Alec to be most concerned when his greatest peace-keeping tool was taken away from him. He had all the confidence of an Alpha in his fighting and in his command, but what he really loved to use the most in any political situation was his Omega. His greatest instrument of calm. "Not work?"

Marvin patted his mate's head. "Did you never notice, honey? Isaac doesn't work on me. Or Ms Trickle. Or, I'm thinking, Trick. Although we haven't really tried yet."

"Work?" Alec looked confused.

"His omega-fu-juice or whatever it is."

"Must we say *juice?*" Kevin made a face.

"Wait, Omega doesn't work on you?" Alec was dumbfounded. "Or you?" He stared at Trick.

Marvin turned to look at his mate, clapped small hands to Alec's cheeks, and pressed in, forcing their great leader to make a pouty face. "Aw, you're so cute when you're confused. How are you so cute? No, baby, it never has. Nor has your adorable highly concentrated Alpha-fu-juice either."

"Could you *please* stop saying *juice?*" begged Kevin.

"All water shifters?" Alec's words were muffled by Marvin still squeezing his cheeks.

"Probably," said Marvin, cheerfully unconcerned.

"Taking Max tonight makes sense then, doesn't it? After all, no one's immune to Magistars," said Colin, looking at Judd, trying to forestall enforcer concern for pack safety. For Alec's safety.

But neither enforcer protested. Max and Bryan were a great security detail. Probably the world's best.

Alec grinned at his pack. "I also called and invited Ms Trickle." His lovely hazel eyes crinkled when he smiled, which he did often. Trick loved that.

Marvin giggled. "Oh you did, did you? That's my smartypants Alpha-poo."

"Marvin, must you? Dignity of the rank and all," growled Kevin.

Trick struggled not to laugh. He was on Marvin's side; Ms Trickle was a smart call.

"She'll be representing the local government's interest, of course, but also..." Alec trailed off.

"She's a kelpie," crowed Marvin.

"And that matters, why?" wondered Lovejoy.

Marvin waggled his eyebrows. "Oh, mermaids *hate* kelpie. This is gonna be *such* fun."

Trick remembered something then. Information that would do him no good to keep to himself and might actually help the pack. "About that mermaid I met."

"Something I don't know?" Alec's focus was laser sharp and immediate.

Trick tilted his head, searching for the right way to phrase it. "Yeah, because Marvin left before it happened. At first I thought she was just hunting sperm. You know how they are. But she said, as she was leaving with her chosen bonk-fest, that she was actually in town for a *conference*."

"A mermaid came to Sausalito for a business convention?"

"No single part of that statement makes any kind of sense."

"But it *might* explain why the Paralia is here," said Marvin.

CHAPTER SEVEN
DIFFERENT WAVELENGTHS

The Past: Patrick at Bay L'Ours without Sato

Apparently, it was some kind of truth or dare. Or spin the bottle. Except it was all about revealing secrets. So, Patrick guessed, just the *truth* part of *truth or dare*.

Mary Charlotte had a foreign exchange student staying with her who had taught her this new game. Mary Charlotte really wanted to play it. Amongst the L'Ours High sophomores, what Mary Charlotte wanted, Mary Charlotte got.

To be fair to Mary Charlotte (although, why should he be?), with enough alcohol sixteen– year-olds will try pretty much anything.

Patrick was actually enjoying himself, but then Patrick always tended to enjoy himself at parties these days.

It was a gift.

Essentially the idea, in this instance, was that everybody sit around the coffee table, lounging on couches and in armchairs and on the floor, and put their hands in the air with all five fingers open. Then everybody shut their eyes.

Then Mary Charlotte would ask a question about whether you'd done some sexual act or another. If you hadn't done it, you could put a finger down. But if you *had* done it you had to keep the finger up.

Then there was another question.

And another question.

Until they hit five questions. Then everybody opened their eyes, and… surprise, we all got to figure out who's the slut in the room!

Patrick was pretty nosy and totally interested in everybody else's sex lives. Also, he was pretty sure that he and Sato had managed most of the things needed to qualify for slut-hood amongst his peers (except actual penetration). Thus he was bound to be both the superior slut every single time and find out how slutty everyone else was. Win win!

"Let's start easy," said Mary Charlotte. "Who here has held somebody's hand in a romantic way?"

Patrick left all five fingers up. That would be a definite *yes*. Not that Sato was a big hand holder, his being webbed and all. But they had done it a few times. Mostly so he could tug Patrick out of the way of oncoming traffic and useful stuff like that.

Patrick still thought it counted.

"Okay, number two," said Mary Charlotte. "Who here has kissed somebody on the cheek that they're interested in dating?"

Patrick thought that one was kind of weird. Who kissed on the cheek at their age? Was Mary Charlotte secretly lusting after a Little House on the Prairie kind of romance? How quaint.

He put down one finger.

Mary Charlotte pressed on. "Who has kissed somebody? Like a proper actual romantic kiss on the lips."

That was an easy one, Patrick left four fingers up.

"Okay, next. Who has French kissed, with tongue and everything."

A few people around the table giggled nervously. Mary Charlotte was having none of it. "It's gonna get worse," she said. "Last one for this round! Who has actually necked?"

Patrick still had four fingers up at the end of the first round. He didn't get the cheek kiss one, but he'd earned a solid four out of five.

Mary Charlotte sounded pleased with how things were going. "Okay, everyone, open your eyes."

Patrick looked around eagerly, just like everyone else. Most of them had three fingers up. That's the thing about being in a small town, nothing else to do. Most kids got sexed-up early. Patrick examined each person's hands, looking for surprises.

Jolene, the super geeky girl with cat eye glasses and too-short bangs, had all of her fingers still up. Patrick thought that was pretty cool. It was always the ones you least suspected. She probably went to comic conventions and such. Everybody knew those places were *wild*. He gave her an approving smile. She made a very embarrassed face. He waved his own four fingers at her. She smiled at him then.

Mary Charlotte noticed Patrick's wiggling hand. "Would you like to confess to which one you haven't done, Patrick?" she needled him.

Patrick would confess to anything, even something he had done, if it amused others and got him attention. Well, *almost* anything. Not his shifter identity, of course. Or his parents' work. But his sex life was pretty much fair game, as far as he was concerned. It was nothing to be ashamed of. Sato was a fantastic boyfriend, all things being equal – thorough and *very* focused, and incredibly intense. Patrick suspected, as first boyfriends went, he'd been spoiled.

He said, "The cheek question was weird. You know that, right? Only old people in twenty-year-long relationships kiss each other's cheek. That's for grandparents or whatever."

Mary Charlotte looked pleased. "So you're saying you've done all of the others?"

Patrick looked at his hand as though it had betrayed him. "Fingers don't lie."

Mary Charlotte giggled and then turned to everybody else at the table. "Some people, we know, are going to brag, and others may be lying, because it's all on you to be honest in this game."

Patrick didn't like Mary Charlotte very much. She gave him attitude all the time. Patrick felt like *attitude* was his responsibility at their school. For identity politics reasons. Yes, yes, he was *the gay kid,* but he was also an otter. Otters were made of pure uncut *attitude.*

Mary Charlotte spread her attention and curiosity around, asking some of the other kids about their experiences and why some of their fingers were down.

Patrick mostly paid attention. He was intrigued, but they were all still teenagers, and they were all, so far as he could tell, regrettably straight.

At that juncture, Patrick realized that he was under scrutiny.

This party was mostly sophomores but there were a few interloping juniors and seniors, and even a lucky freshman or two. But since they all went to the same school, he should know all of them by sight. The kid sitting across from him had all of his teeth and all of his fingers up but Patrick didn't recognize him.

Patrick didn't like mysteries.

So he said, during a brief lull in Mary Charlotte's inquisition, "Who are you?"

Mary Charlotte, the hostess with the mostess, answered for the stranger. "Oh, that's just my cousin from Chicago. He's staying with us for winter break."

Patrick grinned at the Chicago cousin. "Well, hello there. I'm Patrick."

"I gathered as much."

"Chicago, really? That's cool."

"Especially in winter." Oh, this one thought he was a comedian? Patrick was undaunted; he could be charming and funny too.

"This has to be weird for you." Patrick gestured at the assembly but he meant small town, deep South.

"Not really. They've exiled me down here before."

"Lucky you." Patrick wondered why he'd never noticed him. Probably because during breaks he and Sato were usually off swimming.

"I agree with you about the cheek kissing. Weird question." The Chicago boy had a nice soft smile and very blue eyes.

"But you left all your fingers up."

"I believe in trying everything at least once."

A man after Patrick's own heart.

Mary Charlotte apparently did not like Patrick and her cousin talking without her sanction. She called their focus back to herself.

"Shall we play another round?"

Chicago cousin hid a smile and said in a low, soft voice for Patrick's ears alone, "She wants your attention."

"*Me?*" Patrick was startled.

Mr Chicago wiggled his eyebrows.

Really? Patrick had always thought it was obvious that he was gay. Apparently, not to sixteen-year-old Mary Charlotte. *Awkward.* However, she was the queen in charge and he wasn't going to blatantly out himself. Especially when it shouldn't be necessary. That seemed like overkill.

So instead he said, "All right, let's play another round, shall we?"

So they continued with the game. Moving on and through various sexual acts including leaving hickeys, getting hickeys, licking somebody's ear, licking somebody's elbow, kissing hands, nibbling ankles, oral sex, and so forth. Patrick thought the game was more insightful into Mary Charlotte's erotic imagination, which was clearly a little confused about levels of intimacy, but he remained amused enough to play along.

When he opened his eyes at the end of the third round, he and his new friend across the table had all of their fingers up. Kindred sluts. He gave the boy a cheeky wave.

Mr Slutty Chicago grinned at him. He had a nice smile. It crinkled those bright eyes.

Patrick smiled back. "Are all the boys in Chicago fifteen fingers of fun?"

The boy laughed.

There was something about the way he looked at Patrick. It made Patrick wonder if the reason this human could check fifteen things off of the proverbial list was because the two of them were on the same kind of life path. Although Mr Slutty

Chicago's experience in this regard was no doubt with a man much less hot than Sato.

They played another round.

Both of them left all five fingers up.

Patrick wished there was a secret signal for asking if a boy were gay. Like some hand gesture or table-tapping morse code. Instead, he tested the only way he knew how. Which was to lower his eyelids, because he had very long lashes, and then open them again slowly, looking upwards at his new friend. Patrick knew his eyes were by far his best feature. Huge and limpid and dark. Sato called them *fathomless*.

The boy across the table from him looked like he wanted to drown in them. Patrick found this highly gratifying and took it as confirmation of a pro-dick-sucking agenda.

Mr Slutty Chicago had indicated yes to the oral sex question. Now Patrick knew which kind of yes.

Just then, Patrick's cell phone rang. There was only one person who ever called him on that phone, so Patrick leapt up from the table.

"Where are you going?" asked Mary Charlotte, annoyed.

"I'm sorry, I have to take this." Nothing and no one could stop him from talking to Sato, certainly not some two-bit party humans with questionable taste in beer and attire.

"Patrick, you can't leave, the game is just getting started."

Patrick gave her a look. He knew there were tons more sex acts. But he doubted many of the people there had done any of them. Except maybe Mr Slutty Chicago.

Mary Charlotte was just going to make a fool of herself asking questions and then blame them for her embarrassment.

"I have to take this call," he said and dashed out toward the beach.

"Hello?"

"Why are you breathless?" Sato sounded so good. Mostly because he was Sato but also he didn't need to smoke anymore to hide that extra-smooth siren voice of his.

"I had to run out of a party."

"You're at a party?"

"What else do you expect me to do on a Saturday night?"

"It's Saturday?"

Patrick ignored that. Merfolk had a great sense of tide but a notoriously terrible sense of time. "For your information, we were playing a very exciting game."

"Oh, were you? Did you win?"

"Yes, of course. With your help. Apparently you have made me a fourteen-point slut du jour."

"*What* did you just say?"

"Only a slut for you, of course, babe."

"Babe? What are you talking about?" A pause while Sato muttered, clearly to himself, "What are you getting up to without me keeping an eye on you?"

"It's fine, *babe*. I doubt the others actually believe me, and we never got onto the really juicy acts."

"Did we do those, *babe*?"

"Oh yeah, I remember us getting pretty sticky a time or two. There was that one night with the unagi sauce and…"

"Enough."

Patrick couldn't tell if Sato was stopping him because he was annoyed or getting turned on from the memory. Probably a bit of both.

"It turns out some of them might even think I was doing it with a *girl*."

"Really? How bizarre." Sato sounded genuinely amused.

"Right? But enough about me, how are you doing? How's training? What are the other guys like? Is anybody flirting with you? Do I need to swim over there and ruthlessly nibble at my rivals?"

"What are you chittering about? As if anyone but you would ever put up with me. It's fine. I'm fine. I'm not really supposed to talk about it. Which is weird. Because it's mostly stuff that only merfolk would care about anyway. I guess military sea people are just like other military types. Vangill is supposed to exist under a shell of silence."

Sato was saying a lot more than he usually did. Which meant he had a window of phone time without supervision for a change, and wanted to get it all out fast. He wasn't a natural talker, never had been.

Patrick wanted to know whether Sato was getting any better at using his spurs. He wanted to know where Sato ranked compared to the other vangill in training. He bet his boyfriend was at the top of the class. Patrick wanted details on what the training was like. Was it all underwater or did they go up on land? He was full of questions, but Sato abruptly stopped talking. Somebody had come close enough to overhear.

So Patrick asked what he hoped was an innocuous question. "Are they feeding you? Are you eating enough?"

"I'm not a child. I can actually take care of myself. Especially underwater."

"You can't tell me you don't miss your dad's cooking."

"Maybe a little."

"Do you miss me a little too?"

"More than you could possibly imagine." There was a sound of murmuring voices in the background – melodic masculine ones. Then an order was barked out. "I gotta go now."

"Oh wait but—"

Sato swore. "I never asked about your family. Are you okay without me?"

"I don't want to talk about my damn family. I never want to talk about them. I want to talk about you and—" *I'm never okay without you.*

"I have to go."

"When will you call again?"

But Sato had already hung up.

Patrick sighed and pocketed the phone. Mary Charlotte's parents' beach house behind him was all light and activity, cheerful. He felt suddenly lonely.

He'd wandered down to the shore during the course of the conversation. Even though it was late, and there was a house full of humans behind him, he wanted nothing more than to strip and go for a swim.

It really wasn't safe for a small river otter to go swimming alone at night. He only wanted to do it because it would remind him of Sato. But it would probably just make him feel worse and more alone. Better to go back to the party, where he could pretend he was having a good time.

"Important call?" Apparently Mr Slutty Chicago had followed him out and down to the beach.

Patrick had a brief moment of panic, wondering if he'd said anything he shouldn't on the phone. Anything that indicated what he was, or what Sato was. But thinking back, it had pretty much just been banal boyfriend talk.

Then he had a brief moment of fear. This was only a human, but a human boy bigger than him, and Sato was thousands of miles away and Patrick did have a tendency to get himself into trouble.

Patrick decided on a diversionary-tactic-meets-the-always-useful charm offensive. "I didn't even get to tell him about my new job."

Mr Slutty Chicago was willing to be distracted. He approached Patrick carefully, as if Patrick were skittish. "Shall we walk along the water and you can tell me about it instead?"

Patrick always thought it was an odd human thing to walk along the waterfront and stare out at the ocean, especially when you had no intention of going into it. Also he wasn't sure about being alone with a stranger, but if all else failed he could disappear into the ocean. It was right there, after all.

So he allowed himself to be turned gently by the shoulder, and they started strolling together. "So this job you didn't get to tell your… boyfriend?… about?"

Patrick didn't answer the question within the question, simply started chattering. Partly because he didn't really feel like talking about Sato, but also because he was genuinely excited about his new job. Also, it was an excuse to be witty. And he did enjoy the attention. Mr Slutty Chicago was no Sato (who was?), but he was kinda cute.

"There is a new café opening up. I'm going to be their first trainee barista. I'm looking forward to it. I think it'll be tons of fun. Talking with people and making drinks."

"You seem like the sociable type. Is it the town's first café?"

"Like a proper one that does espresso and stuff? Not a diner. Yeah. I think most of the locals will be against it. Especially as it's taking over the old bait shop. And that was *an institution*. But I think tourists will really like it. If the owner does something smart like get donuts, or pie, or some other draw, then the town will embrace it." Humans never could resist pie.

"It sounds like you have a business plan for them."

"Well, this may be my first real job, but I have lived here all my life."

"Do you like it here?"

No one had ever asked Patrick that question. "Honestly? I don't know. It's always just been where I live. But I'm starting to think about getting out. Maybe applying for college, stuff like that."

Mr Slutty Chicago let the quiet draw out for a moment. It reminded Patrick of Sato.

"I'm smart enough." Patrick defended himself against the telling silence. "I mean, I know I seem like a feckless slacker, but my grades are actually pretty good. Plus I do lots of extra- curricular activities. I should look good on college applications. It's just that I have to get a scholarship."

"You're not like most of Mary Charlotte's friends, are you?"

Patrick had a moment of nerves. Did the Chicago boy know Chicago shifters of some kind? Had he been spotted as a fur-sprouter? Was he about to be outed?

"That's an interesting thing to say." He decided to be neutral and flat.

"No offense. I think it's a great thing. Where do you wanna go to college?"

Patrick hadn't really considered it. It was a new idea. He'd opened his mouth and said it because it seemed like something a teenage human from Chicago would understand. "I don't know. I mean I'm only a sophomore. I have time to decide."

"Not a whole lot of time. I mean, you have to think about what size college you want. Where it might be located. Where you have a good chance of getting in. What kind of programs do they have." The human's sharp eyes focused on Patrick. Like his cousin, he clearly had Grand Inquisitor inclinations. "What do you want to major in? Which part of the world do you want to live in?"

Patrick thought about Sato. Sato didn't like large cities. So it would have to be a rural campus. And it would need to be near the ocean, of course.

"Probably something on one of the coasts."

"Do you like the water?"

"Can't really live without it."

"So what about a major? Do you have a department in mind?"

"You're very curious." Patrick was used to being the most inquisitive person in a room.

"You're very interesting."

"Well, I'm kind of into drama. I'd love to go to an acting school."

His companion brightened considerably. "Really? I'm into film studies. I always wanted to go to art school."

"Yeah?"

"I'd love to become a director or a film editor or something like that."

"Do you know where you wanna go?"

"Not only that, I know where I've already gotten in."

"Oh! You're older than me?"

"Senior."

"So tell me?" Patrick was genuinely curious.

"I'm going to Jiggly Yard!" Mr Slutty Chicago said it in such a bright, prideful manner that Patrick had to assume it was a very big and important college, especially if you were interested in film.

"Oh, cool! Is it in LA?" he hazarded a guess.

"You don't know about Jiggly Yard?"

Patrick probably would've been embarrassed, except that he wasn't a human teenager, and nobody in his family had ever considered going to a human university before. He was the first of his siblings to even attend a human high school. Frankly, he was thinking about college because it would be a great way to escape said family. Still, it was genuinely the first time he'd talked about it, which meant he basically knew nothing on the subject.

"Never heard of it, sorry. I'm an ill-educated country bumpkin." *Otter*, he substituted in his own head. "Why don't you introduce yourself to me properly? Then you can tell me all about it." he suggested, knowing he sounded flirtatious. Using it like a kind of weapon. Wanting to be liked by this sophisticated Northern boy. Missing Sato and his devotion like an ache. Wondering if this was what he did when he was trying to fill that void. Defensive flirting.

The older boy laughed happily. "Okay. So, hi. I'm Zach Figg. I'm from Chicago. I'm a senior in high school. I'll be a freshman at Jiggly Yard University, in the film department, starting next fall."

"Patrick Inis. I'm a sophomore and I have no idea what I'm doing with my life."

Zach laughed again, clearly delighted with him. "Maybe I can help you with that. Can I tell you how awesome Jiggly Yard is?"

"That sounds great. I would like nothing more, quite frankly."

"Can I ask you something intrusive first?"

"Sure, I guess." Patrick was unsure about that, feeling a little unsafe.

"You aren't actually interested in dating my cousin, are you?"

Patrick was so surprised he stopped slogging through the sand. "Mary Charlotte? Are you joking?"

"Good, this could get awkward fast, otherwise."

"But I'm not avail…"

"Don't break my heart *right* away, okay? Let me have a little hope for a while."

Patrick closed his mouth and nodded reluctantly. Then gave his brightest smile, aimed to get Zach talking about himself. People always loved to do that. "So, Jiggly Yard?"

"Okay, let's start with the best part, shall we? It's in New York City."

CHAPTER EIGHT

FISHING FOR A COPULATION

The Present: Sato in San Francisco Bay near Sausalito

Sato arrived at the designated meeting spot on time and alone, ahead of the rest of the diplomatic pod. He wanted to scout ahead and Meymey wanted to make a point. She intended to be just late enough to force the land bound to recognize her authority.

A strange group sat on the sharp rocks waiting for them. No otter, unfortunately. Not that he'd really expected to find his otter hiding in a pack.

He wasn't sure what he'd expected, wolves probably. Although werewolves could not speak in their shifted forms.

Only one was a wolf. It was dark, but street lights meant Sato was able to make out features, if not coloring. The wolf was a massive, fluffy creature, mottled and well camouflaged against the rock. Only his bright yellow eyes stood out, supernaturally reflective and focused on Sato.

The wolf stood between two men, both of them quite unassuming.

If Sato was in his human form, they probably would've been around the same size. One of them had the facial features and dark hair of someone from Sato's father's part of the world. He was sitting on a flat rock, lounging back, projecting disinterest like a delinquent teenager. Sato was personally familiar with the attitude. This kind of man should sport a cigarette dangling from two fingers. Sato missed the affectation, even if he didn't miss the taste or the smell.

The other man wore glasses, a polo shirt, and jeans. His hair was a bit messy and his shoulders slightly slumped. He looked like Sato's first human schoolteacher. He couldn't remember the man's name anymore but he did remember that his polos were always smudged with chalk dust and his handwriting had been very tidy. He hadn't lasted very long in that small, sweaty, rural town but he had taught Sato how to read. This man looked like he had tidy handwriting.

The third person on the shore was the merman from before, had to be. Without his tail or his patina, he looked comfortably human. He had hair the color of amberjack and skin like dead coral and big eyes like an anime character. Sato couldn't tell the color in the low light, but he thought they would be similar to his merman form, blue green. He was wearing a silky robe that fluttered in the evening breeze. Sato approved. This land bound merman was ready to swim if necessary. How polite.

They had a woman with them too – easily the largest and most imposing figure there. One of the biggest females Sato had ever seen, likely supernatural, which put Sato on his guard. That was a *very* smart decision from this mysterious Alpha. When dealing with mermaids, truly intelligent two legs utilized *female* politicians. This werewolf Alpha must, therefore, also be a smart politician. He had made arrangements to bring a powerful female with him. Or perhaps she was one of his pack? Or perhaps she *was* the Alpha? Did werewolf Alphas come in a variety of genders? Sato had no idea.

She stepped forward and crouched down at the water's edge, staring at Sato full in the face. Sato could see the strength of water in her eyes. Not the relentless tides and endless pull of the ocean, but the fierce single-minded running of a great river. This woman represented the unsalted waters where Sato's tail did not work.

Instinctively Sato raised up both forearms, pushing himself up and out of the bay as far as he could, showing her the size and power of his tail. Wondered if he should stop Meymey from even approaching. Considered turning and warning her off.

"I'm here as a negotiator, not a threat," said the kelpie showing straight white horsey teeth in a broad smile that did not reach her eyes.

Sato had only ever met one kelpie before and it had been a memorable encounter. Fortunately, the chunk the creature had ripped out of his tail had grown back... eventually. But Sato had worried. He was vain about his tail and it had been a concerning few months of regrowth.

Sato did not like kelpie but he respected them because in the water, they were bigger, faster, and meaner than he was. And that was pretty rare. Those half dragon, half horse heads of theirs were filled with square, razor-edged teeth. There was no sanity in their river-rage eyes, no compassion in those massive front hooves.

Sato looked to the two men. "Bringing a kelpie to meet a mermaid pod is a bit like bringing a gun to a knife fight." He used one of their sayings, picked up from that time he played beach volleyball with a group of Marines.

"Is this a fight?" asked the man with the glasses.

"If she's the gun, then what am I?" asked the other man. The one sitting. The wolf had moved even closer to him after Sato spoke, pressing against one leg. Was the seated man the Alpha?

"You're the semi-automatic, darling," said the merman.

There was mini wave behind Sato and the sound of dripping water as the diplomatic pod surfaced. Sato turned slightly, gave the hand signal to stay back. He hadn't decided on the safety level yet.

Meymey was in charge, but in this she obeyed him. He was, after all, *her* vangill.

Sato said, for her benefit, pointing. "This one is a kelpie. Aren't we honored? That's the merman from before. That wolf is a shifted werewolf. The one standing is the good cop and the one sitting is the bad cop. One of them must be the Alpha."

Meymey looked at the group before her. Tilted her head. "Neither seems very tough."

"They intended it to look that way."

"Then why the kelpie?"

"The fact that they thought her necessary is interesting in and of itself." That was their interpreter, Aqua.

"It's probably Daidai's fault. Vangill make people nervous." There was pride in Meymey's voice. Sato was amused that she thought anyone outside of the sea even knew about vangill.

"Actually," said the teacher softly, "she is here as the local DURPS representative."

"We're registered." Meymey was instantly defensive; they always played by human shifter regulations!

They'd logged all their shells the moment they arrived. Sato had taken them in himself. Stood in line for hours and everything. Sure, he had done it so he could ask if there were any registered otter shifters in the Bay Area. The clerk had said there were not in a tone of voice that doubted their very existence. But the end result was they were officially allowed in the area by the local government. It was all logged into that silly landbound system: twelve mermaids, one merman, all named and accounted for. There was no reason for a representative of DURPS to be meeting them now.

"I know. I checked as soon as Alec texted me," replied the kelpie.

"Are you not going to leave the water to meet us properly? We brought robes." Leather jacket gestured to a pile of fabric on a rock next to him. Of course a wolf pack would have access to thirteen robes!

Meymey swirled the surface of the water with her arms, considering this option. She would have more power over the males if she were on two legs. It would be harder for them to resist her siren song. But on land, Sato was at a disadvantage. Even though he could deploy his spurs, he'd never trained to fight werewolves. Only humans.

Sato hand-spoke to his sister. "Stay in the water."

She gave him the hand flick of agreement.

Sato didn't like their odds either way. Even in the water, he might have to take on a merman and a kelpie, but he could probably distract them long enough for his sister to escape. Out of the ocean? He wasn't sure he could take on any werewolf, let alone an Alpha with pack.

"We will stay in tail," Meymey said to the man with the glasses.

"His spurs won't work on land," explained the merman to his companions, with confidence.

"He has *spurs?*" The seated man leaned forward, wrists draped over his knees, intent on Sato. "Can I see?"

Sato crossed his arms and glared.

"Maxikins, sweetiepie, don't poke at the nice merman," said the other merman. "He's sharp."

The teacher said, "Perhaps introductions might smooth things over?"

Meymey gestured at Sato to speak. Until they knew who had authority, she didn't want to look weak by going first.

Sato said, "Why don't you start, professor?"

"You know me?"

"Educated guess," replied Sato.

"Oh, you're funny," said the seated man, eyes even more intent on Sato. "How interesting."

The teacher gestured. "Ms Trickle, department head at Big Pink DURPs, friend of the San Andreas Pack. Kelpie."

The massive woman raised up one hand. "Greetings, people of the sea," she said, politely.

"Waterhorse," said Meymey with a nod.

One of the pod behind him swam forward, interested. Lana, who was young and from warm waters. Had she never met a kelpie before?

"Sister, control your pod," Sato hummed in siren song.

Meymey whistled hard and sharp.

"What?" Lana pouted but backed away.

"Please don't play with kelpie," said Sato. They take big bites and don't let go."

The kelpie's laugh was a little like a snort. "You've met my kind before."

The professor continued. "That's Max. Human, Beta-mate."

The seated man raised one hand and wiggled all his fingers. His sleeve stretched up, showing scars on his wrist. A fighter? Interesting.

"Bryan, my Beta." The big wolf leaning against Max's side made a chuff noise.

"Alpha-mate Marvin you've met already."

The merman smiled. "Hi, ladies. And mister viral grumpy-pants hotness."

"Pants?" Sato questioned the nickname.

Marvin pursed his lips. "Fair point."

"And I'm Alec, San Andreas Pack Alpha."

"You don't *look* like an Alpha," said Cascade, injudiciously. Meymey turned and glared at her.

"Everyone says that," replied Alec with a soft, sweet smile, untroubled.

Sato gestured to his sister. "This is the Paralia of All Seas."

"No name?" wondered the kelpie.

"Paralia is the correct form of address outside of a sexual encounter," explained Aqua, snidely.

"I'm sorry, *what*?" Max was confused.

Marvin snickered. "Names aren't often needed except for seduction. Best not to trouble your pretty little head about it."

"But your sister?" Alec asked his merman.

"Giselle is a land-walker of a kind, more so than most mermaids. But she is *not* the Paralia of All Seas. She likes me more than most mermaids like their brothers, so she accommodates this world more than most."

Sato did not know any mermaids named Giselle. From Marvin's patina and tail color, he assumed she was a power player in some cold norther pod. They would be allied with the Ogress, not his sister. Still, it was interesting that this merman came from a power-playing pod.

"You'll explain more later, please," said the Alpha to his mate, before turning back to the merfolk. "Nice to meet you, Paralia. And the others?" Alec was trying to understand them, which Sato thought odd. Why so nice?

"Their names are unimportant." replied Meymey. "Except him." She pointed at Max. "A human is fair prey."

Max made a face. "I am most definitely *not* interested. No offense, ladies." The wolf next to him growled. "Also, I'm mated." Max rested one hand on the wolf's head.

The Beta, Sato reminded himself. Second in command.

"That doesn't matter to us," replied Cascade.

"Oh dear. How do I put this?" Max looked up at the starry night sky. "I don't do women."

"But we are *mermaids*," responded Meymey, confused.

"Mer*women*," replied Max.

Sato sensed danger incoming. His sister was now curious. Their collective virtues as mermaids were being challenged. Also, they were being denied access to human sperm. They never liked that. Even if it was just one. They now had something to prove.

Cascade began moving toward the shore. She was currently fertile. It was her responsibility to respond to the challenge.

Max only looked amused.

"Wait!" Meymey's eyes widened, she turned back to Alec. "When you said Alpha-mate about your little merman, you can *do* that?"

"Oh, frequently," said Marvin, grinning.

"No!" Meymey shook her head. "Of course you can do *that*. Anyone can fuck anyone else. The act is unimportant. I fail to see why you would *want* to, with no child possible, but that is neither here nor there. No, I mean *mate*. You have a merman for a *mate*. That is a big deal with wolves, right? You two are conjoined in some symbiotic power exchange of unity. A werewolf and a merman? That doesn't strike you as odd? That doesn't strike DURPS as odd?" She glanced sideways at the kelpie.

The kelpie said, "Leave me and your weird human dick fetish out of it, girl. I prefer females, myself."

Meymey squeaked in shock. "For sex?"

"Yes, for sex."

"And also... mate?"

"Yes."

"Wow." His sister sounded more impressed than offended.

Sato signed for her to get back on topic.

She ignored him.

The kelpie looked sad. "Aw, honey, you're breaking my heart. Just say the word, I'll hook you up. I'm off the market myself but I got lots of friends who'd be happy to open your mind, and heart, and… other parts of you."

Meymey's head was tilting slowly to one side in amazement. "For fun?"

"For pleasure, sweetheart. Or love. Or both."

Alec cleared his throat.

The kelpie whirled on him. "Hush now, the lesbians are talking."

"Yes, Ms Trickle," said the Alpha hurriedly, then pressed his mouth shut.

So, even an Alpha werewolf could be cowed by a kelpie. Sato was pleased he'd identified the biggest threat from the start.

"Tomorrow is Friday. Put on some legs and a pretty dress, and meet me at the cafe across the street, just over there." She turned and pointed. "Same time. Pepper and I will take you into the city."

"But I'm not fertile at the moment." Meymey clearly was losing her grip on the seaweed of the situation. But it was oddly enjoyable to watch her mind being blown right in front of him.

"Exactly, honey. Because that's not the point."

"It isn't?" said Meymey, and then. "It isn't?"

"No, sweetheart."

Sato sang softly, "A word, Paralia?"

Meymey turned to him, blinking as if recovering from some kind of daze. Having been tumbled unexpectedly by a wave of new information about dry reality.

She registered who had spoken and immediately dipped underneath the surface of the water.

Sato joined her. "Is not the purpose of this mission *fertility*?"

He left her beneath the waves to think on that for a moment.

He popped his own head back up and into an awkward

silence.

There seemed to be a stare-off going on between the pack and the pod. He supposed the pack didn't know that merfolk blinked less than land shifters.

Sato apologized, because none of the others behind him knew that they were supposed to. "Please excuse the mermaids their impertinent questions as to the nature of your relationships and orientations."

"And you? Will you tell us your name?" The Alpha took them back to the start of the conversation.

"I am not important."

Meymey resurfaced in time to hear this. "My vangill is here only to protect me."

"A bodyguard?" The Alpha looked very interested.

Marvin said, "I will explain vangill later."

"You most certainly will," replied Alec, sounding, for the first time exactly as Sato expected an Alpha to sound.

Sato used his tail to propel himself backward in the water. Allowing Meymey to float forward until she was directly next to him. After a moment's thought, he shifted sides so that he was between her and the lesbian kelpie. The Bay Area certainly was... different.

The Alpha was still focused on him. Sato respected that. He was the biggest threat to the pack, even if Meymey had all the authority. "You were the one who saved the boy this morning at the pier?"

"Why do the humans let their young wander near open water when they cannot swim?" Meymey asked.

Alec chuckled. "A question for the ages. Humans are unfathomable at the best of times."

"They have so many children, I guess they can afford to be careless with them," added Meymey.

"Is this morning's child okay?" Sato asked, out of polite interest, not real concern.

"He was none the worse for wear," replied Marvin. "Why didn't you stay longer? His parents wanted to thank you."

"Human gratitude is exhausting," replied Sato.

"You've experienced a lot of it, have you?"

"My vangill has many of your *medals of valor*, I believe they are called. They call him a *hero*." Meymey was oddly proud of this.

"You've rescued humans before?" That was Max, the interesting one. The one who asked unusual questions.

"Countless times," answered Sato, because it was true. Even after Hawaii he often answered the call to help. It broke the monotony of his hunting. Sato experienced nothing but endless disappointment from the land, where he had to behave in order to search, not kill. Where he could not lash out every time, it gave him nothing. No Patrick. Their disasters were Sato's opportunity to use speed and sometimes even spurs. It's not so much that he *liked* being challenged by the humans' persistent failure to plan for catastrophe. It was more that adrenaline broke the numbness of Patrick's absence. At least for a brief time. There was always something – some ship capsizing, some bridge collapsing, some ferry run aground.

If Sato Daiki, Vangill of the Deep, was available and nearby, the Paralia allowed him to answer the call. She knew he was good at it. She liked the favors owed. It was as if she collected them.

The humans, however, kept giving him medals as if that were adequate compensation. The paperwork to go with them got registered with DURPS. Sato kept them all in a safety deposit box in a bank in Waikiki. What else could he do with them? Plus he might need to cash them in for those favors. Humans were very into paperwork.

"Where on earth do you pin them?" wondered Max, looking at Sato's bare chest, at his impressive scale pattern there.

"My point exactly!" replied Sato.

Meymey was confused. "What are you talking about now, my vangill?"

"Heroism," replied Sato. "Speaking of which…" he prompted her.

She brightened. "Oh yes. That child. We saved him. You owe us now, don't you?"

"The boy's parents owe you," said the Alpha.

Meymey pretended not to be crestfallen. "No, *you* owe us. You, the San Andreas Pack, custodians of this land and all who dwell here."

Alec said, "The pack claims this territory but we are not responsible for the humans within it. Too many of them to keep track of. I mean, we will help them if asked nicely, and paid properly, but by and large we look after the local shifter population and supernatural affairs. Humans only make that messy."

"I resemble that remark," said Max.

"More than anyone else ever could," replied Alec.

"And yet I am a member of your pack," replied the human.

"A brilliant exception to the rule." Alec had a very soft smile.

Max's answering smile was not soft. It was insincere and a little evil. Max may be human but there had to be a really good reason Alec had brought him to this meeting. Sato thought that reason lurked in the evilness of that smile.

Meymey looked at Sato. "I am sorry you wasted your efforts on a valueless human infant."

Sato shrugged. "It made us look good either way. A favorable first impression. Even if it is only on the local two legs."

"Very favorable," said Marvin. "There are videos and stills of you all over the interwebs now. You have a fan group on WooTube. There is this one long shot of your bare ass on Schlock Tok that has over a million views."

Alec looked at his mate, smile indulgent. "And how many of those million are you?"

Marvin said, without pause, "Enough for me to know he'd fit in your jeans, babe."

"Is that a good thing?" wondered Meymey. She meant Sato's new interweb fame and any benefit it might have on them and their diplomatic mission.

But Marvin said, "Not really. Alec has terrible taste and a limited wardrobe. He only owns four pairs of pants, rotates through them."

"Five," corrected his mate. "There're those stripper ones you insisted on, remember?"

"How could I forget?"

"How could you."

Meymey said, frustrated, "No, I mean is it a good thing that my vangill is popular on your interwebs?"

Alec said, "Shouldn't you ask *him* that?"

Sato hadn't thought much about it. He knew he had a spectacular tail – maybe that meant he had an equally spectacular ass. Patrick had always seemed to appreciate it.

Patrick used to sink his sharp little nails into it while they fucked. Leaving crescent moons of appreciation. Sato loved the sting. They healed over, of course. But Sato had enjoyed admiring them in the mirror after – little red half scales on his human skin. As if Patrick had marked him with the sea.

"My vangill is much admired wherever he goes," said Meymey. "I meant, is that a good thing *for me?*"

Marvin wiggled his head side to side. "Well, that rather depends on how you feel about millions of people checking out your lover's junk."

"That's disgusting." Meymey spoke without thinking about it. "He is most certainly *not* my lover."

The kelpie looked smug. "There, you see?"

Marvin cocked his head. "I thought you all fucked your vangills? Isn't that your *thing?* Aren't vangill the only mermen that mermaids actually *want* to screw?"

"You speak our secrets awfully easily, don't you?" That was Cascade, the only one who had not met Marvin before. Because she had been off hunting and doing her duty for the people of the sea. Harvesting sperm for the continuation of the species. Because she could not get Sato to fuck her.

Marvin said, tone siren-sharp. "Did you miss my introduction? I am Alpha-mate to this pack. The secrets of the deep are not mine to keep, nor do I have any intention of doing so. I remain friendly with my sister's pod, when they deign to visit me, but I am of this *pack* now, not the sea. I owe you nothing, least of all my loyalty."

Sato thought it very brave of him to admit such things openly. Also a little stupid. This was politics. One simply did not give out allegiance information like that and expect to keep playing the game. Now Meymey knew where Marvin stood, and that he wasn't to be trusted. He stood on land, definitively. Had grown roots there. Humans used fish for food and fertilizer. He wondered what werewolves used them for.

But Alec looked pleased and proud of his mate.

Meymey said, "But presumably you would still like to swim in our water?"

"Is that a threat, Paralia?" Marvin sounded casual, but he was something more. Afraid? No. *Angry*.

"Just a statement."

Alec seemed more amused than offended.

Sato thought he should have better control of his mate.

Sato himself was still processing the dynamics. Alpha-mate. Marvin was actually *Alpha-mate*, which meant he and Alec were *together*. Married or the furry equivalent. Remarkable.

Meymey said, "So Alpha Alec, your merman tells me you are the singer here. And you meet me with him, a kelpie, and a human," she pointed at each, "in tow. We must assume this as truth. No matter how odd it is for a four-footed creature to sing for the local seas. Therefore I must apologize. We were remiss in not informing you of our visit ahead of time. Although in my defense, we had assumed notifying DURPS was sufficient. Shouldn't they have told you, if you sing for the San Francisco Bay?"

Alec looked uncomfortable, glancing between Marvin and Ms Trickle.

Finally he said, "Why are you here, Paralia?"

"I am here to attend your marine biology conference. We all are." It was a matter of public record – she had already told DURPS.

The Alpha just stood there, staring at them, apparently dumbfounded.

Sato had no idea why he should be so shocked.

Finally Alec said, "The Oceanic Conference on Threats to Marine Biodiversity and Population Decline?"

"I see you've heard of it."

Another long pause while the Alpha simply blinked at them.

"Why should you be surprised? Are merfolk not a part of marine biodiversity? Do we not have a vested interest in this field?"

"I've just never had merfolk show up to a conference before," replied the Alpha.

Now Meymey was confused. "Why should you know or care?"

Marvin was grinning. Sato narrowed his eyes. In fact, all of those on land now seemed to be deeply amused at Meymey's expense.

Marvin said, "Allow me to reintroduce my boyfriend to you. This is Alec Frederiksen, principal consultant at Super Submersion, Adjunct Professor of Biology at San Francisco State University, whose focus is on Marine Microbial Ecology and Oceanography."

Alec cleared his throat, suddenly nervous. "I'm actually, um, *presenting* at that conference."

Sato couldn't help it, he just started to laugh, it was so unexpected. "I see you married the job."

Marvin flicked him off. "We aren't married yet, but many have said something similar."

Meymey turned to Sato, eyes huge in surprise. "I guess the local werewolf Alpha actually is the singer for the area?"

Alec sighed. "I don't suppose you got tickets? Registered to attend? Anything like that?"

"We were just going to show up," said Meymey.

Alec took a breath, looked briefly up at the heavens. "Uh huh. Looking like that, at a conference with a bunch of biologists? Twelve mermaids? In bathrobes, no doubt."

"Without tickets," agreed Sato, enjoying the werewolf's exasperation.

"I have a suit," chirruped Cascade, from behind them.

Alec slapped his forehead with the palm of his hand. "I suppose I can't tell you not to attend, right?"

Meymey made a face. "Right."

"It starts tomorrow evening," said Marvin, regarding them all with a whole new expression of interest.

"It sure does," said Alec.

"Girls," crowed Marvin, "I'm going to take you shopping!"

Max said, deadpan, "There are twelve of them, Marvin."

Without missing a beat Marvin said, "Girls, I'm going to take you *thrifting!*"

The kelpie started to laugh.

Sato relaxed slightly. "This is the weirdest bunch of shifters I've ever encountered."

CHAPTER NINE

THE SECRET LIFE OF VANGILL

The Past: Sato in Kealakekua Bay without Patrick

Sato hung up the pay phone quickly but reluctantly.

He turned to glare at whoever was pressuring them to return to the cave. It was their *one* visit to the human town. It was his *one* opportunity to talk to Patrick. And he'd been cut short. It hadn't been nearly enough time!

But the person yelling at them turned out to be the Navarch, so Sato really didn't have a choice. And he wasn't stupid enough to complain.

They left the town for the beach, walking double time on their human legs and assembled for a headcount.

Sato's training pod had only twelve members, but still everything had to be done in an orderly military fashion all the time. Sato would've thought such formalities ill-suited to the people of the sea. But the vangill were all mermen with spurs, who would have spent a good portion of their youth on land among humans. Perhaps the disciplinary structure assumed a certain level of humanity. Whatever that level was, Sato didn't have it.

He chafed at the rigid requirements and structured daily routine. But that didn't mean he wasn't willing to play the game. In fact, he was determined to beat it. He needed to get this over with as quickly as possible. He needed to get out. But he also wasn't averse to the skills they were learning. Patrick's family were mostly criminals, after all. Last he heard one set of twins was dealing in black market antiquities, underwater excavations, of course. The other set had something to do with overseas fencing and money laundering. Get it? Launder. And that was just the twins.

All of which meant vangill training, which was essentially bodyguard training, was going to come in handy in his future with Patrick.

Back to the head count.

One of them happened to be missing, of course. So while the Navarch returned to town to hunt down their stray, the remaining trainees loitered on the beach. There were a few local surfers and a couple of adventurous tourists. It was one of those secret beaches that only the locals were supposed to know about, so everyone was giving the tourists attitude.

As a group of very fit mermen who looked like they were a professional sports team in training, they were given a respectfully wide berth by everyone. It was one of the reasons they'd been assigned athletic uniforms to wear when they were on land – if they looked paramilitary or like Olympic hopefuls, they were left alone.

"So who did *you* call?" One of his cohorts, Nix, was actually talking to Sato. How annoying.

Sato looked as casual as he could, not changing his body language or welcoming conversation. "Just a friend."

"Oh yeah? And who uses their one phone call on *just a friend*?" Nix was an easygoing guy, but he did like to gossip. Sato privately thought he might actually be evil. His gossiping had needles to it, like coral that sliced flesh open but only hurt hours later.

Sato didn't feel compelled to answer.

"You seem very protective of this friend. You sure it's not a girlfriend?" Nix pushed.

Sato considered what overhearing just his side of the conversation with Patrick would be like. He couldn't help it, he probably sounded a lot like a boyfriend… because he *was* one. But he didn't think anything he'd said revealed Patrick's gender. Best to keep it that way. There were a lot of expectations and pressures on the vangill, especially considering they were highly regarded as breeding studs. As the only mermen with viable sperm, they were expected to spread it around. They had the reputation for being active and actively admired womanizers. Mermaid-izers? Whatever the correct term, there was a lot of talk in the cave about *scoring* with human females, mermaids, and shifters. The big cheerful fellow who answered to the name of Rus had a scorecard where he was trying to "bag one of each," as he so charmingly put it. The others found this admirable. Apparently fucking as many women of as many different species as possible was considered a desirable personality characteristic amongst the vangill. Sato found pretty much all aspects of the concept gross.

"So what if it is?" he shot back.

Rus came ambling over. "I didn't think you dipped your wick, Speedy."

The Navarch kept insisting on mini competitions – swimming, fighting, racing. Sato kept winning them. It was making him increasingly unpopular and generating a vast number of new monikers, the nicest of which was Speedy.

"I don't."

"Oh, so it's just the one, then?" Nix was relentless.

Rus was mocking. "No action at all? You let yourself get landbound by some human female you met in high school? Dude, you're one of the best of us. Why anchor down so young? Take my advice, dump her now. Then you'll get to swim in the sea of tail that being a full vangill affords you. Once we finish training, of course."

"And who says you're actually good enough to finish training?" the Navarch barked out, reappearing on the beach, dragging their missing stray behind him.

Xanin, the stray, gave them all a cheeky smile and did not explain himself.

Sato was annoyed – now they were off routine and late. He could have had more time on the phone with Patrick.

The Navarch said, "Let's make it a race back to the cave. First one back, if you can beat me, doesn't have to hunt for dinner tonight."

Sato won easily. Swimming was definitely his strongest ability. Having a best friend (and then boyfriend) who was a dobharchú had served him in good stead. He was not only fast, he was incredibly nimble, and he had good peripheral vision for smaller creatures and nearby attacks.

"You're beyond annoying, you know that?" said Nix. "It would, hypothetically speaking, be even more frustrating if you also had a long-term girlfriend to whom you were utterly devoted and with whom you were completely in love."

Sato, as usual, didn't answer.

"I'll take that as agreement, shall I?"

Sato said, since Nix had specified *girlfriend*, "You're wrong, actually.'

"So it isn't really love?"

Sato's smile was all humorless sarcasm. "I didn't specify which part you were wrong about."

The Navarch was suddenly there. "And what exactly happened to make you two think it was time for a chitchat?" His eyes were particularly hard on Sato, like he expected better of him.

Sato merely arched an eyebrow.

"We are going to start spur work today. None of you can activate them at will yet, right? So let's hear it, how did everybody manifest?"

They went around the group with each vangill trainee naming the first incident that caused their spurs. For some of them it had been sexual (or they wanted to *claim* that it was sexual), for others it had been fear, loss, or terror. Finally it was Sato's turn.

"Shark attack," he said simply. After all, the Navarch had said *no chitchat*.

The Navarch had questions, though. "Was anyone with you?"

"Just a friend."

Nix whispered, "Another incident of Sato Daiki's *just a friend*."

Xanin said, "What shocks me is that he *has* friends."

"A friend," corrected Nix, accurately.

The Navarch ignored them and turned away from Sato to question the group. "Have you all noticed the common theme?"

"We were all in states of heightened emotional awareness and adrenaline," answered Nix promptly.

"Of course, you all knew that's what causes spurs before you came here. Have you noticed anything *else* similar between all of your manifestations?"

Everybody stayed silent.

Sato wasn't going to be the one to say it. Not unless he was forced to.

The Navarch seemed to sense that about him. He made a come-hither gesture at him.

Sato didn't want to be seen as perfect in mental acuity as well as physical strength. But he couldn't help it if everyone else was stupid. "None of us were alone."

"Exactly. You were each with somebody, or more than one other person, whom you needed to protect as well as yourself. Spurs are activated by defensive adrenaline, but more specifically, some kind of latent familial instinct, probably an ancient need to protect the pod."

Everyone assembled there looked disbelieving.

Sato thought the idea was preposterous. Mermen were notoriously anti-family. Most mermen, who weren't vangill, went on to live solitary lives on the shores of abandoned beaches in inhospitable parts of the world. They rarely swam with a pod, and if they did, it was only for short lengths of time. There was a reason they were sent away to be raised by their sires in the human world. Mostly sterile, they were considered useless to merfolk society. Having nothing to contribute beyond their adaptability to a land environment and mundane existence, they were used to bridge the gap between ocean and shore.

The Navarch continued explaining, probably because of the incredulous looks, "If you happen to have any kind of relationship or intimacy with your mother's pod, you'll find, when you are around them, you're more likely to deploy spurs. This will happen in the company of a mother, sister, or even lover."

"And what if we don't have that intimacy?" asked Rus, looking not at all cheerful for the first time.

"Then your spurs will deploy whenever you are in water and under stress with *anyone* you care about."

"Is it possible to deploy spurs when one is alone? Or to activate the adrenaline response on behalf of someone I *don't* care about?" asked Nix.

"It's possible for very few of you. And it can take a long time to develop that skill, but it's one of the reasons you're training with me." The Navarch turned and dove swiftly into the water. He bobbed to the surface a little way out, raised up his forearms, took a breath, and focused hard on Sato. Then his spurs appeared up and down each forearm.

He was showing off.

Sato wondered why his teacher felt the need to stare at him.

"Do spurs happen only in our merform?" asked Sato, to make absolutely certain.

The others scoffed at him. Because of course that was the case – like having a tail or gills, the spurs were obviously for underwater use. Except that they *weren't* a tail or gills, they weren't something needed to swim, they were a weapon. They weren't required to function in the water, therefore logically they should also be available on land. A tail or gills were a hindrance outside the ocean, spurs were *not*.

The Navarch flipped himself high out of the water and back onto the shore. His tail shifted to legs mid-air in a spectacular move that Sato instantly wanted to learn how to do more than he had ever wanted to control his spurs.

By the time he was fully ashore, the Navarch's arms were back to human.

The others all hissed appreciatively.

Sato said, "Screw the spurs, how do I learn how to do *that*?"

The Navarch smiled briefly, sharp and tight. "At last, he shows interest in something."

"Sato has a human girlfriend, so he wants to prove himself on land more than the sea," explained Nix confidently.

The Navarch turned and stared at Sato in surprise. "You revealed your identity to her?"

Sato considered. "No part of Nix's statement was accurate in *any* way."

The Navarch blinked slowly, considering. "Well, if you show spur acumen, I'll teach you how to do an airborne shift. But you need to understand that as rare as having spurs is *at all*, the ability to deploy them at will is even rarer. Even the five vangill who protect the Soteria of the Deep are encouraged to form emotional attachments with their sacred mermaids because we need all the help we can get. Instinct will always play a key role in spur deployment."

He continued. "But even if you only ever activate around your home pod, you'll still be incredibly valuable to that pod. The vangill are the only mermen allowed to permanently reenter society. But that, of course, also has to do with your ability in certain *other* arenas."

Many of the trainees smiled smugly. As if this was some kind of prize they had won, when instead it was a freak of genetics that they could sire children.

"First things first, get into the water, shift, and let's start with mental discipline and preparation to intentionally activate the protective instinct."

It turned out that this was by far the hardest part of training. All of the physical testing, all of the racing and weight lifting, all of the running and diving, everything that was actually part of the military aspect of their training was krill compared to simply learning how to activate an instinct.

Sato who, along with everybody else, couldn't seem to master even the beginnings of spurs, became increasingly frustrated as the weeks wore on. He'd been quickly and immediately good at everything else they did. Why, in this one matter, was his own brain fighting him? He'd thought he had good mental discipline. His father, who had declined to give him human affection, had given him that. Plus he always had to be calm and controlled around Patrick, who needed him to be a stable baseline.

But in the matter of spurs, Sato was just as bad as everyone else. And Sato really hated that. To be mediocre was failure. Better not to try at all. But here, he *had* to try.

They did all sorts of thought experiments and tests. Anything that the Navarch could do to get them to mentally put themselves in a state where they had to protect somebody else, as well as defend themselves. They even went out into shark-infested waters. In a few cases, when a shark was spotted, spurs did appear, but that was it. Sato's always remained entirely sheathed. Frankly, he wasn't particularly surprised by this. He was rarely concerned for his own safety, let alone anyone else's – it had only ever been Patrick.

They were given thought experiments where they had to imagine somebody they loved.

Sato tried hard. He imagined Patrick swimming next to him, the shark coming out of nowhere as it had way back when his spurs first appeared.

The idea hurt but it didn't work. Because he *knew* Patrick wasn't there. He felt Patrick's absence as this terrible cold void next to him. Any icy shadow born of absence. He couldn't imagine Patrick there, because all Sato ever felt was the numbness of his not being nearby. Patrick was leagues away across a whole ocean, across a whole continent, probably not even in the water anymore, probably at some party, probably surrounded by human friends, maybe even flirting with other boys and certainly getting into trouble without Sato to look out for him. Sato hated not being there to stand between Patrick and his family, to protect Patrick from the world. Or was it the world from Patrick? And he hated the sea and the other vangill and the Navarch and their merfolk for separating them. Hated them with all the cold strength of a Patrick-shaped void.

Thinking about Patrick didn't force Sato into protective anger launching his spurs. Thinking about Patrick just made Sato feel hard and numb.

Then, almost half a year into vangill training, with everybody getting more muscles and much stronger in terms of physical abilities but only a few of them able to deploy their spurs at all, let alone at will, they had *family visitor day*.

The pods started to arrive first thing in the morning. And they came as full pods, or at least large enough groups to have swum there in a protective manner. Some of them had harnessed dolphins, others must've set out weeks before in order to arrive on that particular day.

Only when the first of the siren calls resonated under the waves, and the first heads began to appear above the surface at the far edge of the bay, did the Navarch bother to explain.

"The womenfolk have been requested to attend our measly efforts and hopefully assist in your training. They do so reluctantly, so be on your *very* best behavior. The pods will hang around in the bay until it's clear which one of them most easily activates your spurs. Then that mermaid will be left behind for a month of focused training. Mermaids are busy with important work – you should be honored they're willing to leave even one pod member behind. Don't waste their time."

To Sato, the visiting ladies seemed the very definition of *not at all* reluctant. In fact, family visiting day was clearly an excuse to engage in mass flirtation with the new crop of eligible vangill males. Sato felt like a delicious and attractive tuna, to be taken down en masse in a coordinated attack.

Mermaid lineage could be told by tail color and either patina or luster. Sato's tail was a distinctive solid dark blue, Patrick called it royal blue. Sato's tendril pattern, his luster, extended up along his spine, bifurcated at the nape to curl over each shoulder along his collarbone and then up each side of his neck around his gills. It was dark blue too and starkly contrasted to his merskin. Patrick always said, with great admiration, that from a distance it looked like Sato had "a really awesome tattoo."

Rus sidled up to him. "What looks dumb on you looks stunning on the females of your line."

Sato followed his gaze. Two dark-headed, blue-tailed, and blue-patterned figures were entering the training cave. In human form, shifted state, a sire's genes dominated – so Sato, his sister, and his mother looked very little like each other on land. But in the water their relationship was undeniable. True form, royal blue, shoulder and collar spirals, there was no denying the family connection.

The beach became crowded with merfolk reunions. Most were formal and stilted.

"Daiki." Sato's mother greeted him, rising out of the ocean and gaining legs in an elegant transition that spoke to her longevity and vitality. Her hair was black like his but it curled and her human skin was the color of dried sugar kelp.

"Mother." Sato inclined his head.

"Daidai!" Then he was slammed into and wrapped up in thin graceful limbs. His arms were suddenly full of a sister he'd barely let himself miss until that moment.

The last time he'd seen her, she was seven. Now, over a decade later, she looked and felt like an entirely different creature. He'd never seen her human form, since he'd only known her as a child before puberty and legs. But there was some memory inside him, and in her, nested in the way she buried her nose into his shoulder and leaned against him – complete faith in his affection.

As kids, his sister had always trailed after him, constantly on his tail, little hands gripping a fin. She'd followed him everywhere. Of course, he'd found it annoying but also endearing. She'd been his pet and his companion. She'd slept curled next to him in the canopies of kelp forests. She'd crooned at him in the language of the ocean currents, hands fluttering with the chatter of the deep, cheerful and curious and endlessly asking questions. She was the one who had trained him for Patrick.

"Meymey," he said, lifting and spinning her gently and then setting her down. A move Patrick had taught him – to make fun of gravity. He bracketed her face with his webbed hands. "Look how much you've grown. Look how pretty you are."

There was something of his baby sister still in those chubby cheeks and huge eyes. Like Sato, she clearly had a father with genes sourced in that surface continent the humans called Asia, but her face was rounder and her mouth fuller. Her sire was unknown and always would be.

"I've grown? Look at you! You're huge!"

Sato wasn't actually all that big (for a human), only Rus was bigger.

Speaking of Rus. Having reacquainted himself with his own female relations, and showing very little interest in them, Rus had ambled over to Sato and was staring a little too hard at his sister.

"Shoo, piranha," said Sato, swatting at him.

Meymey gave Rus an evaluating look.

Sato suddenly felt a little sorry for the merman. Meymey checked Rus over as if she were calculating where best to slice for ideal dismemberment and consumption.

Rus, who was an idiot, preened under the examination. He opened his mouth to say something.

She got there first. "I don't think you *talking* is going to make your case, muscles. Let me see your tail color, and your markings, and how you fight. I'll go from there."

Rus's lips twitched. "Whatever you say, gorgeous."

Then, ignoring Sato, he ambled away.

"I take it you and Mother didn't swim all of this way just for me?"

"Well, it's an honor to be asked, of course. When one of our lineage developed spurs, Mother had the local shells sounded in celebration, but really, in the end, that only increased *her* consequence and made you a desirable proposition for others. It didn't do much for me. No offense, Daidai."

Sato wasn't surprised. She was a mermaid, after all. The female of the species only ever seemed to have thoughts on consolidation of power. That, more often than not, was measured in the preservation and continuation of the species. The two were inexorably linked, like moon and tide. He was certain his mother had achieved a much higher status the moment it was known he'd developed spurs. Still, his sister wasn't allowed to be too blasé. She would reap *some* benefits.

"You're all grown up and very pretty, Meymey, but I think we both know you're that much prettier because I have spurs."

"I forgot how cruel you could be, brother." She was not teasing.

Sato would never understand why people conflated brutal honesty with cruelty. Patrick was the only person he'd ever met who consistently found it amusing rather than offensive. In the end, it meant Sato mostly kept quiet, except around Patrick. He preferred saying nothing over guarding his tongue. But this was his sister.

He tipped his head in Rus's direction. "He's a bit like a shell collector. Only his shells are women of variable species."

"Players are fine. They don't get attached." She waggled her sparse eyebrows at him. Apparently Meymey had questionable standards.

"You're only seventeen!" Sato pretended the expected shock of an older brother.

"Exactly! Time is running out."

Sato almost smiled. He shook his head, amazed at how much she had grown without him around.

She took his wrist and turned those big eyes up at him, demonstrating her abilities to flirt firsthand. "I've been bleeding on legs and land since I was eleven, brother dear. I've voted in the kuriai as an adult since the winter of that year." Mermaids had to take to dry land during their courses. Legs were the curse of puberty. After all, they couldn't swim around bleeding in water – that was a surefire way to attract sharks. Fortunately, they only bled for a day or so each month.

Sato examined Meymey's body thoughtfully. "Have you produced offspring already?" Was he an uncle? How odd would that be?

She blushed and dipped her head. "Not yet. Mother has urged me to be selective and wait for the most viable and valuable prospect."

She left unsaid the fact that she had probably been waiting since they heard he got spurs. Because they knew this moment would come. When she got to swim across the ocean to be united with her brother, but also have her pick of the newest clutch of vangill. The best possible stud prospects.

Sato was strangely proud that he could be of some value to his sister. Since he hadn't been around all these years to see her grow and to protect her from the viciousness of the sea, not to mention their mother's indifference.

"Not Rus, Meymey. See Xanin, over there? He is a better choice. Just as powerful, much more biddable. Plus his home ocean is the Arctic. So he will be far away when the time comes."

"A friend?" she pressed.

"I don't have friends, sister."

Sato had little to say to his mother, and no particular interest in her. Fortunately for both of them, she seemed to feel the same.

Greetings and salutations accomplished, the Navarch announced that if the ladies were willing, they would begin. Some of the mermaids had been flirting with him too, which reminded Sato that their instructor was, himself, an attractive breeding prospect. Older and more reserved, but handsome in a strict angular way.

First the Navarch asked the trainees and their mothers to pair up. He put them through a series of tests designed to endanger the moms. While several of Sato's colleagues reacted gratifyingly quickly, Sato's spurs never made even the slightest appearance.

The Navarch then had those who could, swap for a different female relation – grandmother, sister, aunt, cousin, niece.

Sato looked down at Meymey.

She smiled back.

Oddly, although in their human form they didn't look alike, Sato thought that they probably had the same tight, wicked, smile.

"Think it will work this time?" she asked.

"Maybe."

"Who were you with when they first appeared?"

"My cuter half."

"You have a human girlfriend?"

"Did I say that?"

Instead of getting annoyed, Meymey tilted her head and looked at him, big eyes dancing. Hers were the color of sea lettuce and silt. "You like to be mysterious? How very typical of a merman."

The Navarch called for them to start the second round of tests.

Later when they were analyzing what had happened, the Navarch pointed out that it probably required more stress to activate Sato because he had such an even-keel personality.

Sato thought *even-keel* was a nice way to say *taciturn and antisocial*.

They did manage to get his spurs to deploy in defense of his sister eventually, but it took a lot more stressors than it did any of the other trainees. Took them going out into the open ocean alone, and her being in real danger from shark attack. It was like his spur instincts needed to genuinely believe both of them were at risk. Sato couldn't help but believe, had it been Patrick, it would have happened right away.

The Navarch said, "It probably has something to do with the fact that you see very little as an actual threat."

"Does that mean Sato here really thinks he's better than the rest of us? Does he actually think he can take us on? Me, for example?" questioned Rus.

The Navarch looked at Sato expectantly.

Sato looked away from the small beach fire they had going in honor of their female visitors. He stared out the opening of the cave, toward the open ocean.

"It's not that I think I'm better or more physically fit," he said slowly.

"Oh no?" snapped Nix.

"Let him explain," insisted the Navarch.

Sato shrugged. "I think I'm willing to let things go to an extreme more than anyone else."

"Are you saying that we wouldn't like you when you're angry?"

Sato wondered if he had ever actually gotten angry. Occasionally, Patrick had pushed him into aggravation. Patrick's family, once or twice, had certainly frustrated him. But Sato didn't go into a place of raging heat and boiling anger like the stories described. He went to a cold, dark, still place, like the depths of the ocean, where no light could reach him. He thought if he dwelt too long in that place, that's where the real danger lay – to him and everyone else. That he was obsessed with having Patrick in his life because the little otter shifter was the only speck of warmth he'd *ever* really felt. Only Patrick could swim down to him there, gleaming with air bubbles trapped in brown fur, find him where no one else could. Pull him back up to the surface and the light.

That right now, having been without Patrick for so long, that place looked good to him. Easy. Comfortable. Full of numbness.

The Navarch looked interested and a little worried. "Have you killed a sentient creature, Sato?"

"Not yet. But I think I would find it terribly easy."

"Your walls are built to guard yourself against others? All the more reason to learn to control your spurs and not let fear of them control you."

Sato looked at the Navarch, "Why else do you think I came here?" *But also, why would he be afraid of his own spurs? Why be afraid of others, except where Patrick was concerned?*

"Because you were ordered to, just like everybody else here," said one of the mermaids, from the ladies' side of the fire. She was sitting next to his sister, and they seemed friendly enough. An allied pod?

Sato looked at her. Like with most mermaids, it was impossible to know her age. She could be twenty or she could be a hundred.

"You don't actually think I care about the people of the sea or any pod in it, do you?"

"Clearly you care a little about your sister or she wouldn't have to stay behind to help you control your spurs."

"I suspect I care about her for nostalgia's sake."

Meymey looked a little hurt.

"You need to be pushed harder, and stressed more, because

you're scared of what you might do with your spurs once they're out?" suggested the Navarch.

Sato turned back to him. *Was that it?* Was that why he had to put his own sister into so much danger just to get a part of his anatomy to work the way it was supposed to? That didn't seem right.

"I suppose I'll have to get over that, won't I? Difficult to do, as it seems to be an integral part of my personality."

"We all have shortcomings. Nice to know you have them just like everybody else," said Nix.

CHAPTER TEN

A PLOP IN THE OCEAN

The Present: Trick in Sausalito, hiding under a fancy-pants restaurant

Conversation carries over water, but Trick was still too far away to hear exactly what the pack said to the merfolk. He had to stay downwind and out of line of scent. Bryan was in wolf form and could definitely smell Trick easily, if he got within sniffing distance.

Trick crouched low, hugging a concrete pylon. The restaurant above him was busy. It was a swanky establishment, the kind with tablecloths and too much cutlery. It was just lively enough to make it even more difficult for Trick to hear what the shifters said. So he huddled underneath the building, where it was cold and dank and smelled of old tar, wet wood, and decaying seaweed. The Pacific coast had a different scent from the delta of his youth. He'd never entirely gotten over that.

He dared not go any closer. Werewolves were freaks with their noses and there was nowhere closer to hide than the ocean itself. And if Trick got into the water, he would be in *their* territory.

It was too dark to see much, either.

By the time he arrived they were already in conversation –

Alec, Marvin, Bryan, Max, and Ms Trickle on land, a dozen or so merfolk in the water with their backs to Trick.

The merman was easy to spot. He was closest to shore and substantially bigger than the others.

Trick was to the left, and slightly behind the merfolk, because of the way the restaurant on its little pier jutted out over the bay. He could make out glints of wet hair and scales in the light from the street lamps above the shock rock but that was it. The sidewalk was quiet and free of pedestrians. It was mid week, off season, and cold near the water at night. Plenty of cars drove by, though.

Trick stayed, hugging the cold cement, staring so hard he nearly got a headache. Fixed on the merman, willing him to be something. Willing him to be Sato, or to *not* be Sato. Certain that he wasn't. Surely Sato wasn't as big as this merman. Surely Sato wasn't so active, engaged with protecting a pod, posturing against the landbound threat.

But the way he moved in the water? That was familiar.

It couldn't be Sato, could it?

The merman laughed. And laughter carries over water more and better than other sounds.

Trick knew that laugh. He was the only one who had ever heard it regularly. Sato. His Sato, had only ever laughed for *him*. Had only ever smiled for *him*. It was not a pretty sound, it was a sharp barking noise, like a dolphin's delight.

But that was, without question, Sato Daiki.

Then the pod turned and for a brief moment, before they dove beneath the waves, Trick could see their faces. Or, more precisely, he could see Sato's sharp, beautiful face. Sato's scales stark against the pale flesh of his collar and chest, reflective in the moonlight. The pattern strobed into Trick's memory, rebranding the scar on his heart. The shape was permanently burned there, he hardly needed a reminder. Trick hated himself for still finding it beautiful.

Bryan, still a wolf, threw his head back and howled. Trying to prove something. No doubt at his Alpha's behest. A goodbye and a reminder of the power of a pack, that fish too were prey.

With only a few splashes the merfolk disappeared, diving deep and speeding away.

Sato was gone.

Again.

Trick wondered if he'd hallucinated.

But knew he had not.

He must accept that his past had finally caught up to him.

Trick wasn't sure if he should be sick or euphoric, angry or elated. He shivered. What he felt was cold. The damp barnacle-covered cement under his arms and the winds off the water bit into his human flesh. The familiar smell unpleasant because it was this ocean and not that other one.

He wanted to swim in his otter form but the bay was no longer safe.

No. What he really wanted was to swim a long river in a green land far away. He wanted fresh water and slick, muddy banks. He wanted a different place and a different time. He wanted the otter family that he'd never had, not a pack of wolves and companion misfits. He wanted nothing to do with the people of the sea. Or the predators of the land.

He didn't want Sato who had abandoned him. How dare he want that? How dare he be so weak.

He didn't want to have to confront him. To have to ask why he hadn't been worthy.

He didn't even want to see him.

Except that he did.

He wanted it so badly.

It hurt so much, the memory of Sato *hurt*. It had been so good, that kind of love, that kind of attention. Two things he had never had before. The immersive comfort of all-consuming affec-tion. He thought he had meant everything to Sato, that Sato would do *anything* for him. It had never even occurred to Patrick that Sato wouldn't come back. Until he just... didn't.

Trick had pushed it down and run so hard and so fast for so long that it had become a parasite of fear nested in his soul. A thing that had coexisted but preyed upon him. He had nurtured that parasite because he knew he couldn't face that kind of hurt again. Had built a whole life for himself where he didn't have to. Where the pain was a reminder not to care too much, never to let it happen again.

Here, now, he could be charming and cheerful and utterly untrusting. Here, now, he could have friends and family and a job and a community and still never feel safe.

And then, there Sato was.

In his bay. In his now.

The merman who had abandoned him. The Sato who had *never* come for him. The Sato who had never come *after* him. The Sato who, for their entire childhood, had *always* been there for Patrick. Until he had not.

Of course it was Trick's fault too. Perhaps he hadn't waited long enough. Perhaps it should never have been their dynamic, that Trick so completely relied on Sato for his well-being. That through an accident of fate, when Sato had made his home on land, Patrick had made Sato his whole world. His person. Person of the sea.

Trick had always believed what the sea chose to keep, it keeps forever. He had blamed the Deep. And he had blamed Sato for not being strong enough to resist the inevitable tide. He had blamed Sato for not returning when he said he would. Sato and the sea had conspired against him. And now they had done it again. Casting Sato once more up onto the shores of Trick's existence.

Just when Trick had finally started to relax. With that stupid, warm, welcoming, lovable pack of werewolves.

How dare he, Trick, allow himself to feel even a little bit safe? With this strange group of misfits he had let down his guard. He had found himself surrounded by large, protective shifters who seemed to like him. Who had welcomed him into their home. Who had treated him with gentle respect and cautious care. Who tried to give him space and simultaneously remind him that he was welcome. Who Patrick had never trusted. Because one protective merman named Sato had taken Patrick's home away and left Trick adrift and afraid of protection.

How stupid of Trick for even one moment to think that he

might, finally, have a new home. Perhaps not the one he'd dreamed of, perhaps not one where he had been as welcome as he had in Sato's heart. But some kind of solid thing to hold onto. A place where he did not have to drift alone.

One moment of weakness disguised as hope and there, ten years gone, Sato returned to ruin it before it had even begun. Sometimes, it turned out, the sea spat its treasure back out.

The web of land-bound shifters was vast and powerful. It extended its tentacles even into the sea. Tentacles strong enough to pull a lost merman back to land.

Alec was indeed a powerful Alpha, to summon Patrick's past to the shore with the siren call of a wolf.

The Present: Trick at the San Andreas Pack House

Trick returned to the pack house because he had nowhere else to go.

The pack hadn't really noticed his absence, or perhaps they'd just assumed he'd been out for a swim. They weren't parental about him. They wanted to keep him safe but they understood that as a non-wolf he had different needs and instincts.

It had taken him a long time to unwind himself from the icy concrete pylon. He'd clambered over the shock-rock to the road, shivering and miserable. His brain was full of tangled seaweed – memories and parasitic fear.

He'd thought about just going to the cafe, hiding in the back, sleeping in the stock room. He'd thought about loading up his old car and driving away again. Driving until he found a long river far from the sea.

But the cafe was far too quiet without customers and his car probably wouldn't start.

He needed the warmth of the pack, whether he even trusted it anymore. He still wanted it and resented that fact.

The pack was almost fully assembled in the sunken den when

he arrived home. Only Tank, Isaac, and Max weren't present. Max rarely came inside the pack house if he could help it. Trick didn't know why, but Max was like that, full of quirks. Isaac and Tank worked late nights starting Thursdays at Saucebox, one of San Francisco's best clubs. But Isaac was a ranking wolf. Omega was considered clutch, or so Patrick understood. So this couldn't possibly be a formal pack meeting if the Omega wasn't present.

Trick was going to sneak up the stairs and hide in his room. Colin's old one, which had been gifted to him since the redhead moved permanently in with Judd. But Alec noticed him enter, like always, and gestured for him to join them. Had it been any other pack member Trick would have smiled, pretended to be tired, and continued on his way.

But this was the Alpha, so Trick dutifully trotted over, sitting on the floor near the Beta's feet. Bryan patted his head, Trick looked back at him.

"Tea, cutie?" The Beta reached for the large teapot in the middle of the coffee table and one of the empty mugs nearby.

"You're always trying to foist tea on me. Are you secretly British?"

"No, I just like tea. It's comforting. Are you sure you won't have any?"

Trick shook his head.

Alec glared in mock discipline at his older brother. "As I was saying…"

Bryan interrupted, "Oh, do go on, Great and Gracious Alpha. We await your words of wisdom with bated breath."

The Alpha did just that. "My point is, they've never attended any marine biology conferences before. Why this one?"

"It's rare for them to come to land and interact with humans at all. As a pod, I mean, and not just for sex." That was Judd.

"It's going to be an absolute nightmare. Can you imagine mermaids on the make, swanning around a conference full of geeky marine biologists? Not just because they're, you know, sexy but because they are walking, talking marine life. *Everyone* is gonna want to meet them." Kevin occasionally could be quite insightful.

"Marine-grade celebrities?" suggested Colin.

"Should the conference hire Heavy Lifting?" Alec wondered.

"Werewolf bodyguards, for mermaids. Does that even make sense?" Lovejoy looked amused.

Alec looked at Judd. "You guys aren't under contract at the moment, right?"

Judd shook his head. "We're available. During the day I could even pull in Tank. But are you sure it's necessary?"

"Twelve mermaids at a marine biology conference, who have been dressed by Marvin? Yes, I think it's necessary."

Judd straightened, an order from his Alpha. "I'll make it happen."

Alec continued, "So back to why the mermaids are suddenly coming to this conference. I've been to lots of conferences over the years and they've never shown up before. Why this one?"

The pack started spit-balling ideas, mostly watching Marvin for a reaction.

"Maybe somebody is coming who they want to meet?"

"Maybe someone is presenting on a topic that they are particularly interested in?"

Marvin nodded, serious for a change. "Something to do with the current climate or environmental pollution? You know they have vested interests in that, anything involving garbage in the oceans."

"Or sea level rises."

"Wouldn't the mermaids be in favor of that – more territory for them?"

Marvin said, "I wouldn't put it past the Soteria of the Deep to be that mercenary."

"I don't know about that. A general rise in ocean temperature could be having an adverse effect on merfolk population numbers," said Alec thoughtfully. "I mean, it's pretty much impacting all other oceanic life in a negative way. Why not them?"

Marvin sat up very straight all of a sudden, small face tense. "That would make them desperate enough to come to land. Mermaids are always concerned with breeding and procreating.

It is the Soteria's primary political mandate as well. You know each mermaid owes her pod two children before they're allowed any kind of freedom from that pod? And there is a faction that believes it should be two female children, that boys shouldn't count."

"Mermaids prove their worth with children?"

"Oh yes. And it's not easy to do. Even producing two can be hard. They have to go to land, have legs, seduce some random dude, and it rarely takes. Big part of the lifecycle."

"How do mermen fit into the picture?" wondered Kevin.

"We don't. Mermen are sterile."

"I knew that. Did I know that?" mused Kevin.

Trick relaxed back, letting their chatter and curiosity and inept puzzling abilities wash over him. What he wanted to know was why Sato was here. But he also didn't want to ask. He didn't want to reveal that he had any connection to the merfolk, let alone *these* specific merfolk.

Alec looked at his mate. "So, are they experiencing a population decline?"

Marvin shrugged. "You know I haven't really been in contact with my sister's pod since we moved. But before that, I do remember some chatter. I never hung out with pods all that often. I was only called to meet with you because it was an incident that required interface with the landbound folk. That's the only time mermaids find mermen like me useful. It is our function to be a bridge between sea and shore. That is why we are farmed out to our human sires to be raised during puberty. But you're the marine biologist, babes, what do you think?"

Alec considered his mate's question seriously. "Rising temperature levels are part of my research."

"I thought you focused on microbiomes," said Colin, who would know things. The rest of the pack found Alec's research, and his choice of profession, mystifying. But Colin was a bit of a nerd.

Alec got quite professorial with their youngest pack member, who was still in university. "I do, but what do you think shows population fluctuations first with every tiny increase in temperature?"

Colin's eyes were big, absorbing.

Trick had no idea what they were on about.

"And the merfolk?" asked Lovejoy.

Alec pursed his lips, looking particularly nerdy all of a sudden. "Well, the top of the food chain isn't my specialty, but some of my colleagues are reporting that ocean mammals are showing decreased births. Merfolk are tied, by extension if not classification, to ocean mammals. It's been suggested, and I find some of the research quite compelling, that this has to do both with my own research into the food supply chain, but also breeding viability."

"How exactly?" Even Marvin was curious now.

"Prolonged heat exposure can decrease semen volume, sperm count, concentration, and motility. There's speculation that ocean temperature rises could have exactly the same impact on ocean mammals."

Trick said, "But mermaids breed with humans."

"Indeed. But as usual, such studies have only really focused on male sperm. Eggs could also be impacted."

"Why the bias?"

Alec blinked. "Misogyny still permeates the scientific community. And in the case of mermaids, there's also a lack of data. They simply do not allow themselves to be studied."

Marvin bit his full bottom lip with sharp teeth, then said, "I think this must be why they're here for the conference. The fact that they sent the Paralia makes it even more likely. I don't think you realize what a big deal she is. The merfolk only have five leaders that they look to or respect. In the whole world. Everything else is under the purview of the pods and their endless jockeying for dominance. The Paralia is their one diplomat in charge of all interspecies relations. For her to come herself, with a vangill, to go to this conference, it has to be fertility."

He paused, then added, "But I've always thought it was because the sire needed to carry a shifter gene in a recessive state for infant viability."

The entire pack was now staring at Marvin. They were accustomed to both Alec and Colin talking like academics, but not Marvin.

Trick always suspected that the merman had hidden depths of cleverness and acumen. A kind of brilliance he masked with frivolousness. It was nice to be proven right.

Trick thought about Mr Sato. He didn't seem very shifteresque, but there might be bakemono blood in his background somewhere. Anything was possible, and plenty of shifters were capable of interbreeding with humans and shaking out duds who did nothing but carry the triple helix, never activating it. Dratsie, for example, were pretty notorious for sleeping around indiscriminately. Plenty of people could go through their lives with the ability to shift but never doing so. Not to mention those who required a bite or a skin and just never got triggered into their alternate form.

Marvin said, "I always thought there were a lot more recessives lurking within human populations than anyone realizes."

Trick thought about the fact that the merfolk had their own recessives, like Sato with his spurs.

"So we are in agreement – they are probably here for procreative reasons. Whether practical sperm hunting or theoretical information gathering."

Trick said, because he thought he finally had a sympathetic audience for a thing that had always bothered him, "This whole thing with the legs and the hunting and the breeding seems needlessly complicated, not to mention cruel to mermen." *And the sires*, thinking of Mr Sato a little sadly.

Marvin turned to look at him. "You're right. Also, would we call it *cruel?*"

Trick would, and had. But he realized that to have a firm opinion on this matter was a red flag. Marvin was already looking at him suspiciously.

Marvin's eyes narrowed. The pack stayed silent, waiting for him to speak. He was, after all, the only merman they had.

"Moving on, then, my fuzzy darlings." Marvin stopped staring at Trick, a relief, and waved both arms in the air in excitement. "I'm taking twelve mermaids thrifting tomorrow! Trick, you wanna come?" Marvin batted his eyes rapidly. He looked a little like he was having a seizure.

Trick said quickly, "I have to work."

"Take the day off, darling. The Bean can survive twenty-four hours without you."

"I highly doubt it," said Judd, unexpectedly coming to Trick's defense.

"Floyd would pine," pointed out Colin.

"Floyd *would* pine," agreed Trick, fondly. "But only for my cappuccinos."

"Ah, what you're really thinking is: Who would Kettil fail to flirt with?" Marvin teased.

Trick winced, *Oh right, Kettil.* He'd forgotten about the bear shifter.

Marvin said, too perceptive, "Well, that was an interesting reaction. You okay, honey?"

Trick replied, unguarded. "Will the merman be joining you?"

"I imagine so. He doesn't seem to leave the Paralia's side."

Alec said, "I thought his spurs didn't work on land."

So then Marvin had told Alec all about the vangill. Trick felt a massive sense of relief. At least he wasn't hiding vital information from the pack anymore.

Marvin said confidently, "They don't. But vangill still train to fight on land. Not that they'd be much good against a werewolf."

And now Trick was hiding information again. Because Sato's Spurs *did* work on land. But he wasn't going to tell this pack. Which sucked.

"I really can't join you, much as I love thrifting. Twelve mermaids seems a little overboard. Pun intended," said Trick firmly.

"I'll come," said Colin, who'd recently developed an interest in fashion. "I don't have class."

"Me too," said Judd quickly.

"You hate shopping."

"True. Nothing ever fits me right. But I was thinking more as a de facto bodyguard."

"What about the Heavy Lifting contract for the conference?" pressed Alec.

"Kevin can draw it up,"

"Must I?" said Kevin, wrinkling his nose.

"Yes, dear, sometimes you too must do paperwork," replied Judd.

Marvin was still looking at Trick, a funny expression on his pretty little face. "Well, maybe we will bring the ladies into the Bean after shopping."

"Please don't," said Trick, sharp and firm.

Marvin recoiled.

Trick realized that he had never used that tone of voice with the merman before. He'd never used it with any member of the pack. A mistake to do it now, no doubt.

"Trick, hon, do you have a problem with merfolk?"

"I like *you*," said Trick, quickly.

"I'm not most merfolk."

"Exactly."

"Okay, honey, I won't bring them to your cafe then, don't worry."

Trick felt himself relax noticeably. He was sure they could see it on his face.

"But we should talk about it. Prejudice isn't good. They seem nice enough, for mermaids," added Marvin, making Trick tense again.

Alec said, "Would you like to sit down with Isaac tomorrow? I can ask him to stop by the cafe on his way to work."

Trick blushed to realize so much of his stress was showing that Alec was deploying his Omega.

To see Sato again. To talk so casually of merfolk and their intrusion back into his life. Into their lives. He'd let down his guard.

Alec was sensitive to moods – it was what made him a good Alpha. He also knew how to utilize the skills and personalities of his pack to fix those moods. That was what made him a *great* Alpha.

"It's okay, really," said Trick because he didn't want to talk about it. Not to Isaac, not to anyone. He just wanted to hide in his cafe. He wanted to make drinks and not think about the fact that Sato would be right there, in his area, in his thrift stores. So close. So impossibly far away. "It was just one encounter, a long time ago. Sometimes it's hard to forget." He hoped they would leave things at that.

Fortunately, they did.

Trick didn't sleep much that night. His memories were sun-soaked and humid. They smelled of frying katsu and briny waters. He was cold and alone in Colin's old bed, eyes wide and staring into the dark. He must keep them dry, like the land, because if he cried his tears would taste like the sea.

CHAPTER ELEVEN

WHERE THE CRAWDADDIES SING

The Past: Patrick at Ocean View Cafe

Of course he'd known Sato was coming back that day. They'd managed a couple of phone conversations while Sato was in vangill training. In one of those, Sato had told him his leave dates.

"It would take me at least two weeks to swim all the way there from here, and I only get one week off." Sato said over the spotty connection. "So I managed to persuade my sire to fly me back. That way I'll at least have some time with you."

"I'd offer to pick you up at the airport but you know I don't have a car." Most of Patrick's money went to his cell phone bill and his college fund these days.

"Sire will do it."

"Is he excited to have you home?"

"Sire? Excited?"

"Has he told you what he's going to cook?"

"The real question."

Patrick heard someone in the background yelling something crude about Sato's inability to plow his girlfriend.

"Ooo, am I the girlfriend?" Patrick asked.

"Gimme a sec." Sato clearly put a hand over the phone but

Patrick heard him perfectly when he said, "Just because you wouldn't know how to shift the important bits, let alone use them properly."

"Ooo, he's mad," said a deep sarcastic voice.

"I get *one* phone call. Assholes."

There was some kind of clattering thump noise and then Sato returned.

"Sorry about that."

Patrick was glowing with pleasure.

"I'll come find you as soon as I can get away from sire, which won't take long."

"I'll probably be at the café. They keep giving me more and more hours, so I'm almost always there." Patrick wasn't at home much these days.

"It took over the old bait shop, right? You like it?"

"Yeah, I really do."

"It'll be nice to see you actually doing something useful for a change."

"Oh, charming. Slinging overpriced lattes for tourists is *useful*? As if when I didn't have a job, all I did was cause trouble?"

"Think about what you just said *very* carefully."

Patrick made an exasperated sound at Sato, but did not hang up, because he rarely got to hear Sato's voice and he missed him so badly sometimes it was like one of his limbs had been amputated.

Thus Patrick had known that Sato was coming back that day. He just hadn't known exactly when. So he'd been keeping an anxious eye to the door his entire shift. Of course the one time he actually wasn't watching the entrance, because there was a problem with his most difficult regular, was exactly the point at which Sato walked in.

The cafe's most challenging customer was Eddie McClyck, former owner of the bait shop. He'd sold the building fair and square, but resented the whole town for his decision to do so. He liked shirts without sleeves in primary colors, flip flops, and cargo shorts, and if his style wasn't enough to insult Patrick's sensibilities, he always got dark roast, extra sweet, and then gave himself endless free refills with hazelnut creamer. Even his taste in coffee was repulsive.

Eddie seemed to feel that having once occupied the space, he was entitled to it, and everybody in it. It meant he could be there whenever he wanted for as long as he wanted. It meant that he could insult Patrick as much as he liked, with slurs he pretended were hip modern jokes. It meant he never tipped. It meant he opened sugar packets and scattered them everywhere even though the trash was *right there*. And it meant that any female employees of the café were also de facto *his* property.

Usually when Eddie was around, Patrick made certain that he was the one to go out and clean the tabletops and tidy the chairs. But there had been some sort of scuffle out the back in the alley, and Patrick wasn't going to send Veronica to investigate, because she was a thin-skinned human.

It was late enough in the afternoon that only Eddie was still in residence at his favorite table in the window.

"Stay behind the counter, Veronica. I'm gonna check out back."

Veronica was a glum little thing with graceless movements and stilted speech who did not belong in the service industry. She was of an artistic temperament, and Patrick could foresee her future as either a tattoo artist or an investment banker. She had only recently been hired, so he wasn't ready to make a concrete call either way. But she certainly wasn't familiar enough with Eddie to understand the risk. She was intense and focused and a bit nerdy, but she also clearly thought of herself as more edgy and dangerous than she really was.

"Whatever you say, Patrick." Her tone of voice said *You're not the boss of me* but whatever was going on out back got louder.

Patrick didn't really have time to deal with her attitude.

He wasn't gone very long. Because out back turned out to be a pack of stray dogs. Patrick had merely growled at them, using a bit of his otter side, and they scattered in panicked confusion.

Nevertheless, by the time he got back to the cafe, Eddie had Veronica pinned against the creamer stand, big arms to either side of the girl, a sneer that was meant to be a flirty smile on his lips.

Veronica was head down, using her hair as an ineffectual shield, trembling.

"Now, now, Mr McClyck, are we out of your hazelnut creamer? Or was it more coffee you needed? Let me get that for you."

Patrick attempted to interpose himself between the two humans on the pretext of grabbing for the coffee dispenser that he knew was already full.

"Oh, why don't you leave us alone, faggy boy. Pretty little Veronica and I were just having a nice chat, weren't we, honey?" Eddie petted a finger down one of the purple streaks in Veronica's hair. Pressing closer, so Patrick couldn't squirm between them.

Patrick contemplated leverage and whether he could physically lift the larger human off Veronica. Patrick was stronger than average for his height and weight, because he was a shifter. But that didn't mean he had superhuman abilities. He was only an otter after all, he wasn't a wolf or a bear or anything substantial like that. His people were known for being tricky, and nimble, and fast moving. Not heavy lifting.

"All right, Mr McClyck, if I could just get to the…"

Eddie back-handed him with one meaty arm, hard enough and fast enough to throw Patrick backwards and cut the inside of his cheek on his teeth.

A mouthful of his own blood was not a particularly pleasant sensation. Patrick would've spat it out, but then he'd only have to clean it up later. So he swallowed it down and stood back up.

Veronica gave a little whimper and shrank away, squirming side to side to try to get out of Eddie's arms.

The bell over the door clanged.

Patrick didn't have attention to spare for a new customer. He only hoped it wasn't their boss. She was a slight, sweet little human who liked long flowy maxi-dresses and silver jewelry. She would not be able to handle this at all.

But the newcomer clearly took in and understood the situation, because suddenly there was a large masculine body between Patrick and the two humans. The next thing he knew, Eddie had been half-pushed, half-hurled against his favorite coffee table and Veronica was dashing behind the counter.

Maybe she would listen to him next time he told her not to leave the safety of the barista area.

Patrick realized who was fighting their corner and what might happen next quickly. "Sato, try not to break anything or spill any blood. I'm closing this evening, which means I'll have to clean it up."

Sato didn't turn away from Eddie. Instead he just pointed with one arm so Patrick knew that he too was expected to take refuge behind the counter.

"Fat chance." Patrick refused to move. He wasn't really in danger. "You might need backup."

Sato turned his head briefly and gave Patrick an incredulous look.

Patrick pouted at him.

Sato looked just gorgeous.

Sato made a tongue click of disgust, then returned his attention to Eddie, who was not at all daunted by Sato.

"Who the fuck are you? Another faggot?" He pulled out his knife.

Eddie was one of those guys who might have been former military. Or he might have just liked to play dress-up with weapons. In the South it was hard to tell the difference. Whatever the reason, he always carried a knife on his belt. If asked, he would brag about it or claim that it had to do with gutting fish in a sly way that said he could use it for lots of other things too. It was not a fish knife.

Patrick had a moment to be grateful that it was not a gun. Even Sato could be stopped by enough bullets of the right type. Not that he wanted to see his boyfriend cut to ribbons either.

Eddie seemed actually pretty good with that knife. So maybe he had been in the military after all.

But Patrick had forgotten why Sato had been taken from him and that while he'd been learning how to make milk foam hearts, Sato had been undergoing what amounted to merman military training.

Because Sato defended himself easily.

Eddie seemed to understand his opponent and so changed tactics to focus on the weakest person there. With Veronica behind the counter, that meant Patrick.

He charged toward him.

But Sato now had bodyguard training and had always been incredibly protective of Patrick either way, so he responded by lunging and pushing Eddie so hard the man fell into a table, which rocked on its pedestal but fortunately didn't break.

"Sato! I told you to be careful," griped Patrick, annoyed.

"I told you to get behind the counter," shot back Sato, equally annoyed.

He came over, grabbed Patrick by the shoulders, and muscled him around, looking him over carefully.

"What are you doing?"

"He tossed you. Are you hurt? "

"I'm absolutely fine,. You know I've been through worse a million times over. Get off me." Patrick batted at Sato. "Whoa!"

Eddie came at them again, knife still out.

Sato, looking exasperated, whirled to face him with his forearm up. The knife clanged against something hard and inhuman.

Sato's spurs were out! On land? Was that even possible?

Sato did something that trapped the knife between two of his spurs. Then he flicked and twisted his arm. It snapped the blade in two, leaving Eddie with nothing but the stubby end and a shocked expression.

"What the hell, you bastard?" said Eddie, master of polite speech.

Sato moved behind Eddie, one forearm across his neck, spurs pressed up against his throat like a massive serrated blade. He started frog-walking the bigger man toward the door.

Eddie tried to jerk away.

"I wouldn't do that if I were you. These are very, *very* sharp and your jugular is very, very *close*. Try it and you'll be very, *very* dead."

Eddie allowed himself to be marched to the door.

"Patrick," said Sato, "a little help throwing out the trash."

Patrick dashed over and pulled open the door, gesturing them through with a flourish.

"Hello, is this 911?" he heard Veronica say loudly behind them. She'd called cops? What possible good would they be? "Yes we have a man with a knife. Well maybe two or three knives and more than one man, but only one of them is an asshole. Can you come and..."

Sato shoved Eddie forward, out onto the street. The man stumbled and tripped.

Patrick shut and locked the door behind him, flipping the sign to *closed* even though there were four hours left on shift.

"What do you mean the deputies are all *on lunch break?*" Veronica's voice rose in annoyance. Patrick's shoulders relaxed. Guess the cops were gonna prove his point. "You want us to come in to file an incident report? But it happened *here*. Don't you need to collect evidence or whatever?"

Another pause. Veronica looked around the cafe. "No, nothing is broken. There's no blood or anything. No one is seriously injured."

Patrick patted Sato's face in a condescending way. "Good job there, babe."

Sato crossed his arms and glared. "How do you always get into these situations? How much trouble did you get into while I was away?"

"Welcome home, snookums!"

"Will you please stop with the dumb human pet names?"

Veronica's voice was rising again. "What do you *mean* there's no point and there's nothing you can do. Just Eddie? What the hell, *just* Eddie? He pulled a knife! He touched my— Oh my god, she hung up on me!" Veronica glared at the phone in her hand, dumbfounded.

Patrick hid a smile. "Welcome to small town life."

Sato said, "Nothing ever changes here, does it?"

Veronica looked at Sato, eyes wide and adoring. "And who exactly are you?"

Sato, characteristically, ignored her and focused on Patrick. "You sure you're okay?"

Sato's spurs had retracted. His arms were back to looking like normal human arms, only a lot more muscular than last time Patrick had seen them.

"I'm the one who was groped," grumbled Veronica. "You broke his knife. Were you using sai?"

Patrick glared at her. "Seriously, Veronica?"

"What? Raphael was my favorite." She kept staring at Sato with something akin to hero worship in her eyes. "You're like a ninja or something, right?"

"Or something," said Sato.

Patrick snorted. "Veronica, this is Sato Daiki, friend of mine. Sato, this is Veronica O'Kip, new hire, doesn't listen to instructions."

Veronica gave a funny little bow. "Sato-senpai." She paused, then straightened, shuffling her feet awkwardly.

Patrick blinked at her. What did she think she was doing?

"Look, I'm super into anime." That explained the purple hair. She continued. "So are you an *actual* ninja?"

Sato was still evaluating Patrick for injuries out of lowered eyelids. Or just checking him out. Patrick tsked at him.

Sato turned to give Veronica his attention.

She swallowed and blushed bright pink.

Patrick nodded to himself. He'd gotten that way too, especially early on when they first met, and later when they were first dating. When Sato made that jump from friend to lover. The way he looked when he was concentrating on a person was overwhelming. Patrick wasn't delighted to see that attention focused elsewhere.

"Martial arts training does not a ninja make," Sato explained. Or, no doubt, thought he explained.

"Can I see them?"

"What?"

"Your sai?"

"No."

"They're very well hidden."

"They are."

"Can you teach me?"

"No."

"If you're quite done now…," said Patrick to both of them, pretending to be a lot more annoyed than he was. He knew his eyes were desperately combing over Sato's face. Cataloging how he looked different, logging the shadows under his eyes, and the lines at the sides of his mouth that had never been there before.

"How long are you—?" Veronica looked crushed but determined to still talk to Sato. But the moment Patrick said anything, Sato's attention swiveled entirely back to him.

"I'm fine, stop worrying," Sato said.

Veronica clamped her lips shut, wide eyes darting between Sato and Patrick, growing huge with comprehension, or supposition, difficult to tell the difference.

"Sit down," Patrick ordered his boyfriend, pointing at the table furthest away from the counter. "What can I make you to drink?"

"I don't know, what *can* you make me?"

Patrick knew that Sato didn't enjoy coffee. But he had been raised in a somewhat traditional Japanese household, at least during his teenage years, so Patrick suggested, "Matcha?" He contemplated offering to mix it with fish sauce, but that would probably disgust Veronica and he doubted they had any in the cafe. He thought the idea sounded tasty so he made a mental note to try it himself sometime. Maybe with a hint of seaweed?

"Sure." Sato went to sit where he'd been told.

"I thought you said he was a friend," accused Veronica, "Seems like a lot more than just a friend."

Patrick took a leaf out of Sato's book and chose not to say anything in reply.

He made himself a matcha latte, too. Nothing traditional about it, but he liked the milkiness. "Veronica, I'm taking my break. You can flip the sign back to open if you feel okay to handle the counter by yourself for a bit. Eddie won't be returning anytime soon."

"You're going somewhere?" Veronica looked worried and was clearly still shaken. Patrick thought full responsibility for the counter might be good for her – take her mind off things for a while.

He pointed to where Sato was sitting. "I'll be right there."

"Is he your…?" She let the sentence trail off.

"Whatever it is you're thinking, probably yes." Patrick decided it would be better to have her on their side. She needed the distraction, so he grinned and wiggled his eyebrows. "I did good, right?"

"So sexy," agreed Veronica with feeling.

Patrick grabbed up the two drinks and then leaned toward her conspiratorially. "Hottest thing on two legs." Or more properly, one tail.

"You're a lucky bastard," agreed Veronica.

"Right?"

Patrick flounced over and sat down, set one matcha in front of his boyfriend. Merfriend? Fishfriend? Fuckfish? No moniker seemed to work for what they were.

"Here ya go, babe."

"Babe? Why?" Sato arched his brows.

"What? No one's gonna tease *me*." Remembering their last phone call.

"Those assholes," said Sato with something akin to tolerance.

Patrick felt a stab of jealousy. Did Sato have other friends? *Merman* friends?

Sato sipped the green drink, made a face. "Too sweet."

"This is the South. It's *all* too sweet, hon."

"Hon?"

"You clearly don't like *babe*. Honey? Hanii?"

Sato shifted uncomfortably, glanced over at Veronica who was riveted (there was no one else in the cafe).

"Oh, she knows," said Patrick.

"Knows what, exactly?"

"Just *knows*.'

Sato didn't push, he never did. He always let Patrick keep his secrets and practice his tricky ways. It was very frustrating of him. Patrick had forgotten how annoyingly calm and sanctimonious Sato was. The more teasing and eccentric Patrick got, the more Sato became the opposite.

Sato relaxed back in his chair. It creaked under his newly muscled bulk. Whatever else vangill training was, a great deal of it was clearly physical. Patrick wanted to see what Sato looked like under that tight t-shirt more than anything.

"You can use them on land," he said. They both knew he was referring to the spurs.

Sato looked smug. "Just found that out myself. Your fault. Thanks, I guess." He flipped his forearms over and back again a few times.

"Always blaming me. Will this work in your favor, do you think?"

"Most assuredly," said Sato, even more smug.

"You're really good at it, aren't you? Being a vangill?"

Sato didn't answer that, but he was emitting smug now like sea spray. Patrick had always known that there was going to be a time when Sato became really *good* at something. Patrick was unsurprised it turned out to be merman stuff. Sato had always been more at home in the sea than on land, obligated but uncomfortable among humans. Sato excelled at being a vangill because he excelled at being a merman. It made Patrick jealous and worried. Although he wasn't sure why or what about, exactly.

"Did you miss me?" Sato asked, out of the blue.

Patrick couldn't help but grin. "Of course not, why would I miss you?"

"Liar." Sato let it slide. "How's senior year going?"

Patrick brightened. Oh, right, Sato hadn't heard. Patrick too, could excel. Last time they'd talked he was only applying to colleges.

"I got in!" he crowed, knowing he was grinning like a fool.

Sato seemed genuinely pleased. "Smart boy. Which one?"

Patrick couldn't help but brag. "All of them! But only one gave me a big enough scholarship to actually attend." He pretended to pout.

"Oh? Was it not your first choice?" Sato played along.

Patrick couldn't help himself, he let the grin spread all over his face again. "It was my top pick!"

Sato looked even more delighted. He was almost smiling. "Jiggly Yard?" he guessed.

"Yes! The drama department!"

Sato looked self-satisfied, like it was something *he'd* achieved, not Patrick. "Of course you did." He was not surprised at all. "You're going to be way too popular for my sanity."

"I really am. Plus there'll be so many queer kids around. It'll be awesome."

Sato visibly shuddered. Patrick was well aware that he hated the idea of living in a big human city, but he was prepared to do it for Patrick.

Sato frowned. "Do we use that word?"

"*Queer*? Yeah, apparently it's been *reclaimed*."

"If you say so." Sato didn't look convinced.

"They don't allow you on the interwebs at all during training?"

"Nah. Just the one phone call every few months. I always used that for you." Sato didn't offer further info about what it was like. Patrick wondered how much he'd be able to get out of him about it this week. Or if Sato would remain closed-mouthed about vangill training forever.

"As you should." Patrick was still delighted that Sato used his one call to talk with him, every single time. Sato had given Patrick messages to pass along to his sire about how he was doing. It was why Patrick paid for a cell phone he really couldn't afford. So that whenever Sato got that rare chance to call, he could always reach Patrick.

If Mr Sato minded that his son spoke through a Patrick-shaped mouthpiece, he never complained. He absorbed information about Sato without fuss, as he always had. He'd never once questioned Patrick's presence in Sato's life. Unflappable and uninterested were probably Mr Sato's two defining character traits. Patrick might have been annoyed if it hadn't worked in his favor. He had enough love in him for Sato if his father could not, or would not, care.

Patrick wondered sometimes if Mr Sato even really registered that he *had* a son. Did he think of Sato as his spawn, merfolk style? Were they nothing more to each other than genetics passed along in a single encounter twenty years ago?

"I missed you," said Sato, suddenly, as if continuing their earlier conversation.

Patrick dipped his head, acquiescing to the serious tone. "Fine. Yes. I missed you too."

Sato's eyes darkened. Patrick remembered that look all too well. If they were alone, Sato would've jumped him.

Suddenly nervous, Patrick started to babble. "Was it awful?"

"Missing you?"

"No, idiot, the vangill. Conscription. Military service. Whatever it was pretending to be."

Sato shrugged. "Not really." But that's what Sato always said.

"Was there hazing? Were you bullied?" *Did you bully others?* One never knew with Sato. Patrick was confident in many things, but Sato having a strong moral foundation, without Patrick, wasn't one of them.

"It was *fine.*"

Patrick frowned. "Did any of them flirt with you?"

"Vangill are supposed to be breeder studs." Sato looked over at Veronica, cleaning the slop trays. She didn't seem to be paying close attention to them, but anything was possible.

Patrick made a face. "No gays allowed?"

"Nobody said as much, but it was certainly implied."

Patrick understood. Sato wasn't like him. Sato could pass as *normal.* Well, normal for a merman. "So long as you stayed safe."

"You don't care?"

"Does their opinion or knowing the truth about us count for something? Are they important to you? Do they have to know about me? Do they have to know about you?"

"No."

"Then I don't care. I want you to come back to me whole and undamaged. Nothing else matters."

Silence while Sato stared at him, wanting something more.

"I missed you waiting for me after school. I missed snacks in your bed. I missed you in your bed. I missed swimming with you," Patrick found himself admitting.

"You missed not having my house as a refuge and a pantry."

Patrick grinned. "That too." Also, it was lonely to walk home alone in the dark. It was lonely to swim in the bay without company. He'd taken to swimming more up into the delta waterways, like a true river otter. Except that was where his family swam, so he had to do it at times of day when they weren't around. Like early in the morning. It had been lonely. Soon he'd found himself spending less and less time in his otter form and more and more time as a teenager amongst teenage humans, serving them at the café, partying with them late at night.

But that night Sato got to walk him home in the dark like the old days.

Home being Sato's house, of course. His sire was already in bed, having, surprisingly, remembered to leave the porch light on for them.

The Past: Sato at his sire's house

Sato couldn't believe that he'd arrived home; had to break up a fight at a café over a human female, of all things; and then sit across the table and make small talk with his own boyfriend. When all he really wanted was Patrick naked and underneath him.

Luckily for his sanity, that happened quickly enough once they got home. His sire was a heavy sleeper.

Sato simply dragged Patrick up the stairs, Patrick giggling like a mad thing and suggesting they visit the kitchen first.

"Only if you want to be bent over the counter," snapped Sato.

"I'm a little too short for that."

"There's a step stool somewhere."

"Seems complicated."

"Agreed," said Sato, picking him up and tossing him over one shoulder.

Sato barely registered that everything in his old room was unchanged. Over a year he'd been gone, and the place felt like it had been frozen in time.

He tossed Patrick onto the futon and followed him down. Trying to touch as much of him as he could with every part of his body.

Patrick whined at him about too much clothing.

Their arms got hopelessly tangled as they each tried to take off the other's shirt and pants. They ended up exactly as Sato dreamed. Naked with Patrick flat on his back and smiling up at him. Sato crouched over him like some four-legged land-bound predator.

Patrick's hands were on his waist and up his back. Confident and needy.

Sato fell forward again with his elbows either side of Patrick's neck, almost nose to nose.

Patrick was sparkling up at him, those fathomless dark eyes bright and inquisitive.

"Did you think about anything else but this while we were apart?" His tone was teasing. This was the Patrick that Sato loved so well. Not the capable one at the café.

He answered by kissing Patrick then, melding their mouths. This was a thing they'd learned to do together. This was a thing they were really good at. The way Patrick melted under him. The way Sato could sweep in with his tongue, exploring all the warmth of that mouth, as he might explore an undersea cave. Searching for hidden treasure, but knowing that the treasure was the cave itself.

"Horny bastard," accused Patrick, when they had a breather.

Sato examined his face to see if he was serious. But it was just Patrick being Patrick.

"You're not wrong." He kissed Patrick again. Exploring again.

Letting his hands rediscover every part of this boy that belonged to him.

"What did you get up to while we were apart that makes you so desperate to prove all over again that I'm yours?"

Did Patrick seriously believe that Sato would cheat on him? Would find someone else? *Could* find someone else? Sato never noticed other people. It had only ever been Patrick.

"You really want to discuss what I've been doing, right *now*?"

"Why are you still talking?" wondered Patrick, who was the one who started chatting and teasing in the first place. Who was the one who never shut up. Sato just wanted to kiss him.

Sato took that as permission. He didn't bother to explain himself or the vangill. There was nothing to explain. He had done everything he had been told, to the best of his abilities. Which had, ironically, made him the best there. But he hadn't socialized. He had spent his limited free time thinking about Patrick. How soon he could get back to him. What they would do when he got there. All the different things he wanted to do to this small lithe body, writhing underneath him like it was now. Why did he need to say such things out loud? Patrick should already know all of this. Nothing had changed. He had been this way from the start. Would always be this way. Patrick was the one who had changed. Patrick was the one who needed the reminder of what they were to each other.

This was all Patrick's fault.

Sometimes Sato thought he wanted Patrick so badly it was like he wanted to eat him whole. Actually devour him. Like the rumors surrounding his mermaid ancestors, sea monsters who dragged people down beneath the waves not for seduction but because they enjoyed the taste of human flesh. He didn't think modern mermen were supposed to *want* like he wanted Patrick. But maybe it came with the spurs, as if all of him was a throwback to a time when shifters were creatures of the Deep Dark. When they were the monsters of myth and fairy tale.

Patrick made the best noises in the world when he was turned on. Little trills and chatters and chirps and sighs and moans. He wiggled in the best way, too. As gracefully in bed beneath Sato's hands, as he was in otter form beneath the waves.

Sato gave him all of his weight. Locking him down, letting him feel the new muscles that he'd developed during training. Enjoyed Patrick against him with every inch of his stupid human skin. With all the amazing pleasure, that this, his second form, his second-best form, his inferior self, his incomplete being, could enjoy another thing. A thing that had to take place on land and in this form. A thing that yet, within it, still contained all the motion of the tides – the inevitable push and pull of waves.

Sato realized that making love to Patrick was less like being in the ocean, than it was like being the ocean itself. That he could work Patrick over, and leave him wet and damp and ship-wrecked beneath him. That he could spend himself into exhausted nothingness like the sea did during a storm. Crashing and roaring out pleasure.

He felt that much more calm afterwards. That much more at peace. That much more of the ocean. The storm of them together on land was more true to the sea than swimming in it on a string of summer days full of heat and stillness.

This thing that they did together in Sato's old room, in Sato's sire's house, in the box that was the prison of his exile, in the dry world of an alien species, was more in harmony with Sato's soul than any moment of vangill training. It felt more right than any second he could remember from his childhood, swimming with his mother's pod, his beloved younger sister trailing behind him.

He had missed Patrick more in one day then he had missed his pod during the whole of his landbound exile.

He didn't tell Patrick any of this.

But afterwards, when Patrick lay, quiet for a change, limp and satiated, and cuddled in his arms, Sato made a decision. He would serve his time with the sea people. He would do his duty, as the spurs required of him. But in the end, he no longer belonged to the sea. He belonged to Patrick. He would follow Patrick the way driftwood followed a current, with rings and grains and DNA that recorded where he'd started out but with no concern for where he ended up.

Patrick amused himself trailing a finger through the puddles of spend left on his stomach, mixing the two of their essences together.

Sato watched him with heavy lids.

Patrick glared at him. "Smug," he accused, accurately.

Sato grabbed Patrick's hand and licked the cum off of it.

Patrick gasped, then made a face. "Seriously? Gross."

"It tastes like the ocean. It tastes like us."

Patrick shivered, made the little involuntary throat purr that said he was turned on again. "Why are you so good at this?"

Sato shrugged. *Was he? Was that the nicest thing anyone had ever said to him?*

"Why should I bother to ask? You're good at everything."

"No. I'm good at everything to do with you."

Patrick snorted.

"I don't really care about anything else. So I'm not good at it."

Patrick started playing with Sato's hair. "You've got red streaks in it now? How did that happen?"

"I'm outside all the time on two legs, running on beaches in the tropical sun." Sato held up an arm, the color of wet kelp in the sun now. "I'm a lot tanner than I was, too."

"Has your tail color changed?"

Sato laughed because it was such a surprising question, but he supposed it made a strange kind of sense in Patrick's logical little brain. If his hair lightened from sun exposure, why wouldn't his tail?

"Sun doesn't affect my true form. It's the same blue it's always been."

Patrick let out a long sigh, like he was reassured. Perhaps he was. "Good. Too much of you has changed, something needs to be the same."

But Patrick was the one who had changed. He was independent now. He had learned to survive without Sato. Sato was grateful for that, of course, but he was also jealous and frustrated. He had always preferred Patrick dependent upon him. But now Patrick didn't need him. He had his job, and his human friends, and a whole life that had gone on without Sato. That appeared to have been *successful* without him.

Patrick had plans now. Plans for college. Plans for moving away. Plans that included Sato, but only as an afterthought.

He'd accept it. If it meant that he got to have Patrick. If this was the only way to convince Patrick to wait for him. To convince him that he was worth waiting for. Then Sato would let go of being Patrick's *only*. Let him stray even further into the world of humans. Into the dangers of a big city. Into a place where he couldn't protect Patrick, and couldn't keep an eye on him, and couldn't keep him safe.

This was the price that his people, and the sea, and his spurs demanded of him. For the one millionth time, Sato questioned whether it was worth paying. Whether he was shelling out a cost for his freedom in severing tethers not just to the land, but to Patrick. Patrick who was growing beyond him. Away from him.

But then Patrick wrapped thin, strong arms tight around him and peppered his chest with tiny kisses, made more of those little murmurs of pleasure. And Sato knew that Patrick was worth everything, every risk, and that he would follow him anywhere, even into a concrete city full of loud, angry humans. Sato would pay whatever price his people asked of him, so long as at the end of it he could return to Patrick.

Unfortunately for both of them, the ocean does not honor promises made on land.

CHAPTER TWELVE

LIKE A MERMAID IN A THRIFT STORE

The Present: Sato in the San Rafael Goodwill with way too many mermaids

In the history of bad ideas, of which there were plenty in Sato Daiki's life (mostly via Patrick), going shopping with twelve mermaids, two werewolves, and one very enthusiastic merman had to have been one of the worst. Not that it was his bad idea, of course.

Apparently, some cultures did this kind of thing for fun.

Apparently, some Marvins did it for fun, too.

No one was prepared for them, least of all the San Rafael Goodwill. For one thing, there were only two changing rooms. And there were only two clerks. The clerks were instantly overwhelmed by the combination of mermaids and Marvin's enthusiasm.

The moment they entered it was utter chaos. Fortunately, first thing on a Friday morning, there were no straight men in a downtown thrift store. But a dozen mermaids with an objective of finding multiple outfits, when they had never had such an opportunity before, was a recipe for disaster.

Marvin was running around like a greased priest in leather pajamas. He recruited Sato and Judd to fetch and carry mounds of clothing and kept up a running commentary on the nature of color wheels, draping, and something called the "importance of a power suit."

As far as Sato was concerned, it was all some kind of advanced torture system. Why so many options? And why did Marvin care so much about them? Why was Colin so accommodating? Only Judd seemed to be on his side in this. The two of them took to exchanging increasingly desperate looks. So Sato was now bonding with a werewolf. Who knew?

"Cascade, sweetie darling, not the neon pink '80s suit. Those shoulder pads could become dictators of their own totalitarian regimes. Too far." Marvin rushed over and ripped the suit out of Cascade's webbed hands, putting a mint green pantsuit in her line of sight instead.

Barely had he managed to do that than one of the others distracted him. "Aqua, sweet-cheeks, put the polyester down and back away slowly."

"But it has *squid* all over it!"

"You can't wear a 1960s dressing gown to a marine biology conference, baby-cakes."

"But the *squid!*"

"I thought humans loved a robe," complained Onda, reluctantly putting the silk and lace one she was holding back into the negligee section.

Marvin puffed out his cheeks, then took a deep breath. "I told you on the way here – what matters is the cut and style first! I can't help it if you didn't pay attention. Prints will come into play, but let's find you a suit first. Then we can look for a *blouse* with fish on it. Order of operations, darlings, okay?"

Marvin clapped his hands together, calling everyone's attention like an enthusiastic seal. "Those are the suits over there, girls, please start with those." He pointed to one wall.

A chorus of complaints about how boring the colors were met Marvin's directive.

"But you need to play by human standards when wearing clothing. I explained all of this. I don't make the rules, the two legs do."

"But there are so many other options," protested Meymey, who was flipping through party gowns.

"And if you plan to go out in the evenings you can wear a cute dress or something like that. But you're here for a *scientific* conference. If you want to fit in and be taken seriously, you simply must wear a suit."

"Do we want to fit in?" challenged Lana.

Marvin was getting increasingly frustrated, distracted by yet another flawed mermaid choice. "Doris, darling, no you can't just get naked and try something on in the middle of the store. You have to use a changing room. Colin, hon, would you please explain nudity taboos to the nice mermaids?"

A large part of Sato was annoyed at having to do this instead of hunt for Patrick. Another part of him kept thinking how much fun Patrick would have in this place. His otter had always loved dressing up. What little money Patrick had was often spent on clothes and tons of accessories. Patrick always said accessories were toys he could wear. Sato remembered his stacked bracelet phase. He had enjoyed stripping them off him, dropping them one at a time with a clatter to the floor.

Just to be a dick and throw kelp in the engine, Sato said, "What about accessories?"

Marvin pointed two fingers at him. "Don't you dare start."

Sato simply turned and refocused on his sister. She had moved away from the sparkles and was dutifully flipping through suits. She was in the men's section, but Sato didn't think that mattered.

Behind him, Marvin let out a terrified shriek. Instantly Sato turned back, forearms up. Out of the corner of his eye he saw Judd throw down his armful of clothes and take up a defensive stance.

"Morwenna!" Marvin's shriek resolved itself into vocabulary. "Absolutely not!" He whirled on Sato. "You, vangill, stop her!"

Sato gave him a look. "I do not interfere with the doings of mermaids unless they are in danger."

"She is in very great danger of wearing traffic cone orange as a *redhead!*"

"It's the color of a clown fish," protested Morwenna. "I adore clown fishes!" She pulled out a pair of black and white patterned pants. "Look, like with this."

"You want to wear an orange Hawaiian shirt with zebra print pants?" Marvin covered his eyes and pretended to faint. "I think I might be sick."

Judd sidled over to Sato. "This is insanity." Judd's big frame was hunched and overwhelmed. The werewolf looked like he could lift a tugboat but not, apparently, withstand the weight of one shopping jaunt.

"This was *your* merman's idea." Sato pointed out the truth.

"He's having a blast." Colin joined them. He had a few things to try on, but otherwise seemed content to stick to the fringes of the madness.

"Is he?" Marvin seemed more like a high-strung hurricane.

Colin laughed. "He's probably never been happier."

Sato's feet hurt and he wanted to go looking for Patrick. Marvin and his color wheel could go to hell.

"It's cute," added Colin.

Judd groaned.

Sato was growing to appreciate Judd in a dispassionate way. He came off as grounded and world-weary, steady. Massive, but he seemed decent and protective of his pack.

Judd said, "It's pure torture."

"Worse than vangill training," agreed Sato, surprising himself by making an effort.

"Is it really?" Judd looked interested.

Sato didn't elaborate.

Colin wandered off to advise Rilian on the nature of ruffles.

Sato watched Marvin chase down Tarni and yank a yellow feathered sweatshirt out of her hands, replacing it with a shiny brown suit the color of a damselfish. Too drab. She'd never go for it. She cast it aside without even bothering to try it on. It was the color of Patrick fur swimming in the sun.

Marvin shrieked again.

Sato was used to it now. "Is that *really* enjoyment?" he asked Judd, for clarification purposes only.

"Most definitely," said Judd, his teeth a flash of white against his dark skin. "What's your name, by the way? Or do we just keep calling you *vangill*?"

"That works well enough."

Marvin threw olive satin at Tarni. "Girl! Your taste. You're clearly an autumn, put the spring palette down."

Sato searched for his sister. She was contemplating three different kinds of tweed. Marvin rushed over to explain to her that it was the *wrong season* for tweed. Whatever that meant.

"He's taking this awfully seriously," said Sato to Judd. Patrick had been like that as he got older, always thinking and talking about different styles. Sato hadn't cared too much. He liked it when Patrick dressed in tight things, or in stuff that draped and showed off his collar bones or hips. Pointed bones that Sato wanted to bite.

Marvin was more relentless than Patrick, though. "Yes, Paralia, the pinstripe is a much better choice. Very good, Aqua, that's a great color for you and the cut is lovely. Good little mermaids. Well done, you!"

It took them *four hours*.

Four.

Meymey used something called a *platinum card* to pay. Humans and their obsession with metal. The card was actually plastic, not platinum, but it appeared to be sufficient.

By the time they left, each mermaid had at least one suit and a dress. Or what Marvin referred to as an *evening fun-time outfit*. And most of them had also found and changed into something that wasn't a robe to wear right away.

Marvin insisted on shoes, in some cases high heels. Sato thought that heels were a terrible idea. Mermaids were notoriously clumsy on land already. To put them in high heels seemed asking for trouble. Sato suspected that they would mostly end up barefooted at the convention as a result. But he didn't care much. Meymey had opted for flats.

Judd had solved the problem of transport by driving Heavy Lifting's smallest moving van. It probably would've been easier and faster to simply swim from San Rafael back to Sausalito, but

Marvin wanted to take them all to a place called Tam Junction to eat what he referred to as "the Bay Area's best fish tacos."

Accordingly, all sixteen of them descended upon an unsuspecting taco truck.

The taco truck was extremely popular with all walks of life, including straight human males. It might no longer be lunchtime, but it was still crowded enough to be an immediate problem.

Tacos, it turned out, were a little bit like the food version of mermaids. Which is to say, when mermaids congregated around at a taco truck it was basically the greatest, sexiest, and most exciting thing to have happened in many of these humans' lives.

The efficaciousness of their new outfits was immediately put to the test. There was excessive touching, some making out, and a few popped buttons – and that was just the result of the tacos.

Twelve of the most beautiful women ever seen, hoovering fish tacos and flirting outrageously with any man who came up to them, was like a bad music video.

There was also beer. For the men, not the mermaids, obviously. The werewolves, even trained bodyguards, were having a challenging time of it. Sato didn't much care. His responsibility was to Meymey only.

It was a long few hours, with some mermaid or other disappearing into the bushes with some human male or another, on the theory that even if they weren't in a fertile part of the cycle, it was always best to be on the safe side. The mermaid version of *safe sex* was the opposite of the human version.

Sato stayed away from the fray with eyes on his sister. He sat at the end of a long picnic table munching a poke burrito because for once no one had ruined the fish by cooking it. He watched, unamused, as two men, overcome by the surfeit of tacos and booze, began to tussle over his sister. He wouldn't have intervened except that they were physically tugging her back and forth between them, like sharks with a dead seal.

"Let her go," said Sato, setting his burrito down carefully and wading in.

They were both large humans, much bigger than he was, although not as massive as Judd.

They ignored him and continued tugging.

Meymey was looking mildly perturbed but flattered.

Sato grabbed the hand that was on her upper arm closest to him and simply bent the man's thumb back until it made a pop noise. It was a very satisfying sound.

The man howled in pain and reeled away. A less satisfying sound. Why were humans so noisy?

Sato gave the other one, still attached to his sister, a look.

That human let go and backed quickly away.

Judd came lumbering over. Looked at the whimpering man in confusion.

"Sato, dude, we don't just break humans like that."

Colin added, "Violence should be used in moderation."

"Why?" Sato gave the human clutching his hand a disinterested glance. "Opposable thumbs are a privilege, not a right."

Apparently breaking some strange human's thumb was considered bad form at taco trucks, and the impromptu gathering ended on a sour note. Sato had no idea why. The man was clearly better suited to injury than not.

Marvin insisted that they come to the pack house, so that he could give them all makeovers and makeup tips. Plus he thought it would be fun to do a fashion show for his WooTube channel.

It was a nice big box, the house that the werewolves built. By Sato's standards anyway. Not that he had many where houses were concerned. But he liked this box better than any of the ones he'd lived in or around in his youth. It had large windows and a view of the bay far below. Almost as if he could walk off the deck and float down to the water. He liked that the space was tied to the ocean. It was still a box, of course, but it didn't *feel* so much like a box.

Meymey and her mermaids were having a glorious time, since essentially everybody was fussing over them, but this put them in a quandary over whether they should attend the conference that night.

Alec arrived at the pack house shortly after discussion commenced on the matter.

"Babes, you're early!" Marvin charged at the Alpha and was indulgently swept into a spinning hug.

Sato had never seen two men with such easy displays of physical contact before. It was startling. It made him wonder, had they stayed together or grown up in a different place and time, if he and Patrick would've had that kind of relationship. Patrick had loved to hug him. Draped himself all over him.

"The lab closed early for a change. It's Friday and I have a conference presentation to prepare." The Alpha put his mate down and kissed him softly.

The mermaids were all riveted. They'd never seen affection like this before. Certainly not between two males. The fact that a merman was involved, a merman that they now considered somewhat theirs, or at least their fashion advisor, made it all the more intriguing.

Marvin wound skinny arms around Alec's neck, prolonging the kiss.

Sato felt uncomfortably cold and jealous. Patrick used to do that to him. He wanted to leave. Swim across the bay. Go hunting in the gay bars of San Francisco.

Finally they parted. Marvin gestured to the den, which was full of mermaids in cute thrifted outfits and too much makeup.

"Look, I brought you girls!"

"Wouldn't know what to do with even one of them," was Alec's amused reply. "But I heard your discussion as I was coming in. Paralia," the Alpha focused on Meymey, "I wouldn't bother with opening ceremonies, if I were you. Stay and play here as long as you like. The rest of the pack will be back eventually. We can barbecue something for dinner if you want."

His sister seemed strangely relieved. "We don't have to go tonight? Good, I can meet your kelpie and visit that club."

Alec smiled at her, relaxed and charismatic. "The lesbian one?"

Sato said, "You really want to do that?" It was going to be a long night for him then, more time spent not looking for

Patrick. The one place he definitely wouldn't be was a lesbian bar.

"I do. It sounds *interesting*."

"I don't think it's wise, but if you insist."

"You won't be able to go inside with her, vangill." Judd's tone was casual. They were reasonably friendly now, after a day of torture at the hands of shopping taco-eaters.

Sato said to his sister. "Then you cannot go."

"You can't tell me what to do."

"You want to go, with a *kelpie*, inside a human club *without* me? I think not."

"A kelpie is more than enough protection."

"A kelpie is not a vangill." Sato's voice was hard – she was being unreasonable.

Nervous silence descended over the den.

Judd said, "I didn't think you could challenge her authority."

Technically Sato couldn't, but he'd accidentally slid into older brother mode.

"Ms Trickle is good people," said Alec. "You don't have to worry about her."

Sato narrowed his eyes at the Alpha. "Forgive me for not taking the word of a werewolf where the Paralia's safety is concerned."

"You can't stop me," Meymey said, being pouty and stubborn and very much his spoiled little sister.

Sato took a breath, made an effort to acknowledge her status. "You're right, I can't. But it's a terrible idea."

"How could she possibly be in danger at a lesbian club?" wondered Colin, who was also sitting with them in the den. He had his computer in his lap and was doing something on it.

Sato knew his sister well enough to switch tactics in an attempt to distract her. Perhaps she'd forget about this plan. "It's been a long day without swimming. Perhaps we should go for a dip. We have taken up a great deal of Marvin's time, and space in Alec's house."

"You're more than welcome to stay," insisted the Alpha politely.

Why did he have to be so *nice?*

But Meymey was conscious of her brother knowing more social etiquette than she, and, as he had guessed, she did want to swim. Mermaids were even more tied to the sea than mermen. They normally were only out of the water for a few hours a month of hunting and sex.

So she took what Sato said as an excuse. "Oh yes, forgive us for imposing. We will get out of your hair. Erm, out of your fur. Come along, ladies. Let's go swimming."

The Present: Trick inside Bean There, Froth That, Sausalito

Trick had gotten dressed for work that morning with his own emotional stability in mind. He wanted to look good, because he knew that would make him feel better. He had on a tight, cropped, plaid shirt, oversized black cargos slung low on his bony hips with lots of extra dangling straps from too many pockets. Those straps wiggled becomingly whenever he did. He called it his K-pop boy-band-gone-bad attire. Thus he was playing BTS on the sound system to complement his look.

It was a busy day, but then Fridays always were. Never as busy as Saturdays or Sundays, but enough to keep his mind off *things.* By which he meant *Sato.*

Trick was lucky enough to have weekend help at the Bean. His boss sometimes actually showed up but more importantly there was Joe the part-time high-schooler, full of braces, zits, and ennui. But he was a decent enough worker and he showed up promptly at four on Fridays, which was all Trick could ask of such a creature. It was a bit much that he always had to have a book of terrible poetry in his back pocket. Lately he'd been reciting *Howl* under his breath and that *was* taking teenage angst to an extreme. Even for Trick. Who, as a barista, had a very high tolerance for angst.

By early evening, the front seating area near the big windows was packed with tourists, every table occupied. Floyd and a couple of other regulars sat along the side wall. And the back zone was filling up with crafters, nerds, and lesbians (or all three) because second Friday of the month was Queer Board Game Night.

Ms Trickle arrived unexpectedly.

Trick was pleased to see the kelpie. She was Max's old boss from DURPS and consequently he'd met her at one of their barbecues. He introduced her to Varyenite and the coven of queers at the back, because he thought she was most likely to get along with them. As much as a kelpie can be said to *get along* with anyone.

She ordered a Sea Bream Froth, and lurked in a back corner with an eye on the door, clearly waiting for somebody. Soon, however, she became distracted by the board games and Varyenite. They descended into some deep philosophical conversation about the queer-coded nature of orcs in tabletop RPGs and whether Tolkien could be blamed for this or not.

He left them to it.

Officer Kettil came wandering in next. That was also unexpected. Usually Trick only saw him in the mornings.

"What are you doing here?" he asked, sounding more curt than he meant to.

The bear shifter responded in kind. "I know, right? There's this crowd collected right across the street." He gestured behind him to the window with road, sidewalk, and ocean beyond. Trick squinted against the setting sun. There did seem to be a more-than-usual number of people collected there.

Kettil went on. "Reporters and everything. No permits." He growled.

"What for?"

"Beats me. But it's full of something called vloggers. Most of them female. I need more caffeine to cope." He pouted. "One of them called me an *interfering lascivious lard ball* when I moved her out of oncoming traffic!"

Trick narrowed his eyes, upset on Kettil's behalf. "I suppose you can't arrest somebody for being rude."

Kettil sighed deeply, boulder-like shoulders curving forward. "To be fair, I accidentally touched her ass while I did it. But I really didn't mean to, she was about to get run over!" He grimaced.

"Some crab just crawled up her oyster. Don't fret about it," advised Trick. Once upon a time he would have loved Kettil moving him around by the ass. Once upon a time he would have teased Kettil with just that kind of information. Once upon a time Sato wasn't back. So, yeah.

Kettil made a face. "Must you be crass?"

Trick was about to point out that Kettil went there first, and that it was very gay of a supposedly straight man to be grossed out by accidentally touching female anatomy. Instead, he just gave him a shot of salmon oil with his espresso. The bear shifter looked awfully tired.

"Here you are. Now go sit in the back or something. Stop looming. You're scaring all the customers, big tough berserker like you." He flirted just a little – it was in his nature, after all.

Kettil looked less grumpy. His predator prowess had been praised. "You let Colin hang out here all the time and he's a werewolf."

"Colin is the least threatening werewolf ever to roar at the moon. The kid orders decaf lattes with whipped cream, for goodness' sake."

"*Howl*, you ridiculous creature. Wolves *howl*."

"Whatever."

The bear sighed. "No, I really should go out and deal with whatever nonsense the humans are up to. I hate it when humans get excited. I'm not on the force to deal with humans. I'm only supposed to help with shifters.

"Protect and serve but only in moderation?" suggested Floyd. Who was listening in as usual.

"Do you want me to go check, big guy?" suggested Trick, who admitted to being mildly curious. The weird crowd was right across the street. This kind of thing never happened in Sausalito. He wouldn't mind a little fresh air after all day in the cafe. "Joe can hold down the fort for a bit, can't you, Joe?"

The teenager looked up from refilling the coffee carafe. Gave Trick a baleful look and nonverbal grunt noise. Trick took that as affirmation.

The Present: Sato in the San Francisco Bay, awfully close to Sausalito

The sun set and they had a nice long swim, dining on leopard shark and sea lettuce. The fish in the area were lazy, since there was no resident pod. Easy to catch, especially for Sato. Too easy, because the hunt failed to distract Meymey.

"Let's go back now. I have a date with lesbians," she insisted.

"I hoped you'd forget about it," he admitted.

"I know, but it will be fine, brother."

"I highly doubt that."

"It's your job to be doubtful."

"You realize I will be coming with you?"

"I understand."

They approached Sausalito via the spot where they'd had the initial meeting with the pack. It felt like a lot had happened since then. The sidewalk above, the street beyond, and all the little store fronts on the other side were much busier on a Friday night. The place was lousy with humans, like a completely different town. It made Sato very nervous. Too many two-legs.

They surfaced and moved forward, fighting a strong current.

There were sudden shouts from the sidewalk. People had gathered there, at the top of the shock rock, and were pointing down at them.

Meymey gave a cheery wave.

The excitement got more intense. A few brave humans – or did he mean stupid? – began climbing down the rock-covered embankment toward the water's edge.

Sato wondered what was going on.

He swam a little closer and heard a high-pitched voice say, "That's him! That's the merman!"

There were phones out now. Lots of phones.

There also seemed to be a local news camera crew.

Sato wondered how long they'd been there, trying to spot him.

"I knew this was the best place to wait. The shifter cafe is right behind us," said one of the probable reporters.

"Hello, Mr Merman," another of them yelled, "would you please come and talk to us? You're a local hero."

"You have over three million views on WooTube" yelled someone else from the crowd.

Or my naked ass does, thought Sato.

"Can we interview you?"

"I need to thank you for saving my boy," said a shrill female voice. He supposed that must be the mother.

Meymey was nothing if not amused. "Brother dear, it would appear you are a local celebrity. You have *fans*." She was probably delighted that this was distracting him from her and her plans to go into the city.

"Ignore them," advised Sato, intending to do that himself.

"I don't think they're going to let themselves be ignored. And that cafe behind them is the place I'm supposed to meet the kelpie."

Sato considered. He should distract the group of humans while his sister went to the changing hut. It would be safest that way.

"Fine. You go in. I'll entertain their stupid questions and let them take more pictures and join you shortly. Don't leave for the club without me."

"You really don't have to come. You could just swim away right now. I will be absolutely fine." She knew him too well.

He narrowed his eyes at her. "I'm *your* vangill. I have no idea why you're being so stubborn about this. It is literally in my mandate to stay by your side and protect you when you are on land."

"Suit yourself."

But it didn't suit him at all. "Why are you insisting on going?" he pressed.

"I don't know, but I've never been more curious about anything. This kelpie and her club are fascinating."

"It's a whole different world. Full of danger."

"I know. But also very hot women so I'm doing it anyway." Sato would never have guessed his sister leaned that way. That any mermaid might. Did this kind of thing run in their family?

"You're jeopardizing our mission," he reminded her.

"It will be fine."

"So go do it then, but wait for me before you leave."

She gave him a long look and then fluttered her hands in agreement. Dove down to swim away and resurface near the changing hut. From there she would slip onto shore without being noticed, and dress in one of her cute new thrifted outfits. They'd left them all with the clerk there.

To keep their attention on him, Sato swam closer to the shock rock and the group of humans waiting for him.

They all started asking questions at once.

"Mr Merman, KWYRU radio. What's your intention in rescuing the boy?"

"Mr Merman, Jeff Takke of *Shifter Watch* WooTube channel, four point six million subscribers. Did you mean to cause such a sensation with your lack of attire? Are you planning to pursue a career as an influencer? Have you retained representation?"

One of those gull-like child's voices said, "Mr Merman, I'm Gary, the kid you saved. Ma says I need to say *thank you*. I don't remember you at all but you're very pretty."

Sato said, "You're getting close to the water again, aren't you, kid? I won't bother to pull you out a second time."

"Ooo, he *does* speak!"

"Mr Merman, sir, if I fall in, will you save *me*?" That was a female of some ilk.

"Or me?"

"Or me?"

"Why are you here visiting the Bay Area?"

"What made you rescue the boy?"

Sato scanned the group, wary of threat, uninterested in flirtation or actually answering any of their stupid questions.

There was an ebb and flow to the movement of any crowd. Sato had noticed this before with humans – as a teenager in groups at school and pulling Patrick away from his various parties. Humans had a kind of pod behavior all their own. Different from the symmetry of mermaids swimming together or schools of fish. Humans were more random, less predictable, but they still had a kind of pattern when in a group.

They pressed against each other and then reacted against the group by pulling away. This crowd included a bobbing up and down as the ones at the back attempted to see the famous merman more easily. They were stumbling into each other with words and bodies. As they asked their questions and jockeyed for position, the crowd parted enough for Sato to see the street beyond.

There were a few more people standing there, on tiptoe, trying to see what was going on down at the water's edge. Humans attracted by the enthusiasm and interest of other humans.

Sato locked eyes with one of the curious onlookers standing at the back.

Huge dark eyes the color of deep sea trenches.

Round soft cheeks flushing the color of a conch shell.

In that split second of mutual recognition, he watched Patrick's face lose all its color in horror. A horror that was seeing him.

He watched Patrick, his Patrick, flinch away in real fear.

Watched him turn and run as fast as he could.

Watched a car nearly hit him, slamming on its brakes and horn.

Sato was moving, chasing, hunting, without even thinking about it. His vangill training kicked in. A thousand times he'd practiced that maneuver, because he admired the Navarch's ability. Now he could execute it smoothly. He jettisoned himself out of the water with the strength of his huge tail. He used all its might to propel himself up and forward, converting that tail to legs midair. He cleared the crowd, splashing them with water. He went up and over all their heads, landing in a half crouch on the sidewalk behind them. He bent his knees to take the weight of his human form. Balancing on two legs lightly. On land, he was much less clumsy than a mermaid.

The crowd screamed and scattered behind him. There were splashes as some of them fell off shock rock and into the bay. Some of those on the sidewalk fell to the ground on either side of Sato, shoved out of his way as he landed among them. The sounds of human pain, surprise, and fear were all around him. There was a shriek of car brakes, and the ominous crunch of vehicles hitting each other.

Sato didn't care about any of it.

Patrick.

He pushed through what was left of the bystanders. Dodged around the fender bender blocking the road.

Focused only on Patrick's figure.

Patrick who was running *away* from him.

CHAPTER THIRTEEN

THE IMPERFECT STORM

The Past: Trick's Memories

That one summer before Sato obeyed the vangill summons had been three weeks of bliss a million years ago when Trick was still a child.

Utterly forgotten.

And yet, too often when Trick was sleeping alone in his car on the side of some abandoned road, he thought he could remember every single second of it.

If he tried.

Sometimes, to his shame, he did try.

Because it had been a rosy, sand-saturated, salt-encrusted three weeks of perfect teenage romance. He had been incandescently happy in that way that only the young can be happy. Or maybe that was Sato's magic. Patrick's best and last protector. His greatest champion.

Trick *tried* not to remember that one winter break, when Sato came home from vangill training for the last time. When Sato had used his spurs on a human on land. Sato, who had grown up and changed, but was still very much *his*.

At his worst and most maudlin, Trick might have said *his great love*. When the hunger gnawed at him, when he thought his family might actually find him, when he thought he'd never make it to the West Coast. The place he needed to get to so desperately for no other reason than it meant that he and Sato would be swimming in the same ocean once again.

But who falls in love forever when they're fifteen, anyway?

At seventeen Sato got that break from vangill training and came to visit and they twisted around each other in sheets and sand and sea, like there was no better thing than to share thoughts and flesh and dreams.

But after that? Sato did not come back. For all their promises.

Patrick graduated high school top of his class but Sato did not know because Sato did not come for him. He was supposed to be a free merman by then. Done with the vangill. Done with training.

Three years served for his spurs, duty discharged.

Yet Sato did not return.

Sato and Patrick did not get to swim off into the sunrise together as they'd planned. To the East Coast where Patrick had earned a scholarship to a small artsy college. A scholarship Patrick never used and a college he never even visited. They didn't rent that little off-campus apartment together. Sato didn't get that job with the Coast Guard. He never cooked his sire's katsu recipe for Patrick on the weekends.

Patrick got none of the things that meant love continued eternal.

He got empty beaches and the silence of a vast ocean and the mystery of the Deep. His first love had been swallowed whole without a trace.

He got forgotten affection and the bitterness of foolish childish dreams that were doomed never to come true. How had he not been more guarded? Why had he always let Sato be the guarded one and the one to guard?

He waited past the time he should have gone away to college. He waited while Veronica left him to become an electrician (of all things) and his phone left him to become a brick (there was cheesecake involved – don't ask).

He watched Mr Sato waste away suddenly and rapidly, eaten

up from the inside by, as the man said, *just a touch of cancer*. Patrick knew he had really been eaten away by waiting for his own great love to return, and then for the son he hadn't wanted but waited for anyway.

Mr Sato got tired of waiting and died.

So Patrick was stuck waiting alone in Mr Sato's house, full of memories. Until the landlord noticed and claimed it back. Sooner than he'd hoped.

Then he had to wait in his parents' house. Not very long at all because in a fit of late night horror and self-recrimination, Patrick noticed his family and what they'd been doing. While he'd been distracted by Sato and the sea, cafes and drama clubs, college and impossible futures, his family had moved from trading in moonshine and information to trading in cocaine and antiquities, to trading in heroine and human children.

Which meant Patrick couldn't wait any longer.

He found himself suddenly in motion, in his old beater of a station wagon that he'd paid for with money earned at the cafe. Money that should have gone to college expenses and a new phone. A station wagon that wasn't heading to university, filled with his meager belongings and his vast wardrobe and Sato's sarcastic opinion on the excessive nature of both.

Instead it was filled with scared human children who spoke a language Patrick did not. In the seat next to him sat a teenage girl with terrified dark eyes who spoke a little of both tongues but wasn't sarcastic at all. A girl who was scared of him because he was male. A girl who wasn't Sato.

Patrick could no longer afford to wait.

Because Patrick was not Sato's dad, to measure out his days with the rhythm of a fickle sea, lost to reality.

Sato would have to chase Patrick this time.

But first Patrick would be chased by his own family, three bent cops, and an extremely nasty gang of overly tattooed humans.

Because Patrick had to make his way to places where scared human children would not be turned into profit. Patrick had to learn quickly the right shifters to trust, the right human institutions to consult, and how to escape when his guesses were wrong. Patrick had to learn how to lie. Lie like his family did, lie like he was born to it. Because he was. He had to learn to deceive and avoid trumped-up charges and out-of-state warrants. He had to become slippery like the otter he truly was. He had to survive on his wits and his instincts. Turned out, in the end, he had plenty of both.

He got those kids out.

But Sato didn't chase him because Sato never found him.

So Patrick worked his way slowly and secretly across the country to LA because that sounded like a good place to get lost. And because LA was truly terrible, he eventually dragged what was left of his car and the very last of his cash up Highway 1, ending up in a bougie little coastal town, slinging coffee for tourists and fish-sauce lattes for locals. Because Patrick, it turned out, only really had two life skills – he was a killer barista and he could survive.

Even though he had made it, finally, to the edge of the correct ocean, Sato still wasn't there.

So Patrick Inis changed his name to Trick (no last name, no DURPS registration) and stopped waiting. He stopped trusting in the one thing he had trusted completely. And he learned how to be unsafe.

Because no one gets to keep their first love.

Apparently, the merfolk wanted Sato and cared not one jot for what Patrick wanted, or worse, what Patrick loved.

Who was he to fight the ocean?

What the sea decided to keep, it keeps forever.

The Past: Sato in Kealakekua Bay, heading home to Patrick

Sato was destined to remember little of his years spent training to be a vangill, except the very end.

Oddly, he remembered that ending only because of the

Navarch. His merman trainer had surprised him. Sato didn't surprise easily. That austere presence, that strict disciplinarian, had been nothing if not predictable.

The Navarch had been proud of Sato in his way. Because when Sato returned to him after his last visit home, he was not only able to control his spurs, he was able to use those spurs on land. Sato had done something no other vangill did, chosen an anchor for himself.

It meant Sato would be famous among the vangill. The Navarch's best student. One of the few who could fight on land and sea. Being able to control spurs at all was one thing, but using them in human form? That only happened once a generation.

The Navarch was *proud* of him.

Sato found that very weird and slightly exhausting. Expectations annoyed him.

But when their training was completed and assignments were passed out, the Navarch's pride was shaken. It turned out, Sato had more hidden spurs, the kind that cut with words and decisions. The kind that made even a merman like the Navarch bleed.

Because Sato refused his vangill assignment. "Three years the Deep demanded of me. I gave them to you. I am grateful for your expert training, for I am now a danger to all those around me. I always wanted to be dangerous."

"But you could be the greatest of us."

"No, thank you."

The Navarch licked his lips, confused. "Where will you go?"

"Back to my sire's town. Back to dry land."

"You like it better there?"

"No. I paid three years of penance specifically so the sea would not reject me. I intend never to be a stranger to any ocean. But what I *want* isn't sea-bound."

"What about the children you could sire? What about the next generation?" There was something funny about the Navarch's face as he said that.

"What about them?" Sato asked.

"Will you offer stud services? Accept mermaid visitors? For the good of the species?"

Sato sighed, annoyed and tired of hiding this part. It didn't matter any more. They were all going their separate ways now. He had nothing left to prove.

"No."

The Navarch shook his head, confused and frustrated. "You intend to be faithful to that human girlfriend the others accused you of having all these years?"

Sato laughed. "The one I talk to on the phone that they have never seen? I half expected Nix to follow me home last time. He was *that* curious."

The Navarch was also curious. "So, she exists?"

"Do you need to know?"

"I'm losing my top student. I don't deserve to know the reason for that? Were you taken in by the idea of human romantic love? You don't seem the type. Why did you obey the vangill summons, if you never intended to stay with us and fulfill your fated role? Why did you really use us, use me, for training? That's never happened before. I've never trained a vangill only to have him take his skills elsewhere. Let alone to the surface. Who will you protect, if not your own kind? And why do you so desperately want to protect them?"

Three years and someone had finally asked Sato the *right* question. "There's this boy. He shines."

"A boy." The Navarch did not seem shocked.

"You guessed?"

"You've always been very careful with your pronouns."

Sato fluttered his hands in agreement. "If I can't have *both* Patrick and the sea, I choose Patrick."

"So said with all the confidence of youth."

Sato recognized something in the Navarch then. A wistful bitterness. The reason the Navarch had seemed to like him from the start. The reason the Navarch had always been on his side. And that was what had surprised Sato. That was what he remembered even years later.

"You never took the risk yourself, did you?" Sato asked.

Silence.

Sato understood. The Navarch hadn't found his Patrick. "You never had the opportunity."

The Navarch looked away. "You're perceptive. I'd never have guessed."

"Just because I don't say much doesn't mean I don't see anything." Sato thought maybe he could only see queer in other mermen. Patrick had said Sato had *terrible gaydar*, but maybe that's because Sato had the sonar version.

The Navarch flicked his tail behind him, sending a spray into the air, converting water into rainbows. "Like you, it would have been a man."

"Have you sired children?" Sato wondered.

"That would have been embarrassing for everyone involved."

"So you hide and pay penance by teaching the next generation of vangill?"

"How did this become a conversation about my past instead of your future?"

Sato fluttered his fins, rising up a little out of the water, a dominance play. Showing the full force of his lineage scales. A luster that he would fail to pass along to the next generation. "Come visit us sometime, Navarch. My Patrick will know everyone in the local scene. He'll introduce you to a nice boy." He paused, "Or a not so nice one, if that's your preference."

The Navarch actually laughed. "Maybe I'll do that."

"You'll let me go then?"

The Navarch flicked his hands in sharp agreement and dismissal. "I'll let you go."

The Navarch was strong enough. One of the few who could have stopped Sato. But they both knew that he was letting Sato go because Sato was going to have the life that he couldn't. His pride in his best student would have to stretch beyond vangill abilities and into spaces he had never had the courage to go himself. He would stay proud of Sato, but for different reasons.

So it wasn't the Navarch who kept Sato from returning to Patrick on time.

And it wasn't the vangill.

And it wasn't the sea.

In the end, it was the land that thwarted him.

The humans reported it as an earthquake measuring 7.5 on the Richter Scale. It struck the ocean floor off the Aleutian Islands. Waves traveled across the Pacific at 500 miles an hour, measuring 55 feet high.

Sometimes the earth really could impact the sea.

A local mermaid pod surfed those waves, excited by the opportunity for rapid transit. They also siren-sang a warning from one pod to the next. Faster than the waves. The vangill, who were preparing to depart Hawaii, off to their new assignments, heard about the tsunami shortly before it hit.

"It's coming for us? Here?" said Nix.

"I'm not battling that current," said Rus. "Let's wait it out."

The Navarch addressed the group, "This is an opportunity. The humans are never prepared for tsunamis. They're trying, but they won't be able to evacuate Hilo in time."

"What's that to us?" asked Nix.

"Did you forget? Mermen are the liaisons to the human world. You spent years with your sires, learning their cultures. This is why. Local Coast Guard has asked for our help. We'll be on rescue and retrieval."

"Seriously?" grumbled Rus.

"They knew we were training here?" asked someone else.

Sato looked out at the ocean. It was deceptively calm.

"They call it *humanitarian aid*." The Navarch was openly amused by the term. "We call it *a favor owed*. The tsunami will be here soon. Take to the Deep and float it out well below the surface. I'll meet you at the fourth reef break at sunset, when it's all over."

Sato said, "I will not be meeting you then or there. I'm leaving."

The others looked like they would like to follow his lead.

"Stay, please, Sato. You're the strongest of us." The Navarch humbled himself.

Sato turned back. "This would satisfy any and all remaining obligations I have to you or the Deep?"

The Navarch looked uncomfortable. "The humans need our help." But that was not the point.

Sato was persistent. "The Deep will not make demands upon me ever again?"

"You know the Two Recalls that require you to return no matter what?"

They applied to all mermen but specifically to vangill, so of course he knew. "War and natural disaster."

"Is this not the second?" suggested the Navarch.

"Don't play games, old fish, that means a *disaster* affecting mermaids, not humans."

The Navarch inclined his head. Sato had won that round.

So Sato pressed his luck. "Apart from the Two, I will never be called back after this?"

The Navarch blew out air in a rush, like a whale. "Agreed. You have my word."

So Sato and the vangill spent three days pulling humans, injured and drowning, out of the brink. Sato pushed himself like he never had before, and thus he rescued the most two-legs. When he could, he took to land to try calling Patrick, but the phones were down or busy or washed away. Disaster conditions, the humans called it. Typical of them, their own infrastructure failed when they needed it most.

Then Sato and the vangill spent two weeks searching the nearby Pacific for sailboats and yachts off course. Sato found an adrift cruise ship. Blights on the ocean caused by the human inability to stick to the land where they belonged. He still couldn't get hold of Patrick. Or his sire. When he managed to get through on a phone, neither answered. Patrick's cell rang forever and his sire's landline said mechanically that it no longer existed. Sire had likely forgotten to pay the bill. Again. It's possible they both had.

Sato and the vangill spent another week helping with a coastal rebuild and reclamation, pulling out human objects and sparkles and bodies. All things that the humans, for some reason, treasured and wanted back.

Sato stayed because Patrick would have wanted him to help.

Patrick cared about such things, and Sato wasn't a monster, not really. He assumed Patrick would set off on his own, to plan, and Sato would simply catch up. He stayed because the Navarch asked him. He stayed because the humans would owe him forever because of it.

The humans calculated later that the unexpected assistance of thirteen highly trained mermen had probably saved over two hundred human lives, over a dozen ships, and millions in rebuilding costs. That last bit was probably what they valued most.

There was an awards ceremony. Where, exactly, did one pin a metal on a naked merman chest? And what were they supposed to do with their silly little metal medals afterward? (Mermen always went scaled to televised events, which meant the humans had to accommodate them with a pontoon stage. It was awkward for everyone.)

Sato did not attend. Metal? In the sea? Ridiculous. He was missed. He had made a big impression.

The real end result was that the humans owed the merfolk in a big way. And Sato was six weeks late getting back to Patrick.

He wasn't worried. Patrick would have left his new address with Sato's sire. Sato would swim back to his sire's house, say goodbye, and then swim around Florida and up the East Coast to Patrick.

Sato did get back home eventually – if that tiny human delta town could be called *home*. Only to find his sire dead and Patrick gone. There were strange humans in his sire's house and no address left behind. There were strange humans in Patrick's house too, also without an address. Patrick's family had vanished. Moved on to plague some other delta town.

The neighborhood was sleepy and quiet without them.

Sato went and asked at the cafe about the cute barista who'd once been in charge there. What had happened to him?

Apparently, he'd vanished amidst rumors of human trafficking. Sato had sneered. Who would want to trade in humans? There were so many of them – wasn't that like trying to sell sand to a mermaid? But it did sound like something Patrick would try to fix. It certainly one-upped his own rescuing of humans from tsunamis. If Patrick hadn't made it to college like he was supposed to, it would be because he got into trouble and had to run away, just like always.

Sato heard tall tales of old station wagons and black market ill-fated cheesecake. (Why cheesecake, he had absolutely no idea, but that was classic Patrick.) The rumors were rife, as they are wont to be when someone disappears. And then a whole family vanishes. And then three local cops are done for corruption. And the mayor retires amidst scandal.

But no one knew where Patrick had gone.

He called Patrick's number for months, until it went from unanswered to *no longer in service* to some stranger's voice that Sato hated for not being Patrick.

Sato spent four years looking for Patrick and nothing else. Forgetting to eat sometimes. Driven back to the sea only to hunt and swim and search there, in other deltas, along other beaches, for one small otter.

Sato spent a year searching for every week he'd been delayed. Paying penance for having abandoned his lover to all the sewage that rushed to fill Patrick's life without Sato there to protect him from it.

But Patrick, his Patrick, who sparkled like the sun off scales. His tiny chatterbox with the fathomless gaze. His favorite person. His only person. Patrick had just... vanished. Disappeared into the human world, hidden himself in the dry infinity of the salt-less earth. Patrick was running down dusty pathways that Sato did not understand and going places where Sato could not follow.

Sato had only ever existed on land because Patrick made room for him there. Sato had never understood hugs, only accepted them. Sato had eaten catfish katsu because humans cooked fish, not because he liked it that way. Sato could not wander the world of men asking after the direction of fathomless eyes and chatterbox smiles. There was only nonsense above the waves without Patrick to interpret it for him.

How could he possibly find Patrick, when Patrick had always been his guide?

Still, Sato would have stayed searching, for all he did not know the way to navigate any part of it. Except the only other thing he'd ever cared about called him back to the ocean. And he was so lost and tired and alone by then, he answered the call.

His sister was to become the Paralia of All Seas, the envoy between merfolk and mankind, one of the Soteria of the Deep. She was in need of a vangill. Sato was overqualified for the job. She would be a diplomat, a land-walker, and her brother, who had spurs in both worlds, was the perfect bodyguard.

That brother vowed to use this new role to keep looking for the dobhar-chú he had lost. Keep asking, using any favor he earned as vangill and bodyguard, using all the power his sister allowed him.

But no one he met had ever heard of Patrick Inis. Few even knew the dobhar-chú existed at all.

An otter who does not want to be found, can't be.

Patrick had been swallowed by the earth as surely as Sato was once swallowed by the sea. They had, somehow, managed to abandon each other.

Sometimes, it turns out, what the land decides to keep, it keeps forever.

CHAPTER FOURTEEN
SHALLOW WATERS
RUN FAST

The Present: Trick in Sausalito confronting his past

Sato.

Right there in front of him. Staring at him.

Sato.

A flock of fire-breathing dragonflies was beating wings in Trick's brain. They beat their way down, circling and floating into his throat and from there to his stomach. His gut filled with that beating heat which made him want to throw up.

What he did was run.

He ran, cursing his own curiosity. He rarely bothered to leave the cafe. But with Joe on shift and Kettil's desperate eyes, it had been all too easy to just nip out and see what was happening.

Of course, because this was the way his bad luck worked, there was Sato in the water. Sato's dark eyes found him, focused, held him briefly captive. Recognized him. Of course they did. Filled with desperate, delighted hope. Which *terrified* Trick. Because how could he trust that again? Because how dare he want that? How could he withstand the weight of it a second time?

He knew, because of the noise and the chaos and the tremendous splash behind him, that Sato had left the water to follow him on two legs.

Trick had only his instincts to run on. So he ran on them. Well, and his own two legs, of course. They took him back to the cafe, shaky knees and fire-breathing dragonflies in his stomach. Because the Bean was his territory, his safe place.

Kettil, big lug, was standing where Trick had left him, taking up too much space, decidedly in Trick's way.

Trick dodged around him – or tried to.

Being a cop, Deputy Kettil was focused on the car accident and chaos outside in the street. He wanted answers.

He simply grabbed Trick by the scruff of his neck. One huge hand could easily fit all the way around it. "What's going on?" he demanded in his cop voice.

"Let me go!" whimpered Trick. "Please!"

But it was too late. Sato was bursting in behind him, the cheerful bells clanging unhappily at the force of it. The merman was naked, wet, and glorious. Looking exactly like he had a decade ago and also not looking like it at all. His human skin was paler. He probably didn't spend as much time in the sun on two legs anymore. He was just as muscled as the last time Patrick had seen him, on break from vangill training. His hair was longer, wet strands sticking to his neck.

Behind him the humans were yelling at each other and slamming car doors, waving their hands wildly. Beyond that, there was screaming down by the shore. Friday night lookie-loos had stopped to stare, some with phones out, others just mouths agape.

Sausalito hadn't seen this much action since the selkies and the werewolf country music superstar visited town. And that had been comparatively tame.

A group of reporters was trying to cross through the accident to the cafe.

Trick clocked it all in one brief glance and then his gaze was sucked back to Sato. He struggled hard against Kettil's grip.

But Kettil was a bear shifter and a cop. There was no way Trick was getting free until Deputy Kettil decided to let him go.

"What are you made of, concrete?" Trick demanded.

"What is going on?" Kettil's deep booming voice filled up the entire cafe.

This resulted in dead silence in the Bean.

The tourists at the front tables were riveted, mostly by Sato's naked ass.

No doubt the locals and the gamers at the back were also standing up to see the kerfuffle in the front.

"Shifters are required to wear publicly appropriate attire," said Kettil to Sato. "Anyone got a robe handy?"

Sato ignored him, rushing up to stand directly in front of Trick, taking his face in both webbed hands. "Trick, baby, you're here."

Trick shook his head violently, shook himself violently, desperate to get free of both the bear and the merman.

"Don't touch me!" he yelled. Sato first. He used Kettil to lever himself back, kicking forward at the merman with both feet. Thus realizing he could kick, he also kicked backward at Kettil's legs. It was ineffectual. Oh, he bashed the bear shifter's shins, but Kettil didn't even flinch.

Trick shook his head again. Sato's hands were still on him – damp and cool. Trick hated the familiar feel of the soft webbing between Sato's fingers, the slightly slick rubbery texture. He hated the salt-sweet smell of Sato himself. How dare he smell exactly the same! This was a different ocean and a decade later. Yet Sato smelled the *same!* He smelled like home and safety and things Trick had worked so damn hard to forget. He smelled like Patrick's Sato, but here, in this place there was no Patrick, there was only Trick, and there had never ever been a Sato. But that smell took him back, and he was *Patrick* again, and that made Trick so scared. Scared. Scared!

He didn't want to be Patrick and unsafe and lonely and abandoned and hungry and running all the time. He wanted to be charming Trick who everyone liked and no one really loved. Patrick was scared and hurt. Trick was the survivor.

He turned his head to where Kettil was holding him near his

neck, went chin down and over, and bit down as hard as he could.

"Fuck, he bit me!" exclaimed the cop. Still not letting go.

No one was listening to him. Trick *needed* to get away.

A beautiful woman in a cute ruffled dress with a mouth shaped like Sato's said, "What's going on? Daidai, you were the one who said we had to have clothing when walking among humans. Now you're naked and annoying them."

"Oh, don't worry yourself about that, young lady," said a blue-cardiganed grandma type from the corner window table. "We're fine with whatever he wants to wear. Especially if it's nothing."

Kettil's attention was drawn from her to the window beyond and what was going on outside. "Damn it, the drivers are actually fighting now."

The doorbells tinkled and a group of reporters pushed in, cameras and phones out.

There were so many people, all of them staring at Trick and Sato – his hands now on Trick's shoulders, well out of biting distance. And Kettil would still not let go, even while his arm bled.

But Trick wasn't really aware of the deputy anymore because Sato was right there, staring at him and smelling like the past. All of Trick's body had gone numb now except the spots where Sato's cool hands touched him.

There was a crash at the back of the cafe.

A female voice shouted, "What the hell is going on?"

It was a voice that Trick knew but couldn't name because his ears were buzzing and there was a horrible taste of bear blood in his mouth.

Sato glanced up and then instantly back, his eyes fixed on Trick. "Stay the fuck out of this, kelpie. You too, Meymey. This has nothing to do with either of you."

The beautiful woman, no... mermaid, said, truly shocked, "You speak to me in such a tone of voice, brother? Me?"

But Sato clearly had no more time for her – all his focus only on Trick. "You were here? How long have you been here? Why didn't you *wait* for me? Why were you so hard to find?"

Sato, who rarely ever said anything, the words were pouring out of him. Crashing over Trick, relentless as a tidal wave.

Trick turned his head the other direction and bit Kettil's arm again, this time near the wrist. He bit down as hard as he could, not letting go this time. Desperate to be free.

Sato followed the movement. Seemed to finally really register that Kettil had hold of him. That Trick hadn't simply stopped to talk. "Let him go," he demanded of Kettil. "Who are you to hold him like that? Why do you touch him like he is yours? Let go!"

Sato's webbed hands began clawing at the bear's arms.

Kettil only growled at Sato and tightened his grip. Too tight, he was too strong. It hurt.

Trick hurt. His teeth hurt. The blood in his mouth hurt. His head hurt. His heart hurt. His fucking eyeballs hurt, staring at Sato, cataloging his muscles, his changes, his sameness. Even his stupid nose hurt from the familiar smell. The dragonflies were breathing fire and his gut burned.

Trick said, not to Sato, of course, just to anybody. Just in utter frustration at being too small and too weak. "Get him off me!"

And then Sato became dangerous. What had seemed absurd and unthreatening and sexy, a naked merman, not so big a deal for a town that dealt regularly with werewolves. Suddenly that naked merman had huge spurs sprouting up both forearms from wrist to elbow. Rows of cruel-looking curved spikes, sharp bone-colored thorns, razor-edged and wicked. Like massive teeth.

Sato lunged at Kettil. Those spurs going for the bear's sides. Normally Sato would have gone straight for Kettil's throat, or slashed at those arms holding Trick. But Kettil held Trick in front of him. Sato would never risk cutting Trick – better to go for the cop's unprotected ribs.

It probably saved Deputy Kettil's life.

It certainly saved him from severe injury.

But he was still pretty badly hurt. Wide red punctures opened up, quickly soaking his uniform.

Kettil had his own training and there was no way he was holding on to a small shifter he knew was harmless, when a weaponized unknown creature was suddenly attacking him.

He let Trick go, massive arms up in guard position, ready to defend himself.

Trick, who had been pulling away as hard as he could, stumbled to one side at sudden freedom and fell to the ground. He tried to stand up, slipped, and fell again. Banging his chin on a chair and seeing stars.

Instinctively, Kettil shifted into his bear form, both for protection and to help himself heal. He was even bigger as a bear and the Bean suddenly seemed incredibly small. Several humans ran screaming from the cafe. The film crew dodged but kept their camera and phone focused on the action.

The bear lurched at Sato, narrowly missed stepping on Trick.

Trick rolled to get away but Sato was fast and trained. He got his spurs in the way first, the bear's momentum partly skewering him on them. Sato using his own body to shield Trick from injury.

Sato grunted from the sheer force and weight of the bear.

Kettil lurched off the spurs, undaunted. His bear form had an extra layer of fat for protection and he healed incredibly fast. Plus there was a reason bears were also called berserkers – they retained even less human logic in battle than other shifters.

Sato and Kettil crashed together again.

Trick climbed to his feet and didn't stay. He didn't care. He was free.

There were too many reporters and humans blocking the front door now. Plus all the chaos in the street. The blare of sirens as more cops arrived. Sausalito Police Department saw very little action. This was all quite exciting for them.

Trick headed for the back of the cafe, pushing through the regulars, standing defensively with craning necks. Like a gaggle of confused but brave turkeys.

Floyd's worried face swam before him. "Trick, kid, you okay?" He was holding his knitting needles up like weapons.

Trick shoved past him.

The human lesbian was there with the kelpie and the board game queers. Trick vaguely realized he knew all of them and that they were kind with familiar faces. Faces that had names, but he didn't remember any of them right now. While most of them were friendly, none of them were safe. There was only the roaring in his head, bear blood in his mouth, Sato's desperate face, and dragonflies in his gut. The need to flee.

Trick pushed through all those worried faces and frozen bodies, and into the stockroom, and out the back of the building. He froze for a second, there in the parking lot. Fresh salt air around him. What to do now? Where to go? His otter self wanted water. The dratsie wanted cold, rushing rivers, muddy banks, and slippery, round rocks. A different country. A different time. Trick thought briefly of the ocean. But he could not go to the sea. He was a river otter. The sea was Sato's domain, the merman's world. Patrick was only a visitor. Sato could easily catch him in the ocean.

There were no rushing rivers nearby.

Where else could he run? Where else was safe?

The cafe behind was now a prison.

Where to go?

In that moment, much to his own shock, Trick thought of the pack. Surprising himself with trust.

He thought of a sunken den full of scratch-resistant leather couches and werewolves. Colin's red head bent over a laptop. Lovejoy humming as he puttered about the kitchen. An over-grown yard full of barbecues. Alec's kind hazel eyes. He thought of the neighbor's tuxedo cat who had recently decided that cats owned all things, including werewolves. She had delivered a dead mouse to their doorstep. She liked Trick. She let him scratch her cheeks.

He remembered his rundown station wagon in the garage. The one that had carried him across the country, limping, but reliable. The one that smelled only like him. His old home parked in his new home.

So Trick ran through the streets of Sausalito, heading uphill, away from the water and toward the San Andreas pack house. He had nowhere else to go.

The Present: Sato in Sausalito confronting Patrick's present

Sato had suspected, this trip, he might have to go up against a werewolf, but he hadn't had a bear shifter on the list of probabilities. Certainly not a bear in a small cafe crowded with tourists, reporters, and other shifters. Everyone was tripping over everything and everyone else in an effort to get away from that bear – once it started roaring and bleeding.

Bleeding because of Sato.

Which was quite satisfying.

Sato was no match for most land shifters, but it turned out his training had given him more speed than this bear shifter, at least. But fuck, the creature was strong.

Sato managed to dodge most of the hits, getting in long, cruel slashes whenever he could. But the bear had tons of thick fur and pretty good natural defenses. Mostly what Sato was managing to do was give him an extremely ugly haircut.

He got in a few jabs, and the creature was still bleeding a little from Sato's initial attack, but it was clear those first successful strikes had been a matter of surprise and luck, and both had now run out.

The bear had been understandably surprised by the razor sting of spurs, and then angry, and was now a better fighter than Sato, even if the bear was only operating on animal instinct. All he needed to do was to land one solid hit with all his weight behind it, and Sato was a goner.

Which is exactly what he did.

The bear caught Sato across his right ribs and sent him flying to one side, hard. He hit the news camera and the cameraman behind it, and then a table, the sad wet crunch of his own ribs echoing in his head. Landing hard on that table also knocked the wind out of him. Or maybe that was just the ribs.

Sato lay, shocked and in terrible pain for a moment. He tried first to catch his breath and then to inhale against the sharp shooting burning all over his left side and back. Ribs. Broken, fractured, or thrown out, he didn't know which – probably all three. Stupid fragile human body. He needed his merform to heal from this, but there was no way he was going back to the sea, not when he had *finally* found Patrick.

Patrick! Where was he?

Meymey was leaning over him, pretty face full of shock. "Daidai, are you alright? What's going on? Who is that boy? Why are you fighting a bear? Why are you freaking out over a barista?"

The bear loomed behind her, coming after Sato. He shoved Meymey away, hard.

"Stay back!" Sato managed to cough out the words.

Meymey gave a little shriek and stumbled into the pastry case.

Sato rolled off the table as the bear crashed both massive front paws down on it. It cracked in two.

His sister, little idiot, would *not* stay out of the way. She was suddenly there and seemed to be trying to get between him and the bear.

Sato barely made it to his feet, trying to interpose himself between her and the massive creature. Protect his sister. Protect the Paralia of the Deep. Training.

What the hell was she doing? "Meymey, get away!"

Then he realized that Meymey was trying to meet the bear's gaze so that she could freeze him. Medusa power. One of the mermaid's bag of supernatural tricks, used for protection and seduction.

She might have been equally effective with siren song – that tended to cause land shifters with sensitive hearing to bleed out the ears. But Meymey wouldn't be accustomed to using her song as a defensive mechanism, so she had reached for her other ability, the stoney stare.

It must have looked very strange. Sato trying to engage the bear with his spurs, dodging and slashing, knocking over tables and chairs and tourists and reporters. His sister ducking her head in between the fighters in order to meet that same bear's eyes. This was proving especially hard for her to do, since the bear had a huge, fuzzy face and small, beady, close-set eyes right in the middle of it.

Finally, she caught the creature's gaze.

Fortunately, her power seemed to work on bear shifters, because he froze. She held him in thrall, locked in place.

Sato straightened up, feeling the adrenaline leave his system, forcing him to register the agony in his ribs and the difficulty of breathing. Refusing to let his spurs retract, he looked for Patrick, just in time to see him slipping away through a door marked *staff only* at the very back of the cafe.

Taking short sips of air in an effort to control the pain, Sato dodged around the now frozen bear, intent only on following Patrick.

A frail, elderly human man made a weak effort at attacking Sato with some kind of long pointy silver... *chopsticks* maybe?

"Careful, Floyd!"

Sato brushed the chopsticks aside, snapping one with a twist of his spurs.

"My favorite needle! Get him, Rosie!"

A large human female with shaved sides of her head chucked a very hard pastry at him.

"What good is a scone at a time like this?"

"Scones are the real weapons!"

Someone else drenched Sato in a sticky coffee drink of some kind.

Sato barely registered.

He homed in on the big female kelpie from the night before, there to meet Meymey. She was standing and watching him, but she seemed intent on staying out of the altercation, which was a relief.

The door marked *staff only* led to a dark stockroom.

Patrick was not hiding there.

The heavy bang of another door betrayed his whereabouts.

Sato ran after him, brushing people out of his way with his spurs. Not caring if they cut, kind of liking it because they were between him and Patrick. He burst outside into a back parking lot and dim evening light in time to see Patrick's small lithe form running away, diving into some bushes on the far side.

Sato didn't waste his breath shouting. He needed all of his diminished lung capacity just to breathe through the pain in his side and back. It was incredibly difficult to run and he seemed to be bleeding down one leg where bear claws had caught him, but he couldn't let Patrick out of his sight. Not again.

Never again.

So Sato chased the dratsie through Sausalito. Through yards and up busy streets. He must have made quite the spectacle. The humans were less in awe of him than he might've hoped. He still had his spurs out, but he was naked, bleeding, limping, and puffing. So he shouldn't be offended that they regarded him as some kind of crazy person and not an actual threat. No one cleared out of his way. He had to dodge through and around groups of tourists, dating couples, and gaggles of teenagers, avoiding cars driving the street and trying to park, badly.

Why were there so many humans? Why were they in his way? Why were they between him and Patrick? Why was Patrick so good at running through them?

Sato put on a burst of speed, just to keep Patrick in his line of sight.

Luckily, Patrick seemed intent on leaving the downtown area and most of humanity, eventually running up a much less crowded residential back street. The operative word being *up*.

Now Sato could see him clearly, but they were heading up an extremely steep hill, and Sato had a broken rib or two.

Patrick didn't slow, just kept speeding up that seemingly endless hill. Mountain? Eventually he veered to one side, leaving the road for a driveway.

Sato had managed to close the gap a little. He followed Patrick down the drive into a big circular parking area with a garage on one side. The lot was edged by steep, overgrown hills, down on the left and up to the right. There was a pathway through those trees down the left side, presumably leading to the massive house perched on the hill below. The parking lot was above the house. Strange arrangement.

Patrick paused, clearly undecided as to whether he should hide in the overgrowth, or head for the house, or go for the garage, which was closest.

That was his mistake, because he also looked back to see if he had been followed. Only then realizing that Sato was *right* there. Because Sato hadn't had the breath to yell, Patrick hadn't realized his proximity.

Sato grabbed him from behind in a hug, holding him as close as he could, both arms around his waist. Careful with his spurs – the last thing he ever wanted to do was hurt Patrick.

Patrick struggled against him. His breath short and panting. His familiar voice was wracked with stress and fear. "Just leave me alone."

Sato held on as gently as he could, trying to turn a prison into a cradle. Trying to impart warmth and reassurance rather than threat.

If Patrick had kicked back at Sato's knee, as Sato had once taught him, he probably would've hit him right near where the bear had slashed him open with those claws.

But Patrick didn't.

If he had reached back and twisted Sato over one hip in that old wrestling move, Sato would have been flattened out, for all he weighed twice as much.

Immobilized, hugged, Patrick just slumped forward. Forcing Sato to use some of his fading strength to keep them both upright. Mermen were built for speed, not endurance.

"Why are you still so light? Don't they feed you in this town?"

"Sato-san, get off me!" Patrick braced himself, his slight form stiffened. Stabilized and grounded.

Sato rested his chin gently on Patrick's shoulder. Exhausted. Just so relieved to have him there in his arms. Yes, he hurt, but that pain was somewhat dissipated by an odd fissure of sensation that wasn't adrenaline. What was that? Happiness?

"Am I. Too heavy?" Sato asked. Feeling numb from his injuries, but also not numb at all for the first time in years.

Patrick stamped his foot. "You always think of me as weak."

Sato relaxed, gave him his weight.

Patrick whimpered.

That sound made all of Sato's injuries hurt more.

"What are you so damn heavy? And you're freezing cold."

"Well. I am. Naked," admitted Sato, although he might also be going into shock.

Patrick yelled then, loudly. Top of his voice, "Pack!"

Sato said, still short of breath. "Why. Call. Others? Why. Running? From *me?*"

Patrick said, voice low and trembling, "I called for werewolves. A lot of them. They aren't gonna like it if they find you holding me against my will. Just let me put you down."

"Why. Against your. Will? I've been looking. For you. For so long. Just. Let me. Rest. Here."

"No. Let go!"

But Sato's arms had already dropped, not much strength left in them. Patrick could have easily twisted away.

Sato closed his eyes and pressed his forehead into the curve where Patrick's neck met his shoulder. "I just. Found you. Again. Why. Would I. Let go? Patrick. It's *me.*"

"My pack isn't going to like this."

"Your pack? Since when. Did you get. A pack?"

"Since you left me behind!" Patrick's voice was all high-pitched agony.

A deep voice reverberated around them then. "So who's this, draped over our boy?"

A huge redheaded man wearing very little clothing emerged from the path down to the house.

Sato bristled and straightened. He tried not to appear weak, with his cracked ribs and a slashed leg, bear-marked and broken. But he remained leaning on Patrick a little, for support. And connection.

Trick said. "Hi, Kevin. Little help?"

Sato glared at the man who was, to be fair, quite a bit bigger than him and most likely a werewolf.

Even with his spurs, Sato knew he was no match for this person. He had barely survived the bear and this one moved like a warrior. Like a vangill. Or the werewolf equivalent of a vangill. What were they called? Oh yes, enforcers. Sato was definitely at a disadvantage.

The werewolf named Kevin said, "He doesn't look very dangerous. Do you want me to shift and maul him and get you free that way? Or should we talk about it first, like Alec and Isaac always say I should?"

"You're developing a sense of responsibility and maturity right *now*?" Patrick whined. Sato knew that tone well.

"It had to happen sometime," replied Kevin. "And he doesn't seem to want to actually harm you."

"I would. Never. Hurt. Patrick." Sato defended himself.

"See?" said Kevin.

"Except that you did! You abandoned me!"

Sato was instantly annoyed. "What. Are you. Talking about? I never. Abandoned you. It was you. Who left. Before I got home! You. Did. Not. Wait. You. Abandoned. Me." It was getting harder and harder to talk.

"Well, this is interesting," said another, new voice. A little higher toned, and originating from higher up and to the left, above where Kevin stood. The top of the garage?

Sato glanced over. There was a set of outside stairs just there, which apparently led to an apartment on top of the garage. The human pack member, the one with the scars and leather jackets, seemed to live in that particular box.

He had come out to a small landing and was leaning casually against the railing, staring down at them. He was dressed much the same as he had been previously. In layers of black, covering his body completely from the neck down.

"Hello, merman," he said to Sato. "Nice ass you got there. You always hang it out to dry for all to see?"

The red-headed werewolf, Kevin, sniffed the air in a pointed manner. "Aren't you the smart one, Max? You're right, he sure as shit smells like merman. What's he doing hugging our dratsie?"

"Don't know. Met him last night. He's something they called a *vangill*. What are those things on his arms?"

"Spurs," explained Patrick. "It's what makes him a vangill."

"Cool," said Max, apparently unthreatened and untroubled. This human appeared to be unflappable where all manner of shifters were concerned. Impressive.

As casual as he had been down by the water, Max sat on the stairs and leaned back on his elbows, relaxed. As if the shifters below him were some mildly entertaining TV show he happened to have tuned into.

"Could you, maybe, get him to let me go, Max?" Patrick pleaded. "Kevin wants to talk it out."

"Kevin wants to *talk* when he could have a nice little fight? Kevin, sweet-pea, you feeling all right?"

"Little thing doesn't look up for much, and I'm trying to become a better person," said the redhead, crossing his arms, not taking his eyes off Sato.

"Don't strain anything," said Max, and then, presumably to Patrick, "I'll give it a try, kid. Hey, vangill! Dude whose name I do not know. Why don't you let the cute dratsie go or I'll use quintessence to make your head go all splatty splat?"

"Don't explode his brains," said Kevin. "That would make *such* a mess."

"That's why we do it *outside*, Captain Obvious," replied Max.

"Can you even *do* that?" wondered Kevin. "Without, ya know…?"

"I can certainly try. Been a while since I exploded someone's head, outside of metaphorically, of course. Might be fun."

"One imagines a failed attempt would be even more messy – but okay," said the werewolf.

"You know me, *for a good time call…*," replied Max.

"Do you have to be so cheerful while you're threatening to kill someone?" wondered Patrick.

Sato felt hopeful. Maybe Patrick was worried about him? He leaned on him a bit more. Also, it appeared one of Sato's legs was no longer strictly working properly. Stupid legs, so unreliable.

"Yes," said Max promptly.

"Carry on then, I guess," said Patrick. "You'll owe me a new outfit, though."

Sato relaxed a tiny bit. That sounded a lot more flippant and casual, a lot less tortured and afraid. A lot more like the Patrick he knew and loved.

"Do you *want* him dead?" asked Kevin.

"I don't know. Right now I just want to get away and hide," admitted Patrick, his voice small.

"Well, it doesn't look like he's letting you go without a fight," said Kevin. "So why don't you make introductions before one of us has to kill him."

Patrick relaxed a little bit more.

Sato was grateful to the two pack members. Their weird violent banter seemed to be having a beneficial impact on Patrick. The small frame under Sato's was softening slightly.

Sato risked pressing the length of his own arms against Patrick's shivering ones, trying to warm them. But his own were even colder. He didn't seem to be healing or recuperating as fast as he should. He slumped even more than he intended, rested his cheek on the back of Patrick's neck.

Sato started to shiver. His head felt a little puffy and fuzzy, like Patrick's otter fur. Aftereffects of happiness? Something else? Patrick was so solid and so *there* and it had been so long since Sato had felt anything. Pain, weakness, Patrick. At least he wasn't numb.

Patrick said, "This is Sato Daiki, Vangill of the Deep, merman, and my ex-boyfriend."

Sato said, getting the words out as fast as he was able, "When. Exactly. Did we. Break up?"

"We haven't seen each other in over a decade!"

The redhead said, "Kevin Mangnall, San Andreas Pack enforcer. That is Maximillian Barker, Beta-mate. You've met already."

Max's voice cut through the fuzzy. "While this is entertaining as fuck, is my exploding brains technique necessary when this is obviously a lover's spat? And one half of the spat is equally obviously about to go splat?"

"Oh my god, Sato! Just let me go. You're barely standing on your own anyway." Patrick shifted to better support Sato's weight.

Sato shifted against his back, halfway to a piggyback, chin hooked over Patrick's familiar bony shoulder, eyes heavy-lidded.

"Never. Letting go. Again," insisted Sato, as firmly as he could, tightening his arms as much as he was able. They were not behaving like arms, though, more like soba noodles.

Why were they still talking? Why weren't he and Patrick alone somewhere, preferably fucking? Okay, maybe he didn't have the energy to fuck. Just cuddling would be nice.

Kevin said, "I really think you should let go of our boy."

"Our. Boy." Sato did not like that. "Why. Are. Werewolves. Interfering?" He knew he was whining. "Go. Away. Pack. Or. I will make. You."

"That's rich coming from a man who is butt-naked and bleeding, and looks like he's about to faint," replied Kevin, casually.

"Bleeding? Still?" Now Patrick really did sound worried.

That was *great*. He'd love it if Patrick were worried about him.

Kevin said, "Big old gashes on his leg. Plus broken ribs, I think. Can't you tell from the way he is panting? You ran up a hill, sure. But he's obviously fit. He shouldn't be winded like that."

Max added, "Yes, Trick, *bleeding*. All over your cute outfit."

"Oh, for fuck's sake. *Sato-san!* Let me go. I love this outfit. Let me see how bad you're hurt!"

Sato could feel all of it then. Now that they were forcing him to think about it. It did actually hurt, a lot. It was also causing him to lose his grip on Patrick. Or maybe that was the soba noodles. He wanted to hug him, cradle him close. He didn't want to hold him with spurs out, drooping against him. He didn't want Patrick against his will, he just wanted Patrick.

Did soba noodles have spurs?

Apparently not. His appeared to have retracted.

Two more figures came sauntering up the overgrown path. One as big as Kevin, the other one slighter, but giving off an aura of power and charisma.

Sato knew those two. Alpha Alec and Judd, his enforcer. Judd, his fellow survivor of shopping hell earlier that day.

The Alpha took in the scene at a glance, then turned and yelled, presumably to the house, "Everyone else back inside. There's enough pack here already but it's not safe. That means you, Marvin. Lovejoy, keep him out of this!" There was a muffled squeak of annoyance and the sound of a big door slamming.

Alec turned back to face them and said, sounding much more authoritarian than he had during negotiations the night before, "What *exactly* is going on here? Why are you holding onto our dratsie, vangill? You're losing quite a bit of blood, too. Kevin, is that your fault?"

"Nope," said Kevin cheerfully.

Alec looked up the garage stairs.

"Not me either," added Max. "He showed up already damaged. Should we return him for a refund?"

"Why. Are. Wolves. With *my* otter?" Sato asked. He just wanted Patrick alone to himself, but more and more damn werewolves kept showing up!

That was always the problem with werewolves. They were like dust bunnies – once you spotted one, you knew others were bound to follow.

Alec pondered the situation. "*Yours, is he?*"

"And yet, *we* are his pack," growled Judd, glaring at Sato. Apparently any mutual goodwill they'd built up that morning at, well, the Goodwill, had now evaporated.

"How. Did. My Patrick. Get a pack? He doesn't need you. He has me." Sato's breathing was becoming infinitesimally less labored. It still hurt like hell, though.

Kevin looked annoyed. "Oh, *does* he? So him, driving around in that death trap of a station wagon, starving and desperate, and sleeping in his car – that was *your* fault?"

"What?" Sato tried to see Patrick's face to understand what the hell they were talking about. What was going on?

"Shut up, Kevin," yelled Patrick. "How much is Sato bleeding? Sato, let me go. Are you crazy?"

"I told you. Never. Letting go. Again. That's when everything. Went wrong!" Sato yelled this despite the pain, beyond frustrated. Even though Patrick was right there – he wasn't listening!

Alec said, "Trick, what on earth is going on?"

"Alpha, this is Sato Daiki, my ex-friend-lover-whatever. He seems a bit confused."

Judd said, "Well, well, well, I didn't expect *that*."

"I'm not even *slightly* confused," said Sato for the benefit of everyone there, very carefully trying to string sentences together. "I'm thinking clearly. For the first time. In a decade. And I am. *Absolutely* not. Letting go." In telling them, he wished his arms would also listen.

But then his good leg gave out. He slid abruptly forward, all his weight completely on Patrick.

Patrick stumbled in surprise at the slack heaviness of him, jerked one sharp elbow back as he twisted trying to catch him, hit Sato's side in the region of the broken ribs.

Sato lurched instinctively back from the agony and crumpled to the ground with a wet thud. The soba noodles had completely failed and gravity won.

On land, it always did.

CHAPTER FIFTEEN
IN HAWT WATER

He was free.

Sato's all too familiar grip relaxed enough for him to get away. The fire-breathing dragonflies vanished. His head cleared for a moment in utter relief. Nothing else was in there, of course, but no one had ever described Trick as smart.

Once more the instinct to run and shift and change was overwhelming.

Once more there was no safety or recourse in being a dratsie. Maybe an otter could hide better in the bushes. Maybe. But not so much that a werewolf couldn't sniff him out easily. Especially not here in their territory. And his otter form certainly wasn't fast enough on land to get away from any one of them.

One desperate look around and he took refuge in the only place that seemed even remotely defensible – the steps to Max and Brian's apartment, higher ground.

To be honest, Trick was a little scared of Max. He found him gorgeous, of course. Best thing about his mornings, Max in spandex after his run, getting his absurdly sweet morning coffee. But also a little scary. Max was sharp with his words as well as his abilities, cutting. As if all parts of him had been broken into shards of glass. Max clearly didn't give a fuck if those shards turned into weapons. All of Max could be a weapon, he was *that* powerful.

So Trick only went halfway up the stairs, not too close to Max, and crouched there, not sure what else to do.

He stared at Sato. The merman was bleeding from a long slash, maybe more, in one leg and slumped on the ground. No longer holding onto Patrick, he was trying to hold onto his own side instead. But his arms looked limp. His spurs had retracted. Probably against his will.

Still, he tried to get to his feet, hunched in pain, lurch toward Trick. Focused solely on him as he always had been. That look in his eyes. That lie. The one that said only Trick mattered. That one big lie Trick had believed with his whole stupid little heart.

Bryan, in wolf form, materialized out of the underbrush. He'd been on shift with an EMT team that day, and usually just ran home as a wolf afterward. Trick wondered how long he'd been there. No doubt since before Alec had arrived. Alec was like that. Prepared.

Bryan dropped the uniform he'd been holding in a plastic bag in his mouth, and leapt to guard the base of the stairs.

So now Sato was facing off against Bryan the wolf defending both Patrick and his mate. There was no way Sato was getting up those stairs.

Sato lost it. "More wolves? Get out of my way!"

Bryan's hackles were up and his ruff puffed huge. He growled, low and threatening.

Sato lurched toward him. His spurs back out.

Trick found himself saying, like he was back in high school, "No, Sato, baby, not *that* werewolf."

But it was too late. As it would have been back then.

And why was he even warning Sato? Why was he even worried about him? Why was Sato still bleeding so much? Why was he clutching his side in so much pain? Why hadn't he healed more by now?

Which was when Max finally lost patience with the whole absurd situation. He slid down the stair railing like a child.

Zoomed past Trick, landing at the bottom right next to his familiar with a flourish.

Max buried his hand in the fur on the top of Bryan's head. There was a strong smell of ozone in the air, strong enough for even Trick to sense.

Trick knew, in theory, that quintessence was all around them all the time. But for the first time he could swear he felt it activate. Like there were charged particles in the air, electrified dust motes, and they were all being summoned toward Max and Bryan.

It felt like an awful lot of power. An electrical storm or something. If he were in otter form, his fur would be standing on end.

Sato must have felt it too.

But he just stood there, naked, panting, bleeding, shivering, eyes fixed on Trick, on the stairs. Not even acknowledging the threat of the two directly in front of him.

He lurched forward, as if to simply move around or through them, up the stairs to Trick, as if Trick were the real power, as if Trick had quintessence that was summoning Sato.

"Why won't you just *stop*?" wondered Max. "Is this some kind of obsession? Stalking?"

Sato didn't answer. All his weight on his good leg. Unbalanced.

Max looked down at Bryan, "This is clearly overkill. Why bother to waste the energy?"

Bryan yapped at him in agreement. Then he shifted, right there, into his human form. As naked as Sato and as uncaring. Trick always thought Bryan was the kindest looking of the pack, with his friendly, craggy face, a little scruffy. He was older than Alec and they didn't look alike. Except they had the same gentle hazel eyes.

Sato said, a touch plaintively, "Why are you all so big?"

Naked Bryan interposed himself between Patrick and Sato.

Alec, Kevin, and Judd all came over and joined Bryan and Max. Now there was a wall of men between Sato and Trick.

Sato looked like he was determined to break through that wall, anyway.

"Why. Are there. So many of you? Seriously, Patrick?"

What right did Sato have to take offense? What right had Sato to turn back up in Trick's life right when things were starting to be actually not bad for the first time in a really long while?

"What now?" Kevin asked his Alpha. "Impasse?"

Alec sighed. "Trick, what do you want us to do about him?"

"He's bleeding," was all Trick could think to say.

"We're aware," said Max.

Alec turned and looked at Trick hard for a long moment. Trusting the rest of his pack implicitly to keep an eye on Sato. "I think this might require Isaac. Is he awake?"

"If he isn't, should be soon," said Judd. "He's on shift at nine."

Alec said, "Kevin, go get him, please. Explain that we need an Omega to handle a merman problem." He looked at Sato and Trick. "You two need to talk this out.'

Sato sneered.

Trick said, "But the bleeding?"

Alec gave a huge sigh. "It's a lot harder to be Alpha to non-werewolves. I'm at a loss here." He glanced around at his pack, "Should I use VOICE?"

"You can try," said Bryan. "But why don't I just patch up the merman?"

Trick was shocked to realize he'd momentarily forgotten Bryan was a medic.

"Trick." Alec was speaking to him again. "Hey, Trick? Why don't you go get in your car?"

"What?"

"Good idea." That was Judd. "Familiar territory. Otters have some prey instincts. He probably needs to hide right now."

Alec said, "Not sure it will work as well with a dratsie, but maybe he'd feel safer there. Get some of his brain functioning again. He seems to have gone all spacey."

Trick thought they were talking about him and he was *indeed* feeling spacey but at least Bryan was looking after Sato's wounds now. The Beta was frowning and focused on Sato's leg.

Trick was torn, worried about Sato, wanting to make sure he was okay.

But also that was *Sato*. Yes, he wanted to see Sato badly, wanted him to be healthy, wanted to touch him and get close to him. But he also wanted to get away. Stay away from him. That was the instinct that kept winning and it looked like it might be bubbling up to the surface again.

Now that Sato was getting help, soon he would feel better. Soon he would chase Patrick again.

Then what? Trick heard himself whimpering and his teeth began to chatter.

"He's panicking again," said Judd.

Judd was standing behind Sato now and holding him steady. Holding him upright, but also, holding him away from Trick.

"Try VOICE, Alec," suggested Bryan.

"Marvin said it wouldn't work on water shifters." That was Max.

"Can't hurt to try," insisted the Beta.

Alec said in a bellowing, echoing, rich tone, "TRICK, GO TO YOUR CAR."

Trick thought that was a *great idea*. His sad old car was suddenly the most appealing thing in the world. With its four flat tires and the fact that it probably wouldn't ever start again. He hadn't been inside it in weeks. Not since he moved into Colin's room. But now he should definitely go check on his car. Get inside it.

He stood, legs shaking, and started walking down the stairs.

"What do ya know?" said Max. "Marvin was wrong."

"Wouldn't be the first time. Maybe it just doesn't work on Marvin," said Alec.

Trick was thinking only about his car. The only thing he really owned. The only thing that was really *his* after Sato stopped being his.

Trick sidled past the wolves, hugging the side of the garage. Staying as far away from them, and Sato, as he could.

The pack clustered around Sato, tending to him and entrapping him, keeping him upright and keeping him from following

Trick. Behind those massive bodies Trick caught glimpses of Sato's eyes on him, desperately tracking him. The merman looked so small, surrounded by werewolves.

Sato's spurs were out and his forearms were up.

Sato couldn't fight all of them. But he was going to try.

"Ouch, fuck me, those are sharp." That was Kevin.

Bryan said, "Keep those things away from me. I'm trying to help you, you *stupid* merman. Judd, grab his damn hands and get them behind his back."

"Fuck his *hands*, grab him by the damn balls!" complained Kevin.

Sato wasn't going to be able to follow Patrick no matter what, now.

Which meant that yet again, Sato wouldn't follow him. Like before. No Sato would come after him.

Was that a good thing or a bad thing?

Trick heard Sato's yell and then a kind of keening cry of pain and loss. Not a noise he'd ever heard before. It was the sound a dying dolphin makes.

Alec's voice came again. That terrible awesome bell-like VOICE, "BE STILL, VANGILL."

The garage was cold and musty inside. It wasn't crammed with stuff, just some construction material and tools stacked neatly on the back wall. Mostly it was filled with one very old station wagon, unlocked.

Trick climbed into the way back, curled himself up in his old blanket there. There was a ragged toy there too. A blue fish plushy. Stolen from a convenience store. Left behind by a child with scared eyes a lifetime ago.

The dragonflies were back inside Trick again. No longer breathing fire, they now wielded tiny pickaxes and were intent on beating pinholes behind his eyes. The rest of Trick ached like he'd been running for days, rather than just up the hill home to pack grounds.

Ached like he'd run a marathon.

A marathon that had lasted ten years.

And was now over.

The Present: Sato on pack property dealing with shit

"BE STILL, VANGILL." Alec's tone was lower than when he spoke naturally, oppressive.

Sato thought he could grow to hate that voice even as he found himself subsiding under the weight of it. Could noise be heavy? The sound settled into his bones, making them do what the Alpha wanted despite his objections. It was like being under deep, deep waters, in the middle of a trench made of volume.

"He won't stay under VOICE for long," said Alec.

Sato wondered if this was what it felt like to be locked under a mermaid's Medusa gaze. He wondered how Alec could gauge the effectiveness of his VOICE. Was it like dealing out a wound with spurs? Did Alec instinctively know the depth of vocal injury from experience?

"I'm surprised it worked at all." That was the enforcer, Kevin.

"Me too. Perhaps it's because he has loyalty to Trick and Trick is loyal to me."

"Or perhaps it's because he's vangill, and accustomed to taking orders," suggested Judd.

Sato felt lost and alone. Patrick had walked away. Patrick was out of his sight. Again. When he'd only just found him. Because of werewolves.

"Separation anxiety is strong with this one," said a new voice. Yet another werewolf.

Sato dragged his eyes from the Alpha and onto the newcomer. This one was tall, like the others. although not as tall as either enforcer or the Beta. He had an open, friendly face, with a wide mouth and close-cropped, well-tended facial hair. He was lean like a swimmer rather than bulky like the two enforcers.

"You summoned me, Alpha?" said the man, rather sarcastically for a wolf talking to his Alpha.

Alec didn't seem to mind.

"I think your powers might be called forward, to facilitate conversation."

"My *powers*, you say?"

Alec ignored the sarcasm. "Isaac, this here is a vangill merman named Sato Daiki, Patrick's ex-boyfriend."

Sato wanted to protest because really, when had they broken up? But BE STILL apparently meant his lips must stay still too. Effective.

Except that it wasn't.

The weight left him as quickly as it had settled, perhaps because Alec's attention was diverted or perhaps VOICE had a limited time frame of effectiveness.

He jerked, stumbled, but not much or very far because three wolves still had their massive warm hands on him.

"Patrick?" he rasped, feeling dry and cold and tired and in pain. Lost because he'd finally found Patrick again after all this time, and Patrick had left him.

The Alpha's voice was steady but no longer weighted with compulsion. "He's safe right there in the garage. He hasn't gone anywhere. Just relax. Answer some questions. The Omega will help."

"How?" wondered Sato. Isaac was just another werewolf, although admittedly this time dressed in tight jeans and a black muscle T with the sleeves rolled up and the logo of some bar.

"Omegas always help," said Bryan, with soft confidence.

Isaac stood directly in front of Sato and bent to look into his face. Their gazes met and clashed, in a way that for most shifters would've been misconstrued as a challenge. But this werewolf's eyes were somehow accepting. Not kind, but understanding.

"Tell me about your connection with Trick." Isaac had a mild voice, not too deep but round and resonant. If Sato paid attention to sounds, he might have called it pretty. But for Sato the world above the water had only two kinds of noises, good ones and bad ones. This was a good one.

Sato stayed silent.

Isaac pressed, "You and Trick dated? A while ago?"

Sato considered this. Was *dating* the right word? How could he articulate his past? How was he supposed to explain how Patrick fit into it? Because Patrick *was* his past. All of it. The entirety of who he was formed around Patrick. He wasn't himself without Patrick, because when he lost Patrick he lost the core of himself too. Ever since Sato had performed the act of existing, a surface creature with no depth. The foam on the top of the waves. Under those circumstances, a word like *dating* seemed childish and insufficient. But to say that might make him sound insane, or obsessed, or trying to aggrandize a childhood crush.

"He is my mate." Sato didn't know the *exact* meaning of the word for werewolves, but he thought maybe their language was the best language in this matter.

"Oh, indeed?" Isaac didn't seem disbelieving, just curious.

"Do otters have mates?" asked Kevin.

Isaac looked away from Sato, who was relieved to have those all-knowing eyes off him, and said to his Alpha, "The pack isn't helping. I think you should leave us, Bryan can stay holding him. We'll be fine. I think this is a private matter and Sato here is a private person."

Sato was beyond grateful for the understanding. A weird sensation, because why should he be grateful to the werewolves for anything?

Alec cocked his head a moment, then said, "If you think so. I'm hungry anyway. Inside, boys."

With which the majority of the wolves simply left. Disappearing with remarkable effectiveness into the overgrowth.

Only Bryan stayed behind, holding onto Sato in a way that was both supportive and confining. Sato didn't mind all that much. He wasn't going to struggle. He doubted his stupid human legs were still working anyway. He didn't like being touched by someone who wasn't Patrick, but at least he was still upright.

"*Mate* isn't exactly correct, is it?" Isaac's intensity was focused on him once more.

"Mermen are naturally solitary, or at least that's what I was always told. Your Marvin seems to be an exception," Sato said.

There was something about Isaac that made it easy to talk, even for him.

"The Alpha-mate is exceptional."

Sato frowned. "I'm not. I'm also solitary. The exception for me was always Patrick. From the beginning. I don't need you. I don't need a pack. But I need him and he needs me and he's been lost for so long. I've been searching for a decade."

"You didn't abandon him?"

"Of course not."

"You have a good explanation?"

"If he would listen. I came back. He did not wait long enough."

"Ah, you abandoned each other."

Sato thought about it for a moment. "That seems increasingly likely."

"You're an odd one, aren't you?" said Bryan from near his left ear.

"Said the wolf to the fish," replied Isaac. "I'm just going to step into the garage and see how Trick is doing. You two stay here for a moment."

Silence descended. Bryan did not let go and he did not talk. Sato shivered and was grateful.

A long few minutes later and the garage door went up. Sato was looking at the insides of a box that contained a few assorted objects and one very sad old vehicle. The back hatch was up and Patrick was curled inside the trunk area. Isaac stood outside next to him, arms crossed. Both of them were looking at Sato.

Bryan let Sato go.

Sato stumbled but remained upright, proud of himself for that. He limped slowly – well, stumbled – to the car. Sat gingerly on one corner of the bumper, the opposite side from Patrick.

Talking hadn't been helping him much so far. This time Sato stayed silent and just took Patrick in.

He'd always been a tiny slip of a thing and he was still slender, too much so. His face was leaner. He'd lost all his baby fat, but he still had that big forehead and pretty eyes. There were crinkles at the corners of those eyes that had never been there before. His hair was short now and it had darkened to brown. His amazing smile seemed to have vanished along with the floppy blond hair. Both had been ubiquitous when they were kids.

Sato could hardly believe it, but there were things he'd forgotten. That Patrick's eyes angled down a little at the outer corners. That his lashes were long and his nose slightly too large. That his bottom lip was fuller than his top one, so that when he wasn't smiling he looked pouty. Sato was shocked at having forgotten anything at all about this boy.

The silence continued. The two of them stared at each other.

Finally Patrick shut his eyes and took a deep breath. "What are you doing here, Sato-san?"

"Again with the *san*? You really are mad."

"Ten years, Sato-san. Ten years since you didn't come for me. I waited. I waited until I couldn't anymore and I had to run and you never came for me!"

Isaac said gently, "Give him time to explain, Trick."

"He's had *ten years*!"

Sato moved closer. He was always better at touching than he was at talking. At least with Patrick. Sato put a hand out and curled it around Patrick's ankle.

Patrick jerked away and back into the car.

It hurt.

Isaac turned and looked at him. "And you need to give him space. Ask before you touch."

He retracted his hand. "If you insist. But I am never letting him out of my sight again."

Patrick was truculent. "I'm right here in front of you."

Sato acknowledged this with a curt nod. But he slid back to sit inside the trunk area as well. He coiled back so as not to touch and not to be tempted to touch, as far away as he could while still being in the car with Patrick. The strain of it made his bones ache. Or maybe that was just the aftereffects of a bear fight.

"I see what the Alpha was on about," said Isaac, to no one in particular. Maybe Bryan was still there. Sato refused to look away from Patrick.

Patrick said, finally, still staring at him hard. "Explain then, and it better be a good one."

So Sato explained. He told Patrick about the tsunami, and the rescue efforts, and the rebuild efforts, and more rescuing. About none of the phones working and by the time he got through never getting an answer from Patrick or his sire. He told him about working with the vangill, as a team. He told him about the stupid metal medals that the humans insisted on giving them, even though mermen had nothing to pin awards onto. He told him every detail he could think of, to corroborate his story.

"You could look it up," he said. "I think there are even pictures of us online somewhere. Although it was a long time ago, before the interwebs were really a thing."

Patrick was looking more sad and thoughtful than angry.

Sato continued, "And then I had to swim all the way back to you and my sire. By the time I got there, I was three weeks past the date you said you were leaving for college. Sire was dead. There were strange humans in his house. Your family wasn't there anymore. I assumed you'd gone on ahead but there were crazy rumors about human children, and you being a bad guy, and you vanishing illegally. You had disappeared into the dry world of human roads and endless land. When I asked too much about you, the uniforms started following me. I assumed they were after you, so I returned to the Deep. But I didn't give up.

"I followed you. Or I thought I was following. To that school and that massive city. You weren't there. Or anywhere around there. I searched all the places and things you had mentioned. Other universities in other cities that had drama departments like you wanted. But there was no trace of you at all. It was as if you had died like my sire. I just kept hunting, didn't know what else to do. Then my sister became the Paralia of All Seas. She needed a vangill, and the easiest, best option was me. I thought because she was Paralia at least I would get to have consistent contact with the landbound and other water shifters like dratsie. So every time we came to shore I asked. I looked for you. I looked for any trace of any dobhar-chú whatsoever. Your people are hard enough to find. You alone was harder."

Patrick said, softly, "Dratsie don't like to register with DURPS. We make it a point to avoid such things."

"But you were never like that. You always said you didn't want to be like them. You said you'd go legit. So I checked the registry every DURPS I could. I checked it here when I arrived." Sato wondered how much his Patrick had changed on the inside. Sato had only been noticing outside differences, but perhaps the parts that he could not see were even more altered.

Isaac smiled down at Patrick. "Legal issues? I know how it goes. I was on the run myself for a long time."

"Why didn't you wait for me to get back?" Sato asked. "I know I was late, but I was always going to come for you. When had I ever not? Was it your family?"

Patrick pulled up his legs and hugged them, rested his face inside them so his eye sockets matched up with his kneecaps. He looked very small and Sato wanted to hug him very badly. He pushed himself back until the hard edge of some broken bit of car dug into his back.

When Patrick's voice came again it was muffled and thick. "I ran out of time. And everything got so bad and so crazy so fast. I couldn't risk waiting for you. The things my family was doing, and the people they were paying off, and your father dying, everything came to a head. The only thing I could do was run away. So I ran."

"I wish you'd left a message for me."

"I didn't know where I was going, only that I had to get away."

Isaac said, "So there it is, you two missed each other, and now you're back together again. Is that so bad?"

He was obviously asking Patrick because Sato saw nothing bad with any of this except that he couldn't hold Patrick.

And then Patrick lifted his head and rested his chin on one knee, and the fear was still in his eyes. He carefully looked away from Sato to Isaac.

"Yeah, because of what I became for a long time when he wasn't with me."

"What did you become?" asked Isaac, gently.

"Lost."

"Ah, I see. You fear trusting again when you barely survived the first time parting."

Isaac, Sato realized, was good with words. And understanding. Was that what made him an Omega?

Sato was somewhat relieved. Patrick's fear wasn't of him, it was of losing him again. Missing him after depending upon him.

"So if I just stay close. If I just don't go anywhere. Would you maybe come to like me again? Let me hold you again?" Sato wondered.

Patrick's eyes on him were sad and desperate. "I don't know. Was that bit of me broken a decade ago, or was it, like you, just missing for a really long time? Does the part of me that loved without fear return with you, the source of the pain, or is it gone forever?"

Sato considered this. Considered Patrick. The missing bit of his soul. Possibly his whole soul. Had he felt anything at all since Patrick left, or had it just been the numbness at the bottom of the ocean? He was a solitary creature of some ancient sea-borne lore, a throwback monster with weapons for arms and a heart that had only ever opened one time for one person.

"I guess we will find out, since I'm not going anywhere." He would take any part of Patrick he could get, even if it never returned to what it was. Even if it was only a fraction. Even if what had been a tree was now nothing but driftwood. He didn't have any other choice.

Patrick sighed. "As single-minded and stubborn as ever."

"You may have changed, but I did not."

Isaac said, "Everyone changes."

"If Patrick wants me to change, I will change. If he wants me to come to land and never swim again, that is what I will do. I would have followed him to the big city. I will follow him here into your little town. I will come to your pack lands and court him if that's what's required. I will sleep in this car on the side of a road with him if you do not want us. I would have done all of it back then and I will do any of it now."

"What happened to your pride?" said Patrick, as if he really missed it.

Sato cocked his head. What pride had he ever had? Pride in what? Pride in his tail because it was big and pretty-colored? Patrick was not in the water where he could chase and catch him using it. Pride in his spurs because they were powerful? They had only brought him to the attention of the mermaids who would otherwise have left him alone. The only thing he'd ever been proud of was earning Patrick's love, and he had no idea how he'd done that. The most precious thing in the world was a gift that he'd valued more than anything and still somehow managed to destroy. What right had he to be proud?

"I think you've confused pride with being an antisocial asshole," said Sato, meaning it.

Patrick gave a funny, watery chuckle. Not a sound Sato had heard from him. He missed that unguarded bright bark of laughter Patrick used to give whenever Sato spoke his mind and was accidentally amusing.

"What about your sister?" Patrick asked.

"What about her?"

"You are her vangill. The protector of the Paralia of All Seas. Surely you love her and wish to take care of her. You can't simply abandon her and your duty to pod, and ocean, and family. Can you?"

Sato scoffed. "Have you forgotten how few shits I have to give? If Mother wishes to move their pod here to this little dirty bay of yours, then I will stay her vangill. If she does not, then we will part ways when the diplomatic pod dissolves. I was with her to find you. I have found you. I'm done."

"What if they ban you from the seas?"

"Your Alpha has won rights to this bay. I can swim in it at his discretion. But even if they went so far, I will learn to swim in freshwater."

"You would give up your tail for me?" Patrick seemed truly surprised.

How could Sato possibly make him understand?

"I would give up anything. I don't care. It's just you." He was frustrated. How to voice this so Patrick would truly understand? "There is no alternative. There is only you or looking for you. I have no future plan or place to go without you in it. I was always going to just keep searching until I found you or died trying."

Patrick's eyes were wide on him. Shocked.

"Oh. Did you think I was the strong one? No, baby, that was always you."

Patrick looked briefly away from Sato at Isaac, clearly confused.

"You are his moral compass, I think. He imprinted on you, like a cult leader, and that's all he knows to do. I'm afraid you got yourself a merman whether you like it or not."

"Is that healthy?"

"I'm a bartender, not an actual shrink, you know?"

"Still?"

"Probably not. But of all the shifter species, the merfolk are the most alien to us landbound creatures. One tail compared to four legs – it's nearly impossible to understand. Even Marvin confuses us werewolves most of the time. Including his mate."

"Sato and Marvin are very different," insisted Patrick.

"And yet both, in their way, chose exile. I think, if pressed, Marvin might say the same thing about Alec. It's a different dynamic, of course. But Alec is his world, and has been since high school."

Patrick blinked at him, startled. "I had no idea."

"Yeah, they met way back then, Marvin was this weird goth kid, used to watch Alec's swim practice. Met him again years later when his sister came to land to investigate and brought him along as liaison. But Marvin knew which pack they were going in to talk with. He knew Alec would be there. I think he even made a point of requesting him as point of contact. He'd never forgotten Alec either."

Sato turned his head, looked to the side, considered. "Maybe it takes some of us like that. Or maybe all of us mermen are secretly like that, it's just that most aren't lucky enough to find their… what did you call it… moral compass?"

"You're not mad at being diminished like that?" wondered Patrick.

Sato shook his head. Who was he to be diminished by the truth? He wondered what he might do to get Patrick to accept him again. Or at least to stop huddling like that, cringing and alone.

Time was whenever they were together they would be touching. He missed Patrick's small hands all over him. He missed it so much.

He took a deep breath, turned to the Omega. "Do you have any catfish?"

"Random question. You'd have to ask Lovejoy but he's at work already. It's Friday night – his food truck is catering opening ceremonies for that Marine Biology conference. You could check the freezer, I suppose."

Sato stood. "Show me where."

Isaac blinked at him. "Right now?"

"I need to make katsu."

Patrick's shoulders relaxed. "Katsu?" his voice was less thick, more hopeful.

"Katsu," said Sato, firmly. "And you should come watch me do it and tell me how bad it is and how different from sire's technique and stick your finger into the sauce when I'm not looking like you used to with him and—"

Patrick firmed his mouth, then unwrapped his arms from his legs. "Okay, katsu."

CHAPTER SIXTEEN

THE WORLD IS YOUR OTTER

The Present: Trick in the pack house contemplating katsu

Which is how Sato Daiki reappeared in Trick's life and then took over Lovejoy's kitchen and began to make what turned out to be some of the worst katsu Trick had ever eaten.

A merman, in an oversized yellow waffle robe, frying food for a bunch of werewolves was just surreal enough for those wolves to dutifully push aside Lovejoy's absolutely delicious stew and choke down the overly dry, yet still raw in the middle, piece of fish.

How had he managed to make it both soggy and burned?

Trick did not help Sato in the kitchen. He wanted to be close to him, but also didn't. He needed to keep his eyes on him but also couldn't. So instead, he sat with the pack (the ones currently home) around the big dining table, casting furtive glances at the kitchen more often than he wished.

Thankfully, Lovejoy had already gone to work. They would have to fix the kitchen back to normal later. Tank was getting ready to do the same. Kevin was on patrol. Marvin was getting dressed. Max rarely joined them for meals. The others were all either staring at the merman destroying their small appliances in pursuit of terrible Japanese food, or staring at Trick to see how they were supposed to react to the aforementioned merman's destructive tendencies.

Even Alec looked nonplussed.

Sato managed to dirty every gadget from food processor to air fryer, but in classic undersea fashion, didn't actually know how to use any of them. He forgot lids and didn't understand settings, merely punched at buttons aggressively. He didn't defrost the fish, so when the knives failed to cut the frozen fillets, he deployed and used his spurs, which were effective but only in a stabby-slashy way. This resulted in uneven chunks of still-frozen catfish sliding all over the counter.

Bryan forayed in to make tea. "Did you go at it with a weed wacker?"

Sato glared at him.

Bryan retreated (without tea) and joined them at the table, looking unbowed and amused. "You know what they say about fish and bicycles. I guess it's the same for mermen and kitchens."

"Not a fish," said Sato.

"We know," chorused all the werewolves at once.

Eventually Sato left the kitchen, which had survived without burning down, barely. But it did look like militant chipmunks with a vendetta against breadcrumbs had waged a successful campaign in the Great Panko-Induction War of 1871.

During their school days Sato would never have done any of it. Never have cooked (well, *tried* to cook) and certainly never have sat down with Patrick and a pack of his friends to eat. Sato had never hung out in groups, rarely joined Patrick at parties, he'd just charged in and dragged him away, or waited outside for Patrick to be done. Sato regarded people en masse the way cats regarded water en masse, with deep suspicion and disdain.

For the first time, Trick realized Sato wasn't like that because he was antisocial (although he *was* very antisocial) but because he simply didn't care about anyone else but Patrick. He wasn't sure how he felt about that. It was a little scary but also, oddly flattering.

Sato slapped his plate down across from Trick, since there

were wolves flanking him, Colin one side and Judd the other, and stabbed at the inedible fish with his chopsticks in a way that would have had his sire rapping his knuckles.

He took a bite. Spat it out. "This is absolutely terrible." He reached across and batted the dish away from Trick. "Don't eat that, it might kill you. And I just got you back."

Trick hid a smile. It was just like Sato to spend ages preparing something when he had no idea how to cook, and then acknowledge without embarrassment when it was an abject failure.

A collective sigh of relief came from the wolves around the table.

"Oh good, we don't have to eat it, either," said Alec.

A scraping noise emanated as they all pushed their plates away.

"It's not crispy! What's the point of katsu if it's not crispy?" Judd wondered, not aggressively, just curious.

"I think we have some fish sticks. Do you want fish sticks, Mr Sato, sir? Closest we can get, I think." That was Colin, who knew their stock relatively well, as he was one of the few Lovejoy allowed in his territory regularly.

Sato gave Colin's offer the deadpan stare it deserved.

Trick felt his lips twitch.

Sato had always promised to cook his sire's katsu, but he'd never actually learned how to do so. Sato probably thought that having *watched* Mr Sato was sufficient.

"Darling! I hate to break it to you, but something seems to have objected to the existence of our kitchen," said Marvin, traipsing in and sitting down unceremoniously on Alec's lap.

Judd pointed at Sato. "He cooked for us."

Marvin glared at his fellow merman. "How dare you undermine my carefully cultivated reputation of mermen never cooking."

"Don't worry, that reputation remains intact," said Colin.

"Unlike our kitchen," added Alec, wrapping his arms around Marvin's waist.

Marvin reached for the katsu plate in front of his Alpha.

"Don't eat it!" said several voices at once.

Marvin ignored them all, picked up the whole piece with his little finger sticking out, and sniffed at it ostentatiously. He put it back down with a wrinkled nose, brushing the burnt panko off his fingers.

Marvin turned with purpose and evaluated Sato with narrowed turquoise eyes. "Why are you here, vangill? Trying to poison my pack with bad fish?"

Trick suspected Alec had told them all everything while he and Sato and Isaac were sorting out life history. Marvin was just being a punk-ass on Trick's behalf.

It was sweet of him.

"He's courting our dratsie," said Judd. His voice a defensive rumble next to Trick. Trick realized, then, that Judd was close to him on purpose, to protect him.

From Sato.

"Apparently this is a kind of love offering," added Isaac, clearly not impressed.

"Ooo, no. Not good." Marvin's blue-green eyes went huge with horror.

"Not good at all," agreed Judd.

Marvin looked back at the kitchen. "Lovejoy is gonna have kittens."

"Why would a werewolf—" started Sato.

"Human saying," Trick felt compelled to explain, before Sato made a fool of himself. Well, *more* of a fool of himself.

Sato tilted his head, then asked Alec, seemingly out of the blue, "Do you have cats?"

Marvin perked up. "There're some neighborhood ones who visit regularly. Why do you ask?"

"I like cats – only sensible things on four legs." That was a new thing for Sato. There hadn't been cats around their neighborhood as kids. Also, he rarely liked anything.

Marvin pursed his lips, pleased. "You're not wrong."

"Mermen like cats?" That was Colin, looking very confused.

"Apparently," said Alec. "Would you like a cat, baby?" he asked his mate.

"The best cats happen, they aren't sought out," said Marvin, wisely.

Alec looked over at Trick.

Trick met the Alpha's eyes, scared by the endless compassion he saw there.

Alec shifted his hazel gaze to Sato and finally Isaac. "Is someone going to explain why a strangely weaponized merman is trying to poison my pack with katsu?"

Colin stood. "I'll heat up the stew, shall I?"

"Yes, please," said Judd with feeling.

Colin petted the enforcer's head affectionately and he went to the kitchen. Colin had to wipe down the stovetop before he could put the big pot back on.

Trick quickly glanced at Sato, still trying not to stare at him too much. Sato was trying to look nonchalant. At least his color was back and he was breathing normally. He seemed to be starting to heal at last.

Alec leaned his chin on Marvin's shoulder and looked at Sato without malice.

Trick loved this about the Alpha. There was no anger in his gaze, only curiosity and a willingness to understand and help if he could. Despite the fact that Sato had invaded his territory and threatened his pack, Alec held few grudges and usually attributed hostility to mistakes in communication or fear. Oddly practical, actually, since that was usually true.

Isaac looked to Trick. "It's your responsibility to explain to the Alpha, kiddo. It's your business, of course, but this is his territory, and you brought your business into it. Or Mr Sato did."

"Just Sato," said Sato. "Mr Sato was my father."

Isaac turned to him, fully focused and intent. "Would *you* like to explain then?"

Sato looked over at the Omega for a long moment. "I got lost to human business and human concerns and was too late to help Patrick when he needed me the most." That was Sato in a nutshell, putting everything as succinctly as possible and in the context of his own worldview.

It was true, of course, but also Trick didn't like Sato taking all of the blame. Not now. He didn't like to see him humbling himself. Weirdly he felt compelled to mount a defense.

"He got caught up in disaster relief when that big tsunami hit Hawaii ten or so years ago. His vangill training pod stayed to help with search and rescue. Took so long I wasn't able to wait for him to get back. I found out my family was into some epic-level bad shit and ended up running a kinda rescue mission myself. That pissed off everyone in town, humans and shifters *and* cops. So I had to disappear fast. I did that by going inland, changing my name, and crossing state lines."

"A merman can't find what the land hides," explained Marvin. "Especially not a merman like Sato."

"Why him specifically?" Alec asked his mate.

"He's vangill. The vangill always get swallowed by the Deep. The rest of us mermen can escape, but the mermaids *want* the vangill, so they keep them close. And they keep them forever, or until they're no longer strong and viable enough to be useful."

Colin returned to the table with the pot of reheated stew and a trivet. Bryan got up, retrieved bowls for everyone, and began dishing it out. Colin sat back down next to Trick, green eyes sympathetic.

"Why? Because of those teeth on his arms?" wondered Judd, sounding rather impressed.

Marvin bit his lip. "Spurs. Yes, but that's only a part of it. Vangill can produce viable offspring."

"Stud services?" Judd's forehead creased and his eyes narrowed.

Marvin nodded.

Trick was shocked. He hadn't known that. He hadn't realized Sato would be forced into *that* kind of thing. He hated that idea.

"Arranged marriages?" asked Isaac, who had grown up in a cult where such things were commonplace.

Marvin looked at Sato. "I don't think so. Generally merfolk don't practice any forms of restrictive monogamy. Anything that narrows the breeding pool is unacceptable."

Sato said, looking bored but obviously trying for Trick's sake,

"No marriage, but yes, I've been pursued as a sire since I became a vangill."

Trick felt himself go very hot and then very cold. "Have you sired children, Sato?"

Colin's hand was suddenly in his, warm and dry. Trick's own felt clammy. He worried it would feel like a dead fish to his friend. But Colin didn't seem to mind, his grip supportive.

Sato looked at him, untroubled and not understanding why Trick would be upset by such an idea. "How would that even be possible?"

"Sato Daiki, answer the question!" yelled Trick. Colin squeezed his hand.

Sato rolled his eyes. "Of course not. I told you, there is only you. I refused."

Judd and Isaac both looked relieved.

"You can refuse?"

Sato seemed confused that they should question his autonomy. "Not outright, but I pretended that I got tail elsewhere." He tilted his head slightly, tucked a lock of stiff salt-crusted black hair behind one ear. "It has been increasingly difficult of late. They are remarkably persistent." His dark gaze slid over to Trick. "I would, of course, refuse outright if necessary, especially now."

"Why now?" wondered the Alpha.

"I have no reason to stay with the mermaids anymore. I was only there because the Paralia travels near the shores regularly. I could guard her and continue to look for Patrick at the same time."

"Is she not your sister?" asked Colin.

"She is."

"Don't you want to stay with her because she's family?" asked Bryan, who had stayed with his brother when they moved to the Bay Area.

"I want to stay with Patrick. Nothing else matters."

"Not even your sister?" that was the Alpha.

"Not even her."

Alec nudged Marvin with his cheek. "This lack of familial loyalty is concerning."

Marvin patted the Alpha's head condescendingly. "Don't worry your pretty noggin about it. Remember, I left my sister without a qualm for you, babes. Merfolk aren't like wolves. We aren't naturally loyal to blood or family group. Merfolk are loyal for reasons of politics and survival. The mermaids stay in pods to raise the children and stay safe during migrations. There's no real affection to it. And mermen aren't part of even *that* much. Remember, they abandon us to shore the moment we sprout legs. It is the natural way of things. We are not wolves or humans. We are a different species. We do not act as you might expect."

The Alpha still seemed concerned. His eyes were steady on Sato's face.

Sato met those eyes directly. "So can I stay with you instead of them? Or at least *near* you? For Patrick."

Alec shook his head. "That isn't up to me. That is up to Trick."

Trick felt all eyes on him then. Five werewolves, two mermen, all staring at him expectantly.

He stayed silent. Normally he enjoyed being the center of attention, but this time the hairs on his arms prickled. If he were an otter, he'd be all fluffed up. He wanted to escape again. Run away from having to decide.

Isaac came to his defense. "It's a lot, all at once. He thought he'd been abandoned. He was running a long time before he found us." Isaac understood. Isaac had been running and hiding a long time too, when Tank found him and they fell in love. Isaac had been the opposite of Trick – overly wanted. But they had both been chased, and hounded, and scared. Isaac had hidden for different reasons, but probably understood Trick best.

So Trick looked to him. "What should I do, Omega?"

Isaac sighed. "I hate giving advice. I'm best at listening. But I guess, reconnect? Take your time. Talk as much as you can. Rebuild trust if you think he's worth it."

Alec said, maybe seeing something in Trick's sudden frozen stillness. "You don't have to run again."

Colin added, "We want you to stay."

Trick swallowed against believing that. But some part of him must have – he felt less prickly and unsettled.

He looked over at Sato. Forced himself to focus on that familiar face. The new lines tension had made at the sides of his mouth.

"You're here."

"Finally accepting it, are you?" Sato pushed back his chair and stood, came around the table. Carefully, as if he didn't want to startle Trick. He ended up standing next to his chair. He still smelled like sea salt. That smell had been on Sato's futon the first day they met.

Trick twisted and tilted back, looking up at him. He still looked like Sato, too. Harder, meaner, but Sato. "You're really *actually* here."

"Yes, in this pack house. I made katsu. It sucked." Sato crouched down, lowering himself below Trick's eye level. Those kelp dark eyes of his were intent on Trick's face. That too was familiar. Sato watching him like he was something amazing. Sato had done that from the very beginning. When Trick was a tiny wild chattering creature in Sato's room. Sato had been hypnotized by him. Stayed hypnotized.

"I'm sorry it took me so long."

"To make katsu?"

"This hardly counts as katsu. Please forget I ever tried. No, to find you. You have no idea how sorry I am."

Trick thought to ask, then, a thing he hadn't contemplated until that moment. "Was it bad, all those years, without me?"

Sato hung his head. "Worse for you, I think."

"This isn't a competition over which of us had a shittier time, Sato."

Sato glanced back up at him, then down, then closed his eyes. Like he was having to think too hard. He brought his hands up, fluttered them slightly, the language of the sea. An ineffectual gesture on land.

For some strange reason, Trick remembered the first time he'd hugged Sato. Sato's webbed hands had clenched at his sides, tight and unsure – gripping hard onto emptiness. The last time they had hugged, those hands had clenched in Patrick's shirt, scrunching the material taut across his lower back – gripping hard onto Patrick.

"I don't know," Sato said finally. "There was just looking for you and surviving long enough to find you. There was holding myself together so hard, afraid the currents could break me open or wash right through me. I swam around with an open wound for a decade."

"I'm surprised the sharks didn't get you."

"Me too."

Trick caught his breath. "You fought them." No doubt, Sato had sought them out.

"I did."

"A lot of them?"

"Enough."

Trick sighed. His eyes burned. Why did Sato have to be so very much *Sato*, even now?

While Trick had been running and hiding and scared and longing for Sato. While he had found his cafe and his friends there and this pack, and grieved that they were not Sato. While he had been building a life and nursing resentment. Sato had searched and spiraled. Sato had gripped onto emptiness.

Trick really thought about it then. Their shared past. He had grown into adulthood the sole focus of all Sato's attention. But while the void Sato left when they parted had been vast and cold, it hadn't been empty. For ten years Trick had been unmoored and lonely for one man and trying to fill that void up with other people, but it was Sato who had drifted alone.

Sato spoke then, ignoring the avid ears of the pack around him. He never cared how he sounded. "I didn't know what to do, without you. I didn't know who I was. I didn't care about anything. There's only you, Patrick. It was always only you."

Trick understood then. He'd been an enthusiastic eight-year-old, excited to have a kid his own age, another shifter, move in next door. But Sato had been abandoned and alone in an entirely alien world. Trick had always seen their past as something where Sato was the strong one. This solitary rock in the middle of the ocean that Trick clung onto for dear life. His best friend. His great love. His childhood sweetheart. An uneven distribution of affection – Patrick giving unfettered adoration while Sato gave dutiful care.

Perhaps it had not been so one-sided.

Or perhaps it had been one-sided, but in the opposite direction.

Perhaps for Sato it had not been so much duty as necessity. That he had needed Patrick not just for friendship and eventually sex, but for survival. Perhaps Sato, all along, had been the one clinging to Patrick. He'd thought Sato was naturally solitary; maybe it wasn't natural, maybe it was just cultural conditioning.

Patrick had seen Sato as his port in a storm. His lifeboat. His safety net. All those euphemisms that human sailors had invented to compensate for their discomfort in an environment not made for them. Because Patrick's life was chaotic and full of drama and situations and other people. It always would be. He was a trickster born of a trickster species. A social animal who loved others easily. Sato was none of those things.

Trick was naturally dramatic. He surrounded himself with gossip and amusement in his work and now in his home life. In the end, he had friends and resources because of who he was, *what* he was. Sato had none of those things.

Where had Trick gone when he felt under threat? Not to the water, in the end. Not to the wilderness. No, Trick had gone first to the cafe and then here, to the pack house. To the pack. To a new family that was not even his own species. But were his friends. Where had Sato gone?

Where could Sato go to feel safe? To feel welcomed? To feel loved? People, groups, friends, humans, other shifters were not safe to Sato.

To the ocean? The sea and its people had rejected him. Cast him out at age ten. As an adult they demanded him back, wanting things from him he could not and would not give.

To the land? Certainly not. Sato had never felt secure on land, he always said it was too heavy there. Too loud. Too fast. It was a dry, confusing place, inhospitable.

Perhaps Sato had searched for Patrick his whole adult life because he truly had no other option.

When he had said, *It was always Patrick*. For him there really was *only* Patrick. Sato had meant that *precisely*. Sato always meant what he said.

But perhaps it was also, actually, true.

"I missed you," Trick said to the merman, looking him full in the face, meaning it. And then he worried that now he had spoken those words out loud, the consequence was eternal. They had been dropped like pebbles into still waters. And all water-folk know that ripples had consequences.

So Trick added, "I'm sorry I couldn't stay waiting."

Sato's hand carefully, cautiously, gently, curved over the side of his face. "I'm sorry I was late."

The Present: Sato in the pack house contemplating Trick (and more)

Sato was many things, but he wasn't stupid, certainly not where Trick was concerned. He stood up and held out a hand, impossibly grateful when Patrick placed his smaller one into it. Skin as soft as sea lettuce, and fortunately a lot less slimy.

He hoisted Patrick up all the way out of the chair and into his arms. Patrick melted into the hug, clung onto him with both hands, pushed his face into Sato's shoulder. Sato tangled his own webbed fingers in the soft fabric of Patrick's shirt, breathing him in. Grateful for lungs instead of gills.

Patrick drew back, not letting go, just so he could look up at him. Something in Sato's face reassured him, sure Patrick was the only one in the world to find solace there.

He let go, but when Sato would have stepped away, Patrick tugged him toward the stairs. Sato followed him obediently, not taking his eyes off him. Nevertheless he was aware that the werewolves had been staring at them with interest the entire time.

As soon as they were on the second floor, Sato heard the Pack start talking behind them. Sato did not care, he paid attention only to Patrick.

Patrick dragged him into the small room that was right near the top of the stairs. "This one is mine. And werewolves have supernatural hearing, remember?"

Sato tilted his chin slightly. "Will we be making lots of noise, Patrick?"

"You learned how to tease while we were apart?"

"I don't want to presume" – although he did want to do all the kinds of things to cause Patrick to make noise. He wanted to know what made him squeal with delight. He wanted to rediscover all the planes and angles of Patrick. He wanted him whimpering and under him.

Patrick pushed him gently onto the small bed. Stared down at him for a long moment. Then closed his eyes, small face resolute.

Opening them he looked, determined. He climbed into Sato's lap, straddling him, wrists resting on Sato's shoulders.

Sato felt like he was holding his breath. But also, his hands had a will of their own, smoothing and curving around to grab Patrick's ass, grip tight, pulling him closer.

Patrick moaned.

It was such a dear, familiar noise it made Sato's eyes burn with missing it. Not having had that for so long. It made him ache both in his heart and his cock. It made him want to be fierce and demanding, and also slow and careful and lingering. It made his hands clench reflexively.

Which made Patrick moan again and wriggle against him.

Sato couldn't help it. He flipped him over and flat onto his back on the bed. Patrick bounced and squeaked adorably. But did not let go of his neck. Even dared to dart forward and nibble at his ear.

Sato nearly lost reason, but then remembered his chatty Patrick should be chattering, not moaning. "Isaac said we should stay talking. And I know you like to talk. So talk," he tried to glare at him. "I'll occupy my mouth with other things."

Patrick actually giggled. "If memory serves, you are one of the few who can make me lose my voice."

Sato didn't like the implication that there had been others, but also, he took that as a challenge. Fortunately, and by design, the yellow robe was as easy to get out of as it had been to get into. He was still bloodied and bruised but he was healing. Any lingering pain was being swamped by his need for Patrick. His Patrick, right there under him. Squirming just like he used to.

Patrick's eyes were dark and bright, shining and focused on Sato's body. He liked that. Preened under the attention. Tried not to drown in them. The only place he could drown.

One small hand touched his ribs tentatively. "Do your ribs still hurt?"

Patrick was touching him again. *Patrick.* Sato swallowed a groan. Took a deep breath to slow himself down.

"Why are you still dressed?"

Patrick's hand trailed down his stomach over to his hip and down his leg. "It's already scabbed over. I forgot how fast you heal in this form."

"It's my shifted state, made to be under threat and heal faster, since it's not safe. Your hand should be further up." His cock hurt, he was so hard. Patrick's hands were on him, yes, but still so cautious.

Patrick's gaze drifted and he licked his lips. But Sato wanted to taste Patrick right now. Not the other way around. Yet Patrick was still fully dressed.

So that meant kissing.

He bent, pressed his lips to Patrick's, who turned his head into the kiss, arched upwards a little. Not sloppy and eager as he had been in their youth, but welcoming and practiced.

Sato coaxed with little kisses and nibbles, used his tongue to lick a the seam of Patrick's mouth. Questioning, not insistent. Patrick's chin tilted and he opened to him. Yielding.

Eventually Patrick was inciting kisses. Patrick was making little whimper noises deep in his throat.

Patrick's words between kisses (yes, he was still speaking)

were nonsense now. Words like Sato's own thoughts always were, jumbled by lust.

"It's annoying how good you are at kissing. Did I never tell you that? Merfolk don't kiss. Why should you be good at this?"

Sato just kept slanting over his mouth, tongue delving deeper. Consuming him like he was fresh meat, tender and salt bright, sweet and savory.

"I hate that you're still good at this." Patrick spoke between moans and kisses. "Oh, do I think that because we learned together? So this way seems like the best way?"

Sato moved to his neck. Bit against it, not hard, just soft little nibbles trailing downwards until he was thwarted by Patrick's shirt.

"I missed this," said Patrick. About the bites or the kissing or the making out Sato wasn't sure. But it made him so happy.

Patrick's clothes were different now. More complicated and elaborate, floaty layers of fabric like kelp forests. Sato wasn't sure how to get Patrick out of this style of attire without ripping it. He wanted to tear them away, but Patrick was fond of clothing – that would upset him. But he needed to go slow. Not chase. Be careful. Not scare Patrick into running again. Never that. Sato wanted to destroy and claim, but that need only drove him to move slower.

He plucked ineffectually at the layers of material, trying to worm his hands under and touch skin, but there didn't seem to be any gaps. It was very frustrating.

Patrick laughed at him. "Lemme up."

Sato rolled to one side, reluctant to stop touching, but willing to do anything Patrick wanted that kept them together.

"I really did miss this, but I'm scared.

Patrick stood and began to strip out of the layers one at a time.

"What exactly are you scared of?" Sato asked, hoping he could correct for whatever it was.

Each time Patrick pulled off a garment, he said one thing to go with it. As if he were doling out truth into a growing pile of discarded cloth.

"I'm scared I'll fall for you again, too much, and exactly like before." A feather-light scarf fluttered to the floor.

Sato did not answer because that was what he wanted.

"What happens if you leave me now?" Off came one shirt.

"That will never happen," vowed Sato.

"That's a childish thing to say. We're all grown up now. We know more than anything that we don't control our own fates or futures." Patrick's other shirt came off then. His chest was still slender but less boyish, his skin was lighter toned with a few freckles, and he had more chest hair than he'd had before. Sato's fingers itched to touch. Was it soft?

"I will not leave if I can possibly help it, and I will cut ties so no one else has any sway over me."

"That's such a Sato thing to say. That the solution is further isolation."

Sato wondered what Patrick wanted from him.

"No matter how hard both of us try, it could happen and I can't do it again." Off came Patrick's necklaces and other jewelry from wrists and hands. Patrick could wear rings. Sato could not. They looked pretty on his small hands. "I don't want to run anymore. I want to stay here. I like it here." Off came his shoes and socks.

"I won't do anything to drive you away," Sato vowed.

Patrick stopped, half naked, and glared at him. Sato added, "Fine, I will try hard not to. I will do my very best."

That earned him Patrick's belts and the top layer of whatever was wrapped around his waist.

He was so beautiful. Sato was in agony.

"And if for any reason at all I have to leave here for any length of time, I'll make sure you are safely here, in this box, surrounded by pack. And I will come back to you."

Patrick took off another layer. He was going so slowly.

This was the worst.

And the best.

"I won't make promises back, Sato. I'll need to trust you again. That'll take time."

"I understand." Although he didn't, not really. But at least

Patrick was speaking to him. Telling him things. Taking off his clothing right there in front of him.

Sato tried to sit back and enjoy it. He also tried begging. "Just please don't run away from me. Please try talking first. That should help, right? You're good at talking."

"I thought you had too much pride to beg."

Sato wondered why. What pride? "I will do anything to stay with you," he said. Because it was the truth. Begging was just words. Words may not come easy to Sato, but they cost nothing.

It had been ten years. Sato wanted to touch and taste, not watch and beg. He wasn't a patient person. Despite his best efforts, Sato found himself whining. "Please, just take the rest off and come here."

Patrick's grin was evil. "You can wait a bit longer."

"I waited ten years." He raised himself up on his elbows and watched. Carefully not touching himself – he was too close and it had been too long.

Patrick looked comically disbelieving. Arched eyebrows, big forehead, big eyes. "Did you really?"

What an odd thing for him to disbelieve. What possible incentive had Sato to lie about such a thing?

"There was only ever you for me, Patrick. I *told* you."

Patrick paused and cocked his head. Squinted down at Sato. Nodded once and then continued slowly stripping. Unlike Sato, Patrick had always been a bit of a tease. He was busy activating his power, testing Sato's control.

Sato let him. Held himself back. Whatever Patrick needed to feel secure about him again.

"What if you never found me?" asked Patrick.

"Not an option."

"What if I had died."

"*Definitely* not an option."

"I don't think even your stubbornness can keep someone from death."

"Did you miss the part where I spent years training to be a vangill? It's what I'm supposed to do."

Finally Patrick shucked the last of his clothes. Stood naked before him. Unashamed by his own nudity.

Sato scooted himself to the edge of the bed, reached out and dragged Patrick to him by the hips. Swallowed him down. Using his mouth to rediscover everything about Patrick. The way he tasted. Smelled. The texture of him.

"I forgot how good you were at this." Patrick gasped it out, breathing uneven.

The best kind of compliment, to be praised for something he enjoyed, rather than something he was just good at, like fighting. Still, Patrick was managing to voice coherent sentences. Sato needed to try harder. Be better.

"You know I always kinda of hated that about you. I mean, whose first lover is actually good? Whose first time is glorious? How dare you ruin me for others like that?"

More praise. Sato smiled around Patrick's cock. Occupied his hands rediscovering the rest of Patrick's body, how much it had changed and how much it had not. Where his new erogenous zones were, and if they were the same as the old ones.

Patrick hit him with one tiny fist, ineffectually and with no real intent. "It's so annoying, you know?"

Sato licked all along the shaft, replaced his mouth with one hand. Looked up, confused. Had he missed something? Patrick reached down with one small, soft hand, curled it around the side of Sato's face tenderly.

Sato lost himself in those fathomless eyes.

"What is it?" he asked.

"Why are you so good at sex when you've barely ever done it? Upsetting, actually."

Sato sighed. "You trained me. Stop chattering, Patrick. I know Isaac said to talk but now you're just being ridiculous."

"Then shut me up," suggested Patrick, leaning forward for another long kiss.

Sato gave him that and more. He let his own need take over. He let bits of his own wanting trickle into his actions now. Biting down harder. Digging his nails into Patrick's ass. Muscling Patrick around just because he could and he wanted to.

It was a mixed-up jumble of all the things he had longed for. Plus all the things he had forgotten he longed for. Things he had loved and missed. Patrick's silken movements. The salt-sweet taste of his flesh and his need and his tears overwhelmed Sato. Three different flavors, complementing each other. He tasted like the ocean after a rainstorm.

The little whining eager noises Patrick made overwhelmed Sato's ears. How he talked and talked and then suddenly stopped and inhaled sharply. The way it became Sato's challenge to make him do that.

Sato was driven to take Patrick, the ultimate chatterbox, to places where he had no words and he barely had any breath.

Sato remembered how pleasing it was when Patrick bucked up against him. He was reminded that Patrick liked to lick the webbing between his fingers, that this caused tingles through his body that went straight to his cock. The membrane there was soft and delicate, a memory of the fins in his true form.

He wanted Patrick to ride him. So he could see everything. The slight wince of pain mixed with pleasure as he slid inside. And he also wanted Patrick face down and entirely vulnerable, so Patrick could not see anything, so Sato did not have to look into those fathomless eyes full of regret. He wanted the eternal boy-Patrick of his memories, all angles and hollows, all fine bones and fragility. And he wanted this new Patrick, all lean and sinewy, angles tempered by age, sharpness dulled by life, fragility hardened by dry land, tough but still bendy.

He wanted the long arch of Patrick's back, and the flex of his hips under the webs of Sato's fingers. He wanted the ache of him, the need. He wanted him so close it was like they were trying to crawl inside each other's skin. Patrick would have his tail, and he would have Patrick's fur.

He wanted them coiled and connected at all possible points. Which meant, in the end he had Patrick sitting in his lap, like they had started out. All four of Patrick's limbs wrapped around him. Sato driving up into him from below, using the pure strength of his muscles and bigger body to get any kind of lever-age. His hands on Patrick's hips and ass and lower back, encouraging him to move. His lips pressed against Patrick's until there was no kissing possible, only gasping for air.

Patrick undulated like the open ocean. Cresting and falling over Sato, waves breaking on the shore. Patrick beached himself upon him, landed on Sato like something the sea was rejecting. Turning Sato, creature of the salty deep, into the warm soft sand of an otter's resting place.

If Patrick was Sato's salt water home, his sustenance and reason for existence…

If Patrick could be Sato's whole ocean, if he could dwell in those fathomless eyes…

Then Sato would try to be Patrick's shore. He would be the land for him. He would be the place where Patrick stayed and rested. He would be dry and sun-baked, heavy with too much gravity, if that was what it took to keep an otter.

By the end, Sato lay flat on his back with Patrick plastered against him. As much of them was touching as could possibly touch. Both of them were covered in sweat and Patrick's cum and Sato's. Even spent, neither of them relaxed. Sato found his arms wrapped around Patrick's back, still, his hands gripping Patrick's sides, unable to let go.

But Patrick seemed to be the same. His legs wrapped and locked around Sato's, his arms coiled about Sato's neck.

It was as if their muscles were locked together like that. Knotted and tied, bound by memories and time, resentment and hope, pain and love. The measured balance of it all, the returning rising tides.

Sato was exhausted, every part of him, but still he had this lingering strength in his shifted bones. This need to keep clinging, out of fear and hope. Out of a memory of absence. Out of practice.

Neither of them wanted, ever again, to be the first to let go.

CHAPTER SEVENTEEN

BLOW HIM OUT OF THE WATER

The Present: Trick in the pack house contemplating islands

Trick awoke the next morning and something was different. Something was filled that had been empty before. And not just his ass.

Sato.

Sato was *there*. Sleeping next to him in that quiet way that made him seem almost dead.

Trick was a restless sleeper. Often moving, flipping his pillow, and kicking off covers. Talking sometimes. When they were young, he'd once woken, confused by a sound. A glowering Sato had said, to his amusement, "You were giggling so hard you woke yourself up."

He didn't think he giggled in his sleep anymore. But he was still restless.

He rolled to his side, focused on Sato's familiar face. It was less severe when he slept, but often still scowling. Patrick had studied him like this a thousand times and never got tired of it.

Sato was so still. Patrick put a finger below his nose to check his breathing.

Sato smiled without opening his eyes, as if Trick's hand near his face was all it took. Air currents, like water, activating his senses into wakefulness.

"I'm starving," said Sato, eyes still closed, reaching out and gathering Patrick to him. Patrick was self-conscious, feeling sticky and crusty. They both smelled of sleep and sex. They were surrounded by werewolves with powerful supernatural noses. Everyone would know what had happened. Would they think of him as weak, having let Sato back into his bed? Was he weak?

But he also felt warm and loved in that way he'd only ever gotten from Sato. Like he was the center of something. With Sato he wasn't on the fringes. He wasn't cared for out of pity like some kind of cute stray. Sato had always made him feel utterly wanted. When they were kids, before they became boyfriends, it had been like that. Right up until the moment Sato hadn't come back. Trick had been secure and confident in just that one thing: Sato wanted to be with him. Sato wanted him. More than he wanted anything else. Perhaps that's why it had hurt so much when he didn't come back. A sign not that Sato didn't want him anymore, but that he didn't want him enough. Patrick had been unwanted by everyone his whole childhood, except Sato.

Knowing it had been circumstances and disaster that separated them helped. But accepting that Sato had wanted him and had eventually found him, just been delayed? That reset Trick's universe. Sato hadn't stopped wanting and hunting.

He, Patrick, *had* been enough. Was still the center of Sato's focus. Was Sato's most wanted person. Trick hadn't felt wanted like that in a long time. Since he'd been Patrick.

"Let's get you some food, then." Trick made a pathetic attempt to leave the bed.

"Not Katsu." Sato rubbed Trick's back from nape to ass in long, strong strokes, power-petting to keep him from going anywhere.

"Certainly not. But we should shower first. Werewolf sniffers, you understand?"

Sato buried his own nose in Trick's neck. "Okay. But maybe a swim after food? I miss swimming with you."

"You do? But you had your own people to swim with."

"I missed *you*. Otters play. You're fun."

"I've taken to stealing surfboards. The humans get so confused when an otter absconds with their board and then catches the next big wave." He grinned.

"Of course that's what you'd do."

"There have been articles about me in the local paper. They don't realize I'm a shifter, of course. Much funnier that way."

"Uh huh." Sato's webbed fingers began combing through Trick's hair.

"I missed swimming with you too," Trick admitted, finally.

Sato's stomach growled audibly.

"Okay, let's shower and eat first." Trick started to rise, but Sato wouldn't let him go.

"You know, you were the first person to take care of me, in my whole life." Sato said it like he was still surprised.

Trick thought that was preposterous. His memories were all of Sato taking care of him, pulling him out of some pickle or another. That time he got trapped in the swimming pool. That fight at the house party. Countless other incidents where it was Sato picking him up, dusting him off, giving him a piggyback ride. Sato standing between Patrick and his family. Sato defending Patrick against violent humans or anything else the world threw at him.

"Silly merman. You were always my guardian."

Sato opened his eyes, dark and serious. Frustrated. "That's not what I mean. Not that kind of *taking care*. You're my home. You can't offer it up and then retract it again. Please?"

It was awfully early in the morning for Sato to confess a fear of such magnitude.

Sato was scared of him running away again. Patrick had never run from Sato before, and now Sato, the unflappable, was shaken and unsure.

"I like it here. I'm going to stay here." That was as much as Trick was willing to admit to right now.

Sato breathed out slowly. "If this is where I will be able to find you, then this is where I stop."

There was no time to really talk about that statement, because Colin knocked on the door.

"Hey, guys?"

"You can come in," said Trick, "but it stinks. Be warned."

Despite the warning, Colin's nose wrinkled as he stuck his head inside. "There's a large contingent of semi-naked mermaids in our den, all pretty annoyed and looking for Sato. Frankly, we're at a bit of a loss what to do with them."

"Oh, shit." Patrick whacked Sato's naked shoulder. "The marine biology conference starts today."

Colin sneezed. "You have time to shower first. Don't get distracted, though."

"I recommend feeding them," suggested Trick.

"Of course we're feeding them! We aren't monsters," replied Colin, offended.

The Present: Sato coping with other people

If the size of the facilities were anything to go by, werewolves were obsessed with showering. Odd wolf behavior. Still, this meant Sato got to shower *with* Patrick so it wasn't that bad. He didn't want to let him go and he couldn't stop touching him.

"We'll need to part for the day, Sato."

Sato couldn't stop the involuntary whine.

"You have vangill duties at a marine biology conference. Remember?"

"Not gonna do that anymore."

Patrick tutted at him. "It'll be good for you. Patch things up with your sister."

"Patch? Why patch?"

"She's still your sister. And you dealt her a blow saying you're leaving out of the blue like that. There's no need to be so abrupt about it. Saturdays are busy at the cafe. I don't want you hanging out there getting in trouble with my regulars. They keep grudges. Not to mention the news people coming in and causing a fuss. You're a local hero, remember."

It made sense but Sato wasn't happy about it. "You'll be here when we get back?"

"Yes," said Patrick, voice firm. Sato believed him.

If Patrick wanted him to trot around after his sister one last time, Sato would do it. Especially if Patrick was occupied with other things. He remembered the one time he'd visited Patrick in that tiny cafe back in their hometown. Patrick had been good at it. Cafe-ing.

They exited the shower and dried off.

"No time for that swim this morning?" Sato pressed, hopeful.

Patrick hissed his upper arm. "No time."

Tonight, Sato vowed to himself. He would come back. Patrick would definitely be waiting. It would be okay. They would be together again. Only a few hours this time. It was hard to convince himself not to cling.

Patrick fluffed his short hair vigorously. "Saturday mornings are the one time of the week the owner actually comes to the cafe. It's good for him to experience the pressure and the rush. Reminds him how *necessary* I am."

"You have a boss?" Sato took the towel away from him and used it to gently pat at Patrick's hair.

"Only just." Patrick submitted to his ministrations without protest.

Downstairs everyone was barely coping with mermaids in their midst. The big red-headed enforcer was trying to flirt and failing miserably. Marvin and his friend, the smaller redhead, were watching this with amusement. Because he'd been a threat, Sato remembered the big one was called Kevin. The smaller one had been shopping with him. He struggled to recall his name. Oh right, Colin. Tank, the biggest and apparently quietest of the pack, was also watching but with ill-disguised horror. Sato remembered his name because it suited him.

Alec and Judd were attempting to ignore them all and talking quietly in one corner over a laptop.

A smaller werewolf with a smiley face was puttering around in the kitchen with much greater efficiency than Sato. He was singing softly and cooking something fishy-smelling that made Sato's stomach growl even louder.

Patrick sniffed. "Kippers?" He looked over at Marvin and his friend. "You can get kippers in California?"

"Lovejoy is magic," said Colin, going into the kitchen himself.

Sato asked, "What are *kippers*?"

Patrick said, "A UK thing. I think. I had them at this random British pub in the middle of Arizona once. They're yummy."

The kitchen werewolf, overhearing this, smiled even bigger. He finished whatever he was doing with the frying pan and then brought a large pile of browned, flat fish on a platter to the table. He put a stack of plates and bowls nearby plus some forks, chopsticks, and spoons, then returned to the kitchen. Colin followed, carrying a big pot of something. Then kitchen werewolf again, this time with a tray of lots of little filled bowls. One of them looked like seaweed.

"Congee and toppings," explained kitchen werewolf. "Breakfast of champions." He undid his apron, glanced over at the mermaids in the den. "I made it with shrimp broth and fish sauce, so you should like it. Make sure everything is spotless before you leave. I'm off." He included the mermaids in his instructions. Sato was amused. He'd never seen a mermaid clean anything. Ever. Dishes were going to be hilarious.

Patrick went to sit at the big table and Sato dutifully followed, taking the seat right next to him. Pleased and honored at having gotten it.

"Where are you going?" Cascade asked the kitchen werewolf, genuinely curious.

"Food truck has the Farmer's Market at Larkspur Landing this morning."

Cascade only looked more confused.

"You ate, Lovejoy?" questioned Alec, before his kitchen werewolf could leave.

"While I was cooking, Alpha. Don't worry."

Sato served Patrick a bowl of the congee, which was some kind of white goo, then himself.

"Good luck today and thank you for breakfast," replied Alec politely.

Sato passed Patrick a spoon and chopsticks. They were both longer and fatter than the kind he'd grown up with. Patrick was busy paying attention to the conversation rather than the food.

"My pleasure." The kitchen werewolf waved at the mermaids. "Hope you like it."

Aqua, who had been trained in some human social niceties, said, "I'm sure we will. Thank you for doing the hunting."

The kitchen werewolf grinned. "Oh, sure. I went out and slayed the wild kipper just for you."

The pod looked collectively confused. "You went swimming this morning, wolf?"

"I hunted them down in the wilderness that is our spare freezer."

"Freezer?"

"Icebox," suggested Colin.

"Thank you for… cooking?" suggested Meymey to avoid any further fruitless side conversation.

Sato hid a smile. No doubt she was wondering why the werewolves bothered to cook at all. Merfolk, after all, ate their food raw.

He nudged Patrick. "Eat."

Patrick blinked in surprise at the serving in front of him. "When did you…?"

Sato pushed the tray of condiments over to him. Watched with interest which ones Patrick selected with his chopsticks. Sato served himself the same. Two of them were seaweed. Sato let out a breath of relief. He knew he'd like that part.

"Itadakimasu," he said, bringing his hands together as sire had taught him.

Patrick, unsuccessfully trying to hide a smile, said the same.

It actually wasn't bad. Salty and fishy like the sea, but thick and warm and nourishing.

"This is nice," he said to Patrick, in surprise. Not sure about the texture, but liking the flavor.

"Right?" Patrick bounced a little in his chair in excitement. "Lovejoy is a great cook. He makes this one dish, Moo Palo. It's my favorite."

Sato wondered if Patrick liked it better than his sire's katsu but didn't want to remind him of last night's catastrophe, so he stayed silent and ate his congee.

Patrick broke a kipper in two, placed half of it on the side of his bowl, the other on Sato's.

Sato tried not to preen at the attention. He took a small bite.

"Oh!" he said, surprised. "Yum!"

The mermaids, overhearing Sato's approval, no doubt, all moved in a colorful gaggle to the big table. Rilian was wearing heels and tripped over the step up from the living area to the dining area.

There was much scraping of chairs while they sat. The werewolves winced at the noise.

Kevin joined them. "Let me show you, ladies." He served himself congee, added toppings from the little bowls, then used a fork to drape one of the kippers over it all.

Marvin waltzed over and ostentatiously did the same, only using chopsticks instead of a fork.

After only a slight hesitation, all the mermaids imitated this action, using forks. Then dutifully all sat around the table and began eating, with spoons.

Patrick said, well under his breath, "Thank goodness they didn't opt for chopsticks."

"Can werewolves use chopsticks?" wondered Sato. Who had always felt his webbing gave him an advantage in that regard. Patrick was adept because otters were naturally dexterous.

"Werewolves will use anything to get as much food into their mouths as possible. I assume this pod can't chop a stick?" answered Patrick.

"Not that I'm aware. It's never come up."

It was a hallmark of their youth together that Sato and

Patrick had learned to use chopsticks. Sato winced, remembering the sharp sting on the back of his hand when his sire whacked it with his own chopsticks to correct Sato's mistake. "Further back!" He could still hear sire's strict tone. "You're holding them too close to the tip." Patrick had mastered the skill way faster than Sato, who never understood why utensils were needed in the first place. Because of heat, presumably. Why cook things? It only complicated matters.

Meymey was not participating in the congee experiment with the rest of the pod. Instead she was standing next to Sato at the end of the table, arms crossed, staring down at him.

She had a look on her face that Sato had learned to be wary of. It was all stubborn petulance and self-righteousness. Little sister was annoyed with him.

She gestured at Patrick. "This is the reason, isn't it? The reason you are the way you are? A dratsie! Of all creatures."

Patrick looked up at her, chewed his kipper, unperturbed.

Sato stopped eating. "Yes. He's the reason." Sato wasn't going to deny anything. No point.

"Now you've found him, will you return to normal?"

"He is normal, for me."

"You can't tell me you intend to keep him."

"I intend to keep him. Or, given his residence here, I suspect he will be keeping me. Right?" he looked at Patrick's sweet, familiar face.

Patrick was looking smug. Sato loved that look. Patrick knew what it meant for a merman to challenge the matriarchy. And one of the Soteria. And a sister who ruled a pod. At least, Sato hoped Patrick understood what this meant. The importance. The ramifications.

"Wait. What? You intend to stay here, in this dirty bay? In this dry box full of werewolves?"

"There is no *intend*."

"The Deep will not allow it." Meymey sounded very young and very sure of herself.

Sato wasn't going to play into her fantasy. "You already agreed the Deep has ceded authority over these waters to this

Alpha." He gestured with his hand at Alec, who looked up from the laptop.

"Why are you involving me in your family drama?" the Alpha whined. Then noticed the table. "Oh, right. Breakfast." He shut the laptop, stood, and stretched.

Meymey didn't even acknowledge him. She was blinking at her brother in shock. He'd never directly challenged her before. He'd had no reason to do so. "Water rights are not the point here, Daidai. You are a *vangill*, you belong to the Deep."

"No. I belong to *myself*. It is the only right a merman truly has – solitary autonomy."

"Not *the vangill*, Daidai." She was so sure of herself. And so very wrong.

Judd wandered over, looking quite fierce. "He is your slave?"

Alec walked over too. Face concerned.

All the mermaids were staring at them. But they kept eating.

Meymey looked uncomfortable. She knew she had no power over the werewolves and she was embedded in their den. Plus Sato hadn't stood to protect her as he once would have. Spurs ready. No, Sato stayed sitting next to his dratsie.

Meymey admitted, "Well, no, not exactly. But he was trained by us to use his spurs, so he owes us his service."

"Indenture?" Judd continued to frown, suspicious.

Aqua, sensing a diplomatic incident in the making, abandoned her kipper and said, "Now, now, Alpha, I'm sure she doesn't mean that. You know English isn't her first language."

Sato studied his sister's face. It was full of confusion and pride and embarrassment, that her vangill was misbehaving right now in front of everyone. "Let me be clear, little sister. I have served my time and then some. Before I came to serve you, I was already free. Have you any idea how many favors are owed the Deep because of my actions a decade ago? No. I *chose* to guard the Paralia. You did not choose me."

"I don't understand." Suddenly Meymey looked forlorn and young. But Sato knew that manipulation tactic of hers all too well. It tugged on his heartstrings, what few he had, but he wasn't going to let it work.

"The Navarch's word is on it. You may ask him." He should reach out to the Navarch anyway. Invite him for a visit. Get Patrick to hook him up with someone. He had made a promise, once. "I am sorry little sister, but you are failing to understand why I was with you at all."

Sato curved his hand around Patrick's shoulder. "He's *the reason*. My reason. He's why I stayed with you. So I could go to land. So I could keep looking for him. He's the reason I completed vangill training *at all*. So I could go back, unfettered by the demands of the Deep. So I could protect him. He's my spurs. He's why they happen. I can be recalled to serve under only two circumstances now, war and natural disaster. This is neither."

"Oh, I don't know," said Patrick, cheeky like he used to be when they were kids, "I've always considered myself a bit of a natural disaster."

"Yes, trouble," Sato tapped him under the chin with one finger.

Meymey sighed and looked away from their intimacy, as if it pained her. "I remember. This is your cuter half, Daidai?"

"Yes. He's it. I don't care about anything else."

"Not even me?"

"Of course I care for you. But you are the Paralia of All Seas. You'll get a new vangill. One more willing to stud, no doubt. You'll be fine without me. But this is Patrick. My Patrick."

"He seems to have been fine without you too." She gestured to the pack. All of those who were downstairs were now on alert because Alec was standing and tense.

"But I am not *fine* without Patrick," Sato pushed back. He might not need her to understand why he was leaving her, but he needed her to accept that he was. Sometimes, that was the same thing. "Meymey, this is not a decision you can make, nor is it a situation you can challenge. It just is. Like the tides. You must accept it."

His sister did not look convinced. She was used to getting what she wanted. She was used to him being by her side.

Sato turned back to his food. Picked up his chopsticks.

Holding them delicately near the ends, as his sire had instructed him.

It really was tasty.

Marvin looked pointedly at Meymey, who found an empty chair and was finally sitting down. Marvin's bowl was already empty. Fast eater. Most merfolk were. Survival trait. "So your brother's life was in crisis last night and you went sightseeing at a lesbian bar?"

"Can you think of a better thing to do?" Meymey bit into a piece of kipper, looked impressed. Scarfed the whole thing.

"That's a very lesbian attitude. Ms Trickle must be so proud."

Meymey fluttered her hands in mermaid agreement. "She's pretty great, for a kelpie. Sexy voice. Beautiful," she paused, looking nervously around, "uh, fingers."

Marvin grinned. "And *that* was even more lesbian."

Meymey said, "It's not like I could help Daidai with whatever was freaking him out and causing him to fight a bear. I mean, I tried, but isn't that *his* problem?"

Alec sat down in one of the few free chairs, some distance away from his mate. "Are merwomen always like this?"

Marvin grinned. "Pretty much. So, Paralia, how was it last night? Did you find yourself a nice hot butch or king or stud or...?"

Meymey was intrigued. "Stud? One of the humans of that kelpie's club could get me pregnant? That sounds like fun."

"I'm sure they'd be willing to try." Marvin was almost as cheeky as Patrick. No wonder they got along.

Colin took pity on Meymey. "It's not quite the same kind of *stud*."

Alec looked over at Sato. "Speaking of which, you said *willing to stud*. Does that mean sire children?"

Marvin said, "I thought I explained. Mermen with spurs, like our new friend here, are genetically superior to the rest of us boys with tails in many ways, including procreative. Merman like me are sterile, ones like him are not." He arched thin blond brows. "He's *potent*."

"Must be challenging, if you're gay," suggested Kevin.

"Tell me about it," said Sato, with feeling.

Aqua said, "Wait a second, you never slept with *any* of us. Not one. Not even outside of the diplomatic pod or the Soteria?"

Sato didn't feel the need to answer that.

"What a fucking waste," said Rilian.

"*Lack* of *fucking*, so that would be a *not-fucking* waste," corrected Marvin, clearly amused with himself.

Aqua looked at Meymey. "But doesn't he *have* to?"

"Sire children?" Meymey frowned, her mind no doubt scrolling through the oral histories of the sea people. Sato had already challenged her once. She didn't want to be shamed again. And this wasn't her jurisdiction. Technically, the physical health and well-being of merfolk, including their longevity as a species, was the provenance of the Anax, not the Paralia. Sato knew that part well. He'd asked.

"The Klepsydra would know for certain, but I believe it is a social obligation, not a mandate," she said, after a long moment. Not wanting to cede the point. "One that most vangill perform willingly."

Kevin grinned. "Speaking as the only straight man in the room, fuck, yeah."

Colin glared at his brother. "Why are you like this?"

Alec said, to forestall further brotherly annoyances, "It's about that time, everyone. Conference is opening soon. I'm giving a talk at noon and I need to get there well before to socialize first. Judd, who is coming with us for protection?"

Judd said, "Me, Kevin, Tank. I think that should be enough. Colin, you can stay behind. We don't need tech support this time. Isaac is still asleep. Can't imagine we'll need him."

"Doubt it," said Tank. "Let him rest."

"Rough night?"

"Very inebriated, very distressed bear shifter at the club." Tank glanced over at Sato and Patrick. "Surprise, surprise."

Judd tilted his head. "But you're okay? Enough sleep?"

Tank lowered his gaze. "I'm fine."

Judd took him at his word. "So yeah, three's enough. We'll

stick with the mermaids as a group." He looked over at Sato. "You don't anticipate major issues, do you, vangill?"

Sato cocked his head, "Define *issues*."

Marvin said, "Have you ever been around mermaids let loose on a human population? In this case, dorky scientists? There's bound to be carnage."

Alec tensed.

"Not that kind, sweetie. Bloodbath in the broken hearts kind of way."

Judd sighed at Marvin's theatrics. "Let me put it another way. Is anything going to happen that requires more than three very large, highly trained, werewolf bodyguards?"

Sato imagined that the werewolves, especially Kevin, might be more of a hindrance to mermaid activities than a help. But it was sweet of them to try.

Marvin was grinning. "It's not an ideal ratio. That's one wolf for every four mermaids."

"What am I, chopped liver? I'm there too, remember?" protested Alec. The Alpha.

Marvin came around the table and gave his lover a smacking kiss on the cheek. "You're just there for decoration, babes."

"Alpha, you know how you get at conferences. All focused and nervous about your presentation. Distracted by scientific data and philosophical quandaries," explained Judd, patiently.

"You drop things," said Kevin.

"You lose track of time," added his brother.

"And repeat yourself." That was Tank.

"It's adorable," said Marvin, with another smooch to the other cheek. "But I can't stay to watch this time, gotta go, do..." he paused, "something fabulous and nothing to do with screamingly dull indoor convention centers and human scientists." He shuddered. "Bathe in sequins or something. I wonder what Mana is up to today."

"I've never understood that saying. I mean, chopped liver is delicious," said Colin softly, almost to himself.

Marvin looked at him. "You coming with me in pursuit of sequins and drag queens?"

Colin stood with alacrity. "Why not? But we are doing dishes and cleaning the kitchen first."

Marvin sighed dramatically. "This life I lead as a lost princess entrapped by wolves is so arduous."

"Come along, Cinderella, you can wear the pink ruffled dish gloves."

CHAPTER EIGHTEEN

KETTIL OF FISH

The Present: Trick at the cafe

The cafe was hopping, it being Saturday and all. Trick's boss was looking overwhelmed and long-suffering. The expression of abject relief on his face the moment he spotted Trick was gratifying. Joe was looking like Joe.

"What's your back pocket poet today?" Trick asked as he made his way from the stockroom with necessary supplies.

Joe didn't look up from the dishes. "Robert Duncan."

"Sticking with the Beats for now, huh?"

"They jive with my current life state."

"Puerile?" suggested Trick.

Joe flicked soapy water at him.

The boss finished up his current order and turned on Trick. "Thank fuck you're here. Please, save me."

"I gotcha." Trick swooped into position behind the espresso machine, wishing he'd worn his cape. Yes, he owned a cape – several, in fact.

Boss said in a low, angst-riddled tone. "None of them know what they want! Ninety percent of the time the savory side of the menu just confuses them. I can't find the oat milk and we're *already* out of buns."

"Has Max been in yet?" Trick handed him a fresh carton of oat milk which he'd already retrieved.

"Who?"

"Mr Spandex?" Trick put on his apron with a flourish.

"I recall no major spandex incidents as yet."

"Well, then some truly spectacular buns are incoming."

"Did you just pun me? At—" boss glanced over at the wall clock "—9:30 a.m.? It's far too early for flirting, Trick."

"No such thing!" said Trick, finishing up the latte and giving it to the nice young couple with his best smile. He pivoted and began loading a new batch of sweet scones into the display case to take over for the missing buns, and tipping the bun label down.

"What flavor are these?" he asked.

"No idea."

Trick sniffed. "Ginger something?"

"Apricot," said Joe, not looking up from the dishes.

"Oh, nice combo." Trick scrawled a label. His handwriting was terrible but it hardly mattered, everyone would ask anyway. Scone people liked having a whole conversation during their selection process. Trick was thinking of developing an advanced personality chart based entirely on beverages and pastry choices. There was a best-selling book buried in there somewhere. He knew Isaac did the same as a bartender. "IPA drinkers," he often said, shaking his head in distress. Trick would nod back, all serious "Same as the skinny half-caf people. I getcha."

None of the regulars were there except Floyd. Floyd showed up first thing every day so as to get his preferred small table along the side nearest the serving counter. On the weekends he was extra diligent because tourists didn't know the table *belonged* to him, but the weekends were the best times to be an observer of human nature. Which, Trick theorized, was Floyd's reason for existence. He was like a birdo, just for people. Tourists dominated the cafe on summer weekends.

It's why the other regulars weren't there.

Although Max dropped in briefly just then, wearing his ubiquitous full coverage spandex and looking like the wet dream of gym bunnies everywhere.

Trick's boss said, "Ah, I see your point."

"Late run today?" Trick didn't ask what Max wanted, just made him an iced Slippery Paris Brest. He was in too good a mood to make the poor man order it by name this morning. Amazing what a little reunion sex could do for one's outlook on life. Okay, well, a lot of reunion sex. Sato was pretty insatiable.

Max smirked around the straw. "Bryan kept me up late." Speaking of.

"Explains why he wasn't down for breakfast."

"Can't complain."

Trick agreed wholeheartedly with that sentiment. Although he couldn't imagine going for a long run after a night like the one he'd just had. Max was a tough cookie. "I thought complaining was your forte."

"We all have superpowers," replied one of the most powerful humans on the planet. "Speaking of which, where is everyone?"

"You found 'em, sweet-cheeks." Trick gestured in shock. The Bean was absolutely packed, humming with conversation and activity.

Max sucked down his drink in annoyance. "You know what I mean. The den was suspiciously quiet when I looked in before my run."

"Marine biology conference, remember?"

"*Everyone* went?"

"The enforcers and Tank went as bodyguards. And then Marvin and Colin went to collect Mana for some shopping."

"Of course they did. I suspect glitter is involved."

"Sequins darling, not glitter. And Lovejoy has a food truck thingy."

"Of course he does. Wait. Do I care about any of this?"

"I don't think so. You never have before."

"Fair point." Max finished his drink, plonked the glass down. "Too crowded in here. I'm off." And sped out.

Trick was tolerably certain the entire cafe turned to watch him leave. The man had a spectacular ass. Runners. Unfair.

His boss said, "Beautiful buns, point taken. Still, next week order double of those sticky ones for the weekend."

Trick got defensive. "I already did. They obviously didn't deliver them."

"Don't let them charge us then."

Trick was annoyed. "Boss! Whatcha take me for?"

His boss was instantly recalcitrant. "Of course, you're wonderful. Silly of me to even suspect you weren't on it."

Trick stuck his nose ostentatiously in the air. "Exactly."

The boss was generally quite cowed by Trick and his efficiency, and his spectacular abilities in the arena of drinks, socialization, and gift of the cafe gab. Trick had single handedly turned the Bean into the local hot spot, and everyone knew it.

The boss (if Trick had learned his name, he'd long since forgotten) was a bit of an idiot. Fortunately, he was well aware that his role, as Trick's boss, was to make sure everything stayed well oiled and to sit back and let Trick do the real work. Like the best lube. As a result he'd become entirely dependent on Trick. Also like lube.

As such, he spent most of his time terrified Trick might leave the Bean for better climes. It was the perfect dynamic, so far as Trick was concerned.

"Excuse me, but when it says *fish sauce* is that Vietnamese or Thai style?"

Trick turned to the sharply dressed woman in front of him. She had an elder goth feel to her. Or maybe she was Scandinavian? She was ghostly complected with razor cheekbones. Wide black pants and a textured asymmetrical top, paired with sparse but extremely expensive silver jewelry. The attention to the details of her outfit screamed human, but she was eyeing the shifter side of the menu with interest.

"Vietnamese," said Trick.

"Have you considered making your own garum?"

Ah, a foodie. "I have, actually. But apparently it stinks to high heaven and I have housemates with sensitive noses."

The lady leaned forward a little. "You have a large local shifter population?" She seemed overly focused on the shifter drinks – for a human. Tail chaser maybe? She seemed a bit old for that.

"How perspicacious of you. Yes, we do." Trick was cautious. He didn't mention the pack.

"I will have an iced Sea Bream, please."

"You're sure?" Trick had thought she was human, but maybe she was one of those shifters who hid her identity well. Selkie? But frankly, she just looked a little too old to be a shifter.

She chuckled. "Yes, sötis, I'm sure. Nicely high in protein and low in sugar, like drinking broth for breakfast. How else will I keep my girlish figure?"

Trick turned and began making it. There was no one in line behind her at the moment so she stayed there, clearly inclined to chat with him. Trick didn't mind, he liked chatting.

"So who invents these drinks? I should like to talk to the person responsible for that part of your menu."

Trick wasn't sure he should admit to anything but his boss didn't give him a choice.

"Trick here does. Isn't he brilliant? And no, you can't steal him away from me."

"She can't?" Trick wanted to know.

Floyd piped up. "No, she can't. I'd have to spend years searching for the perfect cap all over again. If you moved, I'd have to follow. And I don't want to sell my house in the current market."

"You'd sell your house because of a barista?" The lady was suitably impressed.

"Can you think of a better reason?" Floyd took his coffee *very* seriously.

Boss waved at Floyd. "See?"

The lady raised up both hands, bracelets tinkling. "I don't want to poach him. I don't run a competing cafe or work for Sunboodle or Perks or anything like that."

"So you *say*." Floyd was deeply suspicious.

Trick handed the lady her drink, then left them arguing, while he served a small family of tourists. Two vanilla lattes and two iced decaf mochas. Humans. So boring.

The lady sat down with Floyd, presumably to wait for Trick to have a free moment. She'd be there a while but she seemed prepared to wait. Floyd brought out his knitting and started asking questions, prepared to be nosey as long as necessary. He was invested in making certain she really wasn't trying to lure Trick away.

Trick was intrigued but also busy. All morning and lunch the cafe belonged to confused visitors and in the later afternoon and evening the teens would take over.

Trick easily handled the current line and then dashed about, cleaning up.

A couple hours in, Trick was still whirling about, having a grand old time flirting and chatting and serving with aplomb. He really enjoyed his job, and he was good at it, and busy days highlighted both. He didn't even mind the tourists.

Marvin and Colin showed up, looking very sparkly. Flushed with success and burdened with shopping bags.

The lady eyed them with interest too. Maybe she really was a tail chaser.

An opportunity presented itself at about two in the afternoon. Things had slowed and she'd been back twice, once to order something to eat and then again to order a normal human drink (espresso shot, a respectable choice) with no opportunity to chat business with Trick.

Trick was going to show her mercy by pulling up a chair to Floyd's table and chatting a bit, but then Deputy Kettil came into his cafe. In uniform this time, and with his partner. Which meant he would behave himself. At least Trick hoped so.

Frankly, Trick had been dreading this bit.

The bear shifter was very subdued, ordering his usual plus one of the last remaining pastries. His partner, Deputy Zarlenga, gave Trick a huge grin and a generous tip even though he only got a black medium roast.

Zarlenga nudged Kettil with an elbow. "Go on."

Kettil huffed. "Sorry."

Trick wrinkled his nose. "For what?"

"I broke your cafe last night."

"Then you should be apologizing to my boss."

The boss glared at the huge man. "One table and three chairs! Do I send the city a bill? Can I get a break on my taxes?"

Kettil mumbled into his chin. "I was off duty."

"That'll be two hundred and thirty-seven dollars then, please."

Joe piped up from the dish station. "I cleaned and locked up last night, but I don't know how to repair furniture so I had to text him what happened."

Trick patted Joe on one bony shoulder. "I know, kid. You're no snitch."

"Yeah, but does that big cop know I'm cool?" wondered Joe, nervous.

"He's a cop. They like snitches," said Trick.

"What about the other guy? He was fighting too," grumbled Kettil, arguing with Trick's boss.

"Sato's body broke the table but you're the one who tossed him into it," defended Trick, wondering if he remembered accurately.

"So we split it fifty-fifty?" suggested the bear, hopefully.

Boss exchanged glances with Trick.

Kettil sighed. "Fine, here's two hundred cash. That's all I carry on me."

"Done," said the boss, taking the wad of bills.

Deputy Zarlenga elbowed his partner again.

The bear shifter glared at him. "Yeah, yeah. Go sit down. I got it."

Trick winced. So the deputy still wasn't out. He clearly hadn't even told his partner why he kept sticking his nose into Trick's business. But Deputy Zarlenga seemed like a decent sort, progressive enough for a cop. He was serving in the Bay Area, after all. Could Kettil not even be out with his partner?

Deputy Kettil turned to Trick. "Can we talk privately?"

Trick narrowed his gaze. "No. Others are already waiting on my time." He gestured to the nice lady sitting with Floyd. She raised her empty cup at the deputy.

Kettil looked startled to be turned down for a woman. He

sighed. "Okay, then. Sorry for sticking my nose in your business last night. I shouldn't have done that."

"Why did you?" Trick pushed, wondering if the bear would admit to anything.

"Well, you seemed to be in an unsafe situation and I *am* a cop."

"Ah, so you would have done the same for anyone?"

Kettil tugged at his ear. "Sure. Yeah." Then he raised his voice so his partner could hear. "You're nothing special."

Trick winced. That hurt a bit. Even though he'd already decided to walk away from Kettil. But at least it showed him it was the right decision. That's where they stood. Kettil still liked him but was too embarrassed to own it. And Trick had returned to his first love, who was entirely the opposite.

Trick respected a man's right not to come out until he was good and ready. But it also justified his own decision. Not that he'd really made one. Sato had shown up and Trick had gone belly up and back to him. Because he was Sato. And Sato was, it turned out, as necessary to Trick as swimming. He'd just forced himself to forget for a decade.

He decided to let the bear shifter off the hook. "Just your natural protective instincts kicking in?" which was bullshit. Well, bearshit. Everyone knew bear shifters had no natural protective instincts.

"Let's call it my cop training," said Kettil, trying for honesty in this one way.

"Sure. Nothing special. I got it. Let's call it that."

But Marvin was close enough to have overheard everything and he never let anything just drop. He was so damn stubborn. Trick wondered if that was a merman thing. He came up to the counter right next to Kettil, leaned his elbows on it tilting forward. "So that's it for you and Deputy Tight-Pants Murder Muffin here?"

"I guess so," replied Trick, not wanting to mention Sato. That seemed too mean.

But Marvin was not so kind. Kind enough to keep his voice low so he didn't out the man to his partner, who was some distance away, talking with one of the other human regulars. But no kinder. "What was he gonna be then, big guy? Your bi-experiment? For a first time, call?" He didn't give Kettil a chance to answer, just kept going, almost hissing he was so mad. "*Nothing special* indeed. Trick is the *special-est*! How dare you! You've liked Trick since he first came to town. How dare you deny it."

Trick knew that Marvin was mad *for* himself too. They were both flaming and femme and high-octane gay. Marvin was in everyone's face about it because he liked it, but also, he could do so safely now, with a pack at his back. But that didn't mean there wasn't a *before* time. That didn't mean that he, like Colin, didn't have a past where it had been dangerous to be himself. When he'd gotten bullied and beaten up for it, because Marvin hadn't had a Sato protecting him. Marvin had been alone and abandoned by his pod too. But unlike Sato he hadn't had Trick befriend him. Marvin had been alone and openly gay. It must have been terribly scary and sad. Trick could understand him lashing out. But perhaps this was something for him to talk to Isaac about, not take out on Deputy Kettil on a Saturday in Trick's cafe.

Marvin continued, "And after fighting over Trick, you just gonna drop him like it meant nothing? Like it *means* nothing?" Marvin glared hard at the bear shifter. "I was always on your side, you know?"

Deputy Kettil hunched forward. Trick had never seen a big man that cowed.

Trick kept his voice very low. "Marvin, I made my choice."

Marvin remained pissed, speaking about the deputy as if he weren't right there. "Yeah, but there's no call for him to be nasty about it. You might have given him a chance if he'd had the guts to openly like you."

Whoa, perhaps all mermen did have spurs. "You think I should have grabbed him and cracked him open like a clam shell? Those get eaten, you know?" Trick tried to make light of it. Voice still low.

"You saying you were willing to sleep with him to get him honest? Dick him into coming out? I suppose it's happened before." Marvin looked sideways at the bear, lip curled. "Maybe you still have a chance, big boy."

Deputy Kettil looked appropriately horrified.

Trick was beginning to feel sorry for the cop. He hadn't realized that Marvin also took care of his pack in his own way. It's just that his weapon of choice was less physical than that of the werewolves.

Alpha-mate indeed.

Trick lowered his voice even more. "It's okay, Marvin." He stopped himself from patting the crestfallen bear shifter on the head. "Look at him, he's wilted. It's not only that he doesn't want to, he can't yet. He's not ready. I know he liked me. Likes me. But I can't handle raw, unformed queer and was never gonna. I'm not as strong as you." Alec had been closeted when he and Marvin got together. "He's gotta know what he is and what he wants before he'll be good for anyone, least of all me."

The bear shifter looked resigned at that. Like he knew it. Like he'd heard it before. Possibly from Isaac.

Trick decided he needed to calm Marvin down more than anything. "Look. Sato may have left me for years, but he's never been shy about being with me. He's always been open about wanting me, claiming me publicly. And you saw him, he could pass as straight easily."

Colin put a hand to Marvin's arm then, reminding them that he was still there. His voice was as soft and gentle as ever, eyes full of compassion. "It's okay. We're all okay. Look at Trick, really look at him. He's actually happy."

Trick had forgotten that Marvin was fighting in Colin's corner too. Colin, who'd tried to hide who he was for most of his life. Colin, who'd been chronically abused and neglected because his queerness was obvious in a family where that was unwelcome.

Marvin stared at Trick for a long moment. Trick wondered what he was looking for, what he saw in his face. Whatever it was, it seemed to resonate. The merman pursed his lips. "Okay, it's your decision."

"Damned right."

Deputy Kettil mustered up the courage to speak at that point, brave man. The deputy's deep voice was low enough so eaves-droppers, especially human ones, would struggle to hear.

Floyd had been getting increasingly annoyed by all of this whispering among shifters that he couldn't hear. Trick wouldn't put it past him to have cranked his hearing aid up all the way up.

Kettil said to Trick, quiet but sharp, "You're snack-sized and irreverent. How was I supposed to know whether to take you seriously?"

"Interesting." Marvin crossed his arms, back on the attack. "Are you saying that you never intended to take our dratsie seri-ously or that you just hadn't gotten around to it?"

"Or are you saying that I'm junk food and not filling enough?" shot back Trick, feeling defensive.

Kettil shook his head and sighed. "My apologies, that was unfair. I don't know what I intended. And I don't know what I'm saying. Or even why I fought with *that creature* last night."

"Because you don't know what you want. You never did. That's the problem." Trick felt suddenly tired from his late night and busy day. He hadn't wanted this confrontation. Sometimes Marvin was too much.

Deputy Kettil pressed on. "Marvin is right, you *are* special. I'm bitter because I no longer get to figure out *how* special. Maybe I really didn't think you were serious, or maybe that is an excuse I'm using to make myself feel better. Maybe I lost because of my own lack of courage. Or maybe I never had a chance because of *him*. Maybe it's all my fault like the Alpha-mate claims. But I also feel like you flirted with me when you were in love with someone else. And that *too* isn't fair."

Trick sighed. "I never thought he would come back. We all have pasts and broken hearts, Deputy."

The bear shifter snorted. "Not all of us."

Colin said, softly, "I guess you do now."

Deputy Kettil cocked his head. "Maybe I do. But this, what-ever it was or could have been, ended before it really got started. Yeah, I'm hurt. But you didn't crush me, kid."

Trick was relieved. And that was decent of the bear to say. Graceful in a way. To take any burden of guilt off Trick.

"You *sure* about that?" muttered Marvin.

Kettil looked suddenly old and tired and also sympathetic. "Even if I'd had the guts and we'd started something, even if I hadn't made any mistakes, it still wouldn't be me, now, anyway. That man took on a bear for you. And a cop. That's not nothing."

Trick considered the possibility of a thing that might have been. Kettil was definitely his type. Dominating and growly and damaged.

But now, like before, Sato took up all of Trick's attention. He never did want anyone else when that merman was around.

"Would you have had the guts, Deputy?"

"I guess we'll never know."

With which Kettil left the Bean.

Trick wondered if he'd ever come back. If the cafe would remain a regular stop in daily rounds.

Colin said, after the door closed behind the bear shifter, "Do you think he really is gay?"

Marvin snorted. "Well, he certainly wanted to fuck Trick here. I think that makes him at least a little bit gay."

Trick sighed deeply. "It's all so awful and complicated."

"Never mind him now. Think about your big, strong... erm... medium-sized sharp... merman hottie instead," suggested Marvin.

Trick tilted his head. "I will. I wonder how the marine biology conference is going."

A plaintive voice came from the side. "Would you be able to talk to me about savory drinks now, sötis?" The stylish Scandinavian lady was still waiting.

Trick would like nothing better.

CHAPTER NINETEEN

A SHRIMP OUT OF WATER

The Present: Sato at The Oceanic Conference on Threats to Marine Biodiversity and Population Decline

Sato trailed behind the pod of mermaids, walking among a pack of werewolves. The result of such a group on a marine biology conference was surreal carnage, like a shark feeding frenzy meets ambulatory jellyfish. Only more psychological.

It was an invasion of sorts. If mermaids waged war it would look a lot like this. Weapons of choice: cute power suits, wild hair, lipstick, and a boundless superiority complex. They really weren't great on legs so they wobbled. Which is why Sato kept thinking about jellyfish.

Judd was grinning. "Are we protecting the mermaids from the biologists or the biologists from the mermaids?"

They kept having to pause while one or another of the diplomatic pod went off to flirt. In the guise of asking unsubtle questions about potency and virility. The mermaids also were quickly learning how to stumble *with purpose*. Which meant random biologists were being forced to "catch a falling mermaid."

Sato listened with mild amusement to the eddies of conversation that resulted.

"Why are they all so beautiful?"

"Who are they?"

Cascade tossed her long blonde hair and batted her eyelashes at some gangly tattooed young man who trembled, his fight-or-flight response engaged. She started to approach with clear intent, but Sato put an arm out to stop her.

"No target acquisition allowed right now, we have a mission. You're too slow at sperm harvesting."

The man bolted.

Cascade pouted. "Spoil sport." Obviously she was still in her fertile cycle.

They continued on through the entrance into the main part of the convention center – the scientists scuttling out of their way like hermit crabs.

Sato wasn't sure what he had expected but this seemed to be a standard collective of adult humanity. No outward signal markers as to them all belonging to a marine biology category of foliage. During his hunt for Patrick over the years, Sato had occasion to observe that some classes of humans dressed alike, those associated with the military or music or sports or being a teenager. Or, for some strange reason, postage. Marine biologists didn't seem to have any identifying scale colors. Although their attire did appear to be somewhat fish themed as a general rule.

Everyone seemed to be finding the mermaids, as a group of twelve gorgeous women, more intimidating than the werewolves – even though there were three of them, six-foot-plus with muscles for days. In this instance, beauty won over brawn.

"Are they models? Actresses?" Sato heard one of the scientists ask. "Where's the film crew?"

"What are they doing here?"

"Did they come to the wrong conference?"

"Perhaps it's cosplay of some kind?"

"What are they cosplaying? LA?"

"Maybe they're booth babes."

"This isn't a gaming convention, Fred! Why would there be booth babes?"

"Can you think of a better explanation?"

"Is that Professor Frederiksen?"

"The microorganism dude? Sure *looks* like Frederiksen. What's he doing with *them*?"

"He's some kind of shifter, isn't he?"

"Is he? You think those are shifters?"

"Makes sense."

"That's *a lot* of women, though. Isn't the triple helix mostly Y chromosomally linked?"

"Shifter genetics is not my field. Nor is it yours."

"Just speculating."

"Funny how a group of people who look like *that* come to our conference and we think it's the supernatural walking among us."

Sato desperately tried to keep his scowl in place.

The pod paused to one side of the cavernous room after completing their entrance process. This involved lines and lanyards and the giving of names. The humans' convention box was cold and very big with too much space inside it. Everything was white and gray and industrial. It was as if his old high school gym had swollen up like a puffer fish. The lighting was unnaturally white and there were lots of signs of different types hanging everywhere. Sato was unimpressed.

His feet were already hurting from the cement floor. Why were human structures just so awful? He missed Patrick and didn't like that he had to be away from him already.

He glared at Meymey, but she barely acknowledged his existence.

Instead his sister said to Alec, "So who do we talk to?"

All the mermaids turned to look at the Alpha expectantly.

Alec tugged on one ear, deeply uncomfortable. "No idea. So far as I know, there's no scientist who studies mermaids in particular. Your kind wouldn't allow such liberties. But everyone here is interested in marine life and population issues. Someone, probably quite a few *someones*, has to know *something* useful."

"We aren't fish," said Onda, firmly. "Just a reminder."

Alec gave her an annoyed look. "No humans will understand that distinction better than the ones at *this* very event. You are, technically, marine mammals, though. Even if you do have a scaled tail in your shifted form."

"No," said Aqua, firmly. "*This* is our shifted state. One tail is our true form."

Alec looked intrigued. "Is that how you think of it? Interesting. I suppose you can talk in either form."

"What does that have to do with anything?"

Alec looked thoughtful. "It just makes you unique among shifters, doesn't it?"

"Of course we are unique among shifters. We are the *People of the Sea*. Never animals. *People*, either way, you silly wolf." Meymey sniffed as if that were perfectly obvious.

Sato thought it was. But Alec looked like he'd only just come to this realization and was shaken by it.

It didn't last because he caught sight of someone across the crowd. He waved a hand at a dapper elderly human. "Doctor Morlunkin! Excuse me a moment, I must ask him a quick question about protozoa fungi." He gave Meymey a funny look. "I suppose you need a cetologist of some sort. Closest I can think of."

"What kind of species of human is a *cetologist*?"

But Alec had already gone off in pursuit of the academic, whose quick steps and nimble dodging through the crowd belied his age.

Meymey looked hopefully at Judd, Kevin, and Tank. "What does a cetologist look like?"

"All humans look the same to me," said Lana.

"Right?" Morwenna fluttered her hands.

Rilian made a lunge at a bespectacled young man hurrying past them with real fear in his eyes. He dodged. She stumbled on her silly heels.

Kevin said, "The Alpha was articulating a *type* of marine scientist, I expect. Unfortunately they don't wear tags saying what they specialize in. Believe it or not, most of them know each other's specialty by their names and publications or something. I've never understood academia. Perhaps we should have brought Colin after all."

"So what does a cetologist study?" asked Tarni.

Everyone was quiet for a long moment. Judd patted a pocket. "I'd look it up but convention centers never have decent wifi."

"Why don't I just ask?" Before anyone could stop her, Meymey sashayed over to a small group of nervous-looking younger humans. Sato suspected they were students of some ilk. "Pardon me, human younglings, would you mind explaining what a *cetologist* is?"

"Uh oh, a quiz already?" said one.

One of the others quickly added, "A marine mammal scientist who focuses on whales."

"Whales?" Meymey looked faintly offended.

One of the others hastened to add, "The scientific order Cetacea also includes dolphins. You aren't actual biologists, right? That means you probably like dolphins. Laymen *always* love dolphins."

"Did you just call the Paralia a lay*man*?" Onda was truly offended.

"Don't insult her!" reprimanded one of the others who Sato didn't catch. Sato suspected Morwenna; she had the worst temper.

Meymey's lip curled. "Dolphins? I can take 'em or leave 'em. They mostly get in the way. Whales and dolphins, you say?"

"And porpoises. Any given cetologists could study any one of approximately eighty species. Did you have a particular cetologist in mind? Or were you looking for someone with expertise in any specific family, genus, or species?" A female of the human group stepped in to take point in dealing with the mermaids.

Wise decision. Best to lead with the feminine when merfolk were around. The pod calmed slightly.

Meymey looked hopefully at Tank, who had moved to keep pace with her. "What is this young human female prattling on about?"

Tank shrugged.

Meymey looked back at the young scientists. "Do you have one in your particular school?" Being a mermaid, she meant the collective social group currently before her, but the students went with the human definition. Sato had to assume that they were, in fact, students. Perhaps graduate students, but they seemed awfully young.

"Is Doctor Wendile here? She's from our university. But population levels aren't her particular focus so she might have opted out of attending."

"Are you reporters?" one of them asked Meymey.

Aqua wobbled over to help. "No, we are just interested – what word did you use? – Oh, yes, lay*women*."

Sato and the enforcers stayed watching the interplay with amusement.

Regularly, Sato let his focus drift over the mermaids as a pod, checking up on them and the crowd beyond. The youngsters had failed to engage their collective interest so the mermaids ebbed and flowed.

Cascade had found herself a confused-looking young man with a large beard, and was slowly backing him up against a set of stairs.

Doris and Morwenna had drifted over to a nearby coffee stand and were flirting with both the barista and any male scientists who came to get a beverage.

Rilian, Tarni, and Zale had found a large fish tank and were apparently riveted by the mantis shrimp inside. Rilian appeared to be telling it off in no uncertain terms, using the language of the sea which was odd to hear and see out of water. Her hand gestures were nice but the siren song was somewhat abrasive in the thin air of a landbound world.

Their werewolves were all wincing from it – sensitive supernatural hearing.

Onda went off with a young man who looked like it was the greatest day of his life. Sato wished him well, but wasn't worried for her safety or timing. She was nothing if not efficient. He expected her back in less than ten minutes. She was also in her fertile cycle, just less flashy about it than Cascade.

Flotty, Hali, and Lana joined Meymey and Aqua. Hali latched onto one of the students and began stroking his arm. He looked like a silverfish stunned by the sun.

"I'm sorry, I don't think there are any cetologists here from our school," said one of the others, hurriedly.

The female student, who remained neither awed nor stunned nor confused by the pod, said, "What about Doctor Luckie?"

The group of youngsters collectively inhaled. "But she's *terrifying*."

One of the others hastened to explain to Meymey, "She's not from our school but she has a wicked reputation."

"So smart it hurts."

Meymey inclined her head. "And she is a cetologist?"

"Her specialty is orcas. But if she doesn't know the answer to your question, she can certainly find out. She's like that."

Meymey looked pleased. "Very good. Please summon this lucky human to us immediately."

"Oh, it doesn't work like that with Luckie."

"*She finds you.*" The tone was hushed with portent.

"Usually when you least expect or want it."

"Like an STD."

"Or a shark."

"Orcas aren't sharks, though, you know?" one of them hastened to explain to the mermaids.

Aqua said, "Of course we *know*."

The students all looked relieved. "Are you celebrities of some kind? Do you host a show?"

"Maybe a *Beauty and the Geek* dating show or something?" asked one of the ones whose arm was being caressed.

"Reality TV would make sense but there is no camera crew. None of them even have their phones out."

"What now?" asked Meymey.

"I've answered your questions. It's now your turn."

Sato was impressed. This scientist girl was plucky.

Meymey pursed her lips, silvery pink with gloss. "It's fair. That's how diplomacy works."

"Who are you and why do you walk amongst us?" asked the one not easily cowed by mermaids.

Aqua said, "We're just, ya know, visiting."

"No one plays tourist at a marine biology conference." A

healthy amount of skepticism colored her tone with sarcasm. Sato admired her even more.

Suddenly, there came an impossibly loud crack noise and chaotic ripple of shocked squeaks from the three mermaids at the fish tank. Also from the small group of courageous scientists they'd gathered around them to flirt.

"Oh, for goodness' sake, what did she say that pissed it off?" Doris's tone was all annoyance.

Flotty was grinning. "Was Rilian teasing the mantis shrimp again?"

"What is it with her and shrimp?"

"You know that notch she has in one fin?"

"The one she's really self-conscious about?"

"Mantis shrimp."

An even louder crack emanated from the tank, sharp like a gunshot. Raised voices followed, and then the high pitch of mermaids shrieking in siren song.

The werewolves collectively clapped big hands to their ears.

The fish tank fractured.

Tarni and Zale managed to dodge, but Rilian and her stupid heels stumbled. So when the mantis shrimp broke through its massive tank, she was completely drenched in salt water as a result.

Enough water for her to sprout tail. Now there she lay, in a puddle on a glass-covered floor, poised to tail-slap the uncowed mantis shrimp.

Judd lowered his hands. "So much for infiltrating this conference incognito."

Sato sniffed. "Were they really blending that well?"

"Should I help?" asked Tank.

"She's not in any actual danger," answered Sato.

"Ooooo," said one of the students. "You're mermaids? That is so cool. Makes way more sense why you're here."

"I've never met a real live mermaid before," said another.

"Have you met a *dead* one?" Meymey turned hostile.

"Oh no! That's not what I meant."

"Good."

A ripple of awe went around the whole convention at the sight of Rilian, now flopping indignantly in the puddle left by the tank. Her damp power suit looked ridiculous all bunched up with a massive tail sprouting out the bottom of the short purple skirt.

"That is glass. She'll cut herself," said Kevin.

"Well, go gallantly rescue her then," suggested Judd.

"Oh, should I?"

"Why are you so bad at being straight?"

Kevin dashed over to rescue Rilian.

"It's as if he spends all his time with a bunch of furry queers," said Tank in that mellow, mild voice of his.

Sato shot a confused glance at Judd.

"Our token straight dude," explained Judd.

"Straight? Why?" wondered Sato.

"We don't get it either."

One of the bystanders dove in at Rilian. But Kevin warded him off with one huge arm. Protecting the vulnerable mermaid.

"Move, you big lug," yelled the man. "Save the shrimp!"

Kevin crouched down, guarding Rilian's prone form with his bigger body, but the scientist truly wasn't interested. He scooped up the mantis shrimp and went dashing for one of the other saltwater tanks in a different part of the cavernous room.

Kevin lifted Rilian easily out of the carnage. She was dripping and annoyed but uninjured. Her makeup (by Marvin) was running and her hair was flat and stringy.

Now they were even more of a spectacle, stunning mermaid cradled in the arms of a massive red-headed hot biker guy. It was like the cover of some romance novel.

Murmurs went all around the convention. Scientists began crowding toward Kevin and Rilian with interest. A group of sexy women in power suits was apparently quite scary, but a *mermaid* was absolutely fascinating. They were *marine* biologists, after all.

Sato looked away from the tableaux and up, only to realize that the railings all around and above the main room were lined with onlookers. Alec had said that's where the presentation rooms were located. Classes must be out.

"A mermaid!"

"A real mermaid!"

"Walking among us!"

"Well, flopping."

"Isn't she *amazing* looking?"

"That tail is incredible. Much bigger than I expected."

"Look at the way the scales go up over her skin, forming a pattern. That is *so cool*."

"Also, her skin doesn't look like normal human skin. More like a dolphin's."

Onda rejoined them looking pleased with herself. Sato consulted the big clock. Sperm acquisition had taken her just under eight minutes exactly. Very efficient.

"What'd I miss?" She was smug and relaxed.

Sato pointed at Kevin, standing in the middle of a large crowd of humans, looking slightly confused about what to do next – mermaid in his arms, the hero of an unexpectedly damp action movie.

"We've been outed."

Onda shrugged. "Pity, but we might get answers and attention now."

"You want *more* attention?" asked Tank, awed.

She raised her chin at him. "Always."

"Someone should talk to that mermaid *officially*. Like representing for the conference," said a tremulous voice out of the crowd.

"Yes, but who? It's like we have a visiting celebrity."

"The organizing committee members?"

"Who's the most prestigious professor here?"

"Ludvong, but he'd be the worst ambassador *ever*. So boring."

"Fair point. Who, then?"

"Professor Macy is our most charismatic speaker. Should we ask her?"

"Isn't her expertise krill?"

"What has that to do with it?"

"Shouldn't it be someone who studies marine *mammals*?"

Frustration came then. "Does anyone know what to do?"

"Have we ever had actual mermaids visit a marine biology conference before?"

"Not that I'm aware."

"Are they *all* mermaids?"

"Not possible. Mermaids hunt alone. They only come to land one at a time."

"But look at that group there. It would explain how supernaturally sexy they all are."

"But previous case studies and social patterns suggest they only don two legs for hunting and procreating – on an individual basis! Group visitation to the land is unheard of."

"Well, I think they're all mermaids."

"Not the males."

"No, you're right, not them. Just the females."

"I still think it's unlikely they'd walk amongst us as a pack like that."

"Pod. A group of mermaids is called a *pod*."

Alec came up to Sato then.

Absolutely no one had noticed the Alpha's return except Sato and the other werewolves. The Alpha, of all of them, entirely blended in with their surroundings.

"I see you've decided to come out." He was clearly amused.

Sato said, "Rilian has beef with mantis shrimp."

"I see, surf and turf war. The shrimp won?" The Alpha looked calm and unruffled.

"Evidently." Sato added, "Bit of advice? Never engage in a fist fight with a mantis shrimp."

"Okay," said the Alpha gravely.

Kevin used his bulk and Rilian's flopping tail to push through the crowd and join the rest of the pod.

"Anyone have a towel?" asked Alec.

Sato said, just to keep them on target, since he'd like to get back to Patrick sooner rather than later, "Do you know a Professor Luckie, Alpha?"

"Of course. *Everyone* knows Luckie. We don't have much to do with each other. She's on the other end of the research spectrum from me. Orcas. Why?"

Sato gestured with his chin. "The young ones said she might be a good person for Meymey to talk to."

Alec looked thoughtful. "About your little —" he glanced around — "spawning problem? I can't think of anyone better. Orca population numbers is one of her areas of interest. I remember this one paper I read about how algae and—"

Sato raised one webbed hand. "Yes, yes, but how do we find her?"

"Oh, look! He has webbed fingers. He must be a mermaid too."

"Merman."

"Aren't they like really *super* rare? Even more so than mermaids?"

"There are fewer of them, I think, but they walk among humans more often."

"Do they really? I've never heard of that."

"Well, do you read up on merfolk?"

"Not regularly, why would I?"

"Exactly. Well, I do. I'm a big fan. Just look at them."

A handsome young scientist with aggressive eyebrows and a reluctant ponytail came over at that point. He seemed quite focused on Sato but he spoke to Alec.

"Frederiksen. I noticed that you had a white paper on the program for today."

"Madible. How nice to see you again. Yes, I do. Honored, of course. Are you presenting this year as well?"

"Not this year. Are these *friends* of yours?"

Alec gave a big sigh. "Of a sort."

"Oh, right! You're something supernatural yourself, aren't you?"

"I don't really talk about it in this context. But yes, Canus lupus sapiens."

"And these are colleagues of your lupine self?" The man's interested gaze swept the mermaids and then came back to focus on Sato.

"I suppose you could put it that way. They're in-laws – of a kind."

Was that how the Alpha thought of them? Interesting.

"Would you introduce me?" asked the newcomer.

"Are you sure?"

The man looked startled.

Alec explained, "They will target you."

"Will they, indeed? How novel. But you know I'm more inter-ested in facts than figures, so to speak."

Alec tilted his head. "I didn't know you were gay."

"Ace, actually. So who's this?"

Alec said, "Sato Daiki, this is Doctor Madible. Madible, meet Sato."

Sato shook hands with Professor Eyebrows. The human kept his grip tight, bringing Sato's hand up so he could look at the finger webbing. "Remarkable. And you have gills in water?"

"Yes." Sato extracted his hand with brute strength. The man looked both put out and impressed.

"But she's in her mer-form and not suffocating?" Madible gestured at Rilian, who was still in tail. Although someone had brought a mound of those horrible brown napkin things from the restroom. The other mermaids were attempting to blot her dry. *Attempting* being the operative word.

Regardless, any second now she'd be dry enough to don legs. Sato suspected she was enjoying the attention or she'd have already forced the shift herself. They could all do it. It just took extra effort when very damp. Plus Rilian, like most merfolk, was proud of her tail – a spectacular iridescent teal color. Since they'd been outed, she might as well show it off.

Sato wasn't one to make small talk or give away information to strange scientists with sharp eyes, no matter how impressive his eyebrows. "As you see, not suffocating."

"I guess the merfolk are about as forthcoming as most shifters," replied the scientist.

Sato inclined his head.

Alec asked, "Have you seen Luckie yet? She's on the program but hasn't shown up."

"Yes, I saw her at breakfast. Impossible woman."

"Know how to get hold of her?"

The man's lip curled. "Certainly not. Say something insulting about killer whales, though, and…"

Alec said, quite loudly. "No, I actually do think orcas are a kind of shark."

"WHAT DID YOU JUST SAY, FREDERIKSEN?" It wasn't werewolf VOICE, but it was as close as Sato had ever gotten to hearing that tone out of a human mouth.

"Like summoning a demon," said Madible. "One must simply use the appropriate invocation."

Meymey bumped up against Sato's side and entered back into the conversation. "Do *demons* regularly attend marine biology conferences?"

"Just me," said the owner of the powerful voice. Who was clearly entirely human, just feared by many.

Alec said, "Ah, good, Luckie. We were hoping you'd show up."

The crowd around them began backing away.

Sato heard one of the outside commentators say, "Professor Luckie would appear to be our ambassador of choice. Worst possible option. She'll cause an interspecies incident."

"Too late now."

Professor Luckie proved to be a stocky human with a powerful frame, short spiked green hair, and lots of silver jewelry piercing various parts of her face. She was wearing some kind of suit, but with lots of dangling strappy bits and very large shoes.

She looked like she belonged to one of the louder tribes of music-humans. Out of place among the biologists.

Sato felt Meymey tense against him and looked down at her curiously. She was staring at the newcomer with an expression he'd only ever seen when a mermaid was focused on hunting. He'd never seen that hungry look on his sister's face.

Interesting.

"You're insane, Frederiksen. No one is ever hoping I'll show up." The female's booming voice was a little husky. "Did you bring that mermaid with you to the conference this year?"

"Indeed." Alec was calm and sanguine.

"I love a man who knows how to accessorize properly."

Luckie looked at the pod with great interest. Sato felt her gaze assess him, find him wanting, move on.

Meymey said, stepping forward and trying to sound confident, "I'm the one in charge."

The professor met Meymey's hot gaze and instantly moved into her personal space. Counterpoint hunting behavior.

Even more interesting.

Sato didn't mind; it put the cetologist within easy reach of his spurs.

Meymey blushed as red as a sea star.

Sato hadn't known his sister could blush in her human form.

Meymey tentatively stuck out a hand, prepared to engage in the human ritual of *the shake*.

The orca specialist took that hand gently in both of hers, glanced down at the webbing, then raised it to her lips.

Interesting gesture. Sato wondered if he should try that on Patrick. His otter would probably find it terribly confusing. Or worse, laugh at him. But Sato liked the ritual feel of it.

Meymey went even redder.

"Nice to meet you, gorgeous merwoman in charge."

Alec snorted. "Are you being *nice*, Luckie?"

"There's a first for everything," agreed Madible.

"Actually I think she's *flirting*," said Alec.

"Gross," said Madible.

Professor Luckie ignored them.

His sister leaned forward to lower the neckline of her blouse. "I understand, as you are an orca specialist, that we could really use your assistance and the benefit of your expertise." She chose her words carefully and batted her eyelashes hopefully. "Would you help us – me – please?"

"Nothing could make me happier. Anything to distract from this pustule of a conference and the ever-present nincompoops pretending to be my intellectual equals."

Alec and Madible exchanged long-suffering looks.

Sato knew that werewolves and other land shifters regularly engaged in pissing contests, both literally and figuratively – he hadn't realized scientists did the same.

"Would you like to step outside and talk privately?" suggested Professor Luckie.

Meymey's eyes shone. "I would love that!"

Luckie placed a solicitous hand to the small of his sister's back and began ushering her toward one of the side exits.

Sato trailed after.

The crowd parted before them.

Professor Luckie noticed Sato, although Meymey did not. "Did I stutter when I said *privately?*" she asked him, chin up.

"Where she goes, I go."

The scientist looked suddenly upset and let go of his sister. "Your significant other?" she asked Meymey.

"My vangill," replied Meymey, and then remembering she spoke with a human who would not know the word, added, "My brother."

"Brother? *Biological* brother?" the professor swooped back in.

"Brother from the same mother."

"His presence will make it harder to flirt."

"You're gonna flirt with me?" Meymey was clearly delighted.

"I thought I had been. You're especially adorable, did you know that?" She held the door for Meymey to go through, not Sato.

Meymey put a hand to her throat. "Am I?"

Sato said, "As awe-inspiring and amusing as this is, Paralia, I must remind you that the purpose of our visit is, in fact, not flirting." He paused. "Well, not *just* flirting."

"*Paralia.* Pretty. Is that your name?" asked Professor Luckie.

"It is my title. I am the Paralia of All Seas, one of the five Soteria of the Deep."

"Royalty?" Professor Luckie was understandably confused.

"More like a type of leader."

"You're the matriarch of your pod?"

Meymey hedged. "Sort of."

Sato interjected, because he was, in his way, proud of his little sister. "More like a matriarch of the whole ocean."

"You're one of the *rulers* of the mermaids?" For the first time Professor Luckie actually looked shaken.

Meymey hastened to add with false modesty, "It's not *that* big a deal."

Sato let himself heave a huge sigh. They were outside, the sea breeze and salt smells were all around them. Calling him to swim. Swim across the bay to Patrick. Could they get on with it? He wanted to see his otter shifter, not hang out watching his sister toy awkwardly with a green-haired orca specialist. "Meymey, ask the expert your questions."

"*Meymey*, is *that* your name, then?"

"Just Mey. He's my brother, you know. It's a special name we use just for family."

"Very well then, beautiful powerful Mey, how can this one academic be of service to the merfolk?"

Meymey blushed again. "We have a problem and could use your help."

"Delighted, what's the problem?"

Meymey's tone lowered. "It's a fertility problem."

"I mean, I'm willing to try as much as you would like, darling, but strap-ons only go so far. Although, once we've moved in together, there's always adoption or IVF to consider."

Meymey smiled, confused into silence.

"I was flirting again, sweetheart. You're too cute when you're confused. What's the merfolk version of a U-haul? A tugboat?"

Blink blink blink went Meymey.

The professor smiled indulgently. "Please explain how your fertility issue is manifesting and the cause."

"You may know that mermaids have to procreate with human males, on land? But over the years we have been able to produce fewer and fewer viable offspring, and the percentage is more likely to be male. They used to number less than ten percent."

"Lower population numbers are a concern, but skewing male, when there was a deficit in the past, that I don't understand. Shouldn't you want closer to fifty-percent for species viability?"

"Males are useless to us."

"Well, of course they are, honey, but what do you *mean* exactly?"

"Most mermen are sterile," explained Sato, because his sister was only getting more flustered.

"How interesting. All of them?"

"No, some are potent, like my vangill here."

"He can produce children with mermaids regularly?"

"Well, he could! He just chooses not to."

Professor Luckie turned to stare at Sato for a long moment. "What's up with you then, if not your dick?"

Sato squinted at her. "I assure you it functions well enough." He considered Patrick's complaining and funny walk that morning. "Sometimes to excess."

Meymey made a face.

Sato sighed again. "I'm not into women."

"Madness," said the biologist, without missing a beat.

Somehow Sato knew she'd say that.

Professor Luckie returned all her attention to Meymey. "Has the sterility amongst mermen also gone up?"

Meymey frowned. "We don't really sing a record of mermen or vangill. They're not considered all that important."

"So you don't know if there have been fewer and fewer vangill born over the years?"

Sato said, "There have."

Meymey looked confused. "How would you know?"

Sato had no idea. "I think the Navarch said something about it at some point during training. He would know."

"I forgot about him. Should I summon him?"

Sato was about to say that likely wasn't necessary and then he remembered he'd once made a promise. He bet Patrick could get the Navarch laid in San Francisco.

"Yes, summon him."

Meymey fluttered her hands, agreeing.

"So you don't know much about the masculine side of your own procreative process?" Professor Luckie sucked in around her teeth. "I know it can be difficult to find the penis interesting or important, but unfortunately it is necessary for producing children, at least, in some capacity or another. We need to know whether your decrease in population numbers has to do with something impacting sperm production or egg production, or the process of fertilization, or fetal viability, or something else I haven't thought of. Things like pollutants and global warming can impact sperm count in particular, but if most of your children are the result of breeding with humans, then there is likely something else in play."

"How do we find out?" asked Meymey.

"I'm afraid that will require lots of tests and most likely human fertility experts. Data analysts. That kind of thing. If you're mostly fucking human males, then the scientists who study human fertility will know the most about such things."

"Not marine biologists? Or—" Meymey grappled to remember the word, "—cetologists like yourself?"

"Sadly, no. But I am absolutely going to help you sort out this problem. No matter how long it takes." Professor Luckie looked like she relished the idea and was making a sacred vow. "You know, those who breed dolphins in captivity use fertility technology developed for humans. I do have some passing familiarity with the technique. And, of course, there're all my lesbian friends."

"Huh?"

"I'm saying I know quite a bit about IVF, sweetheart."

Meymey leaned in, focused. "Oh, good. IVF?"

"In vitro fertilization?"

"Come again?"

"Later, honey. As many times as you like."

Sato shifted from foot to foot. "Yes, but is there no immediate solution?"

Professor Luckie glanced at him, clearly annoyed. "To your fertility problem?" She turned quickly back to Meymey. "You say the ones who are like your brother here, these *vangill*, they're reliably fertile?"

"Predictably so."

"Are there not enough of them to go around?"

Sato wrinkled his nose.

"They do their best. Except my brother, of course."

"Yes, yes, he's gay. Doesn't mean you can't use his sperm. I mean, not you *yourself*, of course, because gross, siblings, but others who are not related to you by blood."

"Didn't you say the penis had to be involved?" Meymey leaned forward.

"Ah yes, I did, for my sins. But it doesn't have to be *intimately* involved. Plus you said some humans are viable too? How about looking for commonalities by comparing his sperm with that of effective human sperm from previous successful baby daddies."

"Sires," corrected Sato.

"Thank you, *sires*. Then you might be able to determine what causes fertilization in mermaids. Most likely latent carriers of the triple helix. I think I read about some fertility clinic doing experimental work to test for that. The land shifters were *not best pleased*. But if you could source human men who had the right genes, as well as using your vangill, you'd stand more of a chance of viable pregnancies. And," she winked, "you wouldn't have to actually fuck them."

Meymey's face went through several emotions all at once – pleasure, excitement, relief.

Sato said, "And I wouldn't have to fuck mermaids?"

"Exactly."

"Fertility clinics, you say? Human ones?" What a blow to mermaid pride. Sato was amused that the solution to the merfolk's fertility problem, at least at the start, was sourced among the humans. Who, so far as he could tell, never had *any* issues procreating. The land was so overrun with them, they took to the oceans regularly to fuck things up there, too.

"I'm afraid so. You'd have to work with us. But I know an excellent clinic on the Peninsula. My friend Bethany and her wife used it. I understand pipettes were involved. They have adorable twins now."

"Twins, you say?" Meymey's eyes shone with interest.

"It won't be cheap, I'm afraid."

"Oh, we have plenty of human money. That's not a concern."

"You're rich, princess? Did I find myself a sugar mama? I'm a poor lowly academic, Paralia of All Seas, but I promise to help as much as I can. And in any way possible."

"Call me Meymey."

"Meymey, beautiful, have I mentioned recently that I'm a dab hand with a pipette?"

Sato said, "Before this gets out of control, can I ask, Professor Luckie, if you're based out of this bay area?"

"Oh yes. Stanford."

Sato grinned. "Welcome to the family."

She had no idea what she was in for. But Meymey had clearly just had a very successful hunt. This was gonna be fun.

And, unless he missed his guess, Meymey and her diplomatic pod were about to take up semi-permanent residence in the San Francisco Bay.

"Good, that's settled. Now, lovely Meymey, have you ever heard of the 1980s teenage orca fad for wearing dead salmon on their heads? Very fashion forward."

Meymey giggled. "Lately I've been hearing that their latest quirk is capsizing yachts."

"Yes, the sea creature version of cow-tipping. You know, among my particular group of friends we used to joke about *my salmon being pinker than yours.*"

"And what does that mean?" Meymey giggled again. Sato was faintly revolted.

"Well, sweetheart, maybe tonight we can meet at this charming little seafood place I love, without your brother around, and I will tell you all about it."

Meymey's eyes were huge. "I would like that."

Alec materialized from the convention center at that juncture. Sato suspected they'd been under observation through the glass doors all along.

"Where'd you come from?" asked Professor Luckie, annoyed.

"I'm presenting in half an hour." Alec turned to Meymey. "You good now, Paralia? Problem solved?"

"I think we have made extremely promising progress," said Meymey.

"Really?" Alec looked like he hadn't actually expected that.

"You doubted me, Frederiksen?"

"Never that, Luckie." Alec's quick eyes caught his colleague's solicitous hand at Meymey's back and her care in helping the mermaid negotiate stairs and confusing glass doors back into the building.

He looked at Sato.

Sato nodded.

"Really?"

Sato nodded again.

"No accounting for taste," said Alec, with feeling.

They rejoined the pod and pack. Sato said, because someone had to explain for the poor wolves, "Apparently something called IVF and a pipette is the answer."

That didn't seem to help. The boys mostly remained confused.

"Sperm banks?" suggested Tank, tentatively.

Cascade said, "Like a sperm whale on a sandbank?"

"Or like offshore accounts?"

"Now you've confused them." Luckie gave Sato a conspiratorial look.

Alec, being a biologist and all, attempted to explain. "Ah, no. Basically the humans have this system where they collect sperm and then use a turkey baster tool to put it inside, oh dear," he blushed very red, "ugh, lady-parts. And then… voi-la, babies."

"Nice try, gay boy," said Professor Luckie, clearly amused.

Sato decided he liked her.

"Why bring turkeys into it? Aren't they huge, flightless birds? Why are they getting involved? They aren't land shifters, are they?" wondered Aqua.

"This sounds like the stories we tell merbabies about pelicans bringing them." The mermaids were off again, chattering about inane things.

Sato sighed. Why were they still here? They had the solution, didn't they? Couldn't they leave now?

"I think you mean storks," said Kevin.

"No, I believe storks are for human babies. Pelicans are for merfolk," Judd explained.

"What's with all the birds all of a sudden?"

Cascade suddenly said, "Wait. Are you telling me the humans have a technology for impregnation without sex?"

"Yes," said Alec, obviously relieved that someone understood.

She pointed at Sato. "With his sperm, if we wanted?"

Alec looked at Sato. "You'd be willing?"

"In theory," replied Sato, carefully.

Judd said, "I'm sure Trick would be willing to help you with the sperm collection part of the equation."

Sato was interested all of a sudden. "Is that an option?"

Alec interrupted them. "Before I go sing for my professional supper, a quick question for you, Professor Luckie."

The professor turned in clear exasperation, dragging her attention away from Meymey. "Yes?"

"Are you in town next weekend?"

"I am."

"It's full moon."

"Oh?"

"Ah, right, why would you care? It means that Sunday we're having a barbecue at my place in Sausalito. Come visit. I'm certain at least *some* of the merfolk will be in attendance. Especially now."

Professor Luckie looked both shocked and pleased. "You're inviting me to your *home*?"

"It's potluck."

"I'll bring seafood kebabs for the grill."

"You do that. Two p.m.?"

"Done." Luckie immediately returned all her attention to Meymey.

Alec sighed and then looked pointedly at Sato. "Ms Trickle is gonna have a field day with this. I bet she knows Luckie already. It's always like that with the power lesbians."

"A new kind of supernatural creature?" wondered Sato.

"Exactly," said Alec.

EPILOGUE
THE FUTURE

Trick and Sato with the San Andreas Pack

Trick and Sato got their swim that night.

And Alec got his barbecue the next weekend. Poor Sato had no idea what he was in for. Trick tried to prepare him, he really did, but Sato was overwhelmed quickly.

"There are so many people. Why?" The merman sounded so plaintive.

Trick laughed. "Well, the pack keeps expanding. I mean, I just added you and kinda Meymey too. And now she's got Professor Luckie and of course her diplomatic pod. That's how it works. Eventually Professor Luckie will bring a few of her friends. It's like a massive smack of jellyfish."

He pointed to the kitsune and their leash of lovers. "Those are our local kitsune. They come from the East Bay with their polycules because of Max. Ms Trickle and Pepper are his fault too. Former coworkers, plus assorted friends. For a self-proclaimed loner, Max sure collected a lot of people."

Max joined them at that moment, drinking some kind of fancy peach spritzer someone had brought. He handed one to Trick without having to be asked. "You taking my name in vain, short stuff?" At barbecues Max was always trying to fizz Trick up. He seemed to feel he owed Trick for all the sickeningly sweet lattes Trick made him over the years.

Trick bounced, delighted. Spilled a bit out the bottle top which Max had kindly already opened for him. Trick didn't like things as sweet as Max did, but he loved being noticed by the Magistar. He secretly felt like Max dismissed most of them as frivolous creatures unworthy of his attention. Which they probably were, but Max only brought *him* drinks at parties.

Sato narrowed his eyes in suspicion. Sato was behaving like his old self, generally scowling at too many people and sticking to the outskirts of the crowd. He'd always been like that, until Trick got into trouble. Then he'd charge in, pull Patrick out, scold him, and take him home. He seemed unsure of his role when they were already home, and the masses had come to them. He'd eaten some of the grilled salmon, determined that on land, Professor Luckie and her sharp tongue made for a better vangill than he under these circumstances, and exited the fray. At some point, some brave soul had handed him a beer. Probably Judd. Sato sipped from it occasionally, winced, stared at it in betrayal, then stood around until he forgot about it, took another sip, winced again.

Trick grinned at Max. "I was explaining how we got so many people coming to eat venison after a full moon."

Max rolled his eyes. "Werewolves collect lost souls. At least this pack does." He looked morosely up at the massive house that was technically his but which he rarely entered. "Gonna need a bigger place if this keeps happening." He brightened. "Could rip that one down."

Bryan came over, slung a big arm over Max's shoulders. "We'll make do with what we got, for now. At least you can sleep well at night knowing your father would hate the renovations, and that it's lousy with shifters and queers."

Max brightened. "Fair point." He looked at Sato. "You know, we had a bet going on Kettil winning over our otter here. You came along and ruined the pool."

Trick took away Sato's beer and handed him the peach soda.

Sato sipped from that. Narrowed his eyes, clearly trying to decide if he liked it.

Trick was charmed. He kissed Sato's cheek in approval.

The narrowed eyes turned on him. A webbed hand brushed some smudge of food off Trick's chin.

"Did any of us bet against Kettil? Short the stock?" Max asked his mate.

Bryan wrinkled his nose. "Isaac said something about us being overly optimistic in this matter but refused to put money on it, since he's been counseling Kettil. Poor showing, if you ask me. He could have won big."

"Anyone close?"

"Colin had the longest time frame. He said it'd take at least three years for Kettil to figure his shit out. But I don't think that counts as winning the bet."

"It's possible that might still come true. Just not with Trick," protested Colin, joining them at that point. "This screaming hot merman threw seaweed in the works."

"Mermen have a tendency to do that," said Trick, proudly.

"You don't think the cop is *actually* straight, do you?" wondered Kevin, joining his brother. A whole bunch of were-wolves (and Max) were now looming and glaring without malice at Sato and Trick.

Trick didn't care. Sato had moved his hand down to cup his neck. His thumb was rubbing along Trick's collarbone, the webbing soft against his throat.

"Shouldn't you know your own kind?" Colin asked his brother.

Kevin made a face. "Doesn't work like that."

Max smirked. "Kevin is terrible at being straight."

Kevin looked morose. He'd just been dumped… again. "I know, right? I spend too much time with you losers."

Bryan's kind eyes were watching Trick intently. Trick met them, unselfconscious about Sato's possessive hand on him. Werewolves were a touchy-feely crew. Sato wasn't and never had been, but in a crowd like this, he clearly wanted everyone to know that Trick belonged to him. Or maybe this was the bit of him that had changed over the years they'd been apart. Less grabbing and dragging away, more soft touches and staying close. He certainly didn't like being separated from Trick for any length of time.

He'd moved into the pack house with something approaching alacrity – for Sato. Of course he was off with the pod whenever Trick was working. He'd been figuring out how to ferry all the mermaids around to various fertility clinics and such. But he came home every evening and collected Trick for a swim, and then spent the night in his bed. Their bed.

Bryan said, "House takes the pot, then. Right?"

A chorus of groans and protests met that. "Unfair, this isn't a casino. Just give us our money back."

Max tilted his head and looked with interest at Sato. For some reason the Magistar was intrigued by Trick's boyfriend. Max, who showed very little interest in anything.

"So, Sato-san, what happens if your sister does get preggo?" Max asked.

Bryan explained his mate's interest, thank goodness, for both Trick and Sato's benefit, "Max is the end result of a rather tortured breeding program."

"Oh, am I prying?" Max did not look at all apologetic.

Sato's eyes stayed narrowed but still without hostility and his hands stayed petting Trick. "She will be happy to be fertile," he said, stating the obvious.

Max huffed, annoyed. "And if the Paralia has a male baby?"

Sato frowned. "As soon as he develops legs, she will leave the boy behind with his sire, of course."

"Ah yeah, babe, that's not how fertility clinics work," Trick hastened to point out.

Sato frowned. "Point taken." He looked down at him, face impassive. But Trick could tell from that very stillness, how important this was. "How do you feel about raising up a merman or two in about ten years or so?"

Trick thought about Sato alone in his room at his father's house. Lost in a world too loud and too dry. Trapped with a disinterested sire who did his best, but nothing more. He thought about what Sato had said – that it was Patrick who had saved him, back then. Patrick who'd been the necessary one – the beacon, the comfort. For the first time, Trick considered all the other Satos, all the other mermen, like Marvin, who had not been so lucky as to have a Patrick to save them. Who had been beached on lonely shores, abandoned by both their cultures. Who existed in that liminal place between land and sea, but were welcomed by neither.

What a good thing it would be to stop that from happening to the next generation. At least some of them. What a great thing to use a whole pack to do so. "There is your sperm to think about too. They want it right, because of your spurs?"

Sato huffed out breath through his nose. "Cascade has already asked."

Sato, of course, hadn't mentioned this.

"And?"

"I said no."

Trick was startled. "Oh? Why?"

Sato shrugged. "I don't like her."

Max actually snorted in amusement. "Oh, I like you, merman."

Sato looked with interest at the most powerful member of the pack. "I like you too, Magistar."

Trick hid a smile by dipping his chin against Sato's caresses, which hadn't stopped.

Colin said, and there was a strange kind of hope in his voice, "But if you do donate and sire a boy, Sato?"

Sato tilted his head and looked up at the pack house, around at the lively yard full of shifters and the people who loved them.

"I guess he would come here?" He looked at Trick, genuinely asking. Hand stilling its movement at last, starting to withdraw.

Trick raised his own hand, covered Sato's, pressed the webbing against his skin. He felt like crying. That Sato would still hesitate when loneliness and safety were on the line.

"Of course," said Trick, making a promise for himself, but also a vow for the whole pack. He glanced around. They, all of them, even Max, were nodding.

Marvin popped up then. "Are we adopting? Meymey's kids?"

"She's dating a ball-busting lesbian scientist – I doubt that would be allowed, Alpha-mate," said Max, acerbic as ever.

Bryan said, "No, we're talking about Sato's kids."

Marvin bit his lip. "Right, he's vangill. I didn't think about that possibility." He rubbed his hands together. "Excellent. We'll have to talk about expanding the house. How about renovating the lower level. But funding...."

Sato was staring at Marvin, eyes wide and startled. "You're the strangest merman I've ever met."

Marvin patted his shoulder. "I know, honey. But just look," he gestured widely at the massive barbecue. "We like adopting strays."

Trick said, "It'd be nice if they didn't end up as lonely as you were."

"I wasn't lonely. I had you."

Marvin said, "But that makes you the lucky exception." And there was bitterness lurking in his tone.

Alec joined them then, their little group ever-expanding. Just like the pack.

"Who's lucky?"

Marvin said, "Sato. Because when he was abandoned by the merfolk, Trick found him."

Alec's hazel gaze on Trick's face was warm. "Very lucky."

Trick was embarrassed. Why did Alec have to be so *good*?

"So it is settled?" the Alpha asked his mate, looking at Sato.

Marvin nodded, face a little scrunched like he was trying not to cry. "We get to take them in. We *will* take them in."

"Of course we will," said the Alpha, like it had all been discussed and settled days ago, which, considering this Alpha, it probably had.

Marvin would have worried about this. Alec would have offered without even thinking about it. Alec was like that. He'd chat with Bryan, and Bryan would have mentioned it to Max, and suddenly the whole pack was on board with the weird system the merfolk had developed, that Sato would participate in, but without perpetuating the damage.

Sato looked confused. "Just like that? You accept a future full of hypothetical boys from the Deep?"

"Yep," said Alec.

Trick smiled at Sato's confusion. "Welcome to the San Andreas Pack, baby."

Sato accepted, because that was his personality. But he did follow up with Trick later, still confused.

They were wearing the pack's ubiquitous yellow waffle robes, preparing to walk down to the water and swim that evening. The color looked great on Sato and terrible on Trick, but Trick hardly cared in this moment. Although he did wonder if Sato could be persuaded to adopt a yukata. Outside, the sun was sinking and the party had quieted into a circle of seated forms, mostly just pack and close friends and lovers, some in each other's laps, chatting and laughing.

Trick and Sato left them, trudging down the steep hill toward the shore. Kevin's massive wolf form appeared briefly to escort them to the edge of the territory, then vanished to patrol the perimeter.

Sato asked, softly, "Were they sincere, the Alpha and his mate, about any boys I may sire?"

Trick had known this question was coming. "They were. Marvin in particular. He doesn't talk about it, but I think, before high school, he was very lonely on land."

Sato dipped his chin, really thinking about it. "He's very social for a merman and he didn't have a Patrick."

Trick took a breath, then said, "Thank you for accepting me then, and for coming back to me now."

Sato stopped right there on the side of the road. Reached and cradled Trick's chin with both hands, webbing soft against his cheeks, encouraging him to look up at him. As if Trick could look away. As if there was ever a time he didn't want to see Sato's face.

Sato said, "I've been thinking maybe you don't quite understand. You seem so surprised that I kept looking for you. I don't know how to put this. I don't think even the language of the sea would work but I'm going to try."

He took a breath.

Trick waited, impatient but still under those hands.

"Patrick, our childhood is the same shape."

Patrick frowned, confused.

Sato sighed, pressed on. He hated being forced to use words. But for Trick, he would. And Trick was honored by his suffering.

"All my best memories have the form of an otter. As if I have been, since I met you, a shifter with three forms, not just two. Back then, I adapted not to the land, but to you. There was never a moment I stopped looking for you. Not because I didn't want to stop but because it simply never occurred to me to do so. I was always coming back to you. Always."

And Trick believed him.

Sato kissed him. Soft. Lips questing. Still searching. Trick tasted salt. He tasted memories. And he tasted the future.

Sato pulled back.

"Can we please swim now?" whined his merman.

Fin

How did Alec the Alpha & Marvin the merman first met? Get it *free* in ebook, printable pdf, or full cast audio by joining Gail's silly monthly newsletter, the Chirrup.

Would you like to know what happened to Mana & Lovejoy? They also have is a short story called *Vixen Ecology* only available to Chirrup members.

Find this and much more fun, silly, comforting stuff at…

GailCarriger.com

AUTHOR'S NOTE

Thank you so much for picking up *The Dratsie Dilemma*. I hope you had as much fun reading it as I did writing it. If you would like more from the San Andreas Shifters, please say so in a review. I'm grateful for the time you take to do so.

Even more welcome are donations to your local LBGTQ centers (time, attention, money, whatever you can give). Mine is the San Francisco LGBT Center. Find them at sfcenter.org. We all spread magic in our own ways, and everyone needs a pack to come home to.

ACKNOWLEDGMENTS

Thanks to Juta, for the pelicans.

Thanks to Joy who stepped into the void and turned this cover around in record time and with consummate skill.

Thanks to Amber, Flo, and the ever-ready flock of Carriger Pigeons for their excellent beta reads and editing. Without my beloved team, everything would take a lot longer and be a lot less tidy.

Finally, thanks to Olivia Wylie and the Parasol Protectorate Fan Group for the *dratsie* tip. I had no idea otter shifters were a thing, and my world is now better for having Trick in it. I hope yours is as well.

ABOUT THE WRITERBEAST

New York Times bestselling author Gail Carriger (AKA G. L. Carriger) writes to cope with being raised in obscurity by an expatriate Brit and an incurable curmudgeon. She escaped small-town life and inadvertently acquired several degrees in higher learning, a fondness for cephalopods, and a chronic tea habit. She then traveled the historic cities of Europe, subsisting entirely on biscuits secreted in her handbag. She resides on the edge of the Pacific, surrounded by fantastic shoes, where she insists on tea imported from London.

GailCarriger.com